Nicola Marsh is a *USA*  multi-award-winning a[...] than losing herself in a [...] a previous life, she now [...] raising two dashing hero[...] [...]pping up delish meals, cheering on her footy team, and writing—her dream job. And she chats on social media. A lot. Come say hi. Instagram, Twitter, Facebook—she's there! Also find her at nicolamarsh.com

New York Times and *USA TODAY* bestselling author **Katee Robert** learned to tell her stories at her grandpa's knee. Her 2015 title *The Marriage Contract* was a RITA® finalist, and *RT Book Reviews* named it 'a compulsively readable book with just the right amount of suspense and tension'. When not writing sexy contemporary and romantic suspense, she spends her time playing imaginative games with her children, driving her husband batty with *what-if?* questions, and planning for the inevitable zombie apocalypse.

If you liked *Sweet Thing* and
Make Me Want, why not try

My Royal Temptation by Riley Pine
Ruined by Jackie Ashenden

Discover more at millsandboon.co.uk

SWEET THING

NICOLA MARSH

MAKE ME WANT

KATEE ROBERT

All rights reserved including the right of reproduction in whole or in part in any form. This edition is published by arrangement with Harlequin Books S.A.

This is a work of fiction. Names, characters, places, locations and incidents are purely fictional and bear no relationship to any real life individuals, living or dead, or to any actual places, business establishments, locations, events or incidents. Any resemblance is entirely coincidental.

This book is sold subject to the condition that it shall not, by way of trade or otherwise, be lent, resold, hired out or otherwise circulated without the prior consent of the publisher in any form of binding or cover other than that in which it is published and without a similar condition including this condition being imposed on the subsequent purchaser.

® and ™ are trademarks owned and used by the trademark owner and/or its licensee. Trademarks marked with ® are registered with the United Kingdom Patent Office and/or the Office for Harmonisation in the Internal Market and in other countries.

First Published in Great Britain 2019
By Mills & Boon, an imprint of HarperCollins*Publishers*
1 London Bridge Street, London, SE1 9GF

Sweet Thing © 2018 Nicola Marsh

Make Me Want © 2018 Katee Robert

MILLS & BOON

First Published in Great Britain 2018
by Mills & Boon, an imprint of HarperCollins*Publishers*
1 London Bridge Street, London, SE1 9GF

Sweet Thing © 2018 Nicola Marsh

Make Me Want © 2018 Katee Hird

ISBN: 978-0-263-26639-9

MIX
Paper from
responsible sources
FSC™ C007454

This book is produced from independently certified FSC™ paper
to ensure responsible forest management.
For more information visit www.harpercollins.co.uk/green.

Printed and bound in Spain
by CPI, Barcelona

SWEET THING

NICOLA MARSH

MILLS & BOON

This one's dedicated to Flo Nicoll and Nicola Caws,

two of the best editors a girl could wish for.

Thanks for your enthusiasm, your support and your
all-round awesomeness.

You rock!

CHAPTER ONE

Abby

D-DAY SHOULD'VE BEEN the happiest day of my life.

I'd envisaged a fabulous eight hours at Le Miel, creating the French pastries I'd grown to adore over the last year, followed by an intimate evening with a bottle of Shiraz and Channing Tatum.

What better way to celebrate a divorce than with a rich red to tantalise my palate and a hot guy strutting across my TV screen?

But my dreams of drooling into my wineglass over Channing turned to crap about an hour into the working day, when Remy King, the best boss in Australia, took a tumble off a ladder and ended up here, in Sydney Private Hospital.

'You don't need to stay,' he said, his blue eyes filled with pain despite being dosed up on enough painkillers to fell an elephant. 'Go back to the shop.'

'Makayla has it covered.' I perched delicately on the edge of his bed and reached for his hand. 'Besides, I finished making the croissants, beignets, éclairs and macarons before you decided to do your lousy circus impression, so there's not much left for her to do but serve.'

He managed a wan smile and winced. 'It was the ladder's fault.'

'Yeah, it just happened to move sideways on that patch of flour on the floor all by itself.' I rolled my eyes. 'If you weren't such a great boss and friend, I'd give you an ass-kicking for being so stupid.'

'And if you weren't the best apprentice I've ever had, I'd sack you on the spot for being so bold.'

I squeezed his hand, thanking God every day that this man had given me a chance when I needed it most.

Apparently leaving my cold, calculating husband after only nine months of marriage 'wasn't the done thing' in the Prendigast family.

Not that my parents had cared why I'd done it. All they'd worried about was their precious reputation as one of the wealthiest families in Sydney, so they had cut me off financially and emotionally to teach me a lesson.

They'd expected me to come running back to their harbourside mansion in the first week.

I hadn't been back in a year.

Yet for all their faults, I missed my folks. My friends too. But I'd left Abigail Prendigast, the perfect daughter in a perfect world who did exactly as she was told, behind that fateful day I'd walked out on my old life and into my new.

'What's wrong?' Remy's eyes narrowed, studying me. 'If it's the patisserie, don't worry, you don't have to handle the place on your own. I've already contacted Tanner, and he'll be happy to help run the place while I'm recuperating.'

I stiffened. While I'd never met Remy's younger brother, I'd heard enough to form an impression. And it wasn't good.

The guy sounded like a flake. A rich flake, who ran nightclubs and bars along the eastern seaboard, made a squillion from them, but spent most of his time flitting overseas squandering his fortune on women.

Yet for some reason Remy seemed to adore him. I'd heard genuine emotion in his voice every time Tanner called from one of his far-flung destinations. Guess I had to give the guy credit for keeping in touch with his brother despite his playboy lifestyle.

I'd seen him once too, while Remy had been chatting to him on a teleconference call. It had been a fleeting glimpse of dark hair, dark eyes and stubble-covered jaw. Handsome if you liked that kind of thing. Me? I preferred uncomplicated, the opposite of Bardley, my ex, and the glower I'd seen on Tanner was enough to tell me he had complication all over him.

'Isn't Tanner overseas?' I asked, sounding way calmer than I felt. I didn't need some stranger who wouldn't know a praline from a peach melba looking over my shoulder. I was confident in my work at Le Miel and didn't need some rich-boy novice slowing me down. 'Because I can handle the everyday running on my own.'

'You can't create and do everything else.' Concern clouded his gaze before he blinked, and I wondered if I'd imagined it. 'Tanner is a great businessman. He's run restaurants. He'll handle things at Le Miel for a month before I'm back on deck.'

'A *month*?' It came out a yell, and Remy chuckled.

'That's what the doc said. Apparently the more I keep off the fractured ankle and rest up the broken ribs, the faster it'll all heal.' He winked. 'Who knew?'

Damn, I should've known he couldn't use crutches to move around the shop when he had three broken ribs too. But when he'd said Tanner would be over-seeing the daily operations, I'd envisaged a week, tops. Now I'd have to put up with the gypsy playboy for a month?

Feeling guilty for my selfishness when my friend was in pain, I squeezed his hand again. 'You focus on healing fast. I'll take care of the rest.'

'Don't you mean *we*?'

A deep voice came from behind me, the kind of voice that invoked images of dark bars, dark choco-late and dark souls. Deep. Rich. With an underlying hint of impudence that immediately put me on guard.

I turned and locked gazes with the devil himself.

Crap. Those eyes. A startling sienna, almost golden, the brown was so light. But it wasn't the co-lour that unnerved me as much as the way they looked at me.

Like I was a tasty *tarte tatin* waiting to be de-voured.

An involuntary shiver crept down my spine as that

hungry stare zeroed in on my hand, where it lay covering Remy's on the bed.

'Isn't this cosy?' His insolent drawl made me bristle. 'Hope I'm not interrupting anything?'

I snatched my hand away as Remy said, 'Don't be a dick. Tanner, this is Abby, my apprentice and the best damn French pastry chef outside of Paris.'

'Next to you, of course, bro.' Tanner's assessing gaze focussed on me and damn if the parts of me that hadn't experienced a guy's touch in over a year didn't zing. In a big way.

'That goes without saying.' Remy beamed, his affection obvious as he beckoned Tanner closer. 'Thanks for doing this.'

'My pleasure.' As Tanner stepped forward, I stood and resisted the urge to scoot away.

As if those eyes weren't enough, the closer he got I realised how big the guy was. Huge. At least six-three, with the kind of build honed from many hours in a gym. Or doing other forms of exercise.

Hell. Where had that come from? For the second time in less than a minute, I'd associated sex with him.

I really needed a bout between the sheets. If I could ever be bothered.

Being celibate since Bardley hadn't been an issue. I'd been too busy assembling a life that didn't involve society high teas, expensive dinners to woo clients and yachting on the weekends. All this squeezed around my business degree. Which I'd also walked away from. Bully for me.

'Actually, your timing couldn't be better.' Tanner dwarfed everything in the room as he propped against the bed. 'I've been looking for a new challenge.'

My skin prickled with awareness as Tanner's daring stare alerted me to the fact he wasn't just talking about Le Miel.

Either Remy was oblivious to the tension sizzling between Tanner and me, or the pain meds were really kicking in, because he waved us away.

'Good. Then why don't you two go get acquainted and leave me to wallow in agony?'

'Your wish is my command, bro.' Tanner leaned down to give Remy a gentle hug, an unexpected gesture that made me like him a little when I didn't want to. 'I'll keep you posted. And don't worry, the patisserie will be fine.'

'Take care, Rem,' I said, skirting the bed to the opposite side of Tanner, before bending down to place a kiss on his cheek. 'Get well fast, okay?'

'I will.' Remy's cheeky grin alerted me to the fact I wouldn't like what he said next. 'You're in Tanner's capable hands now.'

Heat surged to my cheeks as I imagined exactly what it would feel like to be in those hands, literally.

Then I made the mistake of glancing up to see Tanner hold up the hands in question, the corners of his mouth curved in a devastating smile. 'Lucky you.'

Many words could be used to describe how I felt right at that very moment.

Lucky sure as hell wasn't one of them.

CHAPTER TWO

Tanner

I HADN'T BEEN kidding when I told Remy I was up for a challenge. But the cool blonde with glacial blue eyes and an attitude to match wasn't one of them.

A snowman could get frostbite next to that one.

From the first time she'd stared down her snooty nose at me, I had her pegged. Bored rich girl playing at baking goodies for a while. Probably like the ones she'd created in her state-of-the-art playroom kitchen as a kid, envisaging a prince charming with a mega bank account to come along and rescue her.

Yeah, women like her had the fairytale down pat.

Which begged the question: Why had she stuck around for a year?

Remy had given me the basics about his protégé during one of our phone calls about ten months ago. Said that one of his best customers had come into the patisserie one day, wild-eyed and dishevelled, begging for a job. It had been her dream to be a pastry chef apparently.

What a crock of shit.

I had no idea what game this Abby chick was play-ing, but the fact Remy had offered her the apartment over the patisserie while she got her life back together, and she was still there, meant I'd be keeping an eye on her and figuring out what her deal was.

Everybody had an angle. I'd learned that the hard way. So if the ice princess was taking advantage of my brother I'd kick her out on her sweet ass so fast she wouldn't see it coming. And it was sweet. Very, from what I'd glimpsed when she'd bent over to kiss Remy.

It had been a touching gesture, indicating a depth of affection that could be construed as genuine, if I didn't know better.

Women like her were masters at deception, and if her endgame was to fool my brother—maybe into giving her a piece of the action at Le Miel—she was in for a rude shock.

Remy had always been too kind-hearted; that was his problem. Probably one of the reasons Dad had tol-erated him and despised me.

'We should head back to the patisserie,' Abby said as we exited the hospital. 'Makayla, one of the staff, will be run off her feet.'

'Not so fast, Sweet Thing.' My hand shot out, touching the small of her back, and a shock akin to electricity sizzled up my arm. 'We need to get ac-quainted first.'

She stared at me like I'd suggested we get naked to do it, and I grinned. The thought wasn't totally unpalatable, considering how much fun it would be to rattle that impenetrable façade.

'I meant let's grab a coffee at that café down by the water, but if you had something else in mind I'm up for it.' I threw in a wink, knowing it would rile her more than anything else I could say.

Predictably, she drew herself up to an impressive five-ten. Tall for a woman. I preferred them petite and pliable, not big and bristly.

'*Sweet thing* isn't my name,' she said, chin tilted, haughty as hell.

'Would you like it to be?' I leaned in, expecting her to jump back like a startled cat.

When she held her ground and glared at me with those big blue eyes, an unusual azure similar to a glacier I'd seen in New Zealand once, I had to admire her a little.

'Here's the deal. I love my job and I respect your brother. He gave me a chance when no one else would, and I'm not going to screw this up over some big-mouthed Romeo who can't keep it in his pants. Got it?'

She jabbed me in the chest with a finger. She actually *jabbed* me. And I admired her all the more for having the balls to stand up to my in-your-face innuendos to get a rise out of her.

'So quit the bullshit flirting and let's talk business.'

I couldn't resist one more. 'Dirty business?'

'Jeez, you're annoying,' she muttered under her breath as she stomped away.

Okay, so maybe I'd pushed too far but getting her

so wound up had its advantages. Namely giving me an unimpeded view of her ass.

My earlier assessment had been correct. It was sweet. Taut and rounded, highlighted to perfection in the tight black pants worn by staff at the patisserie.

The patisserie...

I'd promised Remy to ensure it ran smoothly in his absence, and I always kept my promises. I might be a prick who didn't let anyone get too close but Remy was different. He was my blood. And I owed him.

Which meant I needed to play nice with little miss sweet cheeks.

'Hey, wait up.' I caught up to her in a few strides. 'Look, you can blame my idiocy on jet lag, considering I only got in from LA late last night.'

She shot me an exasperated glance that indicated she hadn't thawed in the slightest.

'Let's have that coffee, and I promise to behave.' I held up my hands to show I had no tricks up my sleeves. 'What do you say?'

She hesitated, gnawing her bottom lip, and damned if the innocuous action didn't shoot straight to my cock. Contrary to popular belief, I didn't screw everything that walked and it had been a few months since I'd been with a woman.

Time to rectify that if the ice princess got me horny with a simple lip-nibble.

'Come on, Abby, I don't bite.' I refrained from adding, 'only if you ask nicely', because that wasn't helping the hard-on situation.

After what seemed like an eternity, she managed a terse nod. 'Fine.'

But it wasn't. Because as we strolled the last fifty metres to the café I caught a whiff of her fragrance on the wind. An intoxicating blend of vanilla and coconut, and I wondered if she tasted as good as she smelt.

Shit. Remy would castrate me if I screwed around with his protégé. Not that I wanted to. Taunting was one thing, following through another.

But as another gust of wind blew blond strands of hair into her face and my fingers itched with the urge to brush them away, I knew working alongside Abby would be a long four weeks.

I'd craved a challenge.

Looked like I'd got one.

CHAPTER THREE

Abby

I DIDN'T HAVE time for this.

I should head back to Le Miel and make sure Makayla had everything under control.

Instead, I had to play nice with *him*.

'This table suit?' Tanner gestured to the only vacant table for two outside the café. A cosy table.

Swallowing my first retort of 'hell no', I nodded. 'Let's get this done so I can head back to the patisserie.'

'Why the hurry to get rid of me?' He pulled out my chair, a gentlemanly gesture at odds with the raw toughness that radiated off him. 'I told you I'd behave.'

I managed a tight smile in thanks as I sat, well aware that Tanner's version of 'behaving' and mine would be continents apart.

'What'll you have?' He sat and pushed his shirt-sleeves up, revealing heavily inked arms.

I didn't like tattoos. Couldn't fathom what drove

a person to scar their skin like that. But as Tanner leaned his forearms on the table, I couldn't tear my gaze away from the sheer artistic beauty that started above his wrists and wound its way up.

Elaborate vines. Stunning roses. Intricate motifs. Symbols I couldn't decipher from this distance but wanted to get closer to.

I found myself inadvertently leaning forward before realising what I was doing, and when I glanced up Tanner grinned like he knew exactly how fascinating I found him.

'See anything you like?'

'No,' I snapped, sounding uptight and prudish, the situation made worse by the wash of heat flushing my cheeks.

'They extend a lot further than my arms,' he said, his voice low and gravelly, the underlying hint of naughtiness making my thighs clench. 'In case you were wondering.'

'I don't like tattoos,' I said, making a mockery of my supercilious declaration when my gaze strayed to those forearms again.

Strong. Sinuous. Sexy.

Damn.

'Many people don't.' He shrugged, like my opinion meant little. 'They see tats and think bikers and drug lords. They don't get the artistic angle at all.'

'You like art?'

It was the safe thing to say, a conversation starter that would get us off the topic of his tattoos and his body. I hoped.

'I like ink.' He leaned back in his chair and interlocked his hands behind his head, a guy comfortable in his own skin.

Which he revealed more of as the hem of his shirt rode up and I got a tantalising glimpse of more ink on his lower belly. I couldn't make out the design, but it looked suspiciously like a cutlass and a hook.

'A pirate, seriously?' The words popped out before I could stop them and while I was horrified I'd articulated my thoughts, he laughed so loud nearby patrons turned to stare.

'Don't look so shocked,' he drawled, filling our glasses from the water bottle between us. 'I like a good pillage like the next pirate.'

I compressed my lips before I blurted anything else. Like how I'd rather walk the plank than be pillaged by him.

Though that wasn't entirely true, and after my disastrous marriage, I'd made a promise to myself to never lie again—especially to myself.

In less than thirty minutes, Tanner King had made me feel more alive than I had in years. He riled me. He taunted me. His cocky, laid-back attitude annoyed the crap out of me.

But I liked the buzz making my skin prickle and the weird hollow feeling deep in my belly. Like I was missing something. Like I craved something.

Much to my horror, I had to admit that he turned me on a little. A lot. Whatever.

Bastard.

'Let me guess. You're going to make some crude remark about what constitutes the pirate's peg leg.'

He laughed again, the crinkles at the corners of his eyes endearingly cute. 'You're funny. I like that in a woman.'

The natural retort, that he'd like all women, hovered on the tip of my tongue but a waitress appeared and after she'd taken our orders—double shot espresso for him, soy latte for me—I was back to being scrutinised by his intense golden gaze and liking it too much.

I needed to get this meeting back on solid ground. Professional. Far from charming smiles and pirate peg legs.

'Remy told me you've run restaurants?'

A shadow clouded his eyes for a moment, a hint of sadness, before he blinked and I wondered if I'd imagined it. 'Yeah, but nightclubs are more my thing.'

I bet. I could imagine him prowling around a dim room like a panther stalking its prey at night. Senses on high alert. Watching. Waiting. Before pouncing on some poor unsuspecting female.

Though with the amount of testosterone radiating off his taut body, maybe I should amend that to lucky female.

'I haven't seen you around the patisserie?'

He'd been toying with the cutlery on the table and he stilled, like I'd taken a shot at him for not being around for his brother. 'I've been working in London and LA. Helping friends set up similar nightclubs to the ones I run here.'

'How altruistic.' The sarcasm slipped out before I could stop it and I wasn't surprised when he frowned at me. 'Sorry, that sounded bitchy. It's an important day for me and then Remy fell and I was so worried...about him and the patisserie and getting everything done...'

Great, now I sounded like a rambling loser. But to Tanner's credit, he didn't make a joke. In fact, he looked surprisingly serious, the first time I'd seen him like this in our brief acquaintance. I liked it. That he could lose the clown act when called for.

'You won't have to do it on your own, that's why I'm here,' he said, eyeballing me with curiosity. 'As for my big brother, he'll be fine.'

He paused, a glimmer of a frown slashing his brows. 'So it's an important day, huh? What's the occasion? You getting hitched?'

I snorted and wrinkled my nose. 'Been there. Done that. Tore the bouquet to pieces.'

'You're married?'

'As of today, officially divorced.' I made jazz hands. 'Woop-de-freaking-do.'

'Being divorced has gotta be better than being married,' he said, making *married* sound like a dirty word.

'It is when you're married to a cold, heartless dweeb because it seemed the right thing to do at the time.'

Even now I could see that day so clearly. The rear garden of my parents' harbourside mansion converted into a winter wonderland. Massive marquees. White chiffon draping everything. Fairy lights twinkling in the perfectly manicured trees. Five hundred of their closest acquaintances. And Bardley, waiting at the altar, staring at me with avarice, like he'd scored a prized portfolio.

I should've made a run for it then. But I'd been a people-pleaser to the end, and given up my soul in the process.

Never, ever, again.

'I thought women viewed marriage as hearts and flowers and all that crap, not something to do because it's *right*.' He made cutesy inverted comma signs with his fingers. 'Want to talk about it?'

His mouth eased into a sexy smile. 'Tell Uncle Tanner all your dirty little secrets.'

If he only knew.

'No dirt and it's not a secret. Married at twenty-one to a guy I'd virtually grown up with. Family friends. Our folks pushed us together constantly so it seemed like a natural progression to get married.'

My chest tightened at the memory of what had happened after I'd said 'I do'. Of how Bardley had morphed into a sadistic, controlling monster. 'Moved into Vaucluse. Perfect house. Perfect life. Except it wasn't so perfect...'

I trailed off, wondering why the hell I was revealing all this to a virtual stranger. Then again, maybe that was the attraction. I didn't know Tanner and he knew jack about me. Today was a turning point for me. Proof that I'd walked away from my old life. I'd been counting down the days until I was officially divorced and who knew? Maybe once I'd purged all the crap I'd bottled up for so long I might be able to finally accept that the past didn't control me any more.

'Did the bastard hit you?' Tanner growled, and I glanced up, surprised to see his hands clenched into fists. 'I don't care if you're divorced. Tell me where to find the prick and I'll beat him to a pulp.'

'Whoa, he-man.' I held up my hands. 'Bardley was emotionally and verbally abusive, but he never laid a finger on me.'

'That other shit's just as bad,' he muttered, his hands relaxing a little. 'What kind of a dickhead name is Bardley, anyway?'

I smiled, his ferociousness as sexy as the rest of him.

'"That other shit" is why I left him. It got to a point where I couldn't take it any more…' I shook my head, remembering the exact moment I'd taken control of my life.

He'd belittled me in front of his friends, forcing me to try water-skiing when he knew I was petrified of any water above bathtub level. I ended up spraining my wrist after taking a bad tumble the first time I tried to stand on the skis. It had been a suspected fracture. Bardley had mocked me. Been totally indifferent to my pain. Had called me names.

I'd packed with my one good hand that night and taken a cab to a motel. Spent a good hour emptying my bank accounts and maxing out my credit cards by paying a top lawyer most of his fee in advance.

I regretted being a fool. Being the kind of woman

to put up with that treatment from anyone. Then again, I'd been doing it my entire life, so I guess my idiocy had been ingrained from birth.

'So what's the plan?'

'Plan?' I mimicked, coming back to the present, almost surprised to find myself sitting at a harbourside café on a glorious spring day with a seriously hot guy.

'To celebrate your divorce.' He lowered his voice. 'You have got something in mind to celebrate, right?'

'I'd envisaged leaving the patisserie early tonight to kick back with a spectacular red wine and Channing Tatum, but it looks like I'll be stuck working 'til late, taking over Remy's duties and prepping for tomorrow.'

He rolled his eyes, his upper lip curled in derision. 'What is it with women and Channing Tatum?'

'Hot bod. Chiselled jaw. And the guy has the moves. What's not to like?'

'He's a fantasy.' He sniggered, a decidedly wicked sound. 'Wouldn't you prefer a real man?'

I saw the challenge in Tanner's unwavering stare. Taunting me. Encouraging me to say yes.

I knew what he was offering.

A night of debauchery.

A night to wipe away sour memories of my marriage.

A night to come alive.

But I had to work with this guy for the next four weeks. Remy was depending on me, and no way in hell would I screw up his faith in me by screwing his brother.

'I'd prefer if we drank our coffees and got back to the patisserie,' I said, exhaling in relief when the waitress appeared to place our order on the table.

'Fair enough,' he said, but he wasn't done yet. The twinkle in his eyes alerted me to the fact that every second I had to spend with him over the next month would be pure, unadulterated torture. 'But if you want to ditch the fantasy in favour of the real thing, you know where to find me.'

He picked up his small coffee cup and raised it in my direction. 'Here's to a good working relationship, real-life celebrations and finding the elusive peg leg.'

I choked on my first sip of latte and he laughed, a low, sexy chuckle that sent a jolt of longing through me.

Yeah, it was going to be a *long* four weeks.

CHAPTER FOUR

Tanner

I TOOK ONE step into Le Miel and wished I'd said hell no when Remy asked me to help him out.

There was a reason I avoided the patisserie. With its polished honey floorboards, sunlight spilling inside and the tempting aromas of warm yeast and sugar heavy in the air, it reminded me of home.

Of Mum.

I'd been ten when she died, twenty long years ago. My memories of her might have faded with time but I'd never forget standing next to her in the kitchen while she baked. Passing her cups of flour. Gently handling eggs. Having my own board to roll pastry on. Licking icing from my sticky fingers.

Our kitchen had been huge, almost industrial-sized. Mum had run a makeshift cupcake business from home but mostly she'd loved to cook. It was her passion, like she'd been my father's, the French-woman who'd stolen his heart on a gap-year trip to Paris.

Pity the romance hadn't lasted.

From what Remy told me, Dad had taken one look at Claudette Allard and she'd become the number one woman in his life. They'd married in two months, had Remy a year later and I'd arrived five years later. And from what I'd overheard that fateful day Mum had died, everything had turned to shit about then.

Dad avoided the kitchen and even as a youngster I'd been glad. We were happier when he wasn't around, me, Mum and Remy.

I'd loved those days when we'd all be in there together: Mum smacking my hand for sneaking a croissant before it had cooled. Remy helping me with a tricky letter on the icing. Me proudly presenting Mum with her favourite chocolate cupcake that I'd baked from scratch. Just the three of us, laughing and joking around. Happy. Together.

Until that day I'd heard my parents argue, the kind of argument that had imprinted on my brain no matter how many times, how many drinks and how many women I'd used to dislodge it. The day Mum had been so upset she'd rushed out of the house, got in her car and been killed in a crash, leaving us with Dad.

And my hell had begun.

'You okay?'

I glanced down to see Abby's hand lightly resting on my forearm, concern crinkling her brow.

Annoyed I'd let memories get to me, I shrugged off her touch. 'Yeah. Let's get started.'

She didn't believe me. She had this way of staring

at me with those deep blue eyes like she could see right through me. It was disconcerting.

No one saw the real me. Ever.

'You've been here before, right?'

I nodded. 'Not for a while though.'

She didn't ask why but I could see her condemnation in the flattening of her lips.

'I'll show you Remy's office as that's where you'll be working.'

So she didn't know I could cook? Interesting. I could have a lot of fun showing Miss Prim and Proper exactly what I could do with a rolling pin.

'Lead the way,' I said, with a mock bow, biting back a laugh when she gritted her teeth.

This could be fun if I concentrated on baiting my cool co-worker rather than mentally rehashing maudlin memories.

The late-morning crowd had thinned to a few mums with toddlers and an older couple reading the newspaper. From the few times I'd been here over the years, I knew early mornings and lunchtimes were hectic. Remy would have hired staff accordingly but a sliver of worry niggled.

I ran successful nightclubs employing hundreds of people. I'd run restaurants up and down the eastern seaboard. So why the touch of anxiety that I could be in over my head with one patisserie?

Because this place was Remy's pride and joy, and I knew it. I owed my brother a lot. He'd cheered me up when I'd been young and reeling from Dad's subtle hatred, even if he'd been oblivious as to the reason behind my sulks. He'd shown me how to cook, how to play footy, how to be a man by using clever words rather than my fists when kids teased me at school for not having a mum. He'd raised me when the old man had the decency to curl up his toes when I was fifteen, never complaining at being saddled with a recalcitrant teen when most guys were partying at twenty.

Remy was my hero, always had been, and the only person I let get close. So I'd make damn sure that not only did the patisserie continue business as usual, but also that it flourished.

As we passed the gleaming stainless-steel counter, a young guy popped up from behind it, balancing a stack of trays. Abby smiled and the poor guy almost dropped the trays. I didn't blame him. I hadn't seen the ice princess smile much since we'd met but when she did…*kapow*. I felt it like a kick to the guts.

'Shaun, I'd like you to meet Tanner King, Remy's brother. He'll be the boss around here 'til Remy's back on his feet.'

I stuck out my hand. 'Good to meet you.'

'You too.' Shaun placed the trays on the counter and shook my hand. Firmly. Earning him brownie points. 'Abby texted me earlier to let me know he's going to be okay. That's good news.'

'Sure is.' The kid couldn't have been more than eighteen yet for some reason the thought of Abby texting him about anything stung. Pathetic. 'Have you been working here long?'

'Two months,' he said, shooting Abby a scared look, like he expected I'd fire him on the spot. 'I've enrolled at a college to do pastry work, and I need the hours here as part of an apprenticeship.'

'You're in the right place.' I tempered my tone so the kid wouldn't look so damn frightened. 'Remy's the best.'

'He sure is.' A woman sauntered out from the corridor linking the shop to the kitchen.

If Abby was ice, this one was fire.

Flaming red hair, deep blue eyes and the body of a lithe goddess. She moved like a dancer, confidence and strength, like she knew her place in the world and wasn't afraid to flaunt it. A stunner. Yet I felt nothing but appreciation for her as a beautiful woman, whereas Abby turned me on with a tilt of her snooty nose.

Go figure.

'Hi, I'm Makayla Tarrant, waitress extraordinaire.' She held out her hand and I shook it, a little relieved when there was no zing. 'Hope you're ready to roll up your shirtsleeves and get to work. Remy doesn't appreciate slackers around here.'

Abby appeared outraged, shoulders drawn back and icy glare back in full force, and I laughed, liking the other woman already.

'You'll be pleased to know I intend to work as hard as the rest of you while I'm here.' I pushed up my sleeves for emphasis, liking when Abby's gaze drifted to my forearms.

She'd been mesmerised when I'd done it earlier at the café, like she'd never seen ink before. A blush had appeared on her cheeks as she'd studied me, and

I'd had the craziest impulse to strip off and show her exactly how much ink covered my body and where.

'Good, then let's get started.' Abby cleared her throat, oddly brusque, and that blush was back.

Oh, yeah, showing her the rest of my tats could be fun.

'Nice meeting you both,' I said, with a wave at Makayla and Shaun.

Shaun shot me a nervous smile and Makayla nodded, her gaze assessing, like she couldn't figure me out.

Join the long line, honey.

Abby strode down the corridor that led to the kitchen, and I followed, the aroma of sugar and cinnamon and buttery goodness getting stronger with every step.

For a moment, I couldn't breathe.

Sadness clogged my throat. Potent. Disorienting.

When she opened a door marked 'Office' off the corridor, I'd never been more grateful.

I couldn't enter the kitchen right now, not when some strange nostalgia gripped me, making me yearn for a past I'd left behind a long time ago.

'Remy's very organised, so you'll find everything documented in spreadsheets. Supply order forms. Current stock. Online orders. The works...' She trailed off as I slammed the door, wishing I could do the same on the memories swamping me. 'Tell me what's wrong.'

'Nothing,' I growled, annoyed that she was so insightful. 'Continue the induction.'

'No.' She folded her arms, her superiority annoying me as much as the relentless memories of how much I missed Mum. 'For some reason, being here has you rattled, and I need to know why so we can fix it.'

'Babe, you may be many things, a shrink isn't one of them.' I stalked towards her, covering the short distance between us. 'I don't need to be *fixed*.'

'I—I didn't mean it like that.' She took a small step back as I invaded her personal space. 'I want this place to run smoothly while Remy's away and if there's a problem I want it sorted now before it affects business.'

I admired her dedication to my brother. Not many employees would give a rat's ass about their boss's business. But no way in hell would I stand here and be analysed by her ladyship.

'So that's what's all-important to you, is it? Business?'

A tiny dent appeared between her brows, as if she didn't understand the question, before she nodded. 'Of course. Remy gave me a chance when my life was down the toilet. I owe him. And I won't have you breezing in here on the pretext of helping and screwing it up.'

My respect ratcheted up further. I didn't like many people in this world let alone respect them, so I decided to wind her up a little to detract from the flood of uncharacteristic emotions swamping me the last few minutes.

'If you're all business, when do you have time for pleasure?'

Her lips parted in a surprised little O and I took it a step further.

'You do know what *pleasure* is?'

I leaned in, close enough to smell the sweetness of vanilla in her hair, close enough to see her porcelain skin was one hundred percent natural and unadorned by make-up, close enough to kiss her if I was so inclined.

'Back off,' she said, her fighting words at odds with the soft, breathy way she uttered them.

'Make me.' I squared my shoulders, wondering when I'd last enjoyed sparring with a woman this much.

'You're such a...child,' she muttered, and I laughed at how she must've watered down that insult.

'And you're all woman.' I leaned against a filing cabinet, knowing she'd have to push past me to get out. 'But a prickly one. Don't you ever lighten up?'

Anger sparked in her eyes, flecks of vibrant emerald and sizzling sapphire among the blue. 'I haven't got time to lighten up. I work ten-hour days here, five days a week, while attending classes one day a week to complete my apprenticeship. On Sunday, my one day off, I do extensive research to update my blog so that people will know who the hell I am if I eventually save up enough to open my own place one day.'

Her chest heaved with indignation as she tried to shove past me. 'So why don't *you* lighten the hell up and give me a freaking break?'

I should've felt bad for pushing her to this point. I didn't. Because if her icy façade had turned me on, it had nothing on this outraged, furious woman.

She was spectacular.

So I calmed her down the only way I knew how.

I hauled her against me and kissed her.

I caught her off guard, her gasp of surprise all I needed to invade her mouth, my tongue taunting hers as much as my words.

I'd expected her to retreat. To possibly bite me. I didn't expect the low moan that emanated from the back of her throat, like a primitive growl that reverberated all the way down to my soul. Or the way she pushed against me, so hard my back slammed against the filing cabinet.

The ice princess liked it rough and ready. Who knew?

I ravaged her mouth, palming her breast and tweaking a nipple as she writhed against me. Hot. Wanton. Abandoned.

If she didn't stop, I wouldn't be able to and, as much as I'd like to, screwing her on Remy's desk my first day here wasn't part of the plan.

Remy.

With an anguished groan I wrenched my mouth from hers, stunned I'd let it get this far.

What was it about this woman that made me forget boundaries let alone my own name?

'I need to get to work.' I pushed past her like nothing had happened and took a seat behind the desk, adjusting myself as I did so and wishing my brother had the smarts to install a shower at his workplace.

I'd never needed a cold shower so frigging badly.

Abby stared at me in open-mouthed disbelief. I knew the feeling. I couldn't believe we'd just done that either.

'I—you—shit,' she muttered, shaking her head as I tried not to notice her reddened lips and her flushed cheeks, blond tendrils sticking out all over the place.

She looked like we'd done a lot more than kiss, and my cock throbbed again.

'Don't expect me to apologise for that,' I said, waving her away in a cruel dismissal, like the kiss meant nothing.

When in fact I needed her to leave ASAP so I wouldn't be tempted for a repeat. Next time, I might not be able to stop.

'I don't expect anything from you.' The haughtiness was back as she tilted her chin and stared down her nose at me. 'Not a single bloody thing.'

She slammed the door on her way out.

I didn't blame her.

CHAPTER FIVE

Abby

IF THERE WERE awards handed out to people for the art of pretending, I'd have an entire shelf full. A room full. An entire house full. I'd be in the academy's hall of freaking fame.

I'd done it my whole life. Pretending I liked the handcrafted silver jewellery box for my seventh birthday when I'd wanted a backyard cricket set. Pretending I liked having a fully catered disco party for my thirteenth birthday when I'd wanted to have fish and chips on the beach with my only friend. Pretending I didn't mind having a lavish society wedding when I would've been happy swapping vows at the register office.

Yeah, I was an expert at pretence. A goddamn queen. Which was how I managed to get through the rest of the day, creating brioche and baguettes and *pains au chocolat*, like that kiss had never happened.

That kiss.

Six hours later, it still haunted me.

Powerful and commanding and so damned passionate I got damp just thinking about it.

I'd never, ever, been kissed like that.

Like stepping into a raging inferno, consumed by heat from the inside out and not giving a damn.

I'd lost it. The moment his mouth covered mine I hadn't been able to think. Hadn't wanted to, if I was completely honest. Because kissing Tanner King put a full stop on my old life and kickstarted my new.

I'd wanted to celebrate with Channing tonight. Instead, I'd got a brief taste of Tanner and I wasn't disappointed. Angry at myself for letting it happen. Confused why he'd done it. And seriously peed off. But never disappointed.

God, the man could kiss.

If I was the queen of pretending, he was the master of manipulating lips.

My hand drifted upward to my mouth and a fingertip traced my bottom lip. I could swear it still tingled from the way he'd devoured me.

'All locked up, Abs.'

I jumped and spun around, hoping Makayla hadn't seen me. 'Thanks.'

She grinned and pointed to the small table set up in the kitchen where staff took their meal breaks. 'Why don't you sit and tell me all about the dishy Tanner while I fix us a hot chocolate?'

'Nothing to tell,' I said, far too quickly, and Makayla raised a knowing brow.

'You've been avoiding the office all afternoon and blushing at random times for no reason so I beg to

differ, my friend.' Makayla tittered as she performed
a little pirouette, something she did often, as if to
keep her dance training at the forefront of her mind.
'Plus I just saw you staring into space and touching
your lip, so I'm guessing you're fantasising about Hot
Stuff kissing you.'

'You're too damn perceptive for your own good,' I
muttered, but took a seat at the table anyway. 'Make
mine a double.'

'Two giant marshmallows coming up,' she said,
busying herself at the stove. 'Have to say, it's nice
to see you lust over a guy. In the three months I've
been here, you haven't mentioned anyone let alone
been out on a date.'

Was I that pathetic? Considering I'd avoided men
for the last twelve months since Bardley the Bastard,
probably.

'Who said I'm lusting over Tanner?'

Makayla beamed as she poured hot chocolate into
two mugs. 'Sweetie, it's all over your face.'

'Am I that easy to read?'

'I'm good at reading people.' Makayla plopped two
marshmallows in each mug and headed for the table.
'Got a ton of experience at an old job.'

Sadness downturned her mouth for a moment, like
it had been a less than pleasant experience, before her
signature smile was back and she visibly brightened.
Makayla spent all her spare time attending dance auditions and had worked in a few theatre productions.
Maybe she needed to get a read on the competition?

'It's probably my self-imposed year-long drought—'

'You haven't been with a guy in a *year*?' Makayla squealed and mimicked a faint as I rolled my eyes.

'Yeah, I'm that much of a sad case.'

It wasn't until that moment I realised I was. Sad. My marriage might have been bland at best, but I missed the intimacy of having someone to debrief with at the end of a day. Of having a male perspective on life. Of being with a guy, even if the sex had been as lacklustre as the marriage.

Maybe that was why I'd enjoyed Tanner's kiss so much?

Yeah, and downplaying it would make me forget it in a hurry. Not.

'You need to get out more,' Makayla declared, her forehead crinkled in thought. 'A night out on the town. You and me. Drinks. Dancing. Deviously scoping out hot guys.'

'Nightclubs aren't really my thing—'

'Bull.' Makayla waggled her finger at me. 'I'm not taking no for an answer. If you're lusting over our new boss on the first day, you need to get laid.'

'I'm not a guy—'

'Girls have needs too, and after a year? Sweetie, you must be pretty damn needy.'

I laughed as Makayla wiggled her eyebrows.

'There's this fabulous club, the hottest dance venue in Sydney, called Embue. We're going. Tomorrow night.' She did another jig. 'So get your dancing shoes on, baby, because I'm not taking no for an answer.'

I'd seen Makayla like this before, when she'd railroaded me last month into buying an exquisite rose silk scarf I couldn't afford at The Rocks market. And before that, when she'd insisted I attend an art gallery opening that featured the weirdest nude paintings.

She wouldn't give up until I said yes, so I sighed. 'What kind of a weird name is Embue?'

'It means *steamy* in French.' Makayla winked and fanned her face. 'Don't you want to get all steamed up over some guy?'

I already was and that was the problem. Because heading out to some dark, dingy nightclub to scope out men wouldn't make me forget Tanner and the potency of his kiss.

I'd need to meet Channing or his equivalent for that to happen and the odds were a billion to one of any guy remotely coming close to my screen idol.

But I had a feeling Makayla wouldn't let up. She'd asked me out to go clubbing several times since she'd started working here and we'd become friends, and I'd fobbed her off with excuses of homework.

With school holidays coming up and the universities winding down, she wouldn't buy that excuse this time.

I gave a resigned shrug. 'Okay. Let's do it.'

Makayla clapped her hands, excitement making her eyes glitter. 'Two babes out to shake things up. Can't wait.'

I could, but I needed something—maybe even someone—to distract me from this insane attraction to Tanner.

A night out could be just the thing I needed.

CHAPTER SIX

Tanner

I HAD TO hand it to my brother. He sure knew how to run a business. Le Miel turned a handy profit and had the potential to expand if the boutique next door ever accepted his generous offer to buy them out.

I'd studied the spreadsheets yesterday and today, and couldn't find a single weak spot.

Unlike me, who'd discovered a major one: for prim, snooty women who kissed like a frigging dream.

Even now, a day and a half later, I couldn't get that kiss out of my head. Which was plain crazy, considering the number of women I'd kissed over the years. I hadn't been in double figures for a long while so why did Abby, with those weird azure blue eyes and her cool façade, get to me so damn bad?

So I'd done what had to be done. Avoided her. Snuck out yesterday while she'd been in the kitchen with Makayla, and locked myself away in the office all day today.

We'd exchanged civil greetings this morning, that

was it. Suited me fine. I didn't have time to be some society girl's plaything. Her walk on the wild side to celebrate her divorce.

Not that I wasn't interested. Sex with Abby had the potential to be phenomenal. Women coming out of a shitty marriage could go off like firecrackers.

But Remy would bust my balls if I inadvertently hurt her and she quit out of some misguided notion that any future chance meetings between us would be uncomfortable.

It had happened before, when I'd been young and dumb; had opened my first club and slept with my accountant. She'd been looking for more than a good time, despite her reassurances before things started up. When it soured she left and I'd lost the best damn accountant in the business.

No, I wouldn't be responsible for screwing this up for Remy, not when he'd spoken so highly of Abby when I'd called him last night and first thing this morning.

I'd keep my distance. Maybe even apologise for that kiss. Remy's business had steadily increased over the last year and, considering he recorded Abby's progress as part of her apprenticeship, looked like his protégé had been a big part of that.

Le Miel and Remy couldn't afford to lose Abby.

Which meant I had to keep the snake in its cage.

I glanced at the clock. After seven, when I needed to start my own work at nine. No time for a workout to ease the kinks out of my back. Sitting at a desk for twelve hours straight was for fools.

Pressing the tips of my fingers to my eyes, I did a few yoga breaths while rolling my shoulders. I heard the door open and when I opened my eyes, Abby stood in front of me, with a steaming espresso and an almond croissant.

'You've been working hard all day and haven't been out, so I thought you might like a snack?'

'You're an angel,' I said, meaning it, as the pungent Brazilian brew hit my nose and I inhaled greedily. 'Thanks.'

'You're welcome.'

A faint blush stained her cheeks, as if she wasn't used to praise, and damned if I wasn't catapulted straight back to yesterday morning when I'd kissed her.

Her blush had been deeper then, the blue of her eyes so damn crystal clear I could've drowned in them.

My cock hardened in agreement and I inwardly cursed. Remember Remy and Le Miel and a flourishing bottom line?

Down, boy.

She handed me the coffee and placed the plate on the desk. 'At the risk of sounding like a nag, you shouldn't lock yourself away in here all day and not eat.'

'Who said I don't have a secret stash of energy bars in the top drawer?'

She quirked an eyebrow. 'Do you?'

'Nah, but if it stops you nagging, I'll say it.'

She smiled and it softened her features from pretty

to breathtaking. 'I'm heading out soon so are you okay to lock up?'

'Sure, go head.' I tapped my temple. 'The alarm combo is stashed away up here.'

The corners of her mouth twitched. 'Not sure how you can remember any new numbers when you must have a phone book's worth stored up there already.'

I laughed, enjoying this softer side of her. 'Did you just make fun of my little black book?'

She held her thumb and forefinger an inch apart. 'A little.'

Surprised by her lighthearted sparring when I'd expected her to be gauche and standoffish after that kiss, I feigned indignation. 'I'll have you know my mental capacity is much less than you give me credit for, so I keep the thousands of women's phone numbers stored in my cell.'

'Little wonder you have such a big one—' Her lips clamped shut and her eyes widened in horror at her gaff.

'We are talking about my cell, right? Or are you still obsessing over my peg leg?'

The blush returned, deepening her cheeks to a rosy pink. 'It's been a long day. I really should go.'

'And I really should let you.'

But neither of us moved, our gazes locked in some invisible battle of wills while electricity sparked between us.

I had to do something to break this tenuous hold she had on me before I did something monumentally stupid, like kiss her again. And not stop at a kiss this time.

'I'm sorry for kissing you yesterday,' I blurted, not sorry at all. 'It was out of line. Blame it on my jet lag, concern over Remy and your unfailing knack of goading me.'

'Glad to know it wasn't my womanly charms,' she said, her dry response tempered with a smile. 'Honestly? Don't worry about it. Forgotten, just like that.'

She snapped her fingers and damned if my ego didn't take a hit.

Forgotten? That made one of us.

'Anyway, got to go. Makayla's taking me clubbing.' She made it sound like her friend was dragging her for a root canal. 'See you tomorrow.'

'Yeah, see you.' I watched her walk out the door, my gaze riveted to her ass.

She worked those black pants like nothing else and I scowled, snatching up the croissant and jamming it into my mouth.

The buttery goodness melted on my tongue and I wondered if its creator would taste as good.

CHAPTER SEVEN

Abby

I'D ENVISAGED EMBUE being a one-room dive with mirrored walls, strobing lights and ear-splitting techno.

Thankfully, I was wrong.

'Isn't this place the coolest?' Makayla clung to
my arm and did a little jive on the spot. 'I've heard
rave reviews about it but this surpasses my expectations by a mile.'

Mine too. Everything about the nightclub screamed
class, from the polished floorboards and soaring ceil-
ings to the chandelier hanging over the DJ's console,
placed smack-bang in the middle of the dance floor.

The dance floor circled the DJ like a giant shimmering oil slick, with golden velvet lounges in booths
surrounding it. Cream and gold were everywhere,
from the chiffon-covered walls to the coasters.

The entire effect was upscale elegance rather than
downtown disco.

I loved it.

As for the music, I actually recognised the song, an upbeat nineties number that made me sway a little.

I elbowed Makayla. 'Should I make a confession now that I've never been to a nightclub?'

Makayla gripped my arm tighter and swung me around to face her. 'What the... I could've sworn you just said you'd never been to a nightclub?'

I held up my free hand. 'The truth and nothing but the truth.'

'What are you, a nun?' She released my arm, only to slug it. 'Girlfriend, either you've been in a cult or kidnapped by a madman who kept you locked up, because everyone on the planet has been to a nightclub at some point in their lives.'

Being part of the perfect Prendigasts had been like living in a cult, before being virtually kidnapped by Bardley and living in a prison of my own making.

'I got married at twenty-one.'

Makayla shook her head, a riot of glossy red curls tumbling over her bare shoulders dusted in glitter. 'But didn't you ever sneak into a nightclub underage? Go out with your friends from school?'

'I went to an all-girls private school and no, we didn't sneak out.'

We didn't do much of anything bar go on expensive shopping trips and have mani-pedis in the private comfort of our mansions. Not that I could call any of the girls I'd hung out with as friends. They'd been the bitchiest group I'd ever encountered, clones of their mothers whose only ambition was to find a rich, upper-class guy and marry him.

All they'd ever talked about was who had the latest designer bag, who had the most expensive car sitting in the garage for when they turned eighteen and which guys from the elite boys' schools were the best to shag.

How I'd longed to be part of those groups of girls who hung around together at the local shops, swapping frozen yoghurts and gossip while they waited for the school bus instead of Daddy's chauffeur.

Those girls had looked genuinely happy, despite their ripped blazers and holey jumpers. My folks had taught me from a young age that money could buy anything. They'd been wrong. I couldn't buy happiness, the kind I'd seen on those girls' faces.

'Sweetie, you need to start living.' Makayla gave me a gentle nudge towards the dance floor. 'Starting now.'

I wanted to let loose but I caught sight of myself in a floor-to-ceiling-length mirror and baulked.

Whereas Makayla fit in here with her dramatic make-up, sexily mussed hair, towering stilettos and a strapless figure-hugging purple mini, I looked like a grandma with my blow-dried hair, clear lip gloss and mascara, moderate heels and a staple sleeveless LBD that ended at my knees.

Who knew little black dresses had gone out of fashion around the same time I'd gone out of circulation?

'You're dancing. Now.' Makayla shoved me again and this time I let myself be propelled onto the dance floor, joining the throngs of writhing bodies moving in time to an old pop song about spinning around.

I liked music and always had the latest stuff on a playlist while I baked. But bopping around a kitchen and moving my body in front of a bunch of strangers were worlds apart.

Thankfully, nobody gave a flying fig as I started to shuffle my feet. Allowed my shoulders to relax and my hips to sway to the music.

'There you go. You're dancing and the ceiling hasn't caved in.' Makayla put her hand over her mouth in mock horror. 'Wow, you may even start having fun.'

'Bite me,' I yelled above the music, moving my body faster and adding a shimmy for good measure.

Makayla laughed and flung her arms in the air, her body sensual and sinuous as she executed moves I could never dream of pulling off.

After the first song, I lost track of how many we danced to. Daggy songs from the eighties mingled with the latest techno beats as I danced my ass off. Wiggling my hips. Shimmying my shoulders. Not caring that I jiggled in places I hadn't jiggled in a long time.

I enjoyed it. Until an old boyfriend of Makayla's slunk up to us and I quickly realised that three was a crowd.

I tapped her on the arm and gestured towards the bar. 'I'll leave you two alone.'

'You don't have to go.' Makayla's gaze swung between the guy and me and I could tell she was torn.

'Seriously, I'm zonked anyway. I'll just have a drink, then take a taxi home.'

'You sure?'

I nodded. 'Absolutely.' I leaned in and pecked her on the cheek. 'Go have fun.'

Still Makayla wavered. 'But tonight was supposed to be about you and finding some hot guy to end your drought.'

'Another time,' I said, giving her a gentle nudge in the direction of the guy waiting patiently for us to finish our conversation. 'Go. Be naughty enough for the both of us.'

A wicked gleam lit her eyes. 'I think I can manage that.'

I laughed and headed off the dance floor. I'd barely made it onto the polished boards before the guy had swept Makayla into his arms and they were doing some weird ritualistic dance that almost looked obscene.

Makayla was a lovely girl, I liked her a lot, and for one fleeting moment I wished I had half the *va-va-voom* factor she did.

With a sigh, I turned.

And ran smack-bang into Tanner.

CHAPTER EIGHT

Tanner

DOING THE ROUNDS of my clubs after putting in two long days at the patisserie wasn't my idea of fun, but I'd been away for almost a year and I wanted to do a stealth visit to see how the managers and staff were coping.

I needn't have worried. I only hired the best and the four clubs I'd visited so far were operating with precision. Embue was the last on my list and, like the rest, the managers were on top of things and the place was packed.

I'd planned on spending thirty minutes mingling, chatting with staff, getting a general feel where I could liven things up.

That plan shot to shit when I spied Abby. Writhing on the dance floor, arms flung wide, hips swaying, out of time with the music but dancing to some imaginary rhythm in her head.

Damned if it wasn't the most erotic thing I'd ever seen.

So I watched. My cock throbbing in time with some crap techno beat. Wanting her.

I saw some guy sleaze up to Makayla and they started chatting like long-lost lovers, all over each other. Leaving Abby a third wheel and about to leave.

She strode off the dance floor and twenty guys in the vicinity swivelled their heads to watch.

Not that she wore anything revealing. In fact, her modest black dress was practically outlandish in a sea of scantily clad women. But it was the way she carried herself. The set of her shoulders. The tilt of her head. The way her hips moved.

She exuded class. And every horndog in the place wanted to see if they could get behind that cool exterior and see how far she could be pushed to get off.

When one guy put down his drink and walked towards her, I made a move, cutting him off. 'Sorry, buddy, she's mine.'

A possessive statement I had no right making but no way in hell would I stand by and watch Abby have to fend off a bunch of horny pricks.

I reached out to tap her on the shoulder when she spun around and smacked into me.

'Whoa.' My arms shot out to grab her, her look of abject horror at finding me here making me want to tease the hell out of her. 'You've got to stop throwing yourself at me like this.'

She recovered her wits and her balance but I didn't release her. I liked having her this close, her nipples grazing my chest, her palpable heat warming my body, the sweat-slicked sheen to her skin.

She looked radiant.

'What are you doing here?'

'I own the place.' I shrugged, like it meant little, when in fact every club I owned was testament to how far I'd come—and how far I'd proved Dad wrong. 'Haven't been here in a year so after I locked up at the patisserie, I've done the rounds of my clubs, checking up on things.'

To my surprise, she hadn't moved. In fact, now that she'd recovered from the shock, she seemed perfectly relaxed having me hold her arms like I wouldn't let go.

'The diligent boss, huh?'

'Something like that.'

We ran out of conversation, our gazes locked in some kind of invisible heated battle, as I wondered what it was about this woman that rattled my cage.

I wanted her with a fierceness I hadn't felt for a long time. If ever. I dated. I screwed. I didn't do commitment. It worked well for me. Sex as exercise. Sex for fun. Sex with women who knew the score and didn't have any expectations.

Women nothing like Abby.

Abby would be a hearts and flowers kind of girl. She'd told me about her bastard ex and the emotional abuse, but who knew what kind of expectations she'd put on the guy? Maybe he hadn't lived up to her high standards? Maybe he'd lashed out verbally when he couldn't handle it?

The moment I thought it, I felt guilty. Just because I wanted Abby and knew that having her would be a screw-up of monstrous proportions, I was trying to find excuses and maligning her in the process. Not cool.

'I should go.' She tried to back away, and the smart thing to do would be to release her.

I tightened my hold. 'Would you like a tour? You can have a drink and relax in the VIP room, then I'll get you a taxi.'

A refusal hovered on her lips. I saw them tremble with it before she clamped them tight and nodded.

Mentally calling myself everything from putz to dickhead, with a long list of obscenities in between, I led her to a shimmering gold curtain in the back corner and pulled it aside.

'After you.'

She hesitated, as if unsure of my intentions. Smart girl.

'What's wrong?'

She glanced sideways at me and, rather than see trepidation in her eyes, I glimpsed excitement. 'I've danced for about two hours nonstop and I'm about to faint if I don't get a drink. Could we skip the long tour and head straight to the bar?'

I smiled, her honesty refreshing. 'Sure, this way.'

We passed through the VIP room, filled with the usual crowd of elite sportsmen, WAGs, models and a visiting rap star from the US. Abby ogled a little but I had a feeling it was more about the way the women were draped all over the men than in any recognition for the VIPs.

For a woman in her early twenties, she was

strangely naïve. Like she hadn't really lived. Rich
girls like her would've gone to the best private school
and been privy to parties from a young age. Sure,
she might have married young but she'd been single
for a year. She must've let loose over the last twelve
months. So why the air of innocence that hovered
over her like a cloud?

'Through here.' I slid a card over a digital lock and
waited for the beep before pushing the door open.

Though no one used this room but me and I hadn't
been in here for a year, I knew it would be immaculate and well stocked. My staff were nothing but pro-
fessionals and word would've travelled fast from the
other clubs that I'd probably drop by tonight.

'What would you like to drink?'

The door slid soundlessly shut behind us and I saw
her glance at it, hesitate, before squaring her shoulders like she'd come to a decision.

She probably didn't trust me. I understood. But
she had nothing to fear. I wouldn't mess with the status quo, no matter how much I wanted to ruffle that
cool façade. Remy was too important to me, and I'd
already screwed up enough in my lifetime to add yet
another thing to feel guilty for.

'Sparkling water if you've got it, please.'

'For you, babe, anything.' I flashed her a quick
grin, surprised when she smiled back. Maybe all that
dancing had loosened up her reservations? 'Take a
seat.'

But she didn't. Instead, she strolled around the
room, inspecting it. 'What is this place?'

'My hideout.' I grabbed a bottle of mineral water out of the bar fridge, unscrewed the cap and poured it into a long glass, adding a sliver of lemon. 'When hosting a bunch of selfish, spoiled brats in the VIP room, I need a place to escape, and this is it.'

'It's nice,' she said, trailing her hand over the butter-soft black leather sofas, the small glass-topped desk in the corner, the display cabinet where I kept my awards. 'These all yours?'

'No, I mug every sportsman who comes in here and stash the loot in here,' I deadpanned, handing her the drink.

'Thanks.' She took the glass and downed the mineral water in several gulps as I stared at the almost convulsive movement of her throat and desperately tried not to imagine her doing something similar to me.

When she finished, she handed me the glass with a sheepish smile. 'I was parched.'

'Want a top-up?'

'Please.' She turned back to the awards as I poured her another glass. 'You've won a lot of stuff in the hospitality industry.'

'Awards are ego-strokers.' I handed her the glass, forcing myself to look away this time. I couldn't be any harder if I tried, grateful that I'd installed a bathroom in here too so the minute I put her in a cab I could take a cold shower. 'I prefer to see results in profit margins.'

She stilled, sadness creeping across her face. 'My

father used to say that a lot. Always about the profit margins.'

'That's what matters most to savvy businessmen. That and a healthy portfolio.'

She screwed up her nose and damned if it wasn't the cutest thing I'd ever seen. 'Is that what you're all about? Because those tattoos speak more about rebelling against convention than caring about portfolios.'

'What's with you and my tats?' I shrugged out of my jacket, flung it on a sofa and rolled up my sleeves. 'Here. Look your fill. Then judge me some more.'

I had no idea where my outburst came from but I felt like a jackass the moment she blushed in mortification.

'I didn't mean to judge—I mean, I just haven't seen tattoos up close and—'

'And you still haven't,' I muttered, hating that she'd touched a sore spot without knowing it and I'd reacted accordingly.

My tats were more than art.

They defined me.

At a time in my life when I hadn't been comfortable in my own skin, I took on a new one.

And having a woman like Abby judge me as just another deadhead rebel because of my tats really pissed me off.

'This would be looking at them up close,' I growled, trying to tamp down my anger and failing as I unbuttoned my shirt and shrugged it off. 'Here. Take a good look. See if you can figure me out.'

I stood in front of her, hands on hips, defiant and

oddly vulnerable. I shouldn't care what she thought of me. After Remy was back on his feet, I'd be outta here and back on the road, heading to Bangkok or Ibiza or Munich, creating successful clubs that would define me more than my tats.

But I did care. And that was what pissed me off the most.

I shouldn't give a flying fuck what Abby thought of me.

Yet I did.

'I'm sorry,' she said, her apology soft and uncertain, her gaze riveted to my chest. 'I've offended you.'

My anger dimmed a little as she scanned my chest as if studying for an art exam. Her hungry gaze gobbling me up and coming back for seconds. She couldn't look away.

I'd never been studied so closely, her scrutiny disconcerting. It felt like she could see through the tats to the real me beneath, the scared little boy I'd once been, desperate for approval.

'You're beautiful,' she said, taking a step closer to study me, gnawing on her bottom lip a little, the innocuous action making me want to throw her down on the sofa and take her.

Not 'the tats are beautiful', but *you're* beautiful', her simple statement deflating what was left of my resentment.

Had it been a slip of the tongue or had she meant it? Because no one saw past my tats and a few moments ago she'd been like the rest, judging me for them.

'May I?' Before I could react she touched me, the

briefest brush of her fingertips skating across my skin, tracing every inch of ink.

The Buddha. The peace sign outlined in flowers. The phoenix.

Symbols of my past.

My search for clarity.

My quest for harmony.

Rising out of the ashes of my childhood.

I held my breath as she moved lower, skirting around the pirate. Her fingertips light as air but making my skin burn.

'Seen enough?' I said through gritted teeth, regretting I'd let my anger get the better of me and done this.

Because daring her to look and expecting her to blush and turn away was far different from having Abby touch me like she wanted to explore my tats.

All over.

Her gaze lifted to mine and the blatant lust darkening her eyes to indigo blew me away.

Fuck, I was in trouble. So much trouble.

'Not nearly enough,' she murmured before placing her hand flush against my straining cock. 'All these pretty tattoos are an insult to your manhood, so you better show me that pirate's peg leg so my faith in you is restored.'

Laughter burst from deep within me as I held onto the last of my self-control.

'Abby, this is a bad idea. You're Remy's protégé and when this all turns to shit—'

'It won't,' she said, stroking me lightly through my

jeans, shredding the last of my resolve. 'One night. That's all I'm asking for.'

She removed her hand and I inwardly cursed my misplaced chivalry. 'Though in fairness, I should disclose I haven't had sex in over a year so I may break you.'

I could resist the snooty princess.

I couldn't resist this playful, honest woman who stared at me like she could devour me in one gulp and come back for seconds.

'Fuck, Abby, you're making this hard—'

'I sure as hell hope so.' She cupped me again, firmer this time, and I lost it.

I dragged her forward and crushed her to me, grinding against her so she was in little doubt to exactly how this would go.

Hot, sweaty animalistic sex. Fast and furious and so fucking good.

She reacted like I'd set her alight. Slamming her mouth to mine. Pushing me against the nearest wall. Climbing all over me.

It was the hottest frigging thing ever, having someone like her want someone like me so damn much.

Her tongue stroked mine, shy and darting one second, bold and commanding the next, as her hand sneaked between us to touch me.

She kissed aggressively, long, deep sweeps of her tongue totally at odds with the aloof front she usually presented. It turned me on even more, the contrast between fire and ice. Hot and cold. So frigging hot.

She'd go off when I entered her, I just knew it, and my cock ached with wanting to be inside her.

I palmed her breast, rolling the nipple between my thumb and forefinger, drawing a deep groan from her. Sensitive breasts, I liked that. I needed to feast on them, to suck on those nipples until she screamed.

But my mind momentarily blanked as she slid her hand inside my jocks. Wrapped her fingers around my cock. And squeezed.

'I want to see you,' she murmured against my mouth, nipping at my bottom lip while continuing to squeeze me. Stroke me. Undo me.

'Right back at you.' I hissed out a breath as her thumb rolled over the head of my cock, and I stilled her hand, withdrew it before I embarrassed myself.

There was something incredibly hot about a shy, reserved woman taking charge, and having her go for my package served to ratchet up the desire pounding through me to a relentless beat.

'Turn around.'

If my guttural growl frightened her, she didn't show it. Instead, her tongue darted out to moisten her bottom lip before she pouted. 'But I want to see the pirate. *All* of him.'

'You will, babe, trust me.' I flashed a wolfish grin. 'But first, I need to see all of you.'

Uncertainty flickered in her eyes, so I hit the dimmer switch, willing to do anything to make her more comfortable.

Anything but stop.

Because I'd ditched my reservations around the time she'd ditched hers and stuck her hand in my pants.

I couldn't stop this. I didn't want to.

Not when she'd articulated exactly what this was. A rebound fuck. We both knew the score and that made it okay.

She didn't expect hearts and flowers.

She wanted hard and fast.

After over a year of celibacy—I didn't have a frigging clue how that had happened considering how damn gorgeous she was—she wanted to use me to break the drought.

The good girl wanting the bad boy to make it all better, even if it was only for one night.

This I could do.

The moment she'd taken emotion out of the equation and shown me exactly what she wanted, I couldn't say no.

I understood wanting to obliterate the past with something a tad wild, something not entirely good, something to make you forget. Boy, did I understand.

'I want you,' she said, the vulnerability of a moment ago fading as she eyeballed me with unabashed hunger. 'Real bad.'

'The feeling's mutual, sweetheart.' I spun her around and homed in on her zipper. Slid the tab down, the rasp of metal against metal meshing with her soft pants of anticipation.

I imagined expanses of soft, creamy skin. Unblemished. Untarnished. The opposite of mine. When I hit the bottom she whimpered a little. I slid my hands up her back. Pushed the dress off her shoulders.

It pooled at her feet, leaving her in matching black satin bra and panties. French cut. Almost prophetic. I liked everything French. French food. French fries. French kissing. And French panties I could tear off with my teeth to feast on her.

Her skin was as beautiful as I'd imagined and I trailed my fingertips across the top of her ass, skirted her waist, drifted upward, loving how soft she felt. She trembled a little as I unhooked the bra and stepped closer to slide it off her arms.

'Beautiful,' I murmured in her ear as I slid my arms around her from behind to cup her breasts. To savour the weight of them. To flick her light brown nipples with my thumbs. 'I can't wait to taste you.'

She made an incoherent sound as her head lolled back a little and I captured her mouth, plucking at her nipples. A deep tongue-tangling kiss, assertive and greedy, as I marvelled at the sweet taste of her, the hot moistness of her mouth, a prelude to how she'd be when I feasted lower.

'More,' she demanded between kisses, and I was only too happy to oblige.

Without taking my mouth off hers, I spun her towards me and ground my hand against her mound.

She moaned and I pushed her panties down, waiting until she'd kicked them off before sliding my fingers between her slick folds, savouring how wet she was. For me.

'Tanner, please…'

I wanted to prolong this, to go down on her once, maybe twice, before finally getting off. But my own months of celibacy ensured I'd take things slow later.

We had all night.

I zeroed in on her clit. Circled it twice. Stunned when she came apart so damn fast.

I hadn't pegged her for a screamer but she made enough noise to make me thankful for the club's soundproofing in every room.

'Wow,' she said, her head sagging against my shoulder, her body trembling with aftershocks. 'I think I needed that.'

I chuckled, her bluntness refreshing. Women didn't articulate much after sex beyond asking where the shower was and implying they wanted another date.

'Plenty more where that came from,' I said, gently easing her away, unable to stop grinning like an idiot when I took in her tousled hair, flushed cheeks and swollen lips. 'In case you were wondering, I love giving head and I plan on going down on you several times tonight.'

Her mouth parted in a shocked O before I continued. 'But first, I need to fuck you. Think you can handle that?'

Her eyes glittered with desire as she nodded and reached for me.

I'd wanted to shuck my jeans and jocks off in record time, get protected and bury myself to the hilt inside her before I exploded. But I let her call the shots because this was her night.

She unsnapped the button on my jeans and, with unsteady hands, yanked the zipper down.

'Easy, babe. Inflicting a mortal injury on me at this stage won't do either of us any good.'

'I want to see you,' she said, eyes wide as she pushed my jeans down my legs, her hungry gaze riveted to the bulge in my jocks.

'Be my guest.' I toed off my shoes and socks, and kicked my jeans away. 'Though haven't you heard staring too long at a guy's cock makes you go blind?'

'I thought playing with it did that?'

I chuckled. Not so innocent after all. 'You're something else.'

A hint of sadness crept into her eyes and I cursed for inadvertently saying the wrong thing. 'You okay?'

Her teeth worried her bottom lip as she shook her head a little. 'I—I haven't done this a lot. And I'm not very good…'

'That useless prick.' An explosive rage filled me at the thought of what her ex had done to her self-esteem. 'Sweetheart, look at me.'

I placed my finger under her chin and tilted it up, the uncertainty clouding her eyes slugging me in the chest. 'It wouldn't matter to me if you were a frigging virgin. This thing between us is pretty damn hot. Fireworks hot. So when we get to the good stuff you'll forget that bastard who did a number on you because I guarantee any problems you had were with him, not you.'

'How can you be so sure—?'

I kissed her. I wouldn't give her any more time to doubt. I had to show her.

She ignited again, her hands everywhere. Grabbing my biceps. My waist. Moaning into my mouth as she dug her fingers into my ass like she couldn't get enough.

I lowered her onto the sofa and broke the kiss, hovering over her like some goddamn avenging angel as she stared at me in wide-eyed wonder.

'That thing you said earlier? About wanting to do me?' She didn't break eye contact as she shimmied out of her panties. 'Please do it.'

I bit back a smile at her avoiding the F word, considering she was naked in front of me, and I didn't have to be asked twice as my gaze zeroed in on nirvana. I liked a full bush and appreciated that she hadn't gone for the Brazilian job many women favoured these days.

'Now it's your turn,' she said, splayed on the sofa like a wanton sex goddess. 'I want to see all of you.'

I slipped my thumbs under the elastic of my jocks and pushed them down and she gasped as my cock sprang free.

'You're huge!' She blushed as she continued to stare, unable to look away. 'I mean, I haven't seen many before. In fact, only one, and that was less than impressive, but you're quite big...' She wolf-whistled and I laughed to hide my surprise that she'd only been with her ex.

No wonder she had reservations when it came to

sex. If the guy had been clueless in the bedroom he would've shoved his insecurities onto her. Dickhead.

'And why does the pirate only have a torso?' An impish smile curved her luscious lips. 'Would've been so much more fun to make *that* his peg leg.'

She pointed to my cock and I chuckled again. 'You're a very bad girl.'

'Not yet, but I'm hoping to be.' She crooked her finger at me. 'Come here and corrupt me.'

I knew this was her fantasy. To have me, the tattooed bad boy, fuck her to eradicate her boring past. Yet for one crazy, inane moment, I wanted her to see me as more than that.

I wanted her to see past my well-honed tough guy persona and want me, Tanner King. Really want *me*.

Annoyed, I grabbed my jeans off the floor and snagged a condom out of my wallet.

Her tongue darted out to moisten her lips as she watched me roll it on, her expression wondrous.

'You sure you're not a virgin?'

A faint pink stained her cheeks. 'I just haven't done it in this much light before.'

Shit. Her ex really must've been a dickhead not to want to see every inch of this glorious woman as he slid inside her.

With an exaggerated wink, I knelt next to the sofa. 'All the better to see you with, my dear.'

Her lips curved into a naughty smile. 'I want to watch too.'

Which meant I needed to put on a show she'd never forget.

But all my intentions to take things slow shot to shit when she slid her ankles apart and her thighs fell open. Giving me an eyeful of moist folds and exactly where I wanted to be.

I grabbed her legs and half turned her, so she was slumped against the sofa with her legs dangling down. Dragging her towards me, I scooted forward on my knees, positioning myself while trying to stop the urge to drive into her and not stop until she screamed my name.

'It's even bigger close up,' she whispered, her audible awe making me grin.

'Maybe you're looking at it through a side mirror?'

She laughed and damned if it wasn't the sweetest sound I'd ever heard.

I didn't usually swap banter during sex. And I rarely laughed. I got in and out. Got the job done. Got off. Felt good. That was it.

And even though we hadn't got to the good part yet, sex with Abby was different.

We connected beyond the bits fitting together.

It disarmed me.

So I focussed on doing what I did best. Ensuring she had a good time.

'Watch me,' I commanded as I gripped my cock in my hand and pressed the head against her clit. Circling it. Rubbing into her slick folds and back again. Over and over until her breath came in pants and her hips shifted restlessly.

'That feels so good.' She propped up on her elbows to watch and I increased the pressure, gritting my teeth against the tension building in my balls.

I'd already warned her about taking this slower later and it would have to do because right now I needed to be inside her so damn bad.

'More,' she gritted out, sweat beading between her breasts as she started to writhe.

'You got it, sweetheart.'

I gave her clit one last rub and as her orgasm started I slid into her. Hard. To the hilt. Sheathed in tight, wet pussy.

Heaven.

I thrust into her fast, using my thumb on her clit as she screamed, desperate to milk every last drop of pleasure out of her.

She surged upward, bringing her breasts into my face, and I took one in my mouth, laving her tight nipple while thrusting into her.

'Too sensitive,' she gasped, wrenching her nipple from my mouth and leaning back on her outreached arms. 'Want. To. See.'

So I let her.

I slid in and out. Harder. Faster. Oblivious to everything but watching her, watching me.

Damned if it wasn't the hottest frigging thing I'd ever seen.

My balls tightened and my mind blanked the moment before I thrust into her one last time. As far as I could go.

The most intense pleasure crashed over me. Wiping me out. Mindless. Boneless.

Conscious of nothing but this woman.

Abby.

My eyes must've closed at some point because when I opened them Abby was staring at me like I'd just given her the keys to the best patisserie in Paris.

'That was amazing,' she whispered, reaching for me. 'I never knew it could be so good.'

'Just good?' I slid my arms around her, cradling her close. Another first for me after sex. I wasn't a cuddler. 'Guess I better lift my game for the rest of the night.'

I couldn't see her face with it buried against my chest, but I sensed her smile.

But as she continued to hang onto me like she'd never let go, the first feelings of remorse flooded me.

For me, this would be a night of amazing sex and I'd walk away in the morning. Back to being Tanner King, the guy everybody labelled, the guy everybody judged, the guy everybody tried to get close to but couldn't.

No matter how stupendously good the sex, tonight wouldn't change me.

Could Abby say the same?

CHAPTER NINE

Abby

I HURT. In places I've never hurt before.

Even now, fifteen hours since I left Tanner's bed in the wee small hours, my muscles twang as a reminder of what I've done.

And how much I enjoyed it.

I didn't know whether to be relieved or annoyed when Tanner didn't front at Le Miel today. Whatever his reason, I couldn't keep the smile off my face.

What we'd done at the club, and later at his apartment…defied logic.

I should never have had sex with Tanner.

So why did I not give a damn that I had?

When he'd taken me to that private room at his club, I'd anticipated having a drink, then leaving. Then he'd got angry, taken off his shirt and I'd lost it.

I didn't usually ogle guys. Sure, I appreciated a fine male body on Bondi Beach in summer like any woman with eyes in her head, but I didn't fantasise about what guys looked like underneath their clothes.

Yet the second Tanner had shrugged off his shirt in defiance I'd wanted to see more. I'd wanted to see all of him.

I must've said the wrong thing and his misplaced anger had prompted him to strip. That was the point I should've called for a cab. Or laughed it off as a joke. Or done anything other than practically drool all over him.

He'd been a good sport about my naivety. Had tried to put me at ease with banter and I'd appreciated it. What I didn't appreciate was my own stupidity wishing I could have more of him.

When I quashed my voice of reason and my inner vixen insisted I deserved one night of sexy fun, it should've ended there. One night.

But after he'd pleasured me countless times with his mouth, his fingers and his very talented and sizeable appendage, I wanted more.

Of course, I hadn't said anything. Instead, I'd been the epitome of casual, like I had one-night stands every day of the week, when he'd kissed me goodnight. If he'd seen through my bravado act, he didn't call me on it. For that, I was grateful.

Because I'd bolted in the wee small hours when he'd been asleep, and during the twenty-minute ride from his penthouse apartment in the city to my apartment over Le Miel I replayed every single moment of our night together and knew that acting like last night didn't mean anything the next time I saw Tanner would take monumental acting skills I didn't possess.

Bardley had always taunted me for being too readable. But he'd been wrong. If I were that easy to read he would've seen my loathing for him on my face every single day.

Thanks to Tanner, I now knew our lacklustre sex life hadn't been my fault. How many times had Bardley called me frigid or cold or worse? Saying I didn't turn him on. That I was as useless in the bedroom as I was in the kitchen.

I hadn't cared about the sex, but insulting my cooking had been a low blow, particularly since I knew I baked like a dream even back then.

Screw him.

Though thankfully, I'd never have to do that again and courtesy of last night I'd replaced memories of a sad sex life with phenomenally amazing erotic ones.

'You're daydreaming again.' Makayla bumped me with her hip. 'You sure you didn't pick up at Embue?'

I felt heat flush my cheeks but I feigned nonchalance as I scrubbed my station. We'd been busy today, frantic, supplying a local private school with pastries for a teacher conference, so I'd managed to avoid Makayla's interrogation. Until now.

'I'm not the one with a story to tell,' I said, pasting a bright smile on my face. 'You and what's-his-name looked mighty cosy when I left last night.'

Makayla screwed up her face. 'There's a reason you date a guy and don't go back.' She held up her little finger and let it droop. 'I'm smarter than that.'

I laughed, wondering what Makayla would say if she knew that a pinkie wouldn't come close to describing Tanner.

'What about you?' Makayla grinned as she dried her hands on a dishcloth. 'You're not still mooning over our dishy boss?'

If only she knew the half of it.

'Don't be silly.'

'Pity he's working off-site today. He brightens up the scenery.' Makayla pursed her lips and tapped them. 'He's nothing like Remy, is he?'

She got that right. Remy and Tanner might be biological brothers but that was where the similarities ended. I couldn't think of two siblings who were so different.

'Yeah, they're nothing alike,' I said, grateful Makayla had moved off the topic of last night and onto safer ground.

'I'm not just talking about looks.' Makayla struck a strong-man pose. 'Tanner's like this big tough guy who swaggers around, and Remy's soft and gentle.'

Tanner could be soft and gentle when it counted, and I'd counted last night. Many times.

'Do you know much about their background?' Makayla leaned against the bench. 'I don't know Remy that well but you've worked here for a year. What's the story?'

I shrugged. 'We don't talk much about our pasts.'

That was the truth. I'd divulged the basics to Remy about my crappy marriage and my dreams to become a pastry chef. He'd told me he'd opened this place many years ago, had never met the right woman and his only living family was Tanner.

When we chatted during a rare lull in our busy

days, we talked pastries, the latest cooking reality show on TV and gave our critiques of the newest cookbooks.

I valued our friendship, especially since he'd offered me a place to live and a job when I'd needed it most, but we weren't the kind of people to reveal too much. I preferred it that way. Until now. Because I'd give anything to discover what made Tanner tick.

'If Remy hasn't revealed much to you, maybe Tanner will?' Makayla's exaggerated wink made me laugh. 'Don't you love that whole bad-boy thing he has going on?'

'Yeah, he's hot.' I settled for a smidgeon of honesty so Makayla wouldn't think anything was wrong.

Like exactly how much Tanner had revealed to me, and how much I'd liked it.

Makayla blew a raspberry. 'Queen of the understatement.'

'What do you want me to say? That he's so damn sexy I get hot flushes just thinking about him?' I pretended to fan my face and Makayla grinned.

'That's more like it…' She trailed off, as if unsure how to continue. 'I've got a confession to make.'

For an awful moment I wondered if Makayla had slept with Tanner too. The thought made bile rise in my throat and I swallowed, feeling increasingly foolish.

Of course a guy like him would go for a girl like Makayla. She was a bombshell. Not to mention beautiful inside and out.

'What's up?' I tried to fake nonchalance. It didn't work when my voice came out a tad high.

Makayla screwed up her nose, but she couldn't hide the twinkle in her eyes. 'I saw you. Last night. Heading into the VIP room with Hot Stuff.'

I exhaled in relief, unaware I'd been holding my breath.

'So you've been fishing for information this whole time?'

'Gotcha.' Makayla made a mock gun with her thumb and forefinger and fired it. 'Come on, sweetie, 'fess up. Did anything happen between you two?'

I'd never had a best friend. The girls at my private school had been bitches, students at uni in the few years I attended were aloof and Bardley's friends were as bland and boring as him.

In the few months I'd known Makayla I liked talking to her. Liked the way she breezed through life. Liked her exuberance and warmth and genuine enthusiasm for everything.

I could lie to her. Fob her off with some lame-ass vague response.

Instead, I found myself nodding, liking having a female confidante for once. 'We hooked up.'

Makayla squealed and jumped up and down. 'Hooked up as in kissed? Or hooked up as in—' She made lewd bumping gestures with her hands.

'Yeah, that.' I felt heat flush my cheeks. 'But you can't say a thing, okay?'

'Good for you, girlfriend.' She made a zipping motion over her lips, but her silence lasted all of two seconds as she eyed me with obvious admiration. 'The quiet ones are always the worst.'

Considering how I'd screamed the place down last night, I wasn't so quiet.

Makayla slugged me on the arm. 'I want details.'

I shook my head, not willing to divulge anything more. I didn't want Makayla casting sideways knowing glances at Tanner and I sure as hell didn't want him thinking I couldn't keep my mouth shut.

I'd never been the type to blab my personal business and I wasn't about to start now. 'Sorry. I don't kiss and tell.'

'Fair enough.' Makayla sighed, her grin goofy. 'I'm happy for you, sweetie. You deserve to have a little fun. But if he has a brother other than Remy, let me know.'

She made a downward sign with her thumb. 'I'm in a major slump. Both professionally and romantically. I've attended eight auditions in the last fortnight, nada. And my dating average is less than that.'

'Those stage shows must be nuts not to hire you,' I said, defending my friend when in fact I had no idea how good a dancer she was. Sure, she could burn up the dance floor with her disco moves but professionally I didn't know how she performed. 'As for guys, most of them have rocks in their heads, but you're gorgeous and sweet. You'll find a good one soon.'

A surprisingly vulnerable smile tugged at the corners of her mouth. 'Hope you're right, because I don't do so well when I'm in a drought.' She wiggled her eyebrows suggestively. 'I need a good man between my legs offstage so I can use my legs to create great dance moves onstage.'

'Maybe that's the problem? You're after a good man when what you need is a bad man?'

We laughed and I impulsively leaned over to hug her. 'Thanks for taking me out last night. I needed it.'

'The dancing or the bad guy between your legs?'

'Both,' I said, my naughty grin matching Makayla's. 'Now, if you're done interrogating me, can we lock up so I can catch up on some sleep?'

'Sure,' she said, pushing off the bench. 'So he kept you up all night, huh?'

'And then some.'

The way Tanner had touched me, stroked me, caressed me—*everywhere*—had blown my mind. I'd never imagined sex could be so good. He'd driven me to the brink so many times, teasing and tasting, before pushing me over with a skill that spoke of years of practice.

I should've felt jealous at the thought of him using his mastery on countless women in the past. Instead, all I could feel was grateful. Very, very grateful.

'Come on, let's close up before I begin to hate you.' Makayla smiled and bumped me with her hip. 'And a word of advice? Don't overthink things with Hot Stuff. He's not here for long, so you should be in this for a good time.'

Whatever 'this' was. Because right now I didn't have a freaking clue. I'd labelled last night as a one-night stand. But from what I'd read in magazines, you didn't usually have to see your one-night stand again. Me, I'd have Tanner in my face for the next few weeks.

Was I really that good an actress that I could pretend nothing had happened and erase the memories of him licking me all over?

Worse, did I want to?

I throbbed just thinking about what we'd done last night. How much stronger would the urge to jump him be when he was standing in front of me?

Did I have the willpower to resist another shot at achieving mind-blowing pleasure?

With the prospect of Tanner showing up for work tomorrow, guess I'd soon find out.

CHAPTER TEN

Tanner

I KNEW THE second I opened my eyes she was gone.

I should've been ecstatic. I never let women stay over. In fact, I rarely brought women here. Over the years I'd been in Sydney I could count the number of dates I'd brought to my penthouse on one hand.

Then again, Abby hadn't been a date.

She'd been…what? A one-night stand? A chance hook-up? A goddamn mistake? Technically, all of the above, which begged the question: Why the hell did I feel so disgruntled to find her gone?

That was another thing. I'd slept better last night than I had in years. Usually I liked the bed all to myself, hated having anyone encroach on my personal space. Yet after the fifth time we'd fucked she'd spooned me and I'd liked it, to the point I'd fallen into a deep slumber, so deep I hadn't heard her leave.

Shit. Why did she have to sneak out of here like some damn fugitive?

Peeved, I pushed out of bed and headed for the

shower. Alone, when I'd had grand plans for the two of us in my expansive double shower complete with rain head and angled jets. Lots of possibilities with those jets. Especially with how responsive she'd been... I could've turned her to face the back wall, where she would've braced. I could've bent her forward. Adjusted the jets to hit her sweet spot. Taken her from behind...

Swearing, I turned the taps to cold. Ice cold. Jerking off wouldn't ease the desire pounding through my veins like the insistent beat of a drum. Burying myself in Abby would, but that wasn't an option. Not now. Probably not ever again.

Last night had been an aberration. It had to be.

I'd vowed to not touch Remy's protégé but that had shot to shit when she'd come on to me like an eager virgin. I should've had stronger willpower. I hadn't. Not getting laid for months had short-circuited my brain. Both the big and little one.

A lousy excuse because I could've stopped her. I should've stopped her. But I hadn't, and now I had to live with the consequences.

Namely seeing her every day at work and keeping my hands off her.

I wasn't a complete idiot. I knew we couldn't have a repeat. That would be a disaster of monumental proportions.

Women like Abby didn't do one-night stands. They did romance and bouquets and all that crap, no matter how much they protested to the contrary. Especially if she hadn't been with a guy in a year.

That blew me away. How could a beautiful woman who'd come out of a shitty marriage not have wanted to purge her past? Then again, maybe her ex had done such a number on her that she'd sworn off men for a while? Whatever the reason, I'd been the beneficiary, because the way she'd reacted to my every touch had blown my mind.

That was what had me rattled the most. The flashbacks of what we'd done. Her on her front, me entering her from behind. Her with her legs spread, me eating her out. Her riding me like a cowgirl. Her clawing my back and biting my shoulder and tentatively licking my cock like it was the best damn popsicle she'd ever tasted.

'Fuck,' I muttered, towelling off and dressing in record time.

I couldn't go to the patisserie, not today. Couldn't face her. Not without my every erotic thought replaying like an X-rated flick on constant repeat.

She'd know. Then where would we be?

If my willpower had been at an all-time low last night, now that I knew how combustible we were between the sheets, would I be able to resist? Doubtful. Which meant I needed time and space between us to gain perspective.

That meant staying away from Le Miel.

I grabbed a bottled banana smoothie from the fridge and headed out. There'd been a shitload of work I could've done at Embue last night before I got distracted. In the best possible way. The way she'd come on to me in my private room…

Damn, I better hole away in my office and stay

clear of that room. Having wavering willpower was one thing. Deliberately putting myself into a fraught situation another.

I'd try to do the right thing where Abby was concerned but I wasn't a saint, and I knew that keeping her at arm's length until Remy got back on his feet would slowly but surely kill me.

I arrived at Embue, parked in the private underground spot reserved for me and entered the club. All these years later it never failed to give me a thrill that I owned this place. That it flourished. That it continued to grow.

Despite dear old Dad's many dire predictions I'd never amount to anything.

How many times had I listened to his snide comments, berating me, battering my self-esteem, while he deliberately praised Remy when he wasn't around, knowing it would make me feel like shit? How many times had he served me the crusts off the fresh bread loaf while he got the thickest slices? How many times had he given me a shrivelled chicken wing while he ate the juicy breast?

After Mum died, on the rare occasions Remy was home he thought Dad was a mean prick too, but he'd excused his mood swings and anger as grief. But I knew better because Dad saved his own special brand of vitriol for me alone.

Even before Mum had died, I'd felt unworthy. That I was not good enough. That I couldn't do anything right. He treated me like a second-class citizen but only when Mum and Remy couldn't see.

I didn't get it. Had always thought it was my fault, some inherent flaw only Dad could see. Until the day Mum died and I overheard the final argument that drove her to her death. The day the old bastard revealed the truth behind his hatred and I'd vowed to never let his insults or shoddy treatment hurt me ever again.

Because it wasn't about me. It was about him. His ridiculous hang-ups and assumptions that had driven Mum to her death and driven me to be nothing like him.

I'd rejoiced the day the prick had died. I'd attended his funeral out of respect for my brother. Remy never understood my latent hatred of our father, and I'd never told him the truth. Better that one of us had good memories rather than none.

Then again, he'd been five years older than me and already holding down a part-time pastry chef apprenticeship while juggling school at fifteen, so he hadn't been around to witness Dad's ritualistic, systemic torture of me. The son he blamed for his entire miserable life.

It meant nothing now. He couldn't hurt me any more. But every time I strode through one of my clubs I saluted him for giving me the drive, the ambition, to be so much better than he ever gave me credit for.

'Hey, Tanner, didn't expect to see you today.' Hudson Watt, my manager and oldest friend, slapped me on the back as I entered the bar area. 'Aren't you meant to be making pastries or croissants or some other fancy-schmancy shit?'

'Had a stack of stuff I wanted to check up on last

night but didn't get a chance so thought I'd spend the day here.'

Hudson grinned, the same smug grin he'd given me in high school when I'd tried to weasel out of a history assignment by devising an elaborate lie and he'd seen right through me.

'Bit busy last night, huh?' Hudson filled a glass with water and added a lime twist before sliding it along the bar towards me. 'Here. You're probably dehydrated after swapping spit with that hot blonde you had holed away in your private VIP room.'

'What are you, twelve?' I downed the water anyway. 'I don't know what you're talking about.'

'Come on, man, don't spin me some line.' Hudson slugged me on the arm. 'I've seen you sweet-talk more girls out of their panties than the number of mojitos I've served. And considering I've worked here for ten years and filled in on many occasions, that's a shitload of mojitos.'

I chuckled. 'I was giving Abby the grand tour, then I took her home.'

'Her home or yours?'

I could've fobbed Hudson off but the guy was right. We'd been friends for a long time. If anyone knew me, faults and all, he did.

'Mine.' I pinched the bridge of my nose to ease some of the tension building behind my eyes. 'Should never have happened.'

Hudson's eyebrows shot up. 'That's the first time I've heard you express post-coital regret.'

'Bullshit. Remember that time we double-dated those bogan twins from Bundaberg? Disastrous.'

Hudson laughed. 'Don't change the subject. From what I saw, this Abby chick had class stamped all over her. Too cool between the sheets, huh?'

Too hot, more like it. Scorching, soul-searing hot. The type of woman who got inside a guy's head and wouldn't leave, no matter how hard I tried. And I'd tried. Boy, had I tried. But she was there, every time I allowed my attention to wander for a moment. Front and centre. Naked. Wanton. Willing.

Fuck.

'Abby's Remy's protégé and I shouldn't have gone there.'

'Why not?' Hudson's grin turned wicked. 'From the way I saw her draped all over you as you left this place as fast as humanly possible, she was seriously into you.'

'Still too complicated,' I said, shaking my head. 'Anyway, what's going on with you?'

'You don't get off that easy.' Hudson glanced at his watch. 'I was just heading down to Jim's for a quick workout before coming back here to do the books. Want to join me so I can grill you some more?'

'You're still working out at Jim's?'

That place had saved my life as a kid. I'd been fourteen when Hudson had taken me to the run-down gym on the outskirts of Kings Cross, where kids could box for recreation, sport or just to vent their frustration.

I'd done a lot of the latter.

When I couldn't tell anyone about Dad's crappy

treatment at home, I'd take it out at Jim's. First on a punching bag, later in sparring matches with other teens. It had been cathartic, being able to physically vent in a safe place, and I hadn't been back in over a decade.

'Yeah, no better place to spar.' Hudson jabbed a left hook in my direction and feigned a dodge to the right. 'Come on, will do you good. You've drifted off about five times in the last few minutes and that means you've got it bad for this new chick.'

If he only knew. Being with Abby hadn't dampened my attraction to her. If anything it had intensified, and that wasn't a good thing. 'Don't you ever stop with the bullshit?'

Hudson chuckled and this time jabbed me on the arm for real. 'Let's go, champ. It'll be my pleasure to whip your ass.'

'Dream on, dickhead.'

An hour later, Hudson had done exactly that but I felt so much better for the workout and being at Jim's had a lot to do with my lift in mood.

Walking into Jim's was like coming home. The pungent smell of sweat warred with liniment. Four boxing rings flooded with natural light from rows of windows set high in the walls. Free weights and punching bags in the far corner, with an old-fashioned juice bar next to it.

There weren't many guys around this morning. Probably all at work. Where I should be, rather than running from my present into the past.

'You're rusty,' Hudson said, draping a towel around his neck and handing me one.

'And you're soft in the middle,' I said, socking a punch into his solar plexus. He dodged.

'Bet that's not what Abby says to you.'

This time, I aimed harder and he sidestepped easily, laughing so loud a trainer nearby grinned.

'Seriously, dude, if you like her this much, do something about it.'

I hated the flare of hope his words elicited. 'Like what, Einstein?'

'Damned if I know. Do I look like an expert on women?'

'Good point.' I wiped the sweat off my face and towelled my torso. 'Seeing anyone?'

'Nah. Between managing the bar and doing part-time work at the theatre, I don't have much time left for a relationship.'

'Who said anything about the R word?'

He snorted. 'I'm not like you. I like to date women for longer than five hours.'

'I'll have you know Abby stayed the night.'

The second the retort popped out I wished I could take it back.

'And there you go, dude. Proof that she's not like the rest.'

'Back off, bozo.' I advanced on him in mock anger so he'd do just that.

Predictably, Hudson just stood there like the big, blond lug he'd always been. Loyal to a fault. The kind of mate I could depend on.

'Make me, squirt.'

Considering I towered over him by three inches,

it was a hollow taunt, one he'd made many times as a kid, and we laughed.

'Let's get back to the club and you can show me proof you haven't been embezzling me out of a fortune.' I tugged on the end of a glove lace with my teeth, thinking I should do this more often.

Boxing worked off frustration of all varieties, including sexual, like nothing else could.

'Sounds like a plan.' As Hudson took off his gloves and helped me with mine, I knew he wanted to say more but was holding back.

'What's up?'

'It's this place.' Hudson gestured around. 'I don't get back here as often as I like but whenever I do it's like the past crashes over me and I wonder why I put myself through it.'

That was another thing that had bonded us, our crappy childhoods. His father had made mine look like a frigging saint.

'Cut the heartstring crap, bozo, and let's get back to work.'

Hudson blinked rapidly, as if coming back from a place of bad memories, before his signature grin made me sigh in relief. 'After you, big guy.'

As we traded banter while changing, swapping the usual crap guys did, I knew I'd done the right thing in taking time away from the patisserie and Abby today.

But I couldn't play chicken for ever, and come tomorrow I'd be back there, wishing I hadn't complicated matters and wanting her more than ever.

CHAPTER ELEVEN

Abby

AFTER MAKAYLA AND I locked up I'd intended on taking a hot bath and having an early night. But as I entered the small one-room apartment over the patisserie, it didn't offer the comfort it usually did.

I'd never forget the first time Remy brought me up here and said I could stay as long as I liked. That had been over a year ago, the day I'd walked out on Bardley and into Le Miel. In search of comfort via the delicious pastries Remy made, I'd frequented the patisserie often during my marriage, using it as my go-to place to escape home. I'd spent many afternoons sitting at the small table near the counter, sipping at a latte and trying to stop at only one croissant while studying.

Remy would come out from the kitchen occasionally and he'd always stop to chat. As kind-hearted and generous with his time as he was with his magnificent pastries.

I'd never plucked up the courage to tell him that I

also enjoyed baking and that to me he had my dream job. Instead, when he asked, I pretended to wax lyrical about my business degree and how happy I was juggling university with marriage.

If he saw through my brittle smile, he never said; that was the kind of man he was. And that fateful day when I'd found my backbone and had the guts to walk away from Bardley, he still hadn't prodded for information despite me coming in here like I had a pack of wolves on my tail.

On impulse, I'd asked him for a job and once he'd heard my sob story he'd offered me the apartment too.

I'd taken one look at the cosy, light-filled space and fallen in love. Pockmarked mahogany floorboards covered in rugs in the most vibrant peacock blues and crimsons, a faded chintz sofa and chairs, a bookcase overflowing with classics and a kitchenette stocked with everything I'd need to whip up healthy meals for one.

The small bedroom and bathroom had been basic but I hadn't cared. I'd never lived on my own, moving straight from my parents' Double Bay mansion into Bardley's Vaucluse monstrosity gifted to him by his folks when we married. Having the freedom to do whatever I liked in my own space had been heady stuff for a girl like me.

So I'd moved in with the few suitcases I'd packed when I'd walked away from my marriage, had paid Remy six months' rent in advance—a pittance, really, considering the rental prices in this upmarket part of town—and settled into a routine.

Living the life I wanted.

But today, restlessness plagued me and after I'd done a quick circuit or ten of the apartment I decided to go for a drive. Another thing I liked doing that I'd never had much of a chance to do in my past: driving for leisure.

Dad had a chauffeur that had dropped me at school and picked me up, and Bardley roared around in his sports car when he wasn't getting a private car to ferry him around. My narrow-minded husband had never understood my love of driving, had mocked me endlessly for wanting to drive out of the city on a weekend with no destination in my mind.

So I'd rarely done it; hadn't been worth the angst. Besides, it had been difficult to squirrel away any me-time when Bardley demanded I keep up with his hectic social schedule and attend every boring polo party/sailing regatta/race carnival as his arm candy.

These days, on my limited down time, I drove for the heck of it. For the pleasure of exploring new places. For the simple fact I could, without anyone telling me I was an idiot or worse.

It wasn't until I was in my hatchback and cruising the streets did I realise where I was heading.

Home.

Not the harbourside mansion I'd lived in for twenty-one years before I got married, but the suburb. Ritzy Double Bay. Everything seemed brighter here, like a fairy had sprinkled glitter over the entire suburb.

I drove aimlessly along the lush tree-lined boulevards, passing row upon row of incredible palatial homes with manicured emerald lawns, tennis courts and pool houses that could house a large family.

Trendy boutiques I'd frequented when I didn't baulk at the four-figure price tag on a pair of shoes or hold back when signing up for the newest release designer handbag.

Cafés I'd regularly met my friends at, to do nothing but chat about our caviar facials and the latest celebrity break-up. Friends that hadn't given a crap when I'd left Bardley. Friends that hadn't even called.

Past Redleaf Beach, a gorgeous slice of Sydney Harbour foreshore, where I'd sat on the sand for hours sometimes, wishing I could swim like the bathers doing laps in the tidal enclosure but too afraid to bring it up in case Bardley ridiculed me for wanting to learn how to swim at my age and conquer my fear of deep water.

I gripped the steering wheel tighter as I glimpsed a sprawling whitewashed building fringed in lush gardens. The day spa Mum and I used to attend.

Emotion clogged my throat as I homed in on the elaborate gold-embossed entrance, wondering what I'd do if I glimpsed Mum. But she was nowhere in sight and I found myself pulling into a parking spot and killing the engine.

Crazy, as even if I saw her I wouldn't approach her. Not when a hotbed of resentment and hurt festered inside me that not once over the last twelve months had she contacted me. Other than those fraught initial phone calls when she'd begged me to reconsider walking out on my marriage.

Phone calls where she hadn't asked how I was or where I was living or what I was doing to support myself since I'd been cut off financially from Bardley and my folks. Oh, no. Mum's phone calls consisted of cajoling alternating with berating.

'How could you be so stupid, darling? Walking away from your husband? Your home? Your friends?'

'What were you thinking, leaving behind a life of luxury?'

'You've embarrassed your husband and you've mortified us. Return home immediately!'

The latter had been the most laughable because I hadn't had a home with Bardley. Not really. We'd been friends coexisting in a massive house. More like housemates, really, who had lacklustre sex on occasion.

Not that anyone besides us knew the truth. To our friends and family we were the luckiest couple in Australia. Married young. The successful merging of two powerhouse families. A glamorous life filled with the best money could buy, with a fortune guaranteed to keep our offspring in the lap of luxury.

The biggest sham ever perpetuated.

I hated myself for putting up with it for so long. For being a mousy, subservient girl who went along with whatever my parents wanted, including marrying a man I only felt a lukewarm affection for.

I'd allowed myself to get caught up in the euphoria of having some guy pay me attention. Because that was what Bardley had done, wooed me with the express purpose of marriage, as his folks had suggested to him.

While he'd had dollar signs in his eyes, envisaging a family merger that would consolidate fortunes, I'd had stars in my eyes, naively hoping that marriage would provide the excitement I'd been craving.

Instead, Bardley had morphed into the dweeb I'd always suspected he was, with a mean streak that flourished once he had a ring on my finger. And I'd started to lose myself, piece by piece, becoming a listless yes-person who'd do anything to keep the peace and not earn his wrath.

What a fool.

I'd hated being that spineless, mouthless idiot and as I stared at the day spa and watched a mother and daughter exit, heads close together as they gossiped, their blond-streaked hair shiny in the lights flickering on, I realised maybe I didn't miss my old life so much after all.

I couldn't fathom my parents' lack of contact, their complete lack of interest in my well-being now that I wasn't doing what they wanted.

Dad had always been aloof and business-focussed, so I didn't expect as much from him. The only time he'd ever paid me attention—Mum too, for that matter—was when we did something that pleased him. Otherwise, he'd convey his displeasure through angry silences that lasted for days, ensuring that I learned from a young age to make him happy.

So it didn't surprise me that he hadn't contacted me, but for Mum to ignore me too…it hurt. A lot.

I'd rung twice over the last six months, more to touch base and hear a familiar voice. The maid had skilfully diverted my call both times, so I never got to speak to my folks.

They hadn't returned my calls.

Was I stupid to still miss them? To still hold onto a faint hope they'd eventually come around? Maybe, but they were my parents and no matter how crappy their treatment, a small part of me wished they'd understand one day.

A tear plopped onto my forearm, startling me. I hadn't realised I'd been crying. Swiping a hand across my eyes, I shot the day spa a final wistful glance before starting the engine.

I should be happy. Last night with Tanner had purged my past once and for all. I should be rejoicing. Instead, I couldn't help but wish I could have my old life mix successfully with my new.

At least the drive had achieved one objective.

Forget Tanner.

But as I headed back to Le Miel, knowing I'd have to confront him all too soon, maybe this new life I'd craved so much was a lot more than I'd bargained for.

CHAPTER TWELVE

Tanner

'FLOUR STOCKS ARE LOW—same with sugar and butter. We've got a flood of orders coming in that haven't been catalogued. And the front display cabinet looks like something a toddler arranged. What the hell's going on?'

I glowered at Abby, hating the flicker of resentment in those stunning blue eyes that had been filled with passion only two days ago.

I'd been riding her—metaphorically, worse luck—ever since I'd arrived at seven this morning. But I had to keep it up, had to keep emotional distance between us, otherwise I wouldn't be able to keep my hands off her.

Walking in this morning and having her fix me with that cool blue indifferent gaze, like nothing had happened between us, made me want to bend her over the counter and thrust into her until sweet, sensual Abby was back.

I liked that Abby. Liked her willing and wanton and wet. Desperate for me.

But I liked that Abby too much—too much to be good for me—and therein lay the problem.

So I'd donned my poker face and reflected her indifference right back at her. Though it was an act. A forced act we were both perpetuating in the hope neither of us would crack.

I'd known it would be like this. That she would pretend like nothing had happened. Hell, she'd made it painfully obvious she didn't want me ever since we'd met, her disdain palpable. Which only served to dent my ego and make me want to rattle her all the more.

It was like some weird twisted game we were playing. Push and pull. A battle of wills. Too bad for her, I'd never backed down from a challenge in my life. I could out-stubborn a donkey. Because I'd learned from an early age that the only way to cope with Dad's derogatory crap was with indifference.

He'd hated it. I'd done it more. He'd never made me crack. Nobody could. I'd become too hardened, too cynical, too tough.

Too tough for the likes of Abby, that was for sure.

I'd ultimately break her and that wouldn't be good. For her, for Remy, maybe for me too.

Though I was a big boy, I could take it. But Remy would hate me for running off his golden girl and I couldn't let that happen. I didn't care what other people thought of me. Anyone except Remy. His opinion mattered. He mattered. He always had.

So I'd keep up this ridiculous charade no matter how much I wanted Abby.

'I'll get Makayla to check the orders and the front display. As for supplies, today's delivery is late. It happens sometimes.' She glared at me like something she'd stepped in. A particularly nasty something that stuck to her shoe no matter how hard she tried to wipe it off. 'I'll go check in the storeroom. We usually stock extras for emergencies.'

'Fine,' I muttered through gritted teeth, feeling like an ogre as I watched her retreating back and her ass.

I couldn't help it. Remembering the soft curve of her cheeks. The way they felt beneath my hands. How she'd squealed when I'd bitten her.

She paused at the door to the storeroom and glanced over her shoulder.

Damn, sprung, as I dragged my gaze upward but not fast enough.

With a raised eyebrow, she said, 'If your foul mood is a result of what happened between us and you're feeling awkward, forget it.' Her gaze turned glacial. 'I have.'

I wouldn't have been surprised if she'd flipped me the bird as she stalked into the storeroom and slammed the door.

'Fuck.' I dragged a hand through my hair and resisted the urge to kick the nearest counter.

I should leave her to her snit in peace. But that was the thing about never backing down; I couldn't stop my feet from following her even if I wanted to. And I didn't. I wanted her to take back that last remark.

She hadn't forgotten our steamy encounter any more than I had. So she must've thrown it out there in hurt.

And I hadn't wanted to hurt her.

I'd apologise for acting like a jackass. Smooth the way towards a better working relationship. Yeah, that was the plan.

A plan that imploded the moment I entered the storeroom and saw her braced against a table, chest heaving, eyes flashing, chin tilted up in defiance.

'Get out,' she yelled, her hands balling into fists, and she thumped the table.

In response, I kicked the door shut.

Locked it.

'Don't you dare come near me,' she said, not moving a muscle as I advanced on her. She squared her shoulders the closer I got, staring me down. Even when we stood almost toe to toe, she didn't flinch. 'You're a boorish, idiotic, moody—'

My mouth slammed onto hers. Our teeth clashed a little, our noses bumped. A disastrous kiss from an experienced guy like me but I didn't care. I didn't care about anything but savouring the sweetness of her mouth again. Taunting her tongue to match mine. Exploring the crevices of her mouth like I'd never get enough.

Her hands clutched at my shirt, like she wanted to push me away. She hauled me closer, clawing at the cotton, wanting skin.

I knew the feeling.

At my apartment two nights ago, I'd worshipped

her body. Taken my time. A leisurely exploration that had imprinted on my brain. Every dip and curve. Every ticklish spot. Every erogenous inch that I'd licked and stroked and caressed until she'd been mindless with want.

Now there was no time for finesse.

'Hurry up,' she growled in my ear, nipping at the tender skin below it, her teeth grazing my skin with short, sharp nibbles before she licked her way along my jaw towards my mouth.

Sensual Abby was back and I couldn't be happier.

I made short work of her zipper. Pushed her panties down. And slid my finger into moist heat.

'More,' she murmured, and I was only too happy to acquiesce to her demand.

I fished a condom out of my wallet, unzipped and sheathed myself in record time.

I had to be inside her. Now.

With her pants around her ankles, I couldn't spread her legs wide so I spun her around and bent her over the table.

Exposing that gorgeous ass.

'You like doing it doggy style, don't you?' I slid a hand around the front, fingering her clit as I nudged at her slick folds. 'Two times the other night.'

'Too much talking.' She glanced over her shoulder, her eyes flashing indigo fire, taunting me.

I entered her in a smooth thrust that made her gasp.

'Better?' I whispered, leaning over her, making our fit even snugger.

She moaned in response and wiggled her ass.

She wanted more? I'd give it to her.

I slid in and out. Slow at first. Wanting to drive her as mad as she drove me. But I couldn't hang on. Not when I'd been fantasising about this for the last two days. Not when she felt better than I remembered.

My cock pulsed with every thrust, the pressure building, and my finger picked up tempo on her clit until she was pushing back at me as hard as I was pushing into her.

'So good...' She stiffened, a moment before she let out a long, satisfied groan, as her pussy clenched around me.

I came so hard I saw spots.

This time, when she glanced over her shoulder at me, her smile was smug. Satisfied. I knew the feeling.

'Hope that puts you in a better mood,' she said, straightening a little so I had no option but to pull out and take care of business.

'We shouldn't have done that.'

I knew it had been the wrong thing to say when her face fell, but she masked it quickly with a fake smile I was growing to hate.

'Seems like we shouldn't do a lot of things that are bad for us, like eating leftover croissants, but we do it anyway.'

She sounded flippant but I heard the hurt lacing her words.

Damn, I'd done it again. Caused her pain when it was never my intention.

'Look, we need to talk this out—'

'From where I'm standing, there wasn't much talking involved, just the way I wanted it.' She pulled up her pants and zipped up, elegant and nonchalant, whereas I felt gauche doing the same thing. 'We don't need to talk about anything.'

She spun away from me and I grabbed her hand, tugging her back to face me. 'I've handled this badly and I'm sorry. But we do have to work this out, Abby, otherwise it's going to be a tough few weeks.'

To her credit, she eyeballed me, trying to stare me down. 'What are you really sorry for? Being a douche the whole day or not being able to keep your hands off me?'

She packed a punch. I liked that. Liked straight shooting.

'Both.'

To my relief, I saw the corners of her mouth twitch. A mouth I remembered doing wicked things to me a few nights ago and just like that I was hard again, ready and raring to go.

'You don't have to apologise for the…sex.' Damn, she was cute when she blushed. 'I like it. In fact, I think we should keep doing it.'

'Pardon me?'

I could've sworn she'd just said we should keep having sex. Nice in practice, terrible in theory.

'A fling. Short term. No strings.' She eased her hand out of mine before I could react. 'It'll be good for me. Purging my past once and for all.'

Bitterness made my jaw clench. So that was all I was. A fuckable solution to her yearlong celibacy. A way to get back on the proverbial horse. I should be flattered. Instead, all I could think was how I'd never been good enough growing up and I wasn't good enough now for anything more than a short-term fling.

Every guy's dream, having a woman articulate no-strings sex. In reality, how often did it turn out that way? Women tended to want more. More emotion. More commitment. More.

But Abby seemed different. She hadn't been mooning around all day. She'd been nonchalant. All business. Like she didn't give a shit I'd been a grouchy ogre determined to keep her at bay.

So maybe she meant it when she said a no-strings fling. I should be ecstatic. Instead, I couldn't help but feel like yet again I'd come up short somehow. A hollow, empty feeling I'd spent years trying to conquer courtesy of dear old Dad's shabby treatment.

'So I'd be your walk on the wild side? Slumming it before you head back to the real world?'

Guilt shifted in her gaze before she shook her head. 'We're very different, so, yeah, part of the appeal is that bad-boy edge you've got going on. But I like you.' Her blush was back, staining her cheeks a vivid pink. 'I never knew sex could be that good, so call me greedy but I want more.'

Defiant, she took a step towards me and placed her hand on my chest. 'A lot more.'

I gritted my teeth against the urge to bend her over the table again. 'Just sex. No muss, no fuss?'

'I'm not a muss, fuss kind of girl.' She lowered her hand, using it to gesture around the storeroom. 'This

place is my life. I want to complete my apprenticeship, become fully qualified, gain as much experience as I can with your brother, save like the devil
and hopefully have my own patisserie one day. So you
and me? A side benefit I'd never anticipated, but no
way would I let it interfere with my dream.'

'Fair enough.'

She'd said all the right things. Talked the talk. But
when it came to ending things, would she walk the
walk?

'What about Remy?'

Confusion creased her brow. 'What about him?'

'My brother will bust my balls for tangling with
you.'

'Does he have to know?'

'We don't bullshit each other. He's always had my
back and I owe him.'

Damn, why had I spilled that? I should keep my
distance. Sex, I could handle, but there was something about Abby that snuck beneath my defences
and made me want to confide. Disconcerting when
I'd never told anyone the truth, not even Remy.

Another side effect of putting up with Dad's shit
for so long: I was ashamed. Ashamed of who I was
around him, ashamed of the years I'd tolerated his
crap, ashamed at the possibility of anyone ever finding out how much of a goddamn coward I'd been.

'I admire your loyalty.' She tilted her head, studying me with that penetrating stare that made me
squirm a little. 'Family should stick together.'

The slight quiver in her voice, underlined with a

healthy dose of vulnerability, slayed me. 'What about you? Any siblings?'

'No.'

One syllable laced with unspoken pain.

'Hence my parents' high expectations of me. Which also explains why they cut me off the first and only time I went against their wishes.' Her harsh laugh was devoid of amusement. 'Didn't matter that I didn't want a princess party as a ten-year-old. Or a formal ball for my sixteenth. Or to do a business degree.' Her breath hitched. 'Or to marry a guy more a friend at twenty-one. I always did the right thing. The expected thing. Until I walked away.'

She cleared her throat. 'I envy you your bond with Remy.'

'Don't ever envy me,' I said, sounding gruff. 'Remy and I are close from necessity.'

Curiosity sparked her eyes. 'What does that mean?'

Shit. There I went again, giving away too much.

'Nothing.' I made a big show of glancing at my watch. 'We need to get back out there.'

Other women would've badgered me for answers. Thankfully, Abby had more class. Or she really was serious about keeping things between us strictly physical.

'You're right.' She hesitated, a shy smile making something in my chest twang. 'After we finish work, do you want to come up to my apartment? I make a mean fettuccini carbonara.'

I should say no. Because Abby wasn't just inviting me up for pasta and we both knew it. But she'd been honest in asking for what she wanted, blunt in out-lining the terms. Considering how much of a jackass I'd been today, dealing with my rampaging lust for her and not being able to have her, I'd be better off agreeing to her very adult arrangement than having another few frustration-filled weeks.

'I am partial to pasta.' I stepped in close and rested my hand on her waist, my thumb strumming the sliver of bare skin beneath her pants and shirt. 'And you.'

'Good. Glad that's settled.' She kissed me on the cheek, a surprisingly sweet gesture that made my chest tighten again.

But as I unlocked the door and followed her back to the kitchen, I knew deep down that things between us were far from settled.

It scared the crap out of me.

CHAPTER THIRTEEN

Abby

THIS WAS CRAZY.

I wanted this.

I asked for it.

But as I flitted around the kitchen, ensuring the pasta had cooked *al dente*, grating Parmesan into a bowl and uncorking a Riesling, I knew that no matter how nonchalant I acted about inviting a gorgeous guy up to my apartment, inside I was a hot mess.

Tanner had agreed to a fling.

My ovaries were still leaping at the thought two hours later. Then he'd gone and revealed snippets of his past and I'd moved from viewing him as a fine piece of ass to a guy with a soul.

Okay, so that sounded shallow. I'd already known he had deeper layers behind that tattooed front, but when he'd told me about him and Remy being close out of necessity…the pain lacing his voice had slain me.

I'd wanted to wrap my arms around him, to offer

comfort I had no right giving. But I'd seen the inner war he waged reflected in his eyes, a kind of personal agony I had no hope of understanding. So I'd changed the subject. Gone back to work. And begged off thirty minutes early to shower and get dinner prepped.

I hadn't dated as a teen. Bardley had been my first in every way: first boyfriend, first lover, first partner I'd lived with. He hadn't appreciated my cooking, had always mocked my 'homebody tendencies'. He'd preferred to eat out at Sydney's finest restaurants, or get high-end catering in. So after the first week of married life I'd given up in the kitchen and grown increasingly despondent because of it.

Whenever I'd been unable to stay away from the kitchen and indulged my penchant for baking, he'd made snide comments and warned me not to eat any of that 'carb-filled crap' in case I got fat.

I should've bashed him over the head with a skillet when I had the chance.

I'd never really had the pleasure of cooking for a guy I fancied before: a guy who'd want me for dessert rather than the lemon tartlets I'd snaffled from downstairs. In fact, as I dished up the pasta and laid the large serving platter on the table, arranging the salad and Parmesan around it, I wondered if we'd even make it through the main course.

What had happened in the storeroom…indicative of why I'd proposed this fling in the first place. We'd been dancing around each other all day and I'd known his foul mood had been more to do with himself trying to maintain his distance than anything else.

So I'd challenged him, hoping he'd snap. Because working alongside Tanner after that sizzling night we'd spent together was pure torture. Having him brush past me, inhaling his manly scent tinged with citrus, feeling the heat radiating off him, watching those strong hands wrangling a dodgy oven door... I'd been hyperaware of him all day.

And craving him like I'd never craved anything in my entire life.

I'd never been the type of person to want things. I guess having everything I ever needed handed to me on a silver platter did that to a girl. I'd taken it for granted, being spoiled and indulged, even if I didn't ask for it.

So wanting Tanner with every cell in my body was new and I'd handled it as best I could: by throwing myself into work and baking like a maniac. Fulfilling every order for the day and then some, Le Miel's front display overflowing with my signature almond croissants, *bugnes* and *chaussons aux pommes*.

We'd sold out as usual, rarely able to keep up with demand, but today we'd only turned away two people near closing rather than the usual thirty. I'd been high on my success of coping without Remy when Tanner had taunted me, spoiling for a fight. So I'd given him one. Knowing he wouldn't back down and would follow me into the storeroom. Where he'd snapped.

I throbbed at the memory, pressed my hands between my legs to stem the insistent wanting. It didn't work and I knew that when he knocked on the door at any moment, I'd probably launch myself at him.

That was the thing with having average, infrequent sex. When you got the real thing, you were insatiable. We'd done it five times that night we'd spent together, and once today, yet having him inside me was all I could think about. Fantasising about the next time. And the time after that.

I'd turned into a man.

A loud knock made me jump and my palms instantly grew clammy. I swiped them down the sides of the simple cotton dress I'd changed into, wiggled my fingers and shook my arms out. Like a prize fighter warming up for a strenuous bout.

A bout of steamy, sizzling sex, if I had my way.

Anticipation made my body zing as I took my time answering the door.

Yeah, like playing hard to get would work now.

When I opened it, my breath caught. He'd ditched the long-sleeve shirt he'd been working in all day and wore a fitted white T-shirt that outlined every ridge of his muscular body. I could see the faintest outline of the tattoos beneath, tattoos I'd barely studied and wanted to learn in intricate detail. His shoulders stretched the cotton and, with his hands thrust into his pockets, his biceps bulged nicely.

I tried not to stare. It wasn't polite. But as I started at his broad shoulders and worked my way down, I couldn't look away. When I reached his jeans' pockets, and noted the sizeable bulge between, my mouth went dry.

I swallowed, trying to think of something witty to say, something that didn't sound like, 'Take me now.'

'Something smells good,' he said, stepping forward to fill my doorway when all I could think about was him filling me. He lowered his head to brush a barely there kiss on my cheek. 'The pasta too.'

'Come in,' I said, my voice sounding strangled as he stepped inside and I closed the door behind him. 'Hope you're hungry.'

'Ravenous.'

One simple word uttered in a low growl that made the hairs on the nape of my neck snap to attention and goosebumps pebble my skin.

My back sagged against the door as he braced his arms either side of me, pinning me. Like I wanted to move even if I could. He stared at me, his dark eyes glowing with intent and I knew in that instant I'd be reheating dinner later.

'Me too,' I squeaked out before launching myself at him.

He laughed and staggered back a step. I didn't care. I literally tried to climb him as I hooked a leg around his waist and grabbed at his shoulders. Needing him. Wanting him. Desperate for him.

He chuckled, his hands spanning my waist. 'We're not eating first?'

'We are,' I murmured, nipping his earlobe to show him exactly what I'd be feasting on. Him. Every delectable inch.

He groaned a little and, emboldened, I wondered how much more of him I could devour. While he'd gone down on me several delightful times the other night, I hadn't ventured near him with my mouth beyond a tentative lick or two, considering how large he was in my hand.

But tonight was about me taking what I wanted.

I wanted him.

I spun him around and pushed him up against the door. Tugged the hem of his T-shirt out of his jeans. Unsnapped them and lowered the zipper. Slid my way down so I knelt at his feet.

'What are you doing?' His voice was barely above a growl as he laid a hand on my head.

'Having an entree.' I flashed him my best cheeky smile, hoping to convey confidence when in fact I'd never given head before.

Bardley had found oral sex distasteful, so we'd never done it. I was glad. Made it all the more special doing it to a guy I really liked.

'Babe, you're killing me,' he said, his eyes round and slightly glazed as he watched me take him out of his jocks.

He was big and hard in my hand as I stroked from the base towards the head. Leaned forward to lick the tip. Awed by his size up close. Feeling completely out of my depth.

'Just so you know, I haven't done this before.'

His fingers tightened in my hair and I winced a little. 'What the—'

'So I may not be very good at it.'

He swore. 'Abby, whenever you touch me I combust, so whatever you do to me, sweetheart, is going to be frigging phenomenal.'

Emboldened by his confidence in me, I wrapped

my lips around the head of his cock and sucked slightly. He swore again. Easing my lips over him, I licked. Swirled my tongue around. Savouring the velvet-soft skin covering steel, the faint muskiness of him.

I couldn't take him all the way in, he was too big, but as I slid my mouth up and down, sucking as I went, I started to get the hang of it. If the sounds Tanner made were any indication, he was enjoying it too.

'Babe, I need to be inside you. I need…ah fuck.' His hand fisted tighter in my hair as I picked up tempo, sucking like I couldn't get enough.

He came on a low groan that made me feel like a wanton goddess and I'd never felt so sexy.

I'd never understood the articles I'd read in magazines, where women raved about how much power they had over men in the bedroom. To me, kneeling in front of a guy getting him off with your mouth reeked of subservience. But giving pleasure to Tanner this way made me feel good in a way I hadn't anticipated: like I was capable of bringing a guy to his knees, like I could do anything.

When I stood, he stared at me like I'd given him the best gift ever.

'Not bad for a novice, huh?' I couldn't keep the smug grin off my face.

'Not bad?' He reached for me and hauled me against his chest. 'You are stupendous.'

I had no idea how long we stood there, my face buried against him, breathing in the addictive scent of him, him squeezing the life out of me, but the longer he held me the harder I found it to delineate between us being a physical fling and something more.

I didn't have much experience with men. I didn't know if this was normal or not. Bardley had never been a cuddler and Makayla said the guys she slept with were the same, though that had more to do with her kicking them out so they couldn't spend the night than anything else.

But the way Tanner hugged me now, like he never wanted to let go, made me feel...special.

A very dangerous feeling to have around this man.

I knew we were nothing beyond a mutual attraction. Two people thrown together at the right time, willing to slake a thirst.

But for the moment, wrapped in his arms, I found it difficult not to wish for more.

CHAPTER FOURTEEN

Tanner

'THIS IS CATEGORICALLY the best pasta I've ever tasted.' I pushed away my empty plate with a contented sigh. 'You're an amazing cook.'

Abby flushed, her cheeks glowing the same pretty pink they did after sex. 'Bet you say that to all the girls.'

'Only the ones who give me great head before serving up a meal like this.'

She blushed harder but her eyes glittered with triumph, like I'd paid her the best compliment ever. 'I'm glad you liked it,' she said, her tone demure but those damn eyes, big and blue and defiant, alerting me to the fact she wasn't just talking about the pasta.

I liked this side of her. Bold and confident. Taunting and teasing. Allowing her inner flirt to come out and play when I had a feeling she'd rarely done that before.

To think, I'd been the lucky bastard to be on the receiving end of her first blowjob. What kind of a putz had her ex been, a frigging eunuch? How had he not wanted to experience everything with this incredible woman?

Me, I wanted it all. I'd have it all. Taking her on an erotic journey she'd never forget.

I'd wanted to go down on her at the door, return the favour. But she'd sauntered off, citing the food was getting cold, and that we'd have plenty of time for that later.

I'd agreed because it heightened anticipation. And I hadn't been able to think straight with my mind reeling from the impact of coming in her mouth. I'd been hard throughout dinner and, while I hadn't lied about this being the best damn pasta I'd ever eaten, I wanted to eat her.

'Have you spoken with Remy today?'

Just like that, she doused my libido like she'd dumped cold water over me.

'Yeah, the docs are pleased with his progress, but he's itching to get back here.'

'Probably doesn't trust us,' she said, her lips curving in a mischievous smile. 'Considering what we've been up to, I guess he's right.'

'I'm going to visit him tomorrow.'

After what had happened in the storeroom, I'd already made up my mind to come clean. I couldn't lie to Remy. Anyone but him.

Then again, I'd been doing it to him for most of our lives. Before Mum had died, she'd been a buffer between Dad and me, so I'd only been exposed to his hatred a few times. But after she'd died and

Dad's guilt and anger had coalesced into a hard ball
of rage against me, I'd had to lie to Remy on the rare
times I saw him at home.

I remembered those nights vividly, when he'd
come home late after putting in extra hours at a bak-
ery and have a mountain of homework to get through
too. He'd ask how was my day, was I doing okay at
school, then grab a snack and head into his room. He
always bought my trite responses that everything was
fine. If he'd picked up something was amiss, he probably put it down to me missing Mum.

He never, ever suspected the awful truth and I kept
it that way. Remy was a good guy and I didn't want
him feeling bad, even after the old bastard had curled
up his toes and done us all a favour.

Something in my tone must've alerted her to my
thoughts, because her smile faded. 'Are you going to
tell him about us?'

I bit back my first response, 'there is no us', because that would irrevocably hurt her. Besides, there
was an 'us' of sorts, even if labelling our insatiable
craving for sex with each other was 'us'.

I nodded. 'He'll know if he asks me about you,
which he will, and takes one look at my face.' I
clasped my fingers in my lap to stop from fiddling
with the edge of the tablecloth. 'In case you haven't
noticed, I'm kinda goofy when it comes to you.'

Her smile softened the lines of concern bracketing
her mouth. 'You know we're both consenting adults
and what we do in our leisure time has nothing to do
with him?'

'I know, but I don't like hiding something this important from him.'

Damn, it'd been the wrong thing to say, because she'd interpret me as saying our relationship was important when in fact I'd meant our involvement, being Remy's brother and protégé, would be important to him. Yeah, that was what I'd meant. Right?

Thankfully, Abby didn't call me on it. 'If you two are that close, how come you haven't been around much the last year?'

'I travel a lot for work. Acting as a consultant for new clubs around the world takes time.'

It was a trite answer, a vague answer, and we both knew it.

'If you need to tell him, tell him,' she said, with a shrug. 'As long as he doesn't give you or me grief when it ends.'

I knew we had an expiration date. I was counting on it. I would never have started anything unless Abby knew it too. So why did the pasta feel like it had wedged in my chest, giving me a bad case of heartburn?

I pushed back from the table a little, clamping down on the urge to bolt while I still could. 'None of his business and as you said we're both consenting adults, so when this ends it won't be messy.'

I didn't buy her bright, fake smile for a second.

We were kidding ourselves.

No matter how often we articulated this was just physical and we could walk away clean at the end, the more time we spent together, the bigger the potential for fallout.

I should walk away now. Get the hell out before the sex morphed into something more.

But she stood at that moment and held out her hand. 'Ready for dessert?'

'We talking about those lemon tartlets I spied on the counter or something else?'

Her lips curved in naughtiness. 'I thought those tartlets would taste fabulous later.' She paused for effect as she leaned forward to murmur, 'In bed.'

I stood so fast my chair slammed against the wall. So much for making a run for it while I still could. Time to make a last-ditch stand so I could tell my conscience to shut the hell up later.

'When we first met, I had you pegged as some prissy, society princess playing at baking.'

An eyebrow quirked. 'And I had you pegged as a selfish, arrogant playboy who didn't give a crap about anyone but himself. Your point?'

'You may be a princess playing at baking but you're far from prissy.' My gaze boldly raked her body. 'And you're sensational in the sack.'

'Right back at you,' she said, with a haughty tilt of her head, playing up to my initial assessment. 'If you'd care to join me in the sack, maybe we can be sensational together?'

I hadn't put up much of a fight. Hell, it had been a token protest at best. But the time for backing out of this thing between us was long past. Whatever happened from here on in, I'd have to take full responsibility.

Because this was my call.

I knew it; she knew it.

She'd been upfront from the start, labelling me as a way to purge her past. But I hadn't returned the favour.

Because Abby was far more than just sex for me.

I was using her. In a way that would alienate her completely if she ever found out.

'Don't you back out on me now, Bad Boy.' She sauntered towards me, hooked her finger into my waistband and tugged. 'Whatever you're thinking, forget it. We're not invested in this emotionally, so stop second-guessing or feeling guilty or whatever it is you're doing, and come show me more of that beautiful body.'

I blew out a long breath, releasing some of the residual tension making my shoulders ache. 'I'd never have thought you'd be into tats.'

'They're incredible,' she said, tugging my T-shirt over my head and flinging it away. 'I could spend hours studying them.'

I didn't move as her fingertips skated over my skin, exploring, lingering, just as she had that first time in my private room at the club.

Now, like then, lust blinded me, pounding through my body in time with my heart.

I didn't get it. Abby was beautiful, but I'd dated stunning. She was inexperienced, where I'd dated sexpots who knew their way around a guy and then some. She blew hot and cold, whereas I'd been with women who were hot to trot any time of day or night.

But there was something about her that got under my skin in a way no woman ever had.

'What's your favourite?' My skin rippled with awareness as she paused over the four-leaf clover on my right shoulder blade.

And licked it.

'This one.'

'Why?'

'Because every time I see it, I get lucky.'

I laughed as she slid her arms around me from behind in an unexpected hug. 'I like it when you lose the frown.'

'I frown?'

'Quite a bit of the time,' she said, her breath fanning my back. 'It makes you look formidable, when you're really a pussycat.'

'Says who?'

'Me.' She released me and stepped around me, her eyes glowing with wicked intent. 'I think it's time you made me purr.'

I didn't have to be asked twice. Catching her by surprise, I scooped her into my arms and she squealed. Looped her arms around my neck. Proceeded to nip at my shoulder. Pleasurable bites that bordered on painful, accentuating the fine line we trod.

What we did now might feel good, but it had the potential to hurt like a bitch if it went pear-shaped.

I nudged open the door to her bedroom and strode

inside, depositing her on the bed gently. She wanted to purr? I'd make sure of it.

'How did you know this was the bedroom?'

'I stayed here once, sleeping off a bender.' I undid my jeans, snagged a condom, and stepped out of them, along with my jocks.

Once again, her lack of curiosity surprised me. I'd half expected her to ask why I'd stayed here and not at Remy's house, why I'd turned up drunk at the pa-tisserie in the first place. But she didn't say a word. Instead, she crooked her finger at me, shimmying up the bed to rest against the pillows.

'You are the most beautiful male I've ever seen.' She lay back, hands behind her head, studying me with unabashed appreciation. 'I could look at you all night.'

The longer she stared at me with shameless ado-ration, the better I felt. Like I could slay dragons for her. Like I could be the kind of guy she deserved.

But that was bullshit and the moment I thought it I knew I had to shatter this illusion. Because that was all it was. Something that appeared to be wonderful but could never be real.

I wasn't the guy for her. No matter how much I wished I was for this brief moment in time.

'And I could fuck you all night.'

If my crassness shocked her, she didn't show it. She just lay there, a smile playing about her mouth as her inquisitive gaze drifted from my chest, to my belly, to my cock.

'Then what are you waiting for?'

I started at her feet. Massaging her insteps. Tugging her toes. Drifting up to her ankles. Soft strokes that had her sighing with contentment and wriggling like a cut snake.

Holding onto her ankles, I tugged her down the bed a little. And spread her legs.

She wasn't wearing panties.

'Hot damn.' I crawled up the bed towards her, flipped the skirt of her dress up, baring her to me.

Slick folds glistening with how much she wanted me.

The feeling was entirely mutual.

'I love when you look at me,' she murmured, squirming a little when I slipped a finger inside her. 'You make me feel beautiful.'

'That's because you are, sweetheart.'

I slipped another finger in as my thumb found her clit, circling slowly as I watched her face. Shifting expressions of rapture and awe that made her eyes glow and her mouth go slack.

Maintaining eye contact, I lowered my head so I could feast on her. She loved this. I'd discovered that first-hand the other night. And giving her pleasure, no matter how fleeting, had become my number one priority.

I loved the sounds she made as I swept my tongue across her clit, through her folds, repeating the action over and over until she was panting and arching into me.

'Now.' She tempered her demand with a barely whispered 'Please.'

'Your wish is my command,' I said, lapping at her like I could never get enough.

She came hard, her hips lifting off the bed as she screamed my name.

'Lucky the patisserie cleared out an hour ago, otherwise we'd have customers queuing up outside your door to have what you're having.' I slid up the bed to lie next to her and slipped the straps of her dress off her shoulders. 'Maybe you should name the next decadent pastry you create a Screaming Orgasm?'

She mumbled something unintelligible as I peeled her dress off and flung it away, leaving her completely naked. Completely beautiful.

'What was that? You want another already?' I lazily circled a nipple before plucking it as it puckered. 'If you say so—'

'I want you inside me.' She stilled my hand, her gaze trying to convey a message I had no hope of comprehending.

It looked a lot like gratitude tinged with something else, something I dared not label in case it scared the crap out of me. More than I already was.

'Done,' I said, sheathing myself and rolling her onto her side so we were face-to-face. 'I like a woman who knows what she wants and isn't afraid to ask for it.'

'And I like you,' she murmured, hooking her leg over my hip and sliding closer. 'Every inch of you.'

Not breaking eye contact, I slid into her in one smooth thrust and she sighed, the green flecks in her eyes sparking with mutual passion.

She felt so tight, so right, I knew I'd never forget this. Never forget her.

I needed to break eye contact, needed to stop her seeing into my soul, but as we rocked together slowly, sensually, I couldn't look away.

We didn't speak. No murmured dirty pleas. No naughty demands. Just the sound of our heavy breathing as we melded together.

Exquisitely slow. Deliciously drawn out.

Long, deep thrusts that made me mindless with wanting more.

As the first ripples of her orgasm clenched around me, I changed the angle of my hips a little, driving into her with enough force to make our heads bang.

'Oh, hell...' She came on a keen, the sexiest sound I'd ever heard as my balls tightened and I followed her over the edge a second later. Body taut. Mind blank. Stunned by the intensity of it and the ferocity of wanting to do it all over again as soon as humanly possible.

'More like heaven,' I said, disconcerted to find we still hadn't broken eye contact, and in that moment reality crashed over me.

What we'd done wasn't just sex.

We'd moved past that.

The intimacy, the eye contact, the yearning to stay inside her, all added up to one thing.

Trouble.

CHAPTER FIFTEEN

Abby

I USUALLY STARTED baking at six most mornings.

Today I started at five.

Tanner had been snoring softly when I'd woken at four, giving me precious time to study him. A slumbering Tanner was nothing like awake Tanner.

Asleep, Tanner's face softened, making him look younger. Awake, tension bracketed his mouth and made his neck muscles bulge a little. Asleep, his lips relaxed into a semi-smile and his head lolled on the pillow all slack and cute.

It made me wonder, had he always been this uptight or had something happened to put him on alert at all times?

He'd dropped another hint about his childhood, about him and Remy, and while I'd never pry behind his back I couldn't help but wish Remy had spoken more about his younger brother.

I knew next to nothing about Tanner King and I'd been okay with that. Having mind-blowing sex with a guy for a short-term fling didn't demand shared confidences.

But last night had changed all that.

I didn't know if it was having him in my space, the only guy I'd ever let into this apartment. Or cooking him dinner and having him rave about it. Or having him tell me that he'd never spent the night at a woman's place so this would be a first. Or the way we'd connected during the first time we'd had sex in my bed. Or the second. Maybe even the third.

Whatever it was, I knew I was in trouble. Because this short-term fling had started to get to me a little.

I wanted to know what made Tanner King tick.

Realistically, nothing had changed. Once Remy was back on his feet and back at work, Tanner would leave. But I'd overheard him chatting to Makayla yesterday about opening another two clubs in Sydney, which meant he'd leave Le Miel but would still be in town.

After last night, short term had somehow morphed in my head into something possibly a little…longer.

I could lie to myself and say it was the sex. The phenomenal, stupendous, soul-drugging sex. But I'd given up lying to myself around the time I'd walked out on Bardley after finally admitting what a disaster I'd made of my life by kowtowing to everyone and lying to myself that I was okay with it.

So lying was out. Which meant I had to accept the fact I was in danger of falling for my sexy fling. No biggie. I'd have to suck it up, get my game face on whenever he was around and make sure he didn't see beneath my devil-may-care mask. Because I could care given half a chance and if there was one thing I'd learned during my brief time with Tanner, he wasn't the kind of guy to develop anything beyond a transient liking for.

I had clear-cut goals and I'd told him as such. No way would I let a little potential crush derail my plans.

I'd already given up so much in my life, had frittered away too many years being someone I wasn't for people who ultimately didn't give a crap about me. Emotional ties bred dependence and submissiveness and compliance, so no way would I allow myself to get involved with Tanner beyond the physical.

Moving forward, this time was for me. I intended to be selfish and goal-oriented, allowing nothing or nobody to distract me.

Tanner King in all his sexy, tattooed glory was one big distraction just waiting to happen.

So I wouldn't allow it.

After fifteen minutes of indulgent daydreaming, where I envisaged waking up to his magnificent body every morning, I'd slipped out of bed and got dressed as quietly as I could. He hadn't stirred, so I'd left him a breakfast tray next to the bed and a note. He wouldn't think it out of the ordinary that I'd started work at five, though he might take offence at being advised to slip out the back stairs if he didn't want to be spied doing the walk of shame.

In reality, I couldn't face Makayla's inevitable interrogation if she saw Tanner waltz in here wearing the same clothes as yesterday. For the simple fact I didn't know what I'd say.

Accepting I'd been idiot enough to be teetering on the brink of falling for him was one thing, admitting it to anyone else another. I could live with my secret. I couldn't live with Makayla's endless banter if she discovered it.

For now, I needed to focus on my morning routine to get my head back in the game; and away from the sexy guy lying slumbering in my bed, waiting for a wake-up he'd never forget…

'Damn it,' I muttered as a glob of butter plopped onto the floor.

The intricate process of laminating dough to produce my signature Viennoiserie pastries required concentration and skill, neither of which I had this morning if my first effort was any indication.

So I started again. Wrapping a light dough around a layer of butter. Rolling it. Folding it. Rolling it again. Repeating the process over and over to produce a dough with many layers that would result in a puffy light texture that melted in the mouth after baking.

Remy said my almond croissants, *pain au lait* and *chouquettes* rivalled the best he'd tasted in France. I knew his excessive compliments were supposed to encourage me so I accepted them with aplomb, all the while wishing I could be half as good as my mentor.

So I toiled away every day, creating and tasting, buoyed by a lighter texture or a richer buttery flavour. Le Miel sold out on a daily basis so I had to be doing something right. And we often had orders for the almond croissants, which were solely my responsibility.

I'd come so far in a year I could hardly believe I was the same person. Thank goodness I'd had the guts to leave that subservient, pathetic people-pleaser who'd given up my dreams to live someone else's behind.

That was another thing sex with Tanner gave me: empowerment. An intoxicating feeling of power that eradicated the shy girl I'd once been.

Performing my first blowjob might have been intimidating, but the way he'd reacted, the way he'd stared at me afterward…made me feel more powerful than I ever had. I might have been in a subservient position on my knees, intent on giving him pleasure, but the person I'd ended up pleasing was me.

I'd never felt so alive. So dominant. So in control. Heady stuff for the doormat I'd once been.

When I'd first proposed a fling to Tanner, I'd never anticipated that having my sensual side awakened would result in feeling this good. In making my body come alive, he'd also given me something I'd always craved: clout. Command over myself and my choices. The confidence to do what I wanted when I wanted, without regard for anyone else.

Something I'd secretly craved for years but never had the guts to do. Then again, it was easier with Tanner because we didn't have a strong emotional connection. I didn't feel the need to say yes to every little thing with him because our relationship focussed on the physical.

Which was exactly why I'd freaked out and come down here early this morning. Because no matter how many times I mentally recited that we were two consenting adults attracted to each other indulging in a short-term fling, after the way we'd connected last night and my desire to know more about him, I had a sneaking suspicion we could move past that.

And it terrified me.

The closer we got, would I be in danger of reverting to the meek, passive people-pleaser who always put others before herself? The woman who felt good about herself by making others feel good first? A guy like Tanner would hate that acquiescent docility and I'd hate myself for doing it.

Crap.

I concentrated on rolling and folding the dough over layers of butter, focussing on the routine to distract from my worrying thoughts, trying to relax. I liked the methodical approach to baking, the knowledge that following a clearly delineated process should result in an edible end product.

The routine calmed me, something I craved to deal with the riotous, out-of-control feelings ricocheting through me every time Tanner popped into my head.

He was there. A lot. Front and centre. Tanner shirtless and defiant in his private room at the club. Tanner stalking towards me in the storeroom. Tanner licking carbonara sauce off his lips. Tanner naked and sated, sprawled across my bed like he owned it.

Hell.

I opened the oven to slide the first batch of croissants in, the radiant heat not helping my fiery cheeks.

Baking might be comforting, but as a distraction from the hot male in my bed upstairs it left a lot to be desired.

Time to bring out the big guns.

I'd nail the elusive *croquembouche* today if it killed me.

Anything to divert me from the yearning to head back upstairs and have Tanner nail me.

CHAPTER SIXTEEN

Tanner

I HATED SNEAKING out of Abby's apartment like a fugitive, but I wasn't an idiot. She didn't want to face an inquisition from her co-workers and that was exactly what would've happened if I'd rocked into Le Miel wearing the same clothes as yesterday.

Nothing got past Makayla. The woman had eyes in the back of her head and I pitied the guy she set her sights on. Bold ball-breakers weren't my type. I preferred quiet, reserved women who morphed into sex kittens with the barest touch.

Women like Abby.

Leaving me breakfast had been just like her, a thoughtful gesture reeking of unspoken sentiment. Unfortunately, there'd been plenty of that going around last night.

We'd barely spoken once we'd hit the bedroom. Then again, words were superfluous when we both suspected what was going on.

We'd potentially crossed the bonking buddies

threshold into some weird, nebulous territory neither of us wanted to label. Not giving it credence
suited me just fine. Her too, considering she must've
bolted out of bed at some ungodly hour.

So I scoffed my buttery soft chocolate croissant,
drank my OJ and slunk down the back stairs, the
words of her simple note imprinted on my brain.

> *Thanks for last night. Hope you enjoyed dinner.*
> *Must do it again soon.*
> *Back stairs quiet in the morning.*
> *See you later.*
> *Abby*

Interestingly, no X. I thought all women liberally
sprinkled kisses on their missives. Then again, I'd
already established Abby wasn't like most women.

The 'must do it again soon' made me look forward
to tonight in a way I shouldn't. I wasn't dating Abby.
This wasn't a relationship. But dinner had been great
and I'd like to return the favour. By taking her to my
favourite restaurant in Sydney.

I'd never gone out with a foodie before, and considering her wealthy background, she'd probably dined
at the finest restaurants this city had to offer. So I'd
take her to my favourite hangout, a tiny Thai restaurant in the backstreets of Kings Cross, a place I'd
give my left nut as a guarantee she'd never been to.

It wouldn't be a date. Just a friend returning the favour to another friend who'd cooked for me. Simple.

'You're full of shit,' I muttered at my reflection as I shaved, something I hadn't done for the last few days.

I didn't care about stubble as a rule, but Remy had always pulled me up on it ever since I'd been old enough to grow facial hair. Considering Remy would have enough to bust my balls about today, I didn't want to add another thing to the list.

The drive to the hospital took fifty minutes in peak-hour traffic, giving me ample time to come up with a plausible excuse as to why I'd shagged his protégé. By the time I'd parked and made it to the ward, I still hadn't come up with anything other than the truth.

Abby was hot and I had to have her.

Bet that would go down a treat with my brother.

I peeked into his room and saw Remy jabbing at the remote control, idly flicking channels, looking bored out of his brain. 'Hey, klutz, how are you feeling?'

'Better for seeing your ugly mug.' He turned off the TV and sat straighter in bed, wincing.

'Still in pain?'

'Only way these fools will give me the good stuff.' He made looping circles at his temple. 'That morphine makes me a little crazy, in a good way.'

I laughed and leaned down to give him a gentle man hug. 'You're perkier than last time, so that's a good sign.'

'Doc said I'm a model patient.' He screwed up his nose. 'Personally, I find it difficult to take the word of a punk wearing a white coat and stethoscope around his neck when he looks like he graduated from kinder last week.'

'Everyone looks young to you, you old fart.'

He pointed at his ankle and grimaced. 'Considering I'll have to use a walking stick once I'm on my feet, I may be living up to that insult.'

'You're only as old as the woman you feel,' I said, wondering what was Abby's age exactly.

'Sadly, I haven't been doing any "feeling" in a long time.'

When Remy pinned me with a speculative stare, I knew what was coming before he opened his mouth. 'What about you? Are you behaving?'

'I've got my hands full with the patisserie, if that's what you're asking.'

It wasn't and we both knew it, so I rushed on. 'Everything's going well. Customers still streaming in. Pastries sold out by the end of the day. Accounts balancing. Stocks replenished. Staff happy.'

Some happier than others, though Remy didn't need to know how I put a smile on Abby's face.

'You're shagging Abby,' Remy said, disappointment lacing every word as he shook his head. 'Man, I told you to keep your hands off her.'

'Since when have I ever listened to you?'

'You used to, once upon a time.' Remy eyeballed me, making me feel guiltier than I already did. 'You should try it again.'

I remembered the many times I'd listened to Remy, when he'd talked me down after yet another run-in with Dad, even if he hadn't known the reason behind my funk. When he'd persuaded me to stay rather than run away the time he'd found me hiding out in the back shed the week after Mum died. When he'd calmed me with words of wisdom on the day of Dad's funeral, painting a rosy future for us since he was over eighteen and could access the trust fund thoughtfully set up by Mum.

If it hadn't been for that money, and for Remy's calming influence, who knew where I might've ended up?

I owed him the truth. At least about Abby.

'I know I shouldn't have messed around with Abby. I'm not a complete doofus—'

'Could've fooled me.'

'But we both know where we stand so she won't get hurt.'

'You're a dickhead.' Remy snorted, his eyes narrowed in disapproval. 'You didn't see her the day she stumbled into Le Miel, disoriented and lost and sad. She hasn't told me much but her ex-husband must be a first-class bastard to do a number on a sweet girl like that and she's steered clear of men ever since.'

Remy jabbed a finger at me, a deep frown slashing his brows. 'So if she's let you anywhere near her, it means a hell of a lot more to her than it does to you. And you're going to fuck it up, just like you always do.'

A chill swept over me. Remy was my go-to guy. He always had my back. So what did he mean?

'Care to elaborate, bro?' My frigid tone did little to ease the sudden tension between us.

'You've never had a meaningful relationship with a woman. Whenever one of them gets close, you end it. That's what I meant.' Remy pressed his forehead, like he had a blinder of a headache building. 'Abby is different and if you hurt her because you couldn't keep it in your pants, I'm going to personally deck you.'

'Like to see you try,' I said, sounding meeker and suitably chastised.

Remy had never hit anyone in his life. I, on the other hand, had dealt out justice with my fists at high school on a regular basis. Bottled-up rage and a lousy self-esteem didn't mix, not when kids discovered which buttons to push to get me to explode.

'Not that I want to encourage this but, for what it's worth, when you walked in here you looked about a decade younger.' Remy stared at me, studying me with a slight tilt of his head. 'There's something different about you. You look less…stressed, or something.'

'Maybe working in a pastry shop rather than a club is good for me?'

He chuckled at my glib response. 'We both know that's not true.'

'Yeah, I know.' I reluctantly admitted, wanting to get the lowdown on Abby from Remy but knowing he'd be onto me if I pried too deeply. 'Abby's special.'

Remy's eyebrows shot up. 'Special to you?'

'I meant in general.' My clarification sounded lame and I continued. 'Hanging out with her makes me happy in a way I haven't been for a while.'

Remy's gaze turned speculative. 'You're sticking around for a few months, yeah?'

I nodded, trying not to acknowledge the leap of hope that the thought elicited. I'd already pondered the possibility of exploring more with Abby beyond our specified short-term fling, but she hadn't given any indication to wanting more and I sure as hell wouldn't stick my neck out.

I'd suffered enough rejection to last a lifetime.

'So you and Abby might be more than a passing fad?'

'Abby and I will sort out our own business, thanks very much.' I grinned at Remy's faux hurt. 'As for you, you old busybody, get better fast.'

Remy smiled but sadness lurked in his eyes, like he couldn't quite believe my flippant act.

'Both you and Abby mean a lot to me. Don't screw this up, okay?'

'I'll do my best not to.' I saluted. 'Anything else, captain?'

Remy hesitated, as if he wanted to say more, before he shook his head. 'Abby's important to me, professionally and personally, so take care of her.'

Sombreness was catchy as I nodded. 'I will.'

A promise I had every intention of keeping, if she let me.

CHAPTER SEVENTEEN

Abby

I DIDN'T HAVE time to wonder if Tanner had enjoyed the breakfast I'd left him or be grateful when he'd snuck out around six. Because at one minute past nine Makayla checked Le Miel's website and discovered we had a massive order for a ladies' function at Bondi. The kind of order that would send Remy into a tizz because of the possibility of repeat business. The kind of order to garner a week's profits in a day.

'How can we possibly do this?' Makayla printed out the order, her brow furrowed. 'It usually takes you and Remy working like maniacs to fulfil an order like this. Even then, it's touch and go.'

I should say no. It was lunacy even contemplating trying to fill this order. Besides, my first instinct to say yes sent a shiver of fear through me. I'd determinedly set aside my people-pleasing personality a year ago, had worked damn hard to ensure I learned to say no.

Then I glanced at the computer, saw Remy's face

in the corner of our website's home page, and my fear faded.

Agreeing to tackle a big challenge for the man who'd given me a break when I needed it most wasn't being servile. It was a way of helping out a friend who'd helped me, a way of giving back. I owed Remy and I knew without a doubt he'd rather I tackled this massive job than wimp out.

'What time do they need it by?'

Makayla stared at me like I'd lost my mind even contemplating this. 'Delivery at two thirty for afternoon tea at three.'

'Shit,' I muttered, scanning the list and mentally prioritising. 'We can supply the mini-croissants from the lot I baked this morning and put the "Sold Out" sign out front. Then I can make the strawberry tarts, the apple turnovers, the *pains au chocolat* and the beignets—'

'You're crazy. You'll never get all that done.' Makayla gnawed at her bottom lip and rustled the paper at me. 'Seriously. We're going to have to outsource—'

'Remy never does that. He hates putting his name to products he didn't make.'

'I know, but what can we do? We're screwed.'

I heard a footfall behind me. 'What's the problem, ladies?'

My heart leapt in recognition, and something akin to happiness, as I turned to Tanner. 'A massive order just came in. Big profits. And I can't do it without Remy.'

He stared at me, brows furrowed, eyes clouded with an unfathomable emotion I could almost label as fear, before he blinked and swiped a hand across his face. When he lowered his hand, determination accentuated the lines around his mouth, like he'd come to a decision and wouldn't let anything or anyone derail him.

'I can help,' he said, rolling up his shirtsleeves, making me salivate a little at a glimpse of those striking tattoos. 'What do you need me to do?'

I appreciated the offer but I still couldn't shake the feeling he didn't want to be here. Saddened by the thought it could be because of me and our newfound intimacy last night.

'Unless you're a secret pastry chef, there's no chance in hell we can do this—'

'I can cook.' He rubbed his hands together. 'Let's get this done.'

'I admire your tenacity but with all due respect being able to cook a steak on a barbecue and being able to create pastries worthy of the Le Miel name are worlds apart.'

One of his eyebrows quirked. 'You're doubting my skills?'

He made *skills* sound like I doubted his prowess out of the kitchen, and Makayla stifled a chuckle behind me.

'This isn't a joke, Tanner. This is Remy's reputation on the line if we can't deliver—'

'Then stop wasting time and let's get cracking.' He

strode into the kitchen, leaving me gaping after him—
and unable to resist staring at his mighty fine ass.

'Something tells me you two won't need any ovens
in there, you generate that much heat between you,'
Makayla said, her gaze speculative as she stared after
Tanner too. 'Look, we've got nothing to lose. Let him
help. Get as much done as you can and if you can't do
it all I'm sure we can substitute the strawberry tartlets with lemon from the front store, and swap *pain
au chocolat* for *pain au lait* from the massive batch
you made early this morning at some ungodly hour.'

Makayla's eyes narrowed. 'Though why you'd be
down here baking when you could be kneading some
prime male is beyond me.'

I tended to agree with her.

'No time to chat,' I said, and Makayla laughed at
my brusqueness. 'Get in touch with the contact person on that order and ask if they're okay with us sub-
stituting some of the items.'

'Yes, boss.' Makayla saluted, then shooed me towards
the kitchen. 'Now go cook with that delicious man.'

'This is a recipe for disaster,' I muttered, dragging my feet.

I liked Tanner. I liked that he was ready, willing
and able to pitch in at a time like this. I didn't like
having to babysit him while I tried to concentrate on
producing quality pastries in the fastest time possible.

Trudging into the kitchen, I was surprised to see
him with apron on, hairnet and cap in place, with
sugar, butter, flour and eggs in the correct quanti-
ties lined up in front of him on Remy's workspace.

'What are you doing?'

'Making croissants,' he said, like it was the most obvious thing in the world that a nightclub owner could create Viennoiserie pastries. But he still hadn't lost the haunted look, like being in the kitchen terrified him, and it worried me. 'Remy taught me when we were teens, so I've got it covered.'

He waved at my workstation. 'You get started on the rest.'

Stunned, I stared at him as he sectioned the butter and measured out the precise amount of flour.

'Babe, I know you love perving on me, but you're wasting time.' He dusted his hands with flour and blew me a kiss, creating a tiny flour cloud in the air. 'We've got an order to fill.'

Speechless, I headed to my workstation, methodically working through the pastries I needed to make while trying not to sneak peeks at Tanner, who appeared to be an expert in laminating dough and creating the perfect croissant.

I couldn't believe it as he produced symmetrical and equal-sized croissants, filling two trays of fifty each.

'One hundred enough?' he asked, sliding the trays into the oven and setting the timer.

'Yeah,' I said, sounding a little awestruck. 'Is there anything you can't do?'

'Climb the Harbour Bridge.' He wrinkled his nose. 'Afraid of heights.'

'Well, lucky for me you're not afraid of getting elbow deep in flour,' I said, putting the finishing touches on the strawberry tartlets. 'I can't believe you made those croissants.'

'I'm a man of many talents,' he said, puffing out his chest in mock bravado. 'As I'm sure you can attest to.' He came up behind me and placed a kiss on the nape of my neck, sending a shiver of delight through me. 'You're pretty hot when you're concentrating.'

He pressed against me, showing me exactly how hot he found me, and I groaned, rubbing my butt against him.

'Later,' he growled, nipping at my neck, my ear-lobe, before seeking out my mouth for a quick peck. 'I've already pissed off Remy enough this morning. Let's not add to his distress by mucking up this order.'

'You've already been to see him?'

He came around the front of my workbench and I glimpsed worry in his eyes. 'Yeah, visiting hours start at eight, I was there at seven.'

'You told him about us?'

He nodded, the grooves bracketing his mouth deepening. 'It went as I expected. Him warning me off you, me reassuring him I wouldn't hurt you.'

'Then what's the problem?'

He hesitated before shaking his head. 'No problem. My brother's a worrywart, always has been. He thinks this may get more complicated than either of us anticipated.'

I didn't want to tell Tanner I agreed with Remy.

Labelling Tanner the tattooed rebel as prime sex-toy material to purge my past had been fine at the start. But after having dinner with him last night, having him spend the night and now, watching him create incredible pastries like he did it every day of the week, I knew we were in serious danger of moving past a casual fling and into some nebulous, murky area I dared not label for making things *complicated*.

'But right now, our only complication is who's going to make the *pains au chocolat*, and if mine's better than yours, what are you going to do about it?'

I chuckled at his cockiness and jabbed a finger towards his workspace. 'You get started on them, I'll make the beignets.'

'I love it when you're bossy,' he said, with a wink. 'In and out of the bedroom.'

Heat crept into my cheeks and I waved him away. 'We've got three hours to get the rest of this order done. Let's do it.'

'And later tonight, we'll *do it* for real,' he said, his voice low and husky, making me yearn for him to bend me over and fill me in the way only he could.

'Work first,' I said, clearing my throat, my hands shaking a little as I reached for the flour.

'Speaking of tonight, I'd like to take you out to dinner.' He threw it out there, casual as you like, like asking me out on a date was an everyday occurrence. 'Nothing fancy, but my favourite Thai place will soon become yours if you enjoy spicy Asian fusion.'

'Sounds great, thanks.'

How I managed to sound offhand, I'd never know, while inside I did whirls and sidekicks.

'Pick you up at seven thirty?'

'Okay.'

We didn't talk much after that, as we focussed on creating pastries worthy of the Le Miel name. But I was super aware of him working alongside me, the big, bad, baker boy, making delicate pastries with ease, making me crave him something fierce.

Was there anything sexier than a man who knew his way around a kitchen? For me, no. I liked a guy confident with a bowl and spatula, a guy who could combine sugar, eggs and flour and create magic, a guy like Tanner.

I liked Tanner. A lot. Today had solidified my feelings into one crazy, scary ball of longing deep inside.

The way he'd pitched in, the way he'd made a potentially stressful situation fun, the way he'd taken charge, all incredibly attractive.

But it was more than how he looked or how he behaved. Tanner was a good guy, despite doing his best to appear otherwise with the tats and the glower. He attracted me on some subliminal level I had no hope of analysing or explaining.

I wanted Tanner. Perhaps for longer than our short-term fling. Which begged the question: What happened to me at the end of our arrangement when he didn't want the same?

I'd had the guts to walk away from my marriage and had been all set to walk away from Tanner with just as much nonchalance. Easy in theory, much harder in practice.

I'd never wanted to make this difficult. I'd wanted a casual, fun fling to take the edge off my otherwise routine life. I'd wanted to experience steamy sex with a hot guy. But now that we'd potentially moved past that…I had to admit to being worried.

I'd come so far in a year. I didn't want a relationship where I could potentially revert to the meek, compliant woman who'd do anything to keep the peace and her partner happy.

That kind of commitment scared me. I had my goals. If I had Tanner in my life for longer than a few weeks, would I lose sight of them? I didn't want to find out.

Remy had every right to be concerned.

Tanner and I were one big complication waiting to happen.

And there wasn't one damn thing I could do about it.

CHAPTER EIGHTEEN

Tanner

'I DON'T BELIEVE THIS.' I glared at the sign hanging in the window of my favourite Thai restaurant, announcing they were closed for renovations. 'I didn't even think to book because it's one of those walk-in places that rarely requires a reservation.'

'Don't worry about it.' Abby laid a hand on my arm. 'We can eat anywhere.'

True, but I'd wanted to show her a place that meant something to me, to see how she acted in the surroundings. Not a test, as such, just a way of convincing myself that while we connected physically we could never be anything long term.

Looked like the cosmos had punished me for being underhanded and I'd have to resort to Plan B. If I had one.

'Honestly, I'm not fussed where we eat.' She patted my forearm and removed her hand. 'It's been a long day, so I'd be happy with fast food and an early night.'

'You just want to get me naked as soon as humanly

possible,' I said, grinning when she blushed. 'You're so predictable.'

'Am not,' she said, with a defiant tilt of her head. Her nonchalant act would've worked too, if I hadn't glimpsed the naughty gleam in her eyes. 'I am hungry, but if you want to grab something and head back to my place…'

Best invitation I'd heard all day but this date was about proving a point and that was exactly what I'd do. Our strong sexual connection wasn't conducive to showing her how different we were outside the bedroom and how we could never be anything more than bonking buddies.

'How about fish and chips on Manly beach?'

If my subtle change of subject surprised her, she didn't show it. Instead, she nodded. 'It's a long way from the Cross to Manly by car.'

'We'll take the ferry.'

Her eyes lit up. 'Would you believe I've lived in Sydney my whole life and never been on the Manly ferry?'

'Never?'

She glanced away, her shoulders slumping a little. 'I got chauffeured everywhere. By Dad, our chauffeur and later Bardley's driver.'

'*Bardley*. I still think it's such a bullshit name,' I snarled, hating the stab of jealousy at her casual use of her ex's name.

'Totally.' She laughed and slipped her hand into mine. 'I've never eaten fish and chips on the beach either, so I'm in.'

Wouldn't her family have a fit if they knew their little princess was being taken on a no-frills date involving simple food and a ferry? It made me wonder, did she miss her old life at all?

She might hate her ex but it had to be tough living a life of luxury, then leaving it all behind. Considering how hard we'd worked today filling that urgent order, she must do that all the time with Remy. Throw in the small apartment, and it had to be a big comedown from her previous life. I admired her all the more.

'Do you miss your old life?'

She stiffened as we strolled back to the car. 'Where did that come from?'

'Curiosity.' I opened the car door for her and waited until she sat before closing it and getting in the driver side. 'Bit of a comedown, switching from chauffeurs to ferries.'

She took an eternity to answer, as if formulating an acceptable answer. 'I miss my family. And some of my friends. But that lifestyle was never important to me.'

That was where we differed. Every luxury I could afford now was testament to how far I'd come. How far I'd proved Father wrong.

Not that I took my wealth for granted or flaunted it, but I revelled in my hard-earned success. And thanked the old bastard every day for spurring me on to become the man he never thought I could be.

'So you're not in touch with anyone from your old life?'

We stopped at a traffic light and I shot her a glance.

Her lips were compressed and her arms folded, protecting herself from…what? Memories? Sadness? Me?

'No.'

A short, sharp response that clearly meant she didn't want to talk, so I remained silent until we reached Circular Quay, bought tickets and boarded the ferry.

But I couldn't let it go. Gaining an insight into her past would make it easier for me when this thing between us ended. I liked Abby. I didn't want to hurt her. Knowing what made her tick beyond the superficial would ensure I could let her down gently. 'Have you ever thought about getting in touch with your family?'

I expected her to shoot me down again with a death glare. Instead, she stared at the Opera House, lost in thought.

'Yeah, I think about getting in touch with Mum. I miss her.' She dragged her gaze away from the white sails and focussed on me. 'You'll think I'm an idiot, but I even drove past a day spa we used to go to together the other day, hoping for a glimpse of her.'

'You miss her. That's not stupid.' I slung an arm over her shoulder and cradled her close. 'I miss Remy when I'm overseas. It's normal. Family has a way of getting under our skin.'

Though not always in a good way. Dad had been testament to that.

'I can't believe she hasn't reached out after a year,

you know?' She rested a hand on my thigh, a comfortable, intimate gesture that secretly thrilled me.

She trusted me. Trusted me enough to talk about her past. But was I worthy of that trust?

'A whole year without so much as a phone call.' She shook her head. 'What kind of a mother does that?'

I didn't have a clue, considering I had nothing but good memories of mine and our happy times in the kitchen. But I had to offer some comfort, otherwise this date was heading south fast.

'I'm guessing your father rules the roost, so maybe she's doing the best she can, trying to keep the peace in her marriage and not piss him off?'

Respect shimmered in her eyes as she gazed up at me from beneath long lashes. 'Dad is the boss and what he says goes, but she wouldn't have to tell him.'

'If she's anything like you, I can't see her sneaking behind his back. You're far too principled for that and she probably is too.'

'Stop sounding so logical,' she said, her admonishment tempered with a smile. 'Anyway, enough of my depressing family.' Her smile faded and she squirmed a little, appearing uncomfortable. 'I don't know much about your family beyond the fact your parents died when you were young.'

I stiffened, my thigh flexing involuntarily beneath her palm, and she stroked my leg, offering comfort. If she only knew…it would take a lifetime of placating to ease the pain any thought of my parents elicited.

'Is that all Remy told you?'

She nodded. 'Said your mum died when he was fifteen, your dad when he was twenty.' Pity darkened her eyes. 'That means you would've been ten when you lost your mum...must've been tough.'

'You have no idea.'

Mum had been my champion, my rock, my buffer. She kept Dad away from me, sensing his hatred even though he never did anything overt towards me in front of her.

And I blamed the old prick every day for ultimately driving her to her death. Because of me.

'Tell me about her.' Abby spoke softly, her tone laced with gentle persuasion, like discovering more about my family background would somehow give her a handle on me.

Yeah, like that would happen.

But I'd prompted her to discuss her family—the least I could do was give her a snapshot of mine.

'Dad didn't have much time for me, so Mum and I were close. She taught me how to cook. How to choose a good mango. How to core apples for a classic turnover until my fingers ached...' Bittersweet happiness filled me at the memories. 'She was French. Very elegant. Very classy. Wore make-up and perfume every day, even when dropping me off at kinder. Everyone idolised her.'

Except Dad. I'd never known the real reason their marriage soured until I'd heard the hurtful accusations he'd flung at her the day she'd died. But he'd definitely been in the minority, because everyone loved Mum.

'She sounds wonderful,' Abby offered with a smile. 'Was that why you looked a little freaked out when you helped fill that massive order? Did being in the kitchen again dredge up memories of her for you?'

Surprised by her insight, I nodded. 'She was wonderful. And every time I set foot in a kitchen, even at home, I feel it right here.' I thumped a fist over my heart, wishing the simple action could dislodge the permanent ache there whenever I thought of Mum and how much I missed her.

Before I could think up something to change the subject, Abby continued. 'What about your dad?'

'He was a prick.' The words tumbled from my lips before I could stop them and if she heard the venom behind them, she didn't say.

Her hand resumed stroking my thigh. 'How so?'

'He hated my guts.'

Her lips parted in surprise. 'But you were a child. How could a father hate his own child?'

I couldn't tell her the truth. Not when I'd never told anyone, including Remy. So I settled for a watered-down version.

'Their marriage hit a rocky patch. I was the spitting image of Mum. Guess that made me dislikeable.'

Her nose wrinkled in distaste. 'I'm not in the habit of slandering people I've never met but your dad sounds like a real piece of work.'

'Understatement of the year,' I muttered, annoyed that her quick defence meant so much.

This date had been about proving our differences,

not growing closer because of shared confidences. I needed to get back on track, fast.

'Anyway, Remy is the only family I have and he more than makes up for the past.'

I could see the turmoil in her eyes, like she wanted to prod further. Instead, she said, 'Tell me how many women you've taken on ferry dates before.'

Surprised and pleased at her change of subject, I grinned. 'As of today, only one.'

She made a cute scoffing sound.

'You don't believe me?'

'I believe you've been a bad boy since you hit your teens and I imagine you've had a string of girlfriends.' She poked me in the chest. 'So don't try to deny it.'

'I'm not denying anything.' I held up my hands, like I had nothing to hide. 'I just haven't taken any of them on a ferry.'

'Lucky me,' she said, batting her eyelashes with exaggerated coquettishness.

'I'm the lucky one,' I murmured, wondering what she'd do if she could see half the thoughts whirling through my head. 'I know what this fling is about for you. A way to move forward. A way to ditch your past once and for all.'

I squeezed her shoulders. 'I'm lucky you picked me to do it.'

An odd expression flitted across her face. Regret? Anger? Hope? But it disappeared faster than I could analyse it.

She snuggled into me as the ferry chugged its way across the water. We made desultory small talk, about the Harbour Bridge, Luna Park and the mega cruise ships sailing through the Heads. Nonsensical stuff that I didn't give a crap about, but safe conversation. Safe from the possibility of emotions or feelings or deeper truths.

Like how much I wanted her to enjoy this simple date and possibly see the real me. The me beneath the tattoos and smart-ass attitude. The me who could fall for a girl like her given half a chance.

But there was a world of difference between us and if there was one thing I'd learned from Father, it was that I couldn't be a relationship kind of guy.

I couldn't be selfless, not after spending too many years feeling worthless. When he'd died, I'd vowed to use every ounce of bitterness and resentment and hurt to concentrate on being a guy worthy of success. A guy worthy of recognition. A guy worthy of every good thing in life.

Being involved with a woman like Abby would ensure I wouldn't be number one any more. I wouldn't only care about myself and not give a damn about her. I'd need to let her in, let her see the deepest part of me where a smidgeon of that scared, worthless kid still resided.

I wasn't prepared to do that.

'We're here,' I said unnecessarily, as the ferry docked and passengers started disembarking.

'Good, I'm starving.'

She held my hand like it was the most natural thing in the world as we placed our order at the outdoor fish 'n' chip pop-up café, squeezing it when we confessed a mutual hankering for grilled barramundi and extra chicken salt on our chips.

If only it were that simple, that similar taste in food could be the foundation of something more permanent between us.

Because that was the kicker amid all my ruminations. While I didn't want a full-blown relationship that required giving too much of my private self, I wouldn't mind continuing our arrangement for however long I was in Sydney.

But Abby had clearly stipulated a short-term fling at the start. Besides, she deserved more. I'd seen the way she'd started looking at me, and while I liked it I couldn't shake the feeling that Abby developing real feelings for me would only end in heartache.

I carried the paper-wrapped parcel as we strolled towards the beach, in time to watch the sun dip behind the horizon in a blaze of mauve and indigo.

'Wow,' she said, slipping her hand out of mine to bound to the sand. 'I know you're a master of many talents, but organising a sunset like that is too much even for you.'

'Anything for you,' I murmured under my breath, grateful she couldn't hear me.

Sure, I'd wanted her to enjoy this date, to see the simple pleasures I liked, but I'd also wanted to prove a point to myself. That we were nothing alike and she'd probably prefer a Michelin-starred dining experience to this.

But seeing her obvious joy when she unwrapped the paper, snagged a piece of fish in one hand and stuffed hot, salty chips into her mouth with the other made me want her more.

'This is divine,' she mumbled, her mouth half-full, and I laughed. The kind of laugh I hadn't done in a long time. A laugh filled with genuine happiness of being in this moment with this woman.

'What's so funny?' She wiped her mouth with a tissue she'd fished from her handbag. 'Let me guess, I'm not like your previous stick-insect model girlfriends who only ate salad.'

'A fact I'm eternally grateful for.' I offered her more chips, pleased when she took another handful. 'What's with you and my old girlfriends? Jealous?'

'Pfft.' She crammed the chips into her mouth to refrain from answering and I grinned.

'It's okay to like me, you know. Thousands have in the past.'

Her eyebrows shot heavenward. 'Thousands? Eww, that's just nasty.'

I laughed, enjoying the banter we traded. 'Well, I may be exaggerating a little.'

'Phew.' She swiped at her brow. 'I can deal with hundreds. Thousands? Not so much.'

'Interesting that you see me as some shallow playboy.' I leaned my hands back, propped on outstretched arms on the sand. 'Truth is, I'm not a relationship kind of guy, but that doesn't mean I sleep with every woman that walks.'

'Just the ones that drop their panties at your feet,' she deadpanned, her eyes alight with mischief.

I loved seeing her like this: playful and lighthearted.

'The only panties I'm interested in dropping these days are yours.' I deliberately stared at her breasts before sweeping lower to linger where those sensible cotton panties would be.

'Stop that,' she hissed, wriggling on the sand a little.

'Why, am I making you horny?'

Her gaze flew to mine, her lips parted in shock.

'It's okay to admit it, you know.' I crooked a finger at her. 'I'll let you in on a secret. I'm half-hard every time I'm around you, and most times when I'm not, just thinking about you.'

'Oh,' she said, so softly I barely heard it as her gaze dropped to my groin.

Predictably, I stiffened, my hard-on straining against the fly of my jeans. Damn, I should never have started this game.

'Told you we should've grabbed takeout and gone back to my place.' She almost purred, her tone soft and seductive. 'Now we have a long ride back on the water.'

'Fuck that ferry,' I muttered, not pleased that our sweet date had morphed to sexy in an instant, even less pleased that I had to be in blue balls hell for an entire ferry ride back to the city.

'It'll be much more pleasurable to f-fuck me,' she said, turning crimson at saying the F word.

'Stop,' I groaned. 'Why do you choose now to start talking dirty?'

She leapt to her feet and dusted sand off her butt, her grin smug. 'Maybe we should grab a taxi rather than wait for the ferry?'

'Maybe you're right,' I said, bundling up our rubbish and stuffing it in the trash on our way back to the road. 'Better buckle up, babe, because I'm going to tell the driver to break the land speed record.'

A coy smile played about her mouth as she stood on tiptoe and pressed a kiss to my lips. 'Thanks for dinner. It was the best date I've ever had.'

Speechless, I flagged down a taxi and bundled her in, almost tumbling in after her in my haste to get her alone. Where I could show her with actions rather than words exactly how much I'd enjoyed our date too.

CHAPTER NINETEEN

Abby

I USUALLY LOOKED forward to my day at TAFE once a week, a day to take a break from the manic pace of Le Miel and absorb the theory behind creating pastries.

I loved the lectures, the note taking, the practical sessions. The sight of my notebooks covered in scrawl. The sharing of recipes with fellow students. The questions fired at the visiting chefs.

I loved it all. But today I was distracted, seriously distracted. And I blamed a tall, tattooed nightclub owner with a penchant for pastry and me.

Last night had been incredible. A laid-back evening filled with laughs and loving. Making love, that was. I'd never be foolish enough to confuse it with any other type of love.

During our beachside date, Tanner had been more relaxed than I'd ever seen him. He had a softer side to him that was just as appealing as the harder edges. I liked seeing his different facets, like peeling back the layers of an onion and discovering more intricacies beneath.

He'd come back to my place after our beachside picnic and we hadn't left the bed for hours, before falling asleep in each other's arms. When he'd left at five this morning, he'd seemed different. Almost reluctant to depart. More tender somehow.

It had freaked me out a little. I couldn't let Tanner derail my plans. I'd already given up so much of myself in the past and now that my divorce had come through and I was finally free, I needed to move forward. To do what was right for me.

As much as we burned up the sheets and the many ways I craved him, having anything beyond short term with Tanner would be a recipe for disaster.

I knew what would happen. I'd end up getting emotionally invested, wanting to do whatever it took to keep my man happy and end up resenting him, ensuring one of us would walk away. And I'd be catapulted back to twelve months ago, picking up the pieces of my life while struggling to heal, while cursing my lack of a backbone.

After coming so far, I couldn't do that to myself. I wouldn't.

Determined to forget the possible complications with Tanner and focus on today's lectures, I hoisted my backpack higher and headed for the imposing wrought-iron front gates, mentally reciting the day's timetable.

Deep in thought, I stumbled over a crack in the footpath.

And almost slammed into my mother.

'Hello, Abigail.' She helped me straighten, her expression half fearful, half expectant, as she released me. 'How are you?'

'Fine,' I responded by rote, stunned to see her here, torn between wanting to hug her and throttle her.

I'd missed her so much. Had she missed me at all?

A tsunami of mixed emotions swamped me: anger, sadness, hope, regret. A potent combination that made my hands shake and I clenched and unclenched them a few times to get a grip.

I'd envisaged the first meeting with Mum or Dad so many times late at night, when I'd been cradling a Chardonnay and trying to ignore the insistent little voice in my head that recited how much my parents didn't give a damn. In those thoughts, I'd imagined Mum hugging me, squeezing me so tight like she'd never let go. Maybe even Dad apologising and begging for forgiveness.

But there'd been no hug from Mum. No sign that this was anything but an orchestrated encounter for who knew what purpose.

'You look tired,' she said, studying my face, her intense scrutiny not bothering me like it once had.

How many times had I heard her berate me?

'Abigail, you need to use more moisturiser on your frown lines.'

'Abigail, sunscreen is an important part of your beauty regimen. You don't want to wrinkle before fifty, do you?'

'Abigail, those dark circles under your eyes could do with a thicker concealer.'

'Abigail, that shade of coral lipstick makes you look too pale. Try a vivid pink.'

I'd tolerated her beauty advice because it was her thing, like I accepted her criticisms of everything from my wardrobe to my haircut. She was my mother and it'd been easier to acquiesce than cause dissension and ultimately get the silent treatment. I'd hated when she'd ignored me.

Ironic, as she'd given me the ultimate silent treatment over the last twelve months.

If she'd been trying to teach me a lesson, it hadn't worked. The only thing I'd learned was that I should've escaped my parents' shadows and started living my own life a long time ago. And that I couldn't trust those closest to me, despite how much I loved them.

Hoping the emotion clogging my throat wouldn't make my voice shaky, I said, 'I'm busy, so maybe we can catch up another time?'

She wrinkled her nose, considering she couldn't wrinkle her perfectly smooth Botoxed brow. 'You don't have to be busy, you know. Working at that pastry place, going to school here once a week.' She waved her hand at the TAFE, then in front of her nose, like the place stank. 'It's beneath you.'

Ice trickled through my veins. This definitely wasn't how I'd envisaged our first meeting after a year. There were no kind words, no professions of missing me, no hugs.

Instead, it was the same old. Mum telling me what I should and shouldn't be doing.

I crossed my arms across my middle, desperate to quell the hollow ache that her indifference elicited. 'How do you know where I work?'

Not that I particularly cared what the answer was. They'd obviously wanted to keep an eye on me, to ensure I hadn't entered prostitution or anything similarly nefarious that would bring disrepute on the precious Prendigast name.

'You know your father likes to keep tabs on everyone.' She patted my arm, the briefest touch that conveyed nothing but condescension. 'We care—'

'Cut the crap, Mum. If you cared, you would've tried to contact me over the last year. To at least pretend you loved me more than keeping up appearances. To show you were worried about me rather than your reputation.' My voice had risen and several students glanced our way, so I blew out a calming breath. 'Look, arguing is pointless. I need to get to class so—'

'Come home,' she said, her expression dour as she stared at me with distaste. Heaven forbid a Prendigast showed real emotion. 'It's not too late. You can salvage your marriage to that poor boy Bardley, resume the life you should have, repair our name—'

'You don't get it,' I said, mentally counting to ten to quell the rising anger making my hands shake. 'I'm happy. I'm leading the life I want, not the life you want me to.'

'Don't be ridiculous,' she snapped, bitterness

twisting her mouth. 'You're behaving like a child. You've had your fun for a year, time to grow up.'

I stared at the woman who'd given birth to me, with her powder-blue designer suit, perfectly streaked blond hair, immaculate make-up and a handbag that would pay my rent for two years.

My mother.

Who wouldn't know the meaning of the word if it jumped up and bit her on her surgically tightened ass.

A few moments ago, I'd been filled with hope that she'd sought me out to offer a smidgeon of understanding, that she'd finally understood my rationale for walking away from my old life and wanted to embrace me with acceptance.

What a crock.

Bone-deep disappointment shook me to my core. I loved my parents; all I expected was to be loved in return. But this wasn't love. And if I was completely honest with myself, had they ever loved me at all?

Love wasn't controlling and dominant and angry. Love didn't expect me to acquiesce and bow down to the heavy weight of expectations. Love didn't leave me alone for twelve long months, without making the slightest overture to heal a rift.

The ache in my stomach spread into my chest, reaching outward until I could hardly breathe. I needed to escape, to get away from her obvious disapproval.

There was no love here, only judgement, and I couldn't tolerate it a moment longer.

'Bye, Mum. Don't contact me again.'

How I managed to get the words out without breaking down I'd never know, but I did, sounding surprisingly calm when I was a screaming mess inside. A seething mass of emotion that threatened to spurt out of my eyes in a torrent.

My mother drew herself up, squaring her shoulders for a fight that would never come. Because I was done. 'Abigail! Don't you dare walk away from me.'

So I did just that, without looking back.

CHAPTER TWENTY

Tanner

'WHAT THE HELL did you tell those doctors to bully them into discharging me early?' Remy propped on his elbow crutches, grinning at me with newfound respect the following Tuesday. 'On second thoughts, I don't give a flying fig what you said. I'm just rapt to be going home.'

'And back to work as long as you keep off that ankle and just supervise,' I added, playing the solicitous brother to the end and feeling like a fraud because of it.

Getting Remy discharged from hospital hadn't been an altruistic act on my part. I needed him back at Le Miel.

So I could leave.

Continuing to work alongside Abby after this morning was untenable.

For the first time ever, when I'd woken next to a woman after another incredible night of sex, I hadn't wanted to leave.

I'd wanted to stay. In her bed. In her apartment. In her life.

Ensuring I had to leave pronto.

I wasn't a forever kind of guy. I'd end up driving away anyone who got too close. I'd had that drummed into me from a young age, the reason why I'd made such a big effort with Remy to prove Dad's prediction wrong. At least he'd died knowing I was loyal to my brother. I hoped he choked on the knowledge when he looked up at me from hell every single day.

'I can't thank you enough for holding down the fort while I've been in hospital.' Remy cleared his throat as I picked up his bag. 'You've been amazing.'

'Save the mushy crap for someone who cares,' I said, sounding just as gruff as we exited his room and made our way slowly up the corridor towards the exit. 'Do you want me to drop you home or at Le Miel?'

'The patisserie, of course.' He waved one crutch around. 'The ankle feels fine in the boot and these things are okay for my ribs, so all good.'

I'm glad it was all good for one of us. Me? Not so much. I had to extricate myself from the thing with Abby and every time I thought about ending it I felt sick in my guts.

I wanted her in my life.

I'd end up pushing her out of my life.

Which meant the kind thing, the honest thing, would be to finish it now before either of us got invested.

Too late for me. I was already in way too deep and flailing like a drowning guy. Desperate to grab onto the nearest buoy, which happened to be my brother returning to work.

'You wait here and I'll go get the car—'

'What's wrong?' Remy stopped me by stabbing my foot with a crutch. 'Did something bad happen between you and Abby?'

'We're fine,' I said, summoning a latent acting skill I'd honed to great effect as a kid, knowing it would fool Remy. He'd never seen through my fake bravado, from the first time I tried to hide my tears at age eight when Dad yelled at me for looking like 'that useless French slut who trapped me into marrying her' to the many times since Mum died and his systemic verbal abuse made me feel worthless and useless like nothing else could.

At the time, I'd resented Remy for not being around, for not seeing enough, for not doing anything. I'd hated him deep down for being caught up in his apprenticeship and his schooling and his dreams of running a patisserie one day.

But as Dad's emotional torture had escalated, I'd been glad Remy hadn't been around to notice. Dad had ruined my life; I didn't want him tainting Remy's as well. Remy was a good guy. He looked after me when he could. I was lucky to have him as a brother.

After Dad died, Remy had broached the topic of my obvious animosity towards our father once. I'd ended up throwing Dad's prized beer stein against the wall, smashing it to smithereens and laughing hysterically. Remy had put my tantrum down to grief and the teenage hormones of a fifteen-year-old running wild but, thankfully, he'd never brought up the subject since.

So I summoned those infamous acting skills now to force a nonchalant grin. 'It's been great working alongside her.'

Remy's eyes narrowed, pinning me with a glare that said he didn't believe my bullshit, not this time. 'I'm not talking about work and you know it.'

'We've had fun.' I shrugged, feigning indifference I didn't feel, wishing that damn ache in my chest would quit sooner rather than later. 'We're good.'

'Had, as in past tense?' Judgement laced his tone. 'So you're over?'

Feeling like a prick for lying to my brother yet again, I nodded. 'You know me. I'm not built to last.'

'You're full of crap.' Remy snorted, shook his head. 'She's a great girl. You're staying in town. Why not see where this can go?'

I knew exactly where this would go. Down the toilet.

'I'll get the car,' I said, stalking away.

My usual MO and I'd stick to it.

I just hoped Abby would understand.

CHAPTER TWENTY-ONE

Abby

ENJOYING A RARE lull after the morning rush, I sipped on a soy latte in the kitchen, mentally sorting the baking tasks for this afternoon.

However, every time I got to item three on my to-do list, thoughts of Tanner would intrude, ensuring all my concentration focussed on him and him alone.

It was no use denying it any longer. I'd fallen for him.

And I'd almost made the fatal mistake of telling him this morning.

It had been so comfortable, so easy, waking up next to him, making idle chatter about our day ahead. There'd been a moment, a drawn-out fraught moment, where I'd thought he was on the same page as me. He'd stared into my eyes, taken my hand and opened his mouth to say something.

I'd held my breath, waiting for him to say he didn't want this to end. That he wanted to explore a relationship. That he wanted me for more than a few weeks.

Instead, he'd raised my hand to his lips, brushed a kiss across the back of it, before rolling on top of me and consuming me whole.

He did it very well, distracting me with his body, bringing me to life in a way I'd never dreamed possible. So I'd given over to the pleasure, biding my time.

I'd tell him. Soon. And hope to God he wouldn't run.

He'd left my apartment early, citing an appointment, but something had been off. Almost like he'd closed down after our monumental wake-up sex.

Maybe he'd sensed my impending revelation? Maybe he'd been tired from the few hours' sleep we'd got yet again? Whatever the reason, he'd be back to help out any second and I'd keep things strictly professional in the kitchen before asking him to a cosy dinner tonight.

Where I'd lay it all on the line.

The back door creaked open and I straightened, my hand drifting unconsciously to my hair and tucking stray strands into the net holding it off my face.

Tanner strode through the door, his expression unreadable as he held it wide open and waited.

'Hey, what's… Remy?' I squealed as my boss hobbled into the kitchen, a grin as wide as the Harbour Bridge splitting his face. 'What are you doing here?'

I flew across the kitchen to give him a tender hug, surprised but thrilled to see him.

'Doc discharged me early because I'm healing well. So I'm back on deck.' He mock frowned and glared around the kitchen. 'Lucky for you, everything seems to be in order.'

I whacked him on the arm. 'Tanner and I have not only held down the fort, we've filled major orders and turned a handy profit.'

'Remind me to give you a raise.' Remy's eyes twinkled with warmth. 'Seriously, kid, you've done an amazing job and I can't be more grateful.' He half turned to Tanner, who hadn't moved from the door. 'To both of you.'

'He's back to the mushy stuff,' Tanner said, rolling his eyes, and I chuckled. 'Let's get him set up on a stool or chair or something, so he can start issuing orders and be a general bossy pain in the ass.'

The bell from the front of the patisserie tinkled, indicating a customer. 'I'll have to get that. Makayla popped out and Shaun called in sick today.'

Remy waved me away. 'Go. Tanner will get me set up.'

'Great to have you back.' I gave him another impulsive hug before bounding down the corridor towards the front of the patisserie.

And pulled up short when I saw who the customer was.

'What are you doing here?' I half closed the door between the front and the kitchen, not wanting Remy or Tanner to hear me send my mother on her way. 'You need to leave. Now.'

To my mother's credit, she didn't flinch from my icy order. 'I've come to apologise.'

'For what? Twenty-two years of not believing in

me? For wanting me to be your clone? For shoving
your expectations on me, then treating me like crap
with the silent treatment if I didn't give in immediately? For not supporting me through a loveless marriage? For having the gall to ask me to come back
and live in that charade, all for the sake of your precious ego?'

Sadness downturned her crimson-lipsticked mouth
and she shook her head. 'I deserve that.'

'And a whole lot more. But this isn't the time or
place. I'm working.'

'I know.' She glanced around, approval in her
brusque nod. 'I used to love walking past this place,
but I never dared enter for fear of putting on two
pounds just by looking.'

Mum had been past here but never come in? Maybe
she did possess a soul after all and had wanted to keep
an eye on me? Then again, if she really cared, she
would've wanted to talk, to hug, to forgive. Instead,
she'd waited twelve long months before confronting
me at uni, demanding I kowtow yet again.

I hated the flare of hope deep inside when I'd
first spied her here today. Because after all I'd been
through with my parents, I should know better. She
hadn't succeeded in convincing me to bow to the
Prendigast way first time around; today would be
round two.

She walked to the front display cabinet and trailed
her fingers over the glass. 'Everything looks so delectable. Those tiny macarons. The croissants. The
tarts. I'm drooling.'

'I made all that,' I said, squaring my shoulders, expecting a put-down or a backhanded compliment at best. 'It's what I love doing.'

'You're lucky, following your dream.' She cleared her throat and turned back to face me. 'That's why I'm here, actually. To help you.'

'I don't need your help.'

I didn't need anything from her, not after the way she'd abandoned me when I needed her most, then chastised me for it last week, imploring me to come back and 'all would be forgiven'.

As if.

Mum sighed and smoothed an imaginary wrinkle from the hem of her jacket. 'I know there's nothing I can say to make up for staying away this past year. Or the way I treated you when I ambushed you outside TAFE.' She waved her hand towards the display cabinets. 'But I'm hoping that my actions will speak louder than any trite apology I could come up with.'

Curiosity tempered my resentment. 'You're talking in riddles.'

'I came here to extend an olive branch.' Mum took a deep breath and blew it out. 'If being a pastry chef is your dream, I want to help you achieve it. So I'm willing to fund your very own patisserie. Wherever you want. I'll pay the lease for as long as you want. Or I'll buy the building.'

While I struggled to comprehend the words pouring out of my mother's mouth, she continued. 'No strings attached. I don't expect you to forgive me. But I'd like to be a part of your life again. To make up for lost time…' She trailed off, her voice soft. 'I think I was jealous of you, for having the guts to do something on your own, for not always conforming, like I do.'

She shook her head, her blond bob swinging lightly across her shoulders in blow-dried perfection. 'I've been telling myself for years that I'm happy with your father calling the shots, that I lead a full, happy life. But in the end, what do I really have to show for it all, apart from a designer wardrobe, a sports car and killer hair?'

I couldn't help but smile. Mum had always been vain about her sleek blond bob.

'For what it's worth, I'm sorry, Abigail. For everything.' She took a tentative step towards me, unsure of my reaction.

I hesitated, wanting to broach the gap between us, wanting the past to fade away, wanting so much but afraid to be let down yet again.

'Abigail, please…'

I couldn't ignore the wavering plea in her voice or the generous offer. So I walked towards her and into her embrace.

Tears burned my eyes and I let them fall, inhaling my mum's familiar rose fragrance, savouring the comfort of her hug. I'd needed this, needed her. Guess it was better late than never.

When we eased apart, her eyes were bloodshot and she blinked rapidly, as if to stave off further tears.

'So what do you say? Fancy being your own boss?'

Her offer had blown me away but I needed to couch my rejection in terms she'd understand.

'I appreciate the offer, Mum, I really do. But I want to keep learning from Remy and complete my apprenticeship here.'

When her mouth drooped in disappointment, I added, 'But after that, who knows? I'd love to run my own patisserie.'

'That's great.' She held my hands and squeezed. 'I'm sorry it's taken me this long to say it, but I'm so proud of you.'

'Thanks, Mum, it means a lot, coming from you.'

She held me at arm's length, her smile genuine. 'Your father's a stubborn old goat, but I'm hoping he'll come around too.'

'Don't hold your breath.'

My dry response earned a chuckle. 'If he doesn't, I don't want that to affect our relationship.'

'Seriously?' My incredulity was audible. 'Did you ever wonder why I was such a mouthless, subservient yes-girl?'

Mum blushed, sadness clouding her eyes, but if we were to have any chance at a real relationship moving forward, I had to be completely honest.

'I'm sorry, Mum, but I copied you. Dad ruled the roost. Whatever he says goes. And if you didn't agree, he'd treat you with frosty silence. Me too.' I shook my head, let down by the person I'd been, but pleased to have come so far. 'So I started modelling you and it soon became easier to acquiesce with everything than cause problems.'

Tears shimmered in her eyes. 'Your childhood wasn't that bad, was it? We loved you. We gave you everything—'

'Life isn't about having everything. It's about being true to yourself.' I gestured around the patisserie. 'I feel more alive here than I ever did.'

I saw Mum's crestfallen expression but it didn't stop me. She had to know how bad things had been so we could move forward.

'I'm not blaming you entirely, Mum, but growing up in a household where it was easier agreeing to everything ensured I didn't say no when I should've, like agreeing to marry Bardley.'

Obstinacy twisted her mouth. 'But you grew up together. He's a nice boy and you had so much in common—'

'I never loved him and he turned out to be a controlling, verbally abusive prick.'

She didn't flinch at my swearing. Instead, she appeared to wilt before my eyes, her usual proud posture defeated.

'I don't know what to say...'

'I didn't tell you all this to make you feel bad.' I patted her arm. 'I just wanted you to know why I've fought so hard to become independent and to follow my own dreams, not live yours.'

She nodded, her eyes clear with clarity at last. 'You've been honest with me so I'll return the favour. I don't expect your father to come around. He's still livid at your "antics".' She made air quote marks. 'But I'll do my best to make him see reason.'

'Thanks, Mum.'

This time, I leaned in to give her a brief hug. To her credit, she hadn't baulked at my revelations or tottered out of here on her designer heels. Maybe there was some hope for us to re-establish a mother-daughter relationship. A real one, free of domination and subservience and lies.

'I'll be in touch but in the meantime if you need anything you call me, okay?'

'Okay.'

She kissed my cheek, cast me a final confused glance like she couldn't figure me out, before sailing out of the patisserie, leaving a cloud of rose-scented air in her wake.

There'd been no mention of a specific catch-up. No mention of coming home for a meal. But for now, it was enough. I knew my mum and her coming here to offer me my own patisserie had been a big gesture on her part. Huge.

It was a start.

Later, I'd mull our exchange at length. For now, I had a stack of beignets to bake and loads of news to catch Remy up on.

Starting with how his brother had stolen my heart without trying and I had no idea what to do about it.

CHAPTER TWENTY-TWO

Tanner

THE MOMENT I heard Abby's mother offer her a patisserie I should've eased away from the door and headed back to the kitchen.

When we'd initially heard Abby's raised voice, Remy had sent me to the front to investigate but I'd stopped short when I'd peeked around the half-closed door and spied Abby in a standoff with a woman.

I had to admit curiosity had got the better of me when I'd heard Abby call the immaculately dressed, perfectly coiffed older blonde 'Mum'.

So this was the dragon that'd abandoned her daughter for an entire year. She didn't look so bad. Then again, most people had thought my father looked like a frigging saint and he'd had the black soul of a devil.

I'd been so proud of Abby, standing up to her mother. But it sounded like this wasn't the first time they'd met up. I'd heard something about Abby being ambushed outside TAFE.

Which meant she'd lied to me. She'd said her

parents hadn't been in contact over the last twelve months, yet she'd obviously seen her mother. Why would she keep that secret?

If I'd needed proof that she only saw me as short-term fling material, this was it. Obviously I wasn't to be privy to her family dealings, not when we had a clear expiration date.

A date I'd deliberately brought forward today.

I hovered at the door like a goddamn sneak, long enough to witness their happy reunion. Abby had forgiven her mum. She'd accept the patisserie. She'd be welcomed back into the family fold. Who knew? She might even find some other rich prick from her social circle to hook up with.

Wasn't any of my concern. That ache in my chest had to be heartburn from downing three steaming espressos at the hospital.

In a way, Abby's decision made things easier. I'd had a gutful of being second best growing up. This time, I wouldn't stick around to be anyone's second choice. Never again.

Leaving them hugging and in tears, I backed away from the door. Time to hit the road.

When I strode into the kitchen, Remy was flicking through one of Abby's notebooks, covered in her flowing scrawl and overflowing with recipes cut from newspapers and magazines.

I'd teased her about the many notebooks lying around her apartment. She'd said it was her thing, to let it go, but I'd loved watching her sit in her favourite armchair, idly flicking those pages, worrying her bottom lip with her teeth, as a small satisfied smile played about her mouth.

She loved her job and it showed. She'd be a great pastry chef, good enough to give Remy a run for his money. Good luck to her. Pity I wouldn't be around to see her success.

'What happened out there?' Remy flipped the book shut and laid it on the bench. 'Abby sounded upset.'

'It's her mother.'

Remy gaped at me, like I'd announced a visit from the Queen. 'She's here?'

I nodded and jerked a thumb over my shoulder at the front of the patisserie. 'They've made up.'

'Good for her.' The concern clouding Remy's eyes didn't dissipate instantly. 'That family has a lot to make up for, abandoning Abby like that.'

'I agree.' I made a grand show of looking at my watch. 'Now that you're back, bro, I've got a ton of work to catch up on. So take it easy. I'm outta here.'

I should've known Remy wouldn't let me leave so easily. 'But you're coming back, right?'

I could've made up some bullshit story. But this was Remy. I couldn't do it. Not to him.

'No.'

A short, sharp refusal that hung in the air like a stinky pall. Heavy and oppressive. Stifling anyone unlucky enough to be near it.

'You're leaving?' Disgust curled Remy's upper lip. I didn't blame him. I disgusted myself too.

'I'm staying in Sydney but I won't be around here to help any more.' I thrust my hands in my pockets, alarmed to find them shaking a tad. This was it. The break from Le Miel. And Abby. 'You've got it covered. I'll check in on you at home and if you need me for anything, just call—'

'You're running scared. Again.' Remy spat the words out, staccato and stabbing. 'Let me guess. You're not even going to say goodbye to Abby.'

Feeling like a low-life bastard, I shrugged. 'I'll call her—'

'You'll *call* her? How fucking magnanimous.' Remy sneered, his loathing nothing on what I felt myself. 'I can't believe I thought you'd changed, that this time might be different.'

I shouldn't ask. I really shouldn't, but I found the question spilling from my lips. 'Different, how?'

'You've looked lighter, happier, than I've ever seen you.' Some of Remy's anger faded as his face relaxed into an expression bordering on antipathy. 'I knew it was Abby. She was good for you. And judging by the way she lit up earlier when you walked in the door, I'd say the feeling is mutual. But you're going to screw it up again. Run like you usually do. Pretend that you're a big tough guy not affected by your past, when in fact it consumes you.'

'You're talking out your ass,' I snapped, clamping down on the flicker of fear Remy's accusations elicited. 'And keep your psychobabble bullshit to yourself.'

'No. This time you listen.'

I'd never heard Remy like this, his tone low and lethal. Ice cold. Chilling.

'Dad did a number on you. I get it. For some un-
known reason he hated you, and I'm sorry I wasn't
around enough to figure it out earlier. But he's gone.
He can't hurt you any more, so why are you letting
him?'

I gaped at Remy in open-mouthed shock. I'd never
spoken to him about Dad. Had gone out of my way to
put on a brave face the few times Remy was home to
eat dinner with us. Had deliberately pretended I was
fine while he chased his dream and I lived at home
with a monster that blamed me for every bad thing
that had happened in his life.

I could deny it now. But what was the point? Besides, it might do me good to offload some of the
bottled-up crap, considering I was screwing up with
Abby because of it.

'How did you know?'

Remy slumped, aging before my eyes. 'The day
before Dad died I came home early. Heard you two
arguing. Heard some of the stuff he said to you…'
Remy's voice broke and he cleared his throat several
times before he could continue. 'I hated myself for
not knowing, for not being more aware. I was going
to talk to Dad about it, and to you, but then he had
that heart attack the next day and it seemed pointless dredging it all up when you seemed so relieved.'

'Best fucking day of my life.'

Sadly, it could never trounce the worst. The day
I'd overheard my parents arguing, the day I'd learned
why Dad hated me, the day Mum had been so upset

she'd driven off in anger, swerved off the road and hit a tree, dying on impact.

Remy's eyes glittered with realisation. 'Did he ever hit you?'

I shook my head. 'Not punches, just the good old-fashioned wooden spoon on my ass, but the rest was worse...' Then it all came bubbling out, like a lanced boil, filled with putridity. 'He grabbed me a few times, rattled the living daylights out of me while yelling the usual abusive crap. About how I looked like Mum and that was a constant reminder of how he'd made the worst decision of his life to marry her.'

My chest heaved with the effort of subduing sobs. 'But he didn't stop there. Because tolerating his crap and me asking what was behind his hatred was like uncorking a genie bottle; unfortunately for me, vitriol appeared and I sure as hell didn't get any wishes.'

I wanted to tell Remy all of it but I couldn't. If he looked shattered by my partial revelations, the rest would undo him completely and I couldn't be responsible for that.

A derisive chuckle, devoid of amusement, exploded from my mouth. 'When you were around, he behaved normally. When you weren't, he heaped praise on you and acted like I didn't exist. When he wasn't accusing me for being as useless as Mum, that is. I pretended like the constant put-downs meant nothing. That I was impervious to whatever he said. But even now, I still think I'm not good enough. That people can see through me to the unworthiness beneath...' I sounded broken, frail, and it mortified me.

I'd hidden everything from Remy, had not wanted to worry the brother I idolised. Remy had been my rock, the one constant in a crappy childhood. For him to now know how badly I was fucked up… I should've felt better, finally confessing, but it made everything one hundred times worse.

'Fuck, I'm so sorry, I had no idea…' Remy's voice hitched and his face crumpled as he swiped a hand across his eyes. 'Why didn't you tell me—?'

'Not worth both of us having a shit upbringing.'

My eyes burned but I'd be damned if I shed one tear over that old bastard. My brother staring at me like I'd stabbed him in the heart, that was another matter entirely. I wanted to blubber like a baby the longer he gawked at me with pity visible in his tear-filled eyes.

'You really feel unworthy still?'

A question I didn't want to answer because it sounded pathetic articulated out loud. At my core was that bitter young boy, filled with resentment and anger and hatred, but helpless to do anything about it.

When I didn't respond, Remy slumped further, appearing to sink in on himself. 'Shit, I'm so sorry, Tanner. But look how far you've come.' Remy gestured at the door, his eyes glistening with tears I'd caused. Me. It tore me apart all over again. 'Out there is an amazing woman who I'm pretty sure is head over heels for you and you're walking away because—'

'Because she'll ultimately walk away from me. Her mother just offered Abby her own patisserie,' I hissed through gritted teeth, the futility of all this washing over me like an icy wave. 'Don't you get it? I'll never be good enough for someone like her.'

A lone tear trickled down Remy's cheek. 'You are the best—'

'Thanks, bro, but it is what it is.'

I had to get out of here before I lost it completely. Or worse, Abby came back in.

'Say bye to Abby for me.'

I didn't wait around to hear Remy's response as I bolted out the door.

CHAPTER TWENTY-THREE

Abby

I DABBED AT the moisture under my eyes with my pinkies, not wanting Remy and Tanner to interrogate me about the reason behind the tears when I re-entered the kitchen.

I couldn't believe it. Mum making a grand gesture. Seeking forgiveness. Re-establishing contact without trying to direct my life. Despite blaming them for so much, I'd missed my family and after our last confrontation had given up all hope of ever being part of the Prendigasts. But if Mum had made an overture, I hoped Dad would follow and, eventually, we'd be a family again.

Not like before, with me afraid to voice an opinion or following their lead for everything, but in a mature way where we respected each other.

I could live in hope.

I paused at the kitchen door, breathed in and out a few times, before fixing a smile on my face and striding in. Only to find Remy slumped at a bench, head in hands, looking like he'd received devastating news.

Tanner was nowhere to be seen.

Foreboding strummed my spine as I approached him. 'Hey, everything okay?'

When he raised his head and his agonised, blood-shot gaze met mine, I knew it wasn't. In fact, something bad had happened in the few minutes I'd been out front, and I rubbed my bare arms against the sudden chill sweeping over me.

'Where's Tanner?'

He shook his head, his expression so morose I wanted to hug him. 'Gone.'

'Did you two fight?'

'No.' He swore, something he never did, and I pulled up a stool alongside him. 'There's no easy way to say this, but he's not coming back.'

Confused, I leaned closer. 'What do you mean? Not coming back to help here? That was inevitable, but—'

'He's gone, Abby.' He spoke softly, barely above a whisper. 'And he asked me to say goodbye to you.'

It took a second for understanding to dawn, and when it did I slumped against the bench too, filled with horror and disappointment and eventually numbness. An icy, debilitating chill that spread from my chest out, making my arms and legs tingle then shake.

It did little to anaesthetise the pain twisting my gut, making me want to vomit.

'What happened? I was only gone a few minutes.'

I couldn't comprehend it. This morning in bed he

looked like he cared way beyond casual. Now he'd walked away from me without even saying goodbye? It didn't make sense. Sadly, I had a feeling nothing Remy said would clarify my confusion.

'Tanner's in a funk and when he's overwhelmed, he runs.' Remy pinched the bridge of his nose. 'It's what he's always done.'

'Am I the cause of that funk?'

Remy had the decency to meet my gaze when he nodded. 'I think so. I've never seen him so happy. It's why I thought this time would be different.'

A stab of jealousy pierced my sadness. 'So he's done this before with other women?'

'No, he's never let other women get this close.' A deep frown slashed Remy's brow. 'You're a first, which is why I thought he'd make a stand and fight.'

'I don't understand. He's in a funk because he's happy?'

Remy nodded, sorrow turning down his mouth. 'He thinks he's not good enough for you.'

'What?' Incredulous, I pressed my fingers to my temples to try and make sense of all this. 'He's successful, rich and hot. Why would he think he's not good enough?'

A slow-burning anger overtook my indignation. 'And I'm not going anywhere, so why would he think I'd leave?'

Remy faced me, his expression morose. 'Has he mentioned our parents?'

I nodded. 'Yeah. Sounds like he idolised your mum but your dad was awful.'

'Okay, so you know some of it…' Remy shook his head. 'It's not my place to tell you everything I just learned, but let me say this. Tanner has been through a hell of a lot and he's hurting…' He shrugged, a simple gesture filled with helplessness. 'It really messed with his head. Explains why as soon as he inherited his trust fund he rebelled, determined to do his own thing and prove himself to the world.'

A picture formed in my head that broke my heart. A boy losing his parents too young and becoming emotionally stunted because of it. A child with an inherent lack of trust for anyone other than the brother who stood by him through everything. Now that boy had become a man who shunned intimacy because of that lack of trust.

But I'd never given him any indication that I would hurt him.

Other than the clearly articulated short-term nature of our liaison.

Hell. I'd basically told him at the start that I was one of a long line of people in his life who wouldn't stick around. No wonder he'd bolted when he'd thought we might be getting serious.

I muttered a curse under my breath. 'What can I do?'

Remy patted my arm. 'Honestly? Nothing. I know from experience that once Tanner makes up his mind, nothing or no one can change it.'

He glanced away, his furtive look not filling me with confidence. 'He thinks that once you'll open your own patisserie, you'll be absorbed back into your old life and you won't want him cramping your style.'

'What the...?' I shook my head, confused again. 'But I'm not opening my own patisserie. I mean, maybe one day, but I'm happy here.'

Remy's expression lightened as he eyeballed me. 'But he overheard your mum's offer and thought you'd accepted?'

'He misconstrued.' I made crazy circles at my temple. 'That's what happens when you listen at keyholes.'

He managed a wan smile at my dry response. 'So you're staying?'

'For as long as you'll have me.' I leaned over and gave him an impulsive hug. 'You saved me when I needed it most. I'd never betray you.'

'It's not a betrayal to embrace your family again,' he said when we'd sat back. 'I saw how gutted you were when they abandoned you.'

'Honestly? I'm trying to give Mum the benefit of the doubt with her generous offer, but a part of me can't help but feel she's trying to buy my forgiveness?'

He nodded, his brow furrowed in thought. 'You could be right, considering the length of time she's taken to approach you. But she's your mother. Take it from someone who lost my mum far too early and who'd give anything to have more time with her. Don't waste time analysing her motivation. Just give it a chance.'

I reached over and squeezed his hand. 'Thanks. You're a good friend.'

'Anytime.' His smile faded as the frown slashing his brows returned. 'As for Tanner, I think you need to give him time. Space. Let him brood. Sulk. Whatever.'

He held up his hand and crossed his fingers. 'And hopefully this time, he won't screw up the best thing to ever happen to him.'

I valued Remy's advice. But as someone who'd walked away from a relationship without looking back, I hoped Tanner wouldn't do the same.

CHAPTER TWENTY-FOUR

Tanner

'YOU'RE IN A foul mood.' Hudson strolled into my office and perched on the edge of my desk. 'Woman troubles?'

'Fuck off,' I snarled, not wanting to talk about Abby. Now or ever.

'Nice.' Hudson tapped at the screen of his cell and turned it towards me. 'What do you think of this?'

Work I could do. Work would keep me focussed and driven. Work I could understand. Unlike the tumultuous feelings eating at me from the inside out, tainting every waking moment and most sleeping ones too.

It had been three days since I'd walked out of Le Miel. Seventy-two long hours where I'd fought every instinct to contact Abby. To explain. To apologise. To do something to ease the pain she must be feeling.

Because if she felt half of what I was feeling, she'd be in frigging agony.

I squinted at the screen. 'A live show?'

Hudson nodded. 'Lots of the Vegas clubs are doing them these days. Hosting special live events to draw in the crowds.'

'We're not known for being a live venue.'

'Which is why this is so innovative.' He brandished the cell at me again and I swatted it away. 'What's happened to the guy always ready to take a risk?'

I'd taken a risk with letting Abby into my life and look how that had turned out. Risks were for suckers.

'Do a proposal. Set out figures for me. Then email me and I'll take a look.'

'That's the spirit.' Hudson gave me a thumbs up. 'Now how about we hit the town tonight? Boys' night out. Involving copious amounts of alcohol and luscious babes. What do you say?'

The thought of being near another woman right now set my teeth on edge. Crazy, because Abby and I were over. I owed her nothing. But it was too soon.

'Thanks for the offer, but I'll be working late tonight.'

Hudson stood and huffed out a breath. 'Look, at the risk of getting my teeth punched out, you've been locked away in here for three days straight. You snap at anyone who ventures close. The staff are afraid of you. And I'm sick of you treating me like an enemy rather than a friend.'

He jabbed a finger at me. 'So do whatever it takes to lighten the fuck up, okay? Confront what's got you so riled. Get it out of your system. Deal with it.'

The only thing that would lighten my mood was

to see Abby again and that wasn't going to happen. Not in this lifetime.

'Thanks for the pep talk, mate,' I drawled, and pointed at the door. 'Now get the hell out and leave me alone.'

'Dickhead,' he muttered, shaking his head as he strode towards the door, where he paused. 'For what it's worth, I liked you better when you were dating that Abby chick. She made you happy.'

I made a growling noise and stood, my fingers clenching into fists.

Hudson held up his hands in surrender. 'Just saying,' before he closed the door on his way out.

Abby had made me happy but that was over.

The faster I got my head around it, the better.

CHAPTER TWENTY-FIVE

Abby

'WHAT DO YOU THINK?'

I glared at Makayla as my back twanged for the umpteenth time. 'I think Pilates is for pretzels.'

'It's your first class. You'll get the hang of it after a few more.' Makayla interlinked her fingers and stretched overhead. 'It's brilliant for flexibility and core strength.'

'I'll take your word for it.' Wincing, I managed to stand. 'In the meantime, I've got a hot bath with my name all over it.'

'Fancy going out tonight?'

It had become Makayla's standard invitation over the last three days. Ever since Tanner had walked out of my life and I'd let him.

'Thanks, but I'd rather chill.' I rolled my shoulders, hoping they didn't spasm. I had a big croissant order to fill tomorrow.

'A night out might do you good.' Makayla slung

a towel around her shoulders and mopped her face.
'Get him out of your system.'

Nice in theory. Sadly, I had a feeling it would take
a lot of practice to get Tanner out of my system.

'You're a good friend. But I'm okay, honest.'

A total lie, but I'd managed not to shed a tear yet,
and I aimed to keep it that way. Easier to keep busy
at work, then watch mindless sitcom reruns at night
and fall into bed exhausted. I had a feeling if Makayla
started asking questions about why things ended with
Tanner, delved too far beneath my fragile surface, I'd
crack. Once that happened, everything I'd been keeping locked away tight might spill out and that would
be disastrous.

'You don't have to lie to me.' Makayla slumped
onto a bench lining the mirrored wall of the exercise
studio and patted the spot next to her. 'I can see how
much you're hurting all over your face.'

I grimaced as I sat next to her. So much for my
poker face. 'That obvious?'

'I've been there. It sucks.' She shrugged. 'Did he
give you a reason why he split?'

'Uh…we haven't spoken.'

Her eyebrows shot up. 'What do you mean?'

'When Remy got back, he left, and we haven't
spoken since.'

Makayla stared at me in confusion. 'You haven't
called him to ask what's going on?'

'Nope.'

'Why the hell not?'

'Dignity. Pride. Nonchalance. Take your pick.'

'You're nuts.' Makayla elbowed me. 'It's been three days and you haven't wanted to see him? To talk to him?'

I knew exactly how long it had been since I'd last seen Tanner, beyond that fleeting glimpse when he'd brought Remy in. The morning I'd left him sexy and sleepy in my bed. The morning he'd held my hand, stared into my eyes and opened his mouth to say something, possibly momentous, before he'd chickened out.

I had too. I could've nudged him, given him another opportunity. Instead, I'd bolted for the shower and waited until he'd left before coming out of the bathroom. If I'd known that would be the last time I'd see him, would I have done things differently? Probably not. I was lily-livered that way.

I hadn't known what had scared me more that morning: the possibility of Tanner saying he wanted a long-term relationship or me saying hell yeah.

'Remy and I had a chat. He advised I give Tanner some time to brood.'

'Wrong.' Makayla made a buzzing noise. 'Guys like him will retreat into their man cave, mull over the situation, invent reasons to suit their argument, then never call again.'

A sliver of doubt pierced my previous calm. I'd assumed Remy knew best. He'd given me insight into Tanner's state of mind and I understood his need to think things over.

But what if Remy's advice had missed the mark in

this instance? What if I'd played this all wrong, giving Tanner too much time?

It made me wonder. What would've happened if I'd approached my family after I'd left? Would they have been more amenable to hearing my side of the story once the initial shock of my defection wore off? Would we have had some semblance of a relationship rather than this weird standoff that had finally been broken by my mother?

I'd been so busy playing the victim this last year, too busy blaming them, to realise that I could've made the first move.

Establishing my independence was one thing. But I'd let the hurt of being judged and then abandoned by them taint my view.

Once I'd got past Mum's initial rants about ruining the Prendigast name and bringing shame on the family, I could've reached out. Could've explained how downtrodden I'd felt my entire life. How Bardley had made my life hell.

I could've revealed how observing Mum kowtow to Dad on every single issue ensured I did too. That I hated his quick temper when he lashed out for the slightest disagreement. That it was easier to say yes to whatever they wanted than tolerate the emotional shutdown and icy silences that followed the few times I'd tried to take a stand. That being a people-pleaser became so ingrained that it had taken me a year to finally feel like I had a backbone.

Instead, I hadn't told them the truth about how I'd

felt. I'd given them time and space too. Just like I was doing with Tanner.

Hell. Had I made a monumental mistake?

'Listen, honey, you need to talk to him. Three days is too long to leave a guy to his own devices.' Makayla swivelled to face me, tugging on the end of her ponytail, a gesture I'd come to realise meant she was worried about something. 'Who knows what bullshit excuses he'll come up with for you two not to get together?'

She patted my arm, her smile warm. 'And trust me, you two belong together.'

I liked her confidence. Pity I didn't share it.

'Why? Because we're both dysfunctional when it comes to relationships?'

'Because I've seen the way you two are around each other.' She bumped me gently with her shoulder. 'It's like no one else's in the room. You've only got eyes for each other.'

'You read too many romance novels,' I said, knowing exactly what she meant, because that was how I felt when Tanner was around.

Like all he could see was me.

Heady stuff for a girl who'd always been second best to everyone else. Tanner made me feel wanted and cherished and important in a way I never had. And that was during our supposed fling.

What would it feel like to have a real relationship with a guy like that?

Considering how I might have mucked this up, I'd probably never know.

'Go see him.' Makayla nudged me again, more forceful this time. 'Besides, you fought for your independence from your family. You fought to follow your dream to bake. Why wouldn't you fight for love?'

My instinctive response, 'I don't love him', died on my lips.

I hadn't loved Bardley and I'd felt nothing but sadness I'd put up with so much for so long when I'd walked away from him.

I hadn't seen Tanner for three days and I felt like my insides had been ripped out, put through a blender and stuffed back into me in disarray.

If that was love, did I really want any part of it?

Then again, Makayla was right. I'd fought hard to get where I was. I'd fought family expectations, social constraints and a possessive husband to gain freedom.

Tanner had become an important part of my life, no matter how hard I tried to dismiss him as bad-boy fling material to purge my past.

If I didn't put up some semblance of a fight, I'd end up regretting it, and I'd had a lifetime of living with regret already.

Makayla must've seen something in my face, because she smiled. 'Go home. Clean up. Then knock him dead.'

'Thanks.' I hugged her, emotion clogging my throat.

She wriggled out of my embrace and swatted me away. 'And don't forget, I'll expect details tomorrow.'

'If I make it into work.' I winked, knowing I'd

never let Remy down but hoping I wouldn't get much sleep once Tanner and I made up.

'Go get him, girlfriend.' Makayla gave me a thumbs-up sign of encouragement as I tried to quell an aviary's worth of butterflies slam dancing against my rib cage.

I would confront Tanner.

Ensure he wouldn't shut me down.

I had a lot to say and I'd make sure he listened.

CHAPTER TWENTY-SIX

Tanner

FOR TWO HOURS after Hudson had left my office I tried to focus on work. But my concentration was shot and I ended up reading the same spreadsheets ten times, numerous applications for a cocktail waitress that blurred into one, and staring unseeing at the architect's plans for an upcoming venture.

Shit.

I stood and stretched, working out the kinks in my back, feeling like I'd wasted an entire afternoon and had nothing to show for it.

Grunting in frustration, I picked up my keys and cell. Maybe a workout at Jim's would help. But as I drove out from the underground car park, a sparring session lost its appeal. The mood I was in I was liable to knock someone's head off and that wouldn't be good for anybody.

I pulled up at a traffic light, hating the indecisiveness that plagued me. Usually, when I made decisions I stuck to them. But my head was a whirl of dark thoughts, mostly centred on how I'd screwed up yet again.

As the light changed to green, something Hudson had said reared up like a grizzly demanding to be heard.

'Confront what's got you so riled. Get it out of your system. Deal with it.'

Easier said than done. I'd love to confront the prick that'd done such a number on me that I still heard his derisive voice in my head sometimes. Berating me. Castigating me. Putting me down.

A crazy thought pierced my self-pity. There was a way I could confront him. Do something I hadn't tried before to put the past behind me. It wouldn't come close to coming clean face-to-face, but it would be a gesture I could've tried a long time ago.

Feeling like a fool, I headed for the small cemetery on the outskirts of Surrey Hills.

I'd only been to the place once, on the day of Dad's funeral. I hadn't wanted to go. Remy had made me, citing it would look bad if I didn't show and might raise red flags with Social Services that he had no control of me and therefore would be a lousy guardian.

The thought of losing the one person who meant anything to me was enough to scare me into an ill-fitting suit and into the neat cemetery where a handful of mourners had gathered.

It didn't surprise me that hardly anyone turned up for his funeral. He hadn't had many friends. People rarely came to visit. He didn't go out. Maybe if he'd socialised more, he wouldn't have focussed all his attention on me; and not in a good way.

Considering his hatred of me stemmed from Mum, he must've made her life hell too but she'd hidden it from us kids. We'd never gone on outings as a family and he'd kept long hours, coming home late from the building site to sit on the couch in front of the TV, more interested in the news than Remy and me.

We'd done our homework in the kitchen, with Mum pottering around, content to listen to the recount of our days. She'd ply us with snacks and make us laugh, her impulsive hugs growing more frequent the more Dad withdrew.

On the rare Sundays he was home, I had a vague recollection of being shunted into the backyard with Remy to play while they talked in the house. Though Mum wouldn't last long inside and she'd soon join us on the back lawn, where we'd play tag or cricket.

Until that fateful day when I'd heard raised voices and my first instinct was to protect Mum. She never shouted, so for her voice to reach me in the furthest corner of the backyard meant things were bad. Remy had been at a friend's birthday party, leaving me to decide whether I should keep weeding or check if Mum was okay.

I chose the latter. And what I overheard explained so much.

I'd hidden behind the back door as the argument escalated, frozen in shock, wishing I were bigger so I could punch my father and knock him out for saying such hateful things.

Tears had burned my eyes but I'd refused to cry. I needed to be strong. For Mum.

She'd spied me when she'd rushed out the back

door, her eyes red-rimmed and swollen, her mouth trembling. She'd gathered me close, squished me in the way she always did, and I'd felt her shaking. She'd said she had to go for a drive and she'd bring me back my favourite humbug lollies.

She never came back.

Her car had veered off the road and into a tree less than two kilometres from our house. The police hadn't been able to explain the cause of the accident but I knew. She'd been so distraught by the disgusting, vile accusations hurled by my father, she hadn't been concentrating on the road.

Thankfully, brake marks and the pattern of skid showed she'd tried to avoid the tree, because I couldn't have handled the fact she'd been hurting so badly she would've abandoned me to that monster.

That day when she got in her car, I remember being scared, left alone with Dad after what I'd overheard.

Little did I know that hour would turn into five miserable years where I'd tolerated whatever the old bastard dished out, wishing every single day that he'd been the one to die instead of Mum.

Surprised to find my eyes moist with unshed tears, I pulled into a parking spot and composed myself before heading into the cemetery.

He didn't have a fancy gravestone. Remy had opted for a small plaque that simply had his name, date of birth and death, and RIP. Rest in peace my ass. I hoped he was squirming in hell, hopping around to avoid the flames.

I stood over the plaque, glaring at it, resisting the

urge to kick it. Why should he rest in peace when I'd had nothing close to peace because of him?

'You were a piece of work,' I said, thrusting my hands in my pockets, rocking on the balls of my feet as if spoiling for a fight. 'You were a mean, spiteful bastard that made my life hell. Which is where you're at now and I hope you're burning.'

Stupid, talking to a piece of stone, but it somehow felt cathartic. So I continued.

'Remember that time you locked me in the cellar because I didn't eat my broccoli? Well, the joke was on you, because the first thing I did when you let me out was go dip your toothbrush in the toilet.'

I grinned at the memory of my first rebellious act at ten, a few months after Mum died.

'Then there was that time you made yourself a stack of strawberry pancakes and gave me half a bowl of dried apricots? Well, let's just say there wasn't just sugar in your tea every night, because some chalk dust might've found its way into your bowl.'

I'd wished many times it could've been arsenic.

'As for the endless beatings on my ass with that wooden spoon? I have a tattoo of your most precious possession, those stupid orchids, on both butt cheeks so every time I sit down I know I'm squashing them.'

Childish, maybe, but those flowers had been my first tattoo and it'd made me feel so good I'd wanted more.

'I knew you would've hated the tattoos so every time I got another one, it was a real up yours.' I flipped the bird at the plaque, getting into the spirit of things. 'Whenever I lay in that parlour, the needle piercing my skin, I thought of how you'd rant and rave and disapprove, and I didn't feel a thing.'

On a roll, I continued. 'I hate you for destroying my trust in people. For making me believe I was unworthy. For making me feel I wasn't good enough for anything or anybody. But you know what? I'm doing okay. In fact, I'm doing better than okay. And Remy's a good guy. The best. So I guess I can be thankful you didn't screw him up real good too. We're happy. And that's the best form of revenge I know, because you're down there and there isn't one damn thing you can do to me any more...'

I trailed off, my legs surprisingly weak and my arms almost numb, like I was on the verge of fainting. I sank to my haunches, dropped my head and breathed deeply, in and out, until the dizziness passed.

He deserved so much more vitriol, but I felt drained and I couldn't summon any more hatred.

I was done.

Did I feel better? Maybe. Purging the past could only be a good thing.

But I wouldn't come back here. I'd said all that needed to be said. Who knew? Maybe I'd have the balls to confront Abby too now, and give her the closure she needed. It was the least I could do.

Not tonight. Tonight, I needed to head back to the club, immerse myself in work and finish that aged whiskey I'd been keeping for a rainy day.

The way I was feeling right now, it was pelting down.

I stood, staring at the plaque one last time. 'See you in hell.'

I walked away without looking back.

CHAPTER TWENTY-SEVEN

Abby

I FELT LIKE an idiot.

Getting tizzied up in a black miniskirt, green halter-top and stiletto ankle boots, with a liberal dose of mascara and coral lipstick, when Tanner had seen me naked.

But the clothes and make-up gave me some much-needed confidence as I strode towards the VIP rope inside Embue.

'I need to see Tanner King,' I said in my best diva voice, to a muscle-bound ninja who glared at me like I had no right being there let alone demanding audience with his boss.

He cast a cursory glance at the electronic tablet in his hand before shooting me a dismissive sneer. 'You're not on the list.'

'The boss will want to see her,' a guy said from behind me, unclipping the rope and pushing aside the gold curtain. 'Come with me, Abby.'

'Uh, thanks.' I swept past the himbo and smiled at

the tall blond guy who bore a startling resemblance to British hottie Tom Hiddleston. 'I don't think we've met?'

'Hudson Watt, manager at this den of iniquity.' He shook my hand. 'And Tanner's best mate, no matter if he tells you otherwise.'

'Nice to meet you,' I said, those damn butterflies taking flight when we stopped outside Tanner's private room. 'You sure this will be okay? He's not busy?'

'Sweetheart, he needs to see you so bad he doesn't even know it.' With a boyish grin, Hudson knocked twice on the door, swiped a card against the digital lock and opened it.

While my hands shook, he stuck his head around the door. 'You have a visitor.'

Before I could second-guess my wisdom in showing up here unannounced, Hudson swung open the door and gave me a nudge inside.

'Good luck,' he murmured, soft enough only I could hear, as he shut the door.

Leaving me staring at Tanner like a gobsmacked doofus.

Any scintillating opening lines I might have rehearsed on the way over fled as he advanced towards me. Shoulders set, neck muscles rigid with tension, massive glower slashing his brows.

He didn't look pleased to see me.

I managed a pathetic 'hey' a second before he grabbed me and slammed his mouth against mine.

I could've protested, could've cited the fact we

needed to talk, could've accused him of being a gutless jerk for walking away from me without saying goodbye.

But as his tongue entered my mouth and he pinned me up against the door, any fleeting thought of resistance fled.

I wanted this. Wanted him. Like I'd never wanted anything in my life.

Lust consumed me as he unzipped, sheathed and rucked up my skirt. I clung to him, overwhelmed by sensation as he dragged my panties aside and thrust into me.

I gasped as he filled me, savouring the exquisite friction as he slid in and out. Slowly at first. Then faster. Each time he entered me harder than the last. Powerful thrusts. Pushing me higher, quicker, than I'd ever experienced before.

I hooked a leg over his waist and he took it as an invitation to pick me up, holding my butt as he drove into me like a man possessed.

My head fell back against the door with a thud as my muscles tensed, pleasure rippling through me as he angled my hips so he dragged across the most sensitive part of me.

With every thrust my body sparked with heat, burning me up as the beginnings of my orgasm pooled deep.

Long, deep, hard thrusts that made me want to bite down on something to stop from deafening him. He shifted. Drove into me again. Once. Twice. And I came apart, spiralling out of control as he swallowed my scream with a kiss.

He followed a moment later, thrusting into me so deep I almost passed out with the pleasure bordering on pain, his low groan fierce and feral.

Before I could say something light to defuse the moment, he withdrew, leaving me no option but to lower my legs. He didn't look at me as he stalked to the bathroom, returning a moment later to sit at his desk like nothing had happened.

Reeling from his coldness, I tidied myself up and crossed the room to stand in front of him.

'Look at me.'

He ignored my demand, preferring to stare at a computer screen like it revealed the secret to longevity.

'Damn you.' I slammed my palm on his desk and he jumped, his gaze finally locking on mine.

What I saw took my breath away.

Disgust. Regret. And a hopelessness that made me want to cradle him close and never let go.

His throat convulsed as he swallowed, before clearing it. 'You need to leave.'

'Too bad, because I'm not like you, taking the easy way out, running away like some scared little kid.' I perched on his desk, close enough I could smell the alcohol on his breath. 'You don't look drunk but you smell like a brewery.'

'I'm not. I've had four shots.'

'To numb the pain?'

'To wake me up so I can work all night.' He faked a

yawn and stretched, his deep scowl and defiant glare reminding me of a guarded lion taunting his prey before he pounced. 'You're disturbing me.'

'And you're disturbing me with this stupid act.' I jerked a thumb at the door. 'I'd like to think what just happened back there was you unable to keep your hands off me, but I think it was more about you proving a point.'

Fear lit his eyes before he glanced away. 'You don't know what you're talking about. I'm a horny guy. You're a babe. We burn up the sheets. Seemed like you came here for one last fuck, so I obliged.'

Clamping down on the burgeoning hurt making my chest ache, I mustered a sneer. 'If you're trying to shock me into walking out of here, think again.'

I leaned forward, getting into his face. 'I'm onto you.'

He pushed back from the desk and stood, putting some distance between us. 'Look, you knew the type of guy I was right from the start. I don't do emotion. I don't do commitment. And I certainly don't do anything past its expiration date.'

He whirled back to face me, anger bracketing his mouth. 'Remy came back, we were finished, so I made it easy on the both of us. No drawn-out goodbyes. No empty promises to stay friends.' He made a chopping motion. 'A swift break.'

'So you did me a favour and I should be thanking you?' I slow-handclapped as I stood and advanced towards him, projecting an outer calm when inside I was a seething mess of wrath. 'Bravo. Thanks for taking something special and tainting it with your asshat behaviour.'

Surprise widened his eyes imperceptibly before the nonchalant mask slid back into place. 'We had phenomenal sex, babe. Nothing special about that.'

'You're full of crap.' I laughed, a harsh sound devoid of amusement, while I resisted the urge to slap him silly. 'Want to know what I think?'

'No,' he snapped, his lips compressing into a thin line as he feigned boredom, glancing around the room at anything but me. Coward.

'You like to hide behind that bad-boy façade but inside you're so soft you're practically a marshmallow.'

Okay, so it lacked the delivery I'd envisaged in my head but at least it got his attention as he resumed glaring at me again.

'I bet you got those tattoos as part of your quest to be the bad boy, because that's what you believed you were.' I softened my tone as his jaw clenched, wanting to prod him into a reaction but unsure how far to push. 'But you're not bad, Tanner. You could never be bad and I'd like to stick around awhile and prove that to you.'

'Already told you, I've got work to do,' he said, deliberately misinterpreting what I meant.

'Don't do that, make me feel more stupid than I already do for coming here and laying myself open to you.' My voice cracked a little as my bravado faded.

What if I'd misread our relationship entirely?

It took less than two seconds for his expression to

crumple and, relieved, I mentally yelled 'hallelujah'. A breakthrough.

'I'm sorry,' he said, leaning against the back of the sofa, swiping a hand across his face. 'I'm a shit.'

'You're a guy out of his comfort zone.' I perched next to him but didn't touch him, no matter how badly I wanted to. 'But I promise to be gentle with you.'

He flinched like I'd struck him. 'Unlike me. Fuck, I can't believe I took you like a madman before. And you were right. It was to drive you away once and for all. To show you what a prick I really am. But I forgot about the part where I can't get enough of you and...I went nuts. I'm sorry.'

'Do you hear me complaining?'

This time, I risked placing a hand on his forearm. He startled and shrugged it off, like I'd electrocuted him.

'You deserve so much better than me. Can't you see that?' He turned towards me, bleakness darkening his eyes to ebony. 'I'm no good for you.'

'I've spent my entire life having other people make decisions for me and pretending I'm okay with it. No more.' I snagged his hand, holding on tight when he tried to snatch it away. 'Don't you get it? You can't push me away no matter how hard you try. I like you, Tanner King.'

My chest tightened with the magnitude of what I had to say but if I didn't get the words out now, I never would. 'I may even be falling in love with you and if there's one thing I learned over the last year it's to fight for what I want.'

He didn't bolt at the L word, which I took as a good sign. What *wasn't* a good sign was the way all colour drained from his face and for a moment I thought he'd pass out.

'You don't mean that—'

'Stop telling me what to think or say or do.' I squeezed his hand, wishing I could infuse some of my belief into him. 'I'll put up with a lot but not that. Never that.'

I could see the war he waged as every conflicting emotion flickered across his face. Hope with hopelessness. Belief with disbelief. Incredulity with incredible, heart-warming anticipation.

I recognised them because I'd fought the same war over the last few days, but I'd come out on the other side, determined to be a victor.

'You're heading back to your old life. Your family. I'll only drag you down.' He sounded desperate, plucking at any excuse to keep us apart. It meant nothing. I'd faced harsher artillery from the Prendigast firing squad and come out on top.

'If you're going to eavesdrop, make sure you do it properly,' I said. 'I don't trust my family. I'm staying at Remy's.' I leaned closer so he couldn't misunderstand. 'I'm not going anywhere.'

He didn't speak for a long time after that and I let him process.

It had taken me three days to get to this point and even then I probably wouldn't be here if it weren't for Makayla's pep talk.

'I don't think I can be the man you want,' he whispered, sounding so bereft that something inside me shattered.

I knew what I said next could ultimately make or break us so I chose my words carefully, willing him to see the real me, willing him to believe.

'Why? Because you've never had a real relationship? Because you don't trust easily? Because your upbringing mucked you up so badly you don't think you're good enough?'

I slid to the floor, kneeling in front of him, hanging onto both his hands for dear life, imploring him to listen.

'We've both got trust issues. Hell, I didn't trust myself for so many years I can barely trust anyone else. But you showed me differently.' I gripped his hands tighter. 'You think I used you to get over my past? Maybe that was true at the start. But somewhere along the way I changed. Because *you* changed me.'

Emotion tightened my vocal cords and I swallowed to ease the dryness. 'I'm not ready to walk away from us, Tanner. What about you?'

Staring into his eyes was like staring into a fathomless dark pool. I couldn't read what he was feeling. Maybe it was nothing. I hoped it was everything.

When his grasp on my hands tightened, hope sprang to life. He stood and drew me to my feet until we were toe to toe, only the barest whisper of a breath separating us.

'How do I begin to make you understand how fucked up I am?'

Of all the things I'd envisaged him saying, that wasn't it. But I remained silent, hoping he'd continue.

'I want to believe you, Abby. I want to believe in us. But what if we're not enough?' His ragged breathing hitched. 'What if *I'm* not enough?'

I waited, sensing he wasn't finished, not by a long shot. My throat tightened and my eyes stung with unshed tears but I didn't speak, fervently wishing that whatever he had to say would allow us to move forward, together.

'I haven't told anyone this, not even Remy...' He sounded so morose, so heartbroken, I almost told him to stop. But his eyes had glazed, as if lost in painful memories, and I knew he had to purge whatever was bugging him if we were to have any chance. 'My dad hated me. From the time I was old enough to understand, probably around four, I felt it. Like he couldn't stand the sight of me.' Pain darkened his eyes and he blinked slowly, like waking from a coma. 'He did a good job of masking it when Mum or Remy were around, but if was just the two of us...man, the guy was a prick.'

My heart ached for what Tanner had gone through as a kid. My dad might have messed with my head, but at least he'd liked me. He'd never been deliberately cruel or condescending. He'd just expected me to do whatever he said and I'd been the idiot to put up with it.

'As I grew older, I could tell Mum couldn't stand him either and she was putting on a brave face for Remy and me. We'd spend all our time with her, even when he was home. She was probably protecting us but I didn't know it at the time...'

He dragged in a deep breath, released it. 'The day she died Remy was out, I was in the backyard and I heard them arguing inside. I got scared because Mum never shouted, and she was yelling so loud I thought the neighbours would hear. So I snuck up onto the veranda and hid outside the back door.'

A deep frown slashed his brows as he continued. 'Dad was saying some pretty horrific things. Flinging accusations like Mum had been having affairs and that she'd never loved him. Then he got to the good stuff...'

His expression contorted with grief and it took every ounce of my willpower not to haul him into my arms and tell him to stop. But if I did that, he'd clam up and I couldn't risk it. He'd come this far and if he hadn't divulged his secret to anyone before... well, I just hoped it indicated he trusted me and we had a shot in hell at a future once the truth came out.

'Apparently he'd fallen out of love with her since Remy was born but he stuck around for four years. Then when he was going to leave her, she announced she was pregnant with me. He accused her of doing it deliberately, to trap him. And he hated me ever since, blaming me for trapping him in a marriage he didn't want. He would've walked away but child support payments for two kids would've crippled him financially so he stayed and made our lives a misery. Mum fired back, telling him to stay away from Remy and me and keep his hatred to himself. So he called her some pretty shocking names and Mum stormed out. Probably needed some time to cool down, so she went for a drive...'

He shook his head, agony twisting his mouth. 'She never should've driven in that state and ended up crashing into a tree not far from home.'

My throat ached with emotion and I touched his arm, trying to convey my sympathy, knowing it would be inadequate.

'Rather than comforting me after Mum died, you know what the bastard did? He blamed me. *Me*. For making him resentful and bitter, for making Mum have to defend me that day and ultimately being mad enough to have that accident that killed her. Blamed me for trapping him even more, since he'd be saddled with two kids he didn't want. I was ten fucking years old and he lumped all that on me. And it just got worse from there. For the next five years until he died, he treated me like shit. Never in front of Remy, who wasn't around much, but he made me feel worthless and useless, drumming it into me 'til I started to believe it... I cried with joy the day he died. Remy put up with my teenage tantrums for the next few years and I bided my time 'til I hit eighteen and had access to my trust fund to start my life. These?' He brandished his tattoo-covered arms at me. 'Getting inked ensured I was reborn. I was never comfortable in my old skin, so I took on a new one. One guaranteed to keep people at bay, which suited me fine. In a screwed-up way, I identified with my dad, not wanting to ever be trapped in a relationship. So I never let anyone get close. Until you…'

His tortured gaze met mine and I held my breath, silently praying we'd had a breakthrough and that he wouldn't send me packing once and for all.

'You saw beneath my tats.' My chest ached with the effort of holding back a torrent of emotion. When he cupped my face, the breath I'd been holding seeped out in an embarrassing squeak. 'You really see me, the real me…and I don't know whether to hold onto you for ever or run as fast as I possibly can without looking back.'

Hope flared to life but I forced myself to stand still as he released my face, to lower his hands to my hips. He hadn't pushed me away. He hadn't bolted. Yet.

So I tried to convey my sorrow at his atrocious upbringing, knowing I'd come up short but having to try regardless.

'Sorry is so trite now but, Tanner, I can't begin to tell you how sorry I am for what you went through. You shouldered a burden you shouldn't have and were raised by a sadist. Just know that I do see you. And I always will.'

I couldn't hold back the tears, not any more, so I let them fall, wrapping my arms so tight around him he yelped.

The good thing was, he held me too, burying his nose in my hair like he used to do.

The bad thing was, once I started crying, I couldn't stop. It was like all the feelings I'd bottled up for so long came tumbling out in a torrent. He held me until the sobs subsided, strong and stoic, the man I wanted, the man I needed.

When I finally eased away, I glimpsed the first flicker of a smile and my heart soared.

'And you had the audacity to call me a marshmallow?' He kissed the tip of my nose and I knew we'd marched out of the front lines, together. 'You're just a big cry-baby.'

I punched him in the chest. 'But I'm your cry-baby.'

'I guess you are.' He didn't hesitate and joy fizzed in my veins. 'For some inexplicable reason, you see the best in me. You bring out the best in me. And I want to see how far this can go.'

I let out a whoop and he laughed, picking me up and swinging me around.

'But you need to promise me something,' he said, sounding serious.

'Anything.'

'If you're going to walk away at any stage, do me the courtesy of telling me.' He tightened his hold around my waist. 'I don't think I could handle being left hanging.'

'Like you did to me the last three days?'

He grimaced. 'Touché.'

I held up my right hand. 'I promise. Anything else?'

'I...I think I love you too,' he said, gruff and bashful.

'I said I like you.' Grinning, I slid my palms up

his chest to rest on his beautifully broad shoulders. 'Maybe I'm only halfway to loving you.'

Cockiness curled his upper lip. 'You love me. You're just too stubborn to admit it.'

Joy made me cling to him, like I'd float away if I blinked and realised this was a dream. 'Maybe you'll have to kiss a confession out of me?'

'Too easy,' he murmured, a second before his mouth claimed mine.

His lips coaxed and tempted, demanding a response I was only too willing to give. A long, slow, soul-searing kiss that would be the first of many. A kiss filled with hope. A kiss to build a future on.

Reluctant to come up for air, I gently pushed him away.

'Okay, I'll admit it.' I pretend pouted. 'I love you. Happy?'

'Sweetheart, you have no idea how much.'

As he hugged me tight, the pounding of his heart matching mine, I had a fair idea.

Unconditional love.

There was no feeling in the world like it.

Now that I'd found it with this incredible, infuriating man, I had no intention of ever letting go.

* * * * *

MAKE ME WANT

KATEE ROBERT

MILLS & BOON

To Tim.
Second chances make for the best stories.

CHAPTER ONE

GIDEON NOVAK had almost canceled the meeting. He would have if he'd possessed even a shred of honor. Some things in this world were just too damn good for him to be associated with and Lucy Baudin topped that list. To hear from her now, two years after...

Focus on the facts.

She'd called. He'd answered. It was as simple as that.

The law office of Parker and Jones was the same as it had been the last time he'd walked through the doors. The small army of defense attorneys took on mostly white-collar crimes—specifically the ones that paid well—and that showed in every element of the interior. Soothing colors and bold lines projected confidence and created a calming effect.

Pale blue walls and good lines didn't do a single damn thing to dial back the pressure building in his chest with each step.

He usually didn't contract out with law offices. As a headhunter, Gideon preferred to stick to tech companies, various start-up corporations or, literally, anyone except lawyers. They were too controlling and wanted their hands on every detail, every step of the way. It was a pain in the ass.

This is for Lucy.

He kept his expression schooled on the elevator ride up. When he'd known her, she was somewhere around floor six, proving herself by working cases not big enough for the lawyers with seniority to want but that were too big to turn down. Now she was on floor nineteen, only a couple below Parker and Jones themselves. She'd done well for herself in the two years since he'd seen her last. Really well.

The elevator opened into a large waiting room that didn't look anything like an actual waiting room. The more money people had, the more care was required in handling them, and the coffee bar and scattering of couches and trade magazines reflected that. The hallway was guarded by a large desk and an older woman with tasteful gray shot through her dark hair. Surprising. He'd expected a bottle-blond receptionist—or perhaps a brunette if they were feeling adventurous.

But then the woman looked up and he got the impression of a general surveying her domain. *Ah.* They'd chosen someone who couldn't be bulldozed, if he didn't miss his guess. Useful to keep unruly clients in line.

Gideon stopped in front of the desk and did his best to appear nonthreatening. "I'm here to see Lucy Baudin."

"She's expecting you." She turned back to her computer, effectively dismissing him.

He spent half a second wondering at her qualifications—and if she was amiable to being poached for a different company—before he set it aside. Stepping on Lucy's toes by stealing her receptionist wasn't a good way to start off this meeting.

He'd spent the last week trying to figure out why the hell Lucy would seek *him* out. New York was rife with headhunters. Gideon was good—better than good—but considering their history, there had to be someone better suited for the job.

You could have said no.

Yeah, he could have.

But he owed Lucy Baudin. A single meeting wasn't much in the face of the fact that he'd more or less single-handedly brought her engagement down in flames.

He knocked on the dark wooden door as he opened it. The office was bright and airy, big windows overlooking New York, the only furniture a large L-shaped desk and two comfortable-looking chairs arranged in front of it. Gideon took in the room in a single sweep and then focused on the woman behind the desk.

Lucy sat straight, her narrow shoulders tense, as if she was about to step onto a battlefield. Her long dark hair was pinned back into some style that looked effortless but probably took a significant amount of time to accomplish. She raised her pointed chin, which drew his attention to her mouth. Lucy's features were a little too sharp to pass for traditional beauty—she would have made a killing on a runway—but her mouth was full and generous and had always been inclined to smile.

There were no smiles today.

"Lucy." He shut the door behind him, holding his place to let her guide the interaction. She was the one who'd called him here. It didn't feel natural to take his lead from someone else, but for her he'd make an effort.

At least until he heard her out.

"Gideon. Sit, please." She motioned at the chairs in front of the desk.

Maybe she could pretend this was like any other job interview, but he couldn't stop staring at her. She wore a dark gray dress that set off her pale skin and dark hair, leaving the only color present in her blue eyes and red lips. It created a striking picture. The woman was a goddamn gift. She always had been.

Jeff, you fucked things up beyond all recognition when you threw her away.

Focus.

She hadn't arranged this meeting because of their past. If she could be professional, then he'd manage, as well. It was the least he could do.

Gideon sank into the chair and leaned forward, bracing his elbows on his knees. "You said this was about a job."

"Yes." A faint blush colored her pale cheeks, highlighting the smattering of freckles there. "This is confidential, of course."

It wasn't quite a question, but he answered it anyway. "I didn't put together a nondisclosure, but I can do that if you need to make it official."

"That won't be necessary. Your word that it stays between us will be enough."

Curiosity curled through him. He'd had clients insist on confidentiality in the past—it was more the rule than the exception—but this felt different. He set the thought aside and focused on the job. "It would help if you'd describe the position you want filled. It gives me a general idea of what you're looking for, and we can narrow it down from there."

She met his gaze directly, her blue eyes startling. "The position I need filled is a husband."

Gideon shook his head, sure he'd heard her wrong. "Excuse me?"

"A husband." She held up her left hand and wiggled her ring finger. "Before you get that look on your face, let me explain."

He didn't have any *look* on his face. *A husband. Where the fuck does she think I'm going to find a husband?* He opened his mouth to ask exactly that, but Lucy beat him there. "The timing isn't ideal, but gossip has come down the grapevine that I'm being considered for partner at the end of the year. While that would normally be a cause for celebration, some of the old guard have very strong beliefs about single women." She rolled her eyes, the first *Lucy* thing he'd seen her do since he'd arrived. "It would be laughable if it wasn't standing in the way of what I want, but I watched Georgia get passed over for a promotion last year for this exact reason. She wouldn't bend and they chose her male competition instead."

She was dead serious.

Gideon took a breath, trying to approach this logically. Obviously she'd put a lot of thought into the idea, and if she was misguided, that didn't mean he had to verbally slap her down. *This* Lucy, put-together and in control, was a far cry from when he'd seen her last, sobbing and broken. But that didn't change the fact that they were one and the same. He could handle this calmly and get her to see reason.

But calm and reasonable wasn't what came out of his mouth. "Are you out of your goddamn mind, Lucy? I'm a headhunter—not a matchmaker. Even if I was, getting married to secure a promotion is bullshit."

"Is it?" She shrugged. "People get married for much less valid reasons. *I* almost married for love before, and we both know how that ended. There's nothing wrong with handling marriage like a business arrangement—plenty of cultures do exactly that."

"We aren't talking about other cultures. We're talking about *you*."

Another shrug. As if it didn't matter to her one way or another. He *loathed* that feigned indifference, but he didn't have a goddamn right to challenge her on it.

She met his gaze directly. "This is important to me, Gideon. I don't know about kids—I love my job, and having babies would potentially interfere with that— but I'm lonely. It wouldn't be so bad to have someone to come home to, even if it wasn't a love for the ages. *Especially* if it's not a love for the ages."

"Lucy, that's crazy." Every word out of her mouth cut into the barrier of professionalism he fought so hard to maintain. "Where the hell would I find you a husband?"

"The same place you find people to fill the positions normally. Interview. We're in New York—if *you* can't find a single man who's willing to at least consider this, then no one can."

Gideon started to tell her exactly how impossible it was, but guilt rose and choked the words off. He thought this plan was bat-shit crazy, and the thought of Lucy in some loveless marriage irritated him like sandpaper beneath his skin, scratching until he might go mad from it.

But it wasn't his call to make.

And he was partially to blame for her single status right now.

Fuck.

Gideon straightened. No matter what he thought of this plan, when it came right down to the wire, he owed Lucy. He knew that piece of shit Jeff had cheated on her, and Gideon had kept his mouth shut for a full month before he'd told her the truth. That kind of debt didn't just go away. If she was coming to him now, it was because she'd exhausted all other options, and his saying no wasn't going to deter her in the least—she'd find a different way.

Really, he had no option. It might have been two years since he'd seen Lucy Baudin, but that didn't change the fact that he considered her a friend, and he'd never leave a friend hanging out to dry when they needed him. Gideon might have questionable morals about most things, but loyalty wasn't one of them.

She needed him. He'd have found a way to help her even if he didn't owe her.

At least if he was in the midst of this madness, he'd have some ability to keep her as safe as possible. He could protect her now like he hadn't been able to protect her from the hurt Jeff had caused.

If she was crazy for coming up with the plan in the first place, he was even crazier for agreeing to it. "I'll do it."

Lucy couldn't believe the words that had just come out of his mouth. It was too good to be true. Attempting to rope Gideon Novak into this scheme had been her Hail Mary. She was desperate and he was the only one she trusted enough to even attempt something like a search for a husband. But she hadn't thought he'd actually agree to it.

He said he'd help. Shock stole her ability to speak for a full five seconds. *Say something. You know the drill—fake it until you make it. This is just another trial. Focus.* She cleared her throat. "I'm sorry—did you just say yes?"

"Yes." He studied her face with dark eyes lined with thick lashes, which she secretly envied. Gideon had always been too attractive for Lucy's state of mind. His dark hair was always styled in what she could only call "rakish," and his strong jaw and firm mouth would have kept her up at night if he wasn't firmly in the friend zone.

At least, he used to be.

She set the thought aside because going down the rabbit hole of despair that was her relationship with Jeff Larsson was out of the question. It had ended, and her friendship with Gideon had been a casualty of war.

Until now.

Gideon shifted, bringing her back to the present. "How exactly were you planning on going about this?"

This, at least, she had an answer for. Lucy had spent entirely too much time reviewing the steps required to get to her goal with minimum fuss—a husband and her promotion. "I thought you could come up with a list of suitable candidates, I could have a date or two with each, and then we could narrow the list down from there."

"Mmm-hmm." He tapped his fingers on his knee, dragging her attention south of his face. He wore a three-piece suit, which should have been too formal for this meeting, but Gideon managed to pull it off all the same. The pin-striped gray-on-gray gave him an old-world kind of feel, like something out of *Mad Men*.

Thankfully for Lucy, he had better morals than Don Draper.

She fought not to squirm in her seat under the weight of his attention. It was easy enough to be distanced and professional when she'd laid out her proposal—she'd practiced it the same way she practiced opening and closing statements before a trial. Getting into the nitty-gritty of the actual planning and actions was something else altogether.

"I'm open to suggestions, of course." *There—look at me, being reasonable.*

"Of course." He nodded as if deciding something. "We do this, we do it on my terms. I pick the men. I supervise the dates. And if I don't like the look of any of them, I have veto rights."

Veto rights? That wasn't part of the plan. She shook her head. "No. Absolutely not."

"You came to me, Lucy. That means you trust my judgment." He gave her an intense look that made her skin feel too tight. "Those are the terms."

Terms. Damn, she'd forgotten the most important thing.

It doesn't have to be the most important thing. He doesn't know it was part of the plan, so it's not too late to back out.

But if she backed out, the deep-rooted fear from her time with her ex would never be exorcised. She'd spend the rest of her life—and her prospective marriage—second-guessing herself and her husband. It would drive her crazy and ultimately poison everything.

She couldn't let it happen, no matter how humiliating she found asking for Gideon's help with this.

Lucy managed to drag her gaze away from his. She pulled at the hem of her skirt. "There's one more thing."

"I'm listening."

She smoothed her suddenly sweating palms over her desk. "Are you seeing anyone?"

"What the hell does that have to do with anything?"

It had everything to do with things. She'd never known Gideon to hold down a relationship longer than a few weeks, but that didn't mean he hadn't somehow changed in the last two years. The entire second part of her plan leaned heavily on the assumption that he *hadn't* changed.

The Gideon she'd known before had been her friend, yes, but he'd also been a playboy to the very definition of the word. He hadn't dated seriously. He'd never mistreated women, but he hadn't kept them around for long, either. Lucy had heard the whispers in college about his expertise in the bedroom—it was legendary enough that most women ignored the fact they had an expiration date from the moment he showed an interest in them.

To put it simply, he was *perfect* for her current situation.

She just had to find the strength to speak the damn words. She forced her hands still. "I'm going to need...lessons."

"Lucy, look at me."

Helpless, she obeyed. He frowned at her like he was trying to read her mind. "You're going to have to explain what the hell you're talking about."

It was so much harder to get it out while looking at him. She pressed her lips together. She'd faced down some of the most vicious prosecutors New York had to offer. She could damn well face Gideon Novak down, too.

You know these words. You've practiced them often enough.

"I need lessons of the sexual nature." He went so still, he might as well have turned to stone, so she charged on. "This might be an arranged marriage, so to speak, but it would be a true marriage. And, as I don't cherish the idea of being cheated on by yet another fiancé, that means sex needs to be part of the bargain. It's been a long time for me, and I have to brush up on my skill set."

Not to mention the only man I ever slept with was Jeff, and he never missed an opportunity to tell me how uninspiring he found our sex life.

Or that he blamed his cheating on my being unable to meet his needs.

She didn't let what Jeff thought dictate her life anymore, but Lucy would be lying if she pretended his words didn't haunt her—that they hadn't been instrumental in her two-year celibate streak. She'd enjoyed sex. She'd thought Jeff had enjoyed it, as well. If she could be so terribly wrong on such a fundamental level before, what was to stop her from failing at it again?

No, she couldn't allow it. If she trusted Gideon enough to secure his help finding a husband, then she trusted him enough to create a safe space to teach her something she obviously needed to know to be an effective wife. His rumored sex prowess just sweetened the bargain, because he was more than experienced enough to walk her through a crash course in seduction.

He still hadn't said anything.

She sighed. "I know it's a lot to ask—"

"I'm going to stop you right there." He stood and adjusted his jacket as he buttoned it. "I will charge you for the husband hunting—the same rates of a normal client. I'm not a sex worker, Lucy. You can't wave a magic wand and acquire lessons in fucking."

She did her best not to wilt.

You knew it was a long shot.

"I understand."

"That said..." He shook his head like he couldn't believe the words coming out of his mouth any more than she could. "Come by my place tonight. We'll talk. After that, we'll see."

That...wasn't a no. It wasn't a yes. But it most definitely wasn't a no.

"Okay." She didn't dare say anything more in fear that he'd change his mind. *I can't believe this is happening.* He didn't look happy to have offered the invitation. In fact, Gideon looked downright furious.

He pinned her with a look. "Seven. You remember the address."

It wasn't a question but she still nodded all the same. "I'll be there."

"Don't be late." He turned and stalked out of her office, leaving her staring after him.

What just happened?

A thrill coursed through her. What just happened

was that Gideon Novak had agreed to help her. Professionally he had a reputation for always getting his man and, personally, he had everything required to get her pending marriage off to the right start.

He said yes.

With him in her corner, there was no way she'd fail.

The promotion was hers. She could feel it.

CHAPTER TWO

GIDEON SWAM LAPS until every muscle in his body shook with exhaustion. It didn't help. All he could see was Lucy's earnest expression as those sinful lips spoke words he would have killed to hear before. *Teach me.* His attraction for that woman had never brought him anything but trouble, and apparently he was doubling down because he hadn't told her no like he damn well should have. Instead he'd told her to come to his place.

So they could talk.

About him giving her lessons in fucking.

He pulled himself out of the pool and climbed to his feet. He'd been prepared to tell her no—to both the husband hunt and the lessons. Instead he'd invited her over tonight. What the hell was that about?

You know what that's about.

Gideon wanted Lucy.

He'd wanted her from the moment he'd seen her across that crowded bar in Queens six years ago. She'd been so fresh-faced and, even too many shots in, he'd known there was something special about her.

Unfortunately so had Jeff Larsson, and that bastard

had beaten him to the punch—meeting Lucy, dating Lucy, proposing to Lucy.

Gideon had tried his damnedest to be happy for his best friend—and to table his desire for his best friend's woman—but it had never quite gone away. It didn't matter how many girls he'd dated, because his heart had never been in it. When Jeff had made a passing remark on Gideon's tendency to find willowy brunettes with freckles, he'd shelved dating completely and restricted his interactions to one night.

He showered and dressed quickly. It would be tricky getting back to his place before she arrived, but he'd had to do something to take the edge off or he was in danger of throwing caution to the wind. The temptation of Lucy in his bed, even for such a shitty reason…

He'd be a bastard and a half to do it.

No, Gideon would grab takeout, sit her down to her favorite Chinese and explain all the reasons why sex between them wasn't an option. He'd be calm and reasonable and use whatever arguments he had to get his point across. She didn't need *lessons*. No man with a pulse and a working cock was going to have a problem with anything Lucy had to offer.

His step hitched at the thought of someone else waking up next to her every morning. Of the long nights buried between her thighs and the friction of sweat-slicked skin and—

Fuck.

He glanced back at the gym, seriously considering calling the whole thing off and spending the next three hours back in the pool. Maybe if he was too exhausted to move, his fury at the thought of her with another man would subside.

He knew better.

If he hadn't been happy that his best friend was with her—even before the idiot had started fucking around—he wasn't going to be pleased with a stranger. There was no help for it. Lucy would charge ahead with this plan of hers whether he agreed to it or not. He might be able to talk her out of the sex bit, but he wouldn't be able to convince her that she didn't need a husband.

He'd failed her when it came to Jeff. Even as his best friend, Gideon had missed the warning signs until it was almost too late—and then he'd hesitated a full month before breaking the news to her. He'd well and truly fucked up across the board and it had cost him her friendship—something he'd valued more than he could have dreamed.

He wouldn't fuck up again.

She wanted a husband? Well, then, Gideon was going to find her the most honorable man he could to make her happy. He owed it to her to do so.

He barely had time to drop the takeout on the kitchen counter when a knock sounded. He skirted the couch and opened the door. "You're early."

"I hope you don't mind. Your doorman remembered me, so he didn't bother to buzz you." She gave a tentative smile that pulled at him despite his determination to do the right thing.

Lucy must have made it home because she'd

changed into a pair of black leggings and a light-weight slouchy shirt that seemed determined to slide off one shoulder. She saw him looking and bit her bottom lip. "I know we talked about lessons, and this isn't exactly seduction personified, but I went through my closet and, aside from work clothes, I don't think I *own* anything that's 'seduction personified.'"

For fuck's sake, she was killing him. Gideon stepped back and held the door open. "You look fine."

"Fine." She frowned. "I know you're cranky about being cornered with this whole thing, but you don't have to damn me with faint praise. I asked you to do this because I trust you to tell me the truth. I've always trusted you to tell me the truth."

If she'd taken out a knife and stabbed him in the heart, it would have stung less. Gideon closed the door carefully behind her, trying to maintain his control. It didn't matter how honest she thought he was, he wouldn't agree to take her to bed. He couldn't. "This won't work if you're going to jump down my throat every time I say something. I said you look fine. You do. I didn't tell you to dress for seduction, Lucy. I said to get your ass over here so we can talk. That—" he motioned at her clothes "—is perfectly adequate for a conversation between two friends."

"Right. Okay. I'm sorry. I'm nervous." She pulled at her shirt, which caused it to drop another inch down her arm.

Gideon had never found shoulders particularly provocative before but he wanted to drag his mouth over the line of her collarbone. *Keep it together, asshole.*

He cleared his throat and looked away. "You don't need lessons, Lucy. Not from me. Not from anyone. You're beautiful and any man would be lucky to have you in his bed."

"If you don't want to teach me, that's fine. I did say that this morning." She wandered farther into his apartment and circled the couch he'd bought six months ago. It was slate gray with dark blue accents, and the saleswoman had insisted it would pull the room together in a way he'd love. He was still waiting to love it. Lucy picked up one of the ridiculous blue throw pillows and hugged it to her chest. "I'm not fishing for a compliment, by the way, but thank you. Though, beauty only goes so far. Since you haven't... We haven't..." She huffed out a breath. "Can I be perfectly frank?"

"You weren't before now?" If she was franker, she might actually kill him.

"Jeff might be a cheating bastard, but that doesn't change the fact that even before he started sleeping around, he was never...satisfied. Since he obviously found that satisfaction with those other women, it's impossible to blame the entire problem on him."

Gideon watched her pick at the tassels on the pillow while he dissected what she'd just said.

"You've been with other men since him."

"No." She still wouldn't look up. "I almost did once. But I kept hearing *his* voice in my head with those nasty little comments that he always wrote off as a joke and I just couldn't. I know that's pathetic, but after a while, the risk of finding out that Jeff was really right all along wasn't worth the potential pleasure. So I focused on work instead of dating—and now here we are."

Gideon wished he could go back in time and deliver a few more punches to Jeff's perfect face. He'd known things weren't perfect with Jeff and Lucy, but he hadn't realized just how much of a dick his friend had been. "He's a piece of shit."

"I'm not arguing that, believe me." She gave a faint smile. "Thank you again for saving me from marrying him. I don't know if I ever said it before, but it couldn't have been easy to say something. You two had been friends for so long."

Gideon scrubbed a hand over his face. He read people for a living—both his clients and the people he found to fill the open positions. He was damn good at it, too. That skill made him the best in the business and ensured that he almost always got the secondary bonus for the position still being filled for a year after the initial contract.

Every instinct he had was insisting that Lucy's sheepish smile covered up a soul wound. If he was a good man, he'd let someone else help her heal from that—someone who'd be there for the long term. Likely that theoretical husband he was supposed to find her. But Gideon wasn't a good man.

He didn't want it to be anyone else.

He wanted it to be *him*.

"Sit down."

She dropped onto the couch, still clinging to the pillow. "Okay."

There wasn't a convenient playbook for how to go

about this, but they *did* need to have a conversation before it went any further. "I will give you…lessons. On two conditions."

"Agreed."

He shot her a look. "Hear the conditions first and then decide if you're good with them. First—you communicate with me. You like something? Tell me. You aren't into it? You need to speak up. You fake anything and we call the whole thing off. I can't help you if you aren't honest with both yourself and me."

She wrinkled her nose. "Fine. I'm an adult. I can talk about sex."

He didn't comment on the fact she seemed to be trying to convince herself. The confidence and ice queen bit she'd played in the office was nowhere to be seen now, which made him wonder who was the real Lucy—the cold and professional lawyer or the unsure woman sitting in front of him now.

Gideon leaned forward. "Second condition is that you're not with anyone else for the duration."

"Why?" She held up a hand. "I have no intention of being with anyone else, but I'm curious."

"It's respect." *Liar. It's jealousy.* He smothered the snide little voice and kept his tone even. "We're exclusive—both of us—until the expiration date."

"Exclusive." She said the word as if tasting it. "When's the expiration date?"

Never. Fuck, he was already in over his head and sinking fast and he hadn't even touched her. "When you decide on a candidate for a husband, we end it."

Lucy nodded. "That seems reasonable. Should we start now?" She reached for her shirt.

"Holy fuck, slow down." He made an effort to lower his voice and held out a hand. "You want lessons? We start with the basics. Come here."

She reluctantly let go of the pillow and rose to cross over to his chair. Lucy eyed his hand, but ultimately placed hers in it. Gideon drew her down slowly, giving her plenty of time to see where things were going. She obliged him by climbing into his lap, though she held herself so stiffly she felt downright brittle.

He kept hold of her hand and set his other on her hip. It would have been innocent if not for the fact that she was straddling him and his cock had not gotten the memo about moving slow.

She shifted, her eyes going wide. "Ah…"

"Are you uncomfortable?" He spoke before she could think too hard.

"No…" She bit her lip. "Right. Honesty. Okay, yes, this feels weird. Awkward. I don't know where to put my hands and I can feel you, and it's making me nervous."

She was right. It was awkward as fuck. But Gideon wasn't going to throw her off the deep end on the first night, no matter how surreal this whole thing was. She trusted him to take care of her and he'd do whatever it took to be worthy of that trust. *Do whatever it took to keep her from changing her mind.* He kept his voice low so as not to startle her. "I'm going to kiss you now."

"Okay." She licked her lips and carefully tilted forward.

Gideon moved his hand from her hip to cup her jaw, guiding her down as he leaned up to brush his mouth against hers. She smelled of citrus and he had to fight to keep a growl internal. *Nice and easy.* He nipped her bottom lip and then soothed it with his tongue. She placed her hands on his biceps and relaxed against him, bit by bit. Gideon took it slow. He kissed her, keeping it light, until she shifted restlessly against him.

Then, and only then, did he slip his tongue into her mouth.

His first taste of Lucy went straight to his head. He used his hand on her jaw to angle her to allow him deeper and stroked his tongue against hers. Slow and steady was the name of the game.

Lucy whimpered and went soft against him. Her body melded to his, her breasts dragging against his chest with each inhalation. She shifted her grip and tentatively sifted her fingers through his hair. As if she wasn't sure of her welcome.

He wanted her sure.

Gideon shifted back to lean against the chair. The move settled her tighter against him as her knees sank into the cushion on either side of his hips. She gasped into his mouth and he ate the sound. He kissed her like he'd wanted to since that first night, when he'd heard her infectious laugh across a crowded bar. She tasted just as sunny as she smelled, as addicting as a summer's day in the midst of winter.

He couldn't get enough.

CHAPTER THREE

LUCY'S AWKWARDNESS WENT up in smoke the second Gideon kissed her. She'd expected… Well, she wasn't sure what she'd expected. For him to take her into the bedroom and strip them down and just go for it. Preferably with the lights turned off to hide her mortification.

He stroked his hands up the sides of her face and tangled his fingers in her hair. The move pulled her out of their kiss, but Gideon didn't let the distance stand. He dragged his mouth down the line of her neck, raising goose bumps in his wake.

A deep, hidden ember inside her burst into flame.

She was doing this. She was straddling Gideon Novak with his mouth on her skin and his hands on her body. Something she'd never even allowed herself to *think* about until she'd come up with this plan.

"You're thinking too hard."

"I can't believe this is happening."

He set his teeth against her collarbone. "If you change your mind—"

"I won't." She'd never dared fantasize about him—

she hadn't let herself cross that line, even in her mind—but she wasn't missing this opportunity for the world. Warmth flared with each breath, the heat centered at her core, where she could feel his cock lining up right where she wanted it.

I want it.

The realization startled her, though it shouldn't have. Gideon was sex personified and having all his considerable attention focused solely on her was a heady feeling. She wanted... More. All of it. Everything he could give her. She moaned. "More."

Gideon took her mouth. There was no other way to put it. He claimed her, establishing dominance with a stroke of his tongue, engulfing her entire world in that single contact. He tasted like peppermint—a shocking sensation against her tongue. Unexpected.

Just like the man himself.

It wasn't enough. There were too many clothes between them. She could feel his broad shoulders flexing, could test the definition of his muscles as she slid her hands down his chest, but his button-up shirt barred her from the skin-to-skin contact she craved.

Her breasts felt too tight, her nipples pebbling until they almost hurt. At least her yoga pants didn't offer much in the way of a barrier as she rocked her hips against him. His slacks did little to hide the size of his cock, and that little movement felt deliciously good. Intoxicating. So she did it again.

Gideon dropped one hand to her hip. For one horrifying moment she thought he'd stop her—maybe tell her that grown adults did not dry hump in the middle of one's living room—but he just urged her on. He never stopped kissing her, never stopped exploring her mouth. As if kissing was his be-all and end-all rather than just the first step to get to sex.

God, I am so messed up.

He squeezed her ass and nipped her bottom lip. "How we doing?"

"Good." Was that her voice? She sounded like she was doing something requiring a whole lot more exertion than kissing Gideon Novak. *If this is what kissing is like, am I going to survive actual sex?*

Who cares? It'd be a glorious way to go.

He used his grip on her hip to pull her closer yet, lining up his cock with her clit. "And now?"

She hissed out a breath. *Please don't stop.* She could come like this if they kept it up. "Really good. But—" She didn't want to talk about it, didn't want to do anything to make this stop, so she went in for another kiss.

Gideon tightened his hold on her hair just enough to prevent her from moving. "But?"

His insistence on honesty had seemed like a good idea at the time—how could she improve if she didn't know what she was doing wrong?—but in practice it felt like he was stripping her bare in a way that had nothing to do with sex. She closed her eyes, because it was easier to answer when she wasn't meeting his gaze. "Isn't dry humping kind of juvenile?" *Are you going to mock me if I orgasm from this? Maybe make a joke about cobwebs or how long it's been for me?*

His chuckle pulled at things low in her stomach. "Does this feel juvenile to you?"

"No." It felt hotter than it should have and even a little dirty. She wanted it too much, and that was the problem. She forced herself to open her eyes and found him watching her with a contemplative expression. "What?"

"Pleasure isn't something you can put limits on, Lucy. There isn't a right way to go about it. Would you tell someone who was eating one of those double-chocolate-death desserts you love so much that they were eating it wrong if they did it differently than you?"

"Of course not." She blinked. How had he possibly remembered her favorite dessert?

"Then why is *this* wrong?" He urged her to rock against him again. "Feels good to me. Feels good to you. No reason to overthink it."

When Gideon put it like that, it sounded so simple. Deceptively simple. She started to ask another question but forced herself to silence it. This insecurity wasn't her. This was the ghost of her relationship with Jeff coloring the current interaction.

Exactly what she'd been afraid would happen.

"Thank you for agreeing to this, Gideon. You didn't have to and—"

"Lucy." He framed her face with his big hands, preventing her from looking away. Those dark eyes were so incredibly serious. "Stop thanking me for this. The matchmaking shit? Sure. Not this. You're crazy if you think I'm not getting something out of it—same as you. Enjoy it. Enjoy *me*. It's as simple as that."

Easier said than done. The malicious voice that had spent far too many years lurking in the back of her mind wouldn't be silenced. Not completely. *Pity fuck.* She pressed her lips together. "I want to have sex now."

"No."

She frowned. "What?"

"No." He sat up, forcing her to grab his shoulders to stabilize herself, and then stood, taking her with him. "You want me to teach you? Then we're doing this on my terms. You were enjoying the hell out of this and something tripped you up." He laid them down on his ridiculously comfortable couch. She sank into the cushions as his weight settled over her. It felt good. Right.

It scared the shit out of her.

"Gideon."

"My terms, Lucy." He kissed her again. Before it had been sweet, and then intense, but she hadn't realized he was holding back until that moment. Gideon kissed her like he owned her. He took her mouth, urging her to meet him halfway.

She held back for all of one second; it was impossible to maintain distance with his very presence overwhelming her. So she let go, tangling her tongue with his. The second she did, he started to move.

It had felt good when she was on top, but it was nothing compared to him pressing her into the couch as he stroked his cock against her clit. One long slide up and then another back down. The desire that had been put on hold while she'd let her insecurities get the best of her seared her—with interest. As if it'd been waiting for her to just let go and enjoy this moment for what it was. *Pleasure. No questions asked.*

She arched up to meet him. "That feels good."

Gideon hitched a hand beneath her knee and drew her leg up and out, opening her farther. He kissed her again and kept up that slow drag that had sparks dancing at her nerve endings. Her body wound tighter and tighter with each stroke until she teetered on the brink. Lucy writhed against him, trying to get closer, to get him where she needed him, to do whatever it took to reach that edge. "Gideon, *please.*"

He shifted back and she sobbed out a breath at the loss of him. But he didn't make her wait long. He slid a hand beneath the waistband of her yoga pants and into her panties. His rough curse would have made her smile under other circumstances, but she was too busy holding her breath. *So close. Please just touch me.*

He did.

He made a V with his fingers and slid it over her clit in the exact same motion he'd been doing with his cock before. She lasted three strokes before she came apart in his arms, her pleasure drawing a cry from her lips and blanking out her mind into delicious static. He softened their kiss to the barest brushing of lips and then shifted to the side so his weight wasn't completely on her.

Lucy blinked at the pale gray ceiling and tried to reconcile what had just happened with reality. *I just came. Without pressure. Without having to force it or fake it.* A world-ending orgasm and *Gideon* was the one who'd coaxed it from her. "Wow." As soon as the word popped out of her mouth, she cringed. *What a stupid thing to say.* She was hardly a virgin and she wasn't an idiot teenager, no matter what they'd just done.

Gideon gave another of those low laughs. "All flavors, Lucy."

Against her better judgment, she couldn't help comparing what they'd just done to her experiences with Jeff when they'd first started dating. Night and day. Even though it'd taken her and Jeff a bit to work up to sex, he'd always had an air of impatience about him when they were intimate—like he couldn't wait to get to the next step. Add that to his competitive need to make her come multiple times every time they were together and the pressure had twisted with the desire until it made her jumpy every time they'd been alone together. Things had changed a little once they'd finally had sex, but then other elements had come into play.

Boring.

Uninspired.

Like fucking a doll.

"Lucy, look at me." Gideon's voice drew her out of the horror show that was her past.

She shook her head. *God, I can't even do this right.* What they'd just done was so incredibly perfect and she'd had to go and ruin it by letting her issues with her ex creep in. "I'm sorry."

"No, I'm sorry." He stroked a hand through her

hair, the move so tender, her stomach tried to tie it-self in knots. His dark eyes took on a distance as he looked at something she couldn't see. "I knew Jeff was an asshole, but if I'd known what a piece of shit he was, I would have warned you off before he got his hooks into you."

"It wouldn't have mattered." Six years ago, in the midst of her headlong rush into adulthood, she was so sure that she knew better, she hadn't listened to anyone. Not her sister, not her friends, not her fledg-ling instincts. As nice as it was to think otherwise, she wouldn't have listened to Gideon, either.

Being this close to him, talking like this while her body still sang from the pleasure he'd given her... It was too intimate. Too revealing. Just plain too much.

She slid off the couch and stood. A quick look at the front of his slacks confirmed that he was still, in fact, painfully hard. *Nice job, Lucy. Bask in your post-orgasmic bliss and ignore the fact he's still in need.* "Do you want me to...?"

"These lessons aren't about me." He sat up. "They're about you. And you need space."

Yeah, she did. His airy living room was suddenly too small, the walls closing in even as her heart beat too fast. "I asked for this."

"You don't have to explain." He gave her a half smile that didn't reach his eyes. "We poked at some old wounds tonight. If that means you need some distance from the whole thing, then so be it. You're being honest, and fuck if I'm going to punish you for that." He grabbed his phone off the coffee table. "But if you're headed home, I'm calling you a cab."

She should push back. She was more than capable of calling her own damn cab and the subway would be running for hours yet. But if Gideon could respect her need to flee without his pride being injured and throwing a fit, she could respect his need to get her home safe. "Okay."

He made the call quickly and set the phone down. "What's your schedule look like tomorrow?"

The change in subject left her discombobulated. "I have court in the afternoon, so I'll be doing last-minute preparations beforehand." It was as close to an open-and-shut case as such things got. The cops had mishandled the evidence and the lead detective had an established vendetta against her client. She had every intention of getting the whole damn thing thrown out.

"I know that look on your face. You have this one in the bag."

Her stomach gave another of those flutters that wasn't altogether uncomfortable. He'd said that with such confidence, as if there wasn't a single doubt in his mind that she would win. Lucy tucked a strand of hair behind her ear. "I should be free in the evening." *For another lesson?* She didn't know if she'd look forward to it or dread it. *Liar. You haven't even left yet and you're already craving another hit.*

"Good." He stood, suddenly taking up too much space. She tensed, half expecting him to touch her. But Gideon headed for the door. "I'll have a list of preliminary candidates ready for you, and we'll go over them at dinner."

"That I'll pay for." She cast a pointed look at the way his jaw tensed at her words. "Don't be like that. If I was a normal client, I'd pay and you wouldn't blink because that's how things are done."

"You aren't a normal client, Lucy. There's nothing *normal* about this." He motioned between them.

She couldn't really argue that, but that didn't mean he'd win this battle. "I'll handle the reservations and text you the details."

"Stubborn."

The twisting in her stomach took on a sour edge. Jeff had thrown that word at her like a curse more often than she could count. *Stop it. Oh, my God,* stop. *He's in the past and he's staying there.* "It's my best trait."

"I wouldn't dream of arguing that." He held the door open for her. "Until tomorrow."

"See you then."

She headed for the elevator, stopping several steps down the hallway and leaning against the wall as she tried to calm her racing heart. She hadn't known it could be like this. He'd just…taken care of her. Both physically and emotionally. Bringing her to orgasm and recognizing and respecting the panic driving her to leave. Lucy hadn't expected that. She didn't know what to do with a version of Gideon who was different than she'd expected.

What did I get myself into?

CHAPTER FOUR

"YOU'RE FUCKING CRAZY."

Gideon didn't look up from his computer. "You don't have to tell me that."

"And yet I'm telling you all the same. What the hell are you doing? *Matchmaker*? For *Lucy Baudin*?" Roman Bassani paced from one side of the room to the other, his restless energy irritating as fuck.

"I know we're supposed to have lunch, but this came up and can't wait. I'm going to have to take a rain check." Gideon wrote down another name and moved to the next candidate on his preliminary list. When Roman paced another lap around the office, he cursed. "Sit down or get out. You're distracting me."

"You need the distraction. Hell, you need a god-damn intervention." Roman threw himself into the chair across from the desk and slouched. He would have been at home in some artsy perfume ad with his brooding good looks and the way he seemed to pose without noticing he was doing it. On any other man, the affected attitude would have pissed Gideon off, but with Roman it was just… Roman. He was too honest, too brash, too comfortable in any space. It was part of what made him so good at his job—he had never met a challenge he wasn't fully confident he could tackle.

Whether his confidence was misplaced or not was an argument for another day.

"Gideon, why are you doing this? Wait—don't tell me. You're not still feeling guilty because you didn't tell her what a douche Jeff was immediately? Look, we all fucked up. You're the only one who stepped in, and that's something I have to live with." He made a face. "I convinced myself that it wasn't my place or my business."

"Jeff's good at spinning any situation to benefit him." He'd sure as hell laid on the guilt and idiotic bro code heavy enough to give even Gideon pause at the time.

"Changes nothing." Roman shrugged. "Including the fact that you are not qualified to be a matchmaker, let alone for Lucy. She's a good girl and, damn it, she deserves a professional. I know a few in the city. I can call in a favor and get her shoved to the top of the list and wrap this whole thing up without anyone crossing any lines."

He tried to be rational and actually consider it. He fucking failed. The line had been crossed last night and there was no going back now. "No. She asked me, so I'm the one who'll do it. And don't get any funny ideas, Roman. You meddle in enough people's lives. I have no interest in being added to the list."

"As if you'd let me." Roman affected a sigh. "You're as mean as a junkyard dog."

"And you're wasting my time. Unless you have something worthwhile to add to the search, get out."

He realized his mistake the second his friend perked up. "Who's on the list?"

Fuck me. "No."

"Come on." Roman shot to his feet, towering over the desk, and snatched the paper from beneath Gideon's hand. His hazel eyes went wide. "Shit, Gideon. You put Aaron Livingston on here. Shooting for the stars, aren't you?"

"She's worth it." He grabbed the paper.

Roman studied him for a long moment. "Interesting."

"For fuck's sake, Roman, don't you have some business to buy up or small children to terrify?" He still had several hours' worth of work to do before he met up with Lucy tonight. The address she'd texted him wasn't far, but rush hour would be a bitch to navigate, so he'd scheduled in extra time. That didn't mean he was going to dick around with this damn list.

His friend pointed to two names on the list. "Take Travis and David off the list. They're fuckheads with women, though they both hide it well."

Gideon crossed out their names. "I hadn't heard."

"Why would you? You don't date, and that handsome mug of yours might have people intrigued, but it's from a distance. People aren't rushing to confide in you because there's a solid chance you'll rip them a new one for wasting your time."

Gideon glared. "Are you finished?"

"Not yet." Roman gave a lazy grin. "My point is that people talk to me, so using that as a resource is a smart thing to do. Aaron Livingston is as straight as they come. If that guy has any skeletons in his closet, they're buried deep. The other two left on the list are up in the air. I'll find out what I can and let you know."

He fought down the need to snap back. The truth was that Roman was right. People didn't open up to Gideon. His clients only cared that he got the job done and had one of the highest ratings in the industry. The people he placed for his clients only cared about their endgame in a company that would pay them well to do what they loved. Friends? He had them. He just preferred them at a distance.

Roman had never been able to take that hint.

"Fine. Look into them."

"It's charming that you think I need your permission." Roman grinned. "I'll come by in the next few days and let you know what I dig up."

A call would have been preferable, but Gideon knew Roman well enough to know that arguing was pointless. His friend did what he wanted, when he wanted. He sighed. "Fine."

"Chin up, Novak." Roman paused. "All joking aside, if you're going to do this, do it right. I know your history with Lucy is complicated, but playing this straight is the only way. Otherwise, there are a lot of potential complications that could arise."

Last night had been nothing if not one long, agonizingly good complication. Even almost twenty-four hours later, he could still taste her in his mouth. It made him crave more, which was a dangerous path to walk.

Lucy wasn't for him.

He had to remember that.

If she'd wanted *him*, she would have said so. Even this almost-timid version of her wouldn't have balked at putting it out there. She was direct, as evidenced by her plan existing in the first place. But she hadn't brought him into her office to ask *him* to step into the role of husband.

Husband.

What would that even look like?

Gideon shook his head and focused on his friend. "I have it under control."

"Keep telling yourself that." Roman headed for the door. "I'll check in tomorrow, but in case I don't see you before then, we still on for Friday?"

"Yeah." They had a standing reservation in Vortex's VIP lounge on Friday nights. It was one of the only social appointments he held consistently, despite occasionally running into Jeff there. But that asshole had started coming less and less in the years since he and Lucy had broken off their engagement. People had started to see through his charming act and called him out when he was acting like a douchebag—which was often.

"See you then." Roman opened the door and paused. "You should bring her."

Gideon tore his gaze away from the list of names yet again. "What?"

"You should bring Lucy on Friday. I know Aaron Livingston since we worked together last year. We can orchestrate a non-pressure meeting. You're on your own with the other two, but I don't think Aaron would agree to a blind date for shits and giggles."

Since Gideon had only met him in passing, he couldn't argue that. "Do it." He spoke before he had a chance to think up half a dozen reasons why it was a bad idea. It *wasn't* a bad idea. It was his issue if he didn't want to see her with someone else—not hers.

He waited for Roman to shut the door behind him before he grabbed his phone. Both Mark and Liam were acquaintances he'd come across in the last few years who had seemed like upstanding guys. He'd feel them out for interest and then take the list to Lucy to see where she stood with all of it.

The knowledge that she'd likely end up with one of these men sat in his stomach like a rock. He hesitated, his contact list staring back at him. It would be the easiest thing in the world to sabotage this. All he had to do was feed some false information about Lucy and they'd say no. Or feed her false information about *them* to prove New York had a shitty dating scene.

"No." He'd promised her to do his best and he'd damn well do his best. Gideon had lied to her once before and it had almost destroyed them both. He wasn't going to do that to her again.

Fuck, he was in this situation *because* of what happened before.

Gideon would do right by Lucy. He'd have to be a heartless bastard to do anything else. The only option was to find her a damn husband.

No matter what it cost him to do it.

* * *

Lucy was on her second glass of wine by the time she caught sight of Gideon's familiar form moving toward her table through the darkened room. He towered over the tiny host and the poor man kept shooting looks over his shoulder as if he expected Gideon to club him over the head. The thought made her smile and was almost enough to distract her from her nervousness.

She'd woken up this morning from the single hottest dream of her life, starring none other than Gideon Novak. It started identical to their encounter last night, but they hadn't stopped until they were naked and in his bed, both shaking from their respective orgasms. Her body flushed at the memory and she took a shaky sip of wine.

What was the protocol for greeting a man who'd used his fingers to make her come on his couch the night before? They weren't dating, so a kiss seemed inappropriate. They weren't even really friends anymore, so a hug was likely presumptuous. A handshake was just absurd.

Gideon saved her from having to decide by sitting before she had a chance to stand. He shot a look at the host. He probably meant it as a polite dismissal, but it actually looked scathing. Lucy watched the man nearly run from the table. "You really have to work on your attitude."

"My attitude is fine."

"Without a doubt, but you have a very intimidating persona. You know most women judge a man by how he treats the waitstaff on their first date—and you would have just nixed the possibility of a second date and we haven't even had appetizers yet."

Gideon raised his eyebrows. "Good day in court, I take it."

"We're not talking about me." She leaned forward and lowered her voice. Enjoying poking at him a little. "Though that was a very smooth change of subject."

The corners of his lips twitched upward. "Yes, it was. We're not here to talk about my dating prospects. We're here to talk about yours." He looked up as a waiter approached and she actually saw the effort he put into forcing a smile. It looked downright pained, but it was better than nothing. "I'll have a seven and seven." He glanced at her half-full wineglass. "Another?"

"Sure." She didn't drink more than two glasses often, but she'd busted her ass on today's case and the judge had been persuaded to dismiss the entire thing. It was a coup that should have been the tipping point for her promotion, but when Rick Parker had come by her office to congratulate her, he'd made a comment about the big, broody man who'd been in to see her yesterday. Because, of course, who she was or wasn't dating was just as important as her professional skill set.

Well, damn it, Parker's crappy attitude wasn't going to ruin her night.

"Tell me about the case."

She almost refocused the conversation, but the truth was that she didn't have anyone to talk to about it. Her sister was supportive and wonderful, but Becka had her own thing going on and couldn't be less interested in law. Get together for drinks and chat about life and what their parents were up to? Sure. Hash out the details of whatever case Lucy was working on? Not a chance. And Gideon actually looked interested.

She picked up her wineglass. "I got the entire case thrown out today. All they had was circumstantial evidence and a bad attitude about my guy's priors. They were so certain he did the crime, they didn't look at anyone else. Anyone on the outside would have come to the same conclusion, but it's always a crapshoot with Judge Jones."

"That's great, Lucy. Congrats."

"Thanks." She smiled and then took a drink. "How was your day?"

"Productive." He leaned over and pulled a tablet out of his briefcase. "I have some things to show you."

Disappointment coated her tongue when he slid the tablet across the table to her. They'd barely gotten their conversation started and now they were back to business. *You hired him as a business decision. You don't get to have it both ways.* It wasn't fair to ask him to go back to being her friend along with her being his client.

She picked up the tablet and found pictures of three men. She clicked on the first one—a blond guy with a close-cropped beard and a seriously expensive suit— and found a file. "'Aaron Livingston, born May thirteenth...'" He'd compiled a list of information ranging from where Aaron was born to where he graduated high school and college—and his GPA at both. There was also a notification about possible likes and dislikes. "Wow, Gideon. You really don't do anything halfway, do you?"

He had compiled the same information for each of the other two men. Interestingly enough, all three of them were local and had gone to prestigious business colleges, graduating close to the top of their class. All three had moved on to respected companies and seemed to be doing well for themselves.

Using their information and ignoring their pictures, she wouldn't have been able to pick any of them out of a lineup. "This... Wow."

"You said that already." He frowned. "Is something wrong? I assumed that you were looking for someone in the same financial class as you, and leaning toward white-collar businessmen. That *is* why you came to me, correct?"

Yes, at least in theory. In reality, this whole thing was playing out much differently than she'd expected. It didn't make a bit of sense, especially because it was proceeding *exactly* how she'd hoped. "No, it's fine. They're excellent candidates."

Seeing them laid out like this, the situation just became so much more real. In a very short period of time she'd be sitting across the table from one of these men, rather than Gideon. She'd be torturing herself with wondering if they'd kiss her after dinner—if maybe they'd expect more to happen.

I'm not ready.

She took a gulp of her wine. "Can we get dinner to go?"

CHAPTER FIVE

NERVES STOLE LUCY'S voice as she and Gideon walked to her apartment. She'd intentionally picked a restaurant close to her place so that they wouldn't have to worry about a cab ride to get from point A to point B. She nodded at the doorman as he held open the door for them and then she strode to the elevator and pushed the button.

Gideon followed her inside and leaned against the elevator wall. The food in the paper bag smelled divine, but her craving was solely for the man holding it. She clasped her hands together to keep from touching him. "I want to progress tonight."

He raised his eyebrows. "I'm listening."

Why was it so challenging to say these things aloud? She was an adult. She should be able to express her needs honestly without fear of being laughed out of the building—or rejected. Lucy fisted her hands and raised her chin. The mirrors in the elevator walls and door reflected a version of her that looked ready to go several rounds on the courthouse floor. "I don't want to wait anymore. I want everything."

That predatory stillness rolled over him and his eyes seemed to flare with barely banked heat. "Bite-size steps are the smart option."

"Nothing about *this* is smart, and I think we both know that." Last night had made her skittish in a way she hadn't expected, and if she was shrewder and less stubborn, she would have called the whole thing off as a result. Instead she was pushing them toward something neither could take back.

The elevator door opened and she wasted no time walking into the hall and down to her door. There were only four apartments on this floor, each occupying their respective corner of the building. Hers faced southeast, so she often woke to the early morning sunlight streaming through her windows. At least on the days she wasn't up before dawn.

She unlocked the door and held it open for Gideon. He stopped just inside the entranceway, barely leaving room for her to slide inside behind him. She tried to see the place through his eyes. The open floor plan showcased the big floor-to-ceiling windows. The kitchen lay just to the right of the front hall, the white cabinets set off with little turquoise handles she'd found online. The living room contained a decent-size TV that she rarely used and two short couches arranged in a loose V. Her cat, Garfunkel, lifted his head and gave Gideon a death stare.

Gideon moved to the kitchen counter—white marble shot through with pale gray—and set the bag of food on it. He turned and crossed his arms over his chest. "Why the change of pace?"

"Maybe I just want you." It was the truth, but not the full truth.

He shook his head. "Honesty, Lucy."

Why had she agreed to that particular term? She pulled at the hem of her fitted blue dress. "I'm nervous. Last night was good, but I didn't expect that level of reaction, and I'm afraid if we don't get it over with, I'm going to change my mind."

"Get it over with," Gideon murmured. "Sex isn't something you 'get over with.' If you think of it that way, there's a problem somewhere."

A problem he was determined to fix if the expression on his face was anything to go by. She sliced her hand through the air. "No problem. That's not what I meant at all. My issue is that the anticipation, the will-we-or-won't-we, is driving me nuts. I want to rip it off right now—like a Band-Aid."

He stared at her for a long moment and then burst out laughing. "A Band-Aid. Fuck, woman, you really are going to kill me." He ran a hand over his face. "The anticipation is meant to be enjoyed."

She could think of a lot of words to describe how she felt standing in her apartment with Gideon and knowing they were alone and could do what they wanted for hours. *Enjoyment* didn't top the list. Her body was too hot, her lungs too tight, her core aching from need. But she knew that look on his face. If she didn't do something rash, he was going to put the brakes on and sit her down and coax her to talk through it. For someone with such a ruthless reputation, Gideon was overwhelmingly careful with her.

She knew why—he had residual guilt over not telling her immediately about Jeff's cheating ways. But she didn't care about any of that right now.

All she cared about was getting through this interaction so she could go back to breathing normally again.

Before she could talk herself out of it, Lucy unzipped the side of her dress and slid it off. She didn't look at him as she kicked the silky fabric to the side. If she thought too hard about the fact that she stood in front of him in only a pair of nude-lace panties, she might die on the spot.

A second passed. Another.

Still, he didn't say anything.

What is he doing?

Probably looking for a way to gracefully exit that wouldn't have her throwing herself from the nearest window. *Stop that right now.* She was stronger than this. Lucy looked good. She ate relatively well and hit the gym at least three times a week. Last night Gideon's physical reaction had proved that he'd wanted her. He might not have taken his release, but he wasn't remotely unaffected.

So why was he standing there without saying a word?

Stop waiting for him to make the first move.

Do it yourself.

Gathering her courage, she lifted her head and looked at him. Her first step took more effort than she could have dreamed, and the intense look on his face didn't help her any. He held himself perfectly still, every muscle coiled. Though, for the life of her, she couldn't tell if it was to keep from jumping her or to stop himself from fleeing.

Only one way to find out.

She took the last few steps that brought her close enough to touch. Tentatively she reached out and laid her hands on his chest. *Why isn't he saying anything?* She waited another few seconds but the only sound in her kitchen was the soft rush of their quickened breathing.

Maybe she'd misjudged the situation. *Oh, God, what did I do?* "If you've changed your mind, just tell me. We can pretend this whole thing never happened."

Gideon couldn't look away from Lucy. She was fucking perfect. He'd known that, of course, but seeing it without clothes barring his vision was something else altogether. Her breasts were small and high, capped with dark rose nipples. He forced himself not to reach for her as she stroked her hands down his chest and back up again.

"Gideon?"

She'd asked a question, hadn't she?

"What?" His gaze snagged on her narrow waist and the nude-lace panties that were so sheer, he could see a shadow of her slit beneath them. He cleared his throat and jerked his attention back to her face.

She frowned a little. "Did you change your mind?"

"No." He finally allowed himself to move, reaching up and covering her hands with his. "Fuck me, but you can't expect a man to be faced with the sight of you naked and still be able to hold down a conversation."

"That's sweet."

But she thought he was lying. He could read it all over her face.

It struck Gideon that he'd been playing this wrong. He'd known Jeff had hurt Lucy with his actions, and then she'd told him that she hadn't been with anyone since, and he'd gone straight to treating her like an innocent virgin. She was innocent in some ways, but by being so careful with her, he'd created room for her to doubt herself—and him.

Fuck that.

He guided her hands to his shoulders and then started unbuttoning his shirt. "You don't believe the words, and I don't blame you for that. But if you won't listen to me when I tell you that you're a fucking goddess personified, then I'll show you."

She kneaded his shoulders slightly, her eyes glued to his hands as he finished with his shirt and started on the front of his slacks. "I believe you."

"You don't." He kicked off his shoes and shoved down his pants. Lucy shook her head as if fighting off a daze and pushed his shirt off his shoulders. He let it fall to the floor and then the only barriers were their respective underwear. He snagged the lace with a single finger. "These have to go."

"Yours, too."

He took a step back and hooked his thumbs in his boxer briefs. A single, smooth movement and he stood before her naked. Watching Lucy's jaw drop was ridiculously gratifying. She took in each part of his body, starting with his head and moving over his neck, his shoulders, his chest, his stomach and, finally, settling on his cock. He grew harder in response to her hungry expression.

Gideon had never had a woman look at him the way Lucy did. As if he was a present she'd found under the Christmas tree—just for her. It threatened to turn this interaction into something it could never be, so he smothered the thought. She wanted him physically. End of story.

"Gideon, you're beautiful." She shucked off her panties, never taking her gaze from him. "I mean, I'd seen you in a swimsuit, but this is different." She closed the distance between them once more, a small line appearing between her brows. "Is it weird, though? I never considered you a brother or anything like that, but you were family."

Family.

He'd forced himself to forget that feeling of belonging that Lucy seemed to extend wherever she went. When he'd hung out with her and Jeff, he'd never felt like a third wheel—he'd just been part of the unit. Of all the things he'd missed when she'd cut off communication between them, that might be the highest on the list. "I never saw you as a sister."

"I know." She laughed softly. "I'd catch you watching me sometimes—not often—and you never made it weird. But… I know."

He thought he'd hid it better than that. Gideon shoved the past away just like he shoved aside so many inconvenient feelings that seemed to arise the more time he spent with Lucy. "It's not weird."

"I guess it's not." She carefully slid her hands up his chest and around his neck, taking that last step to bring them chest to chest. He rested his hands on her waist, but she felt too good to limit the contact. Gideon stroked up her back and down again to cup her ass.

There was nothing left to say. They'd reached the point of no return the second Lucy's dress had hit the floor. Gideon lifted his head. "Bedroom."

"This way— *Oh!*"

He swept her into his arms and strode across the living room to the door she'd indicated. Her bedroom was purely Lucy: a pretty wood headboard, more pillows than one woman should require, and a bright yellow floral bedspread that brightened the room even in the low light of the single lamp she must have left on.

He laid her on the bed and settled between her thighs. Gideon had every intention of slowing things down and having a very specific conversation about how this would proceed.

Every. Intention.

But Lucy wrapped her legs around his waist and arched up to meet him, and that honorable plan disappeared as if it'd never existed. Maybe it hadn't and he'd just been lying to himself all along. It didn't matter. There was only her soft skin beneath his palms, her body sliding against his and her mouth on his neck.

He kissed her. Gideon might never get enough of

her sunny taste, and he wasn't about to miss a chance to immerse himself in the feel of her. This was happening. They would cross the line he'd never once considered anything other than insurmountable.

He stroked a hand down her waist to squeeze her ass and hitch her up to fit tighter against him. The temptation to sink into her was almost too much, but this wasn't about him, his wants, his needs.

This was about Lucy.

Gideon hadn't leashed himself and his desire for her this long to skip over for anything less than the full experience. He didn't want to miss a single thing. He kissed down and across her collarbone and palmed her breasts. "Perfect. Every single thing about you is fucking perfect."

She laughed a little nervously. "You said that before."

"I'll say it again." He tongued one nipple. "Pretty and pink and...fuck. Just fucking perfect."

"Don't stop." She laced her fingers through his hair and drew him back down. "Harder."

He set his teeth gently against her nipple and then increased the pressure slightly when she went wild beneath him. Through it all, he kept his eyes open. Gideon wanted it all, every nuance of expression, every reaction. All of it.

A flush stole across her freckled cheeks and over her chest, and her small breasts heaved with each sobbed breath. He moved to give her other nipple the same treatment but kept stroking the first, pinching it with the same amount of pressure he'd applied with his mouth.

She shuddered against him, her hips grinding. "Gideon. Oh, God. I think I could come from this alone."

"I'm not done yet." He pressed one last kiss to each nipple and then slid back until he knelt on the floor next to the bed. He grabbed her hips and jerked her to the edge. This close, he could see every part of her. Gideon drew his thumb over her slit. "You need more."

"Yes."

He used his thumbs to part her. "Next time, you'll tell me exactly what you want."

"Next time?" She lifted her head to give him a dazed look. "Why next time?"

"Because I'm a selfish bastard." His mouth actually watered being this close to the most private part of Lucy. Her pussy was as flushed as the rest of her skin, wet and wanting and practically begging for his tongue. There wasn't a single damn reason *not* to give her exactly what he wanted. "I hope you're ready."

CHAPTER SIX

LUCY HAD NEVER enjoyed oral. Not really. It was yet another area where Jeff's competitiveness soured any inkling of pleasure she might get from the act. He had a series of moves he'd go through, the goal being to get her wet enough for sex. Truth be told, she'd always suspected he didn't like the act any more than she did, but the one time she'd brought it up, it had been one of the worst fights they'd ever had.

The first rasp of whiskers against Lucy's inner thigh drove thoughts of her ex right out of her head. Gideon didn't immediately go for her clit. Instead he dragged his cheek against her other thigh, using the motion to spread her legs farther.

She lifted her head just as he dipped down and drew his tongue over her in one long lick. Then he did it again—as if she was his favorite flavor of ice cream. Considering their frenzied making out, she'd expected this to be just as quick…

Should have known better than to make assumptions about Gideon.

Especially after last time.

He spread her folds and thrust his tongue into her, his low growl making the act unbearably erotic. Lucy's thoughts slammed to a halt and her mind went gloriously blank. "Holy shit."

He didn't appear to hear her. Gideon fucked her pussy with his tongue as if he couldn't get enough of her taste. He gripped her thighs with his big hands, holding her open to his ministrations even when her muscles shook with the effort to react, to move, to do *something*.

She thrashed her head from one side to the other, the sensations too much and not enough—and she didn't know how to put it into words. *Honesty.* Words crowded in her throat, too raw and vulnerable to give voice, but then she felt his teeth and they burst forth in a rush. "My clit. Gideon, suck on my clit. Use your teeth." Like he had with her nipples. Like he was doing right now with her labia.

Her entire body coiled at the thought, and the feeling intensified when he did exactly as she asked. There was no macho posturing or telling her that he was more than capable of pleasing her without an instruction manual. Gideon just...listened.

He sucked her clit into his mouth and set his teeth against the sensitive bundle of nerve endings. She arched almost completely off the bed, and he used the move to slide his hands under her ass and lift her so he could feast more effectively.

Because that was exactly what he was doing— feasting.

There was nothing gentle or teasing about his

touch now. He went after her clit in a way that was just shy of pain, sending little zings of pure bliss through her. Her body coiled tighter yet, so close to the edge, she didn't know how much longer she could hold out.

Gideon lifted his head just enough to speak, his lips brushing her heated flesh with every word. "Do you want to come like this?"

Asking that question was the single sexiest thing anyone had ever done to her. Choice. Control. Who knew it could be such a turn-on?

She almost said yes. Lucy was so close to orgasm, she shook with need and had to focus entirely too hard to create verbal words beyond *yesyesyesyesyes*. Did she want him to keep doing what he'd been doing? Hell, yes.

But she wanted him inside her more.

She licked her lips. "I want…" How did she want him?

Every way.

Right now, though? "I want to ride you."

A muscle in his jaw ticked and his grip on her thighs twitched. "You have condoms."

"Yes." She pointed a shaking finger at her nightstand.

The ones she'd bought after her breakup had expired ages ago, victim of her self-esteem issues, so she'd picked up a new box this morning. She'd also unwrapped the box so they could save time. It had felt presumptuous in the extreme when she'd been sitting alone on her bed, Garfunkel staring at her in feline judgment. Now she wished she'd already had one of them on Gideon.

He slowly released her, as if it pained him to move away. She sat up and scooted back so she could watch him pull open the top drawer. It wasn't until his dark eyes flashed that she remembered what *else* was in the drawer. "Ah..."

He held up her pink vibrator. "We'll talk about this later." He dropped it back in the drawer and pulled out a condom. "Scratch that. We're not going to talk. I'm going to stroke myself while I watch you use it."

Her eyes went wide at the image his words painted. Him, sitting against the headboard with his cock in his hand. Her on her back with her legs spread, using her toy. Her core clenched. "I want that. Later."

"Later," he agreed. He ripped the wrapper open and proceeded to roll the condom down his length.

She stood and pushed him to sit on the edge of the bed. "Like this." Lucy climbed into his lap and reached between them to notch his cock at her entrance. With her desire driving her, it was easy to speak things that would have stoppered her words with embarrassment in any other situation. "Kiss me while I ride you."

"You have no idea how fucking sexy it is that you know exactly what you want." He scooted back enough that she could brace her knees on the mattress. Then he hooked one arm around her waist while he dug his other hand into her hair. He tugged a little. "Yes?"

She moaned. "Yes." She loved when Gideon didn't

treat her like she was breakable. He didn't so much as hesitate when she urged him to bite her harder, to grab her tighter. Things she hadn't even known she craved until he gave them to her.

Lucy slid down until he was completely sheathed inside her. She had to pause to adjust to the almost uncomfortable fullness. The sensation passed quickly, dissipating to sheer pleasure as her body accommodated his size. She wrapped her arms around his shoulders and kissed him as she started to move. Their position had him rubbing against her clit with every stroke and, despite trying to hold out, her orgasm loomed all too soon.

Her strokes went choppy. *"Gideon."*

He shifted his hands to her hips, helping her maintain the rhythm that would get her where she needed to go. "You feel so fucking good."

"You...too." She opened her eyes, not sure when she'd closed them, and the expression on his face stilled her breath in her lungs. *Possession. Desire. Need.* It was too much.

Lucy cried out his name as she came. He kept her moving, kept the orgasm going, until her muscles gave out and she slumped against him.

He carefully pulled out of her and shifted them back onto the bed. Gideon spooned her, lightly stroking her arm, her hip, her stomach. She stared at the art print on the wall next to her bed for several long moments while she relearned how to breathe. Gradually she became aware of a very specific part of him pressed against her ass. "You didn't come."

"Not yet."

Not yet.

Who knew those two little words would be the sexiest thing she'd ever heard?

Gideon kept up his light touching until Lucy arched back against him. Judging her to be recovered enough, he hooked one knee and lifted her leg up and over his legs, leaving her open to him. He slid a hand carefully between her thighs, testing her tenderness. "Tell me what you want."

"You."

He kissed the back of her neck. "You have me." *For now.* "Tell me what other fantasies you've been harboring." The image of her using that toy on herself would be enough to keep him up at night for the foreseeable future. He was a goddamn idiot for feeding his imagination more images, but he craved them the same way he craved her.

"You want my sexual bucket list?" Her amused tone turned into a gasp as he idly stroked her clit. "You can't expect me to think when you're doing *that*."

"Consider it inspiration." He liked the idea of being the one who helped her cross items off that type of list. Fuck, he liked the thought that he was in her bed right now and would be for as long as she felt he had something to teach her.

Lucy reached back to sift her fingers through his hair. "I haven't really thought about it."

"Liar." He took the move for an invitation and

slid his other arm beneath her so he could palm her breasts. "There's at least a few things you have lurking in the back of your mind about this—something you've always wanted to try." Something he could be the only one to ever give to her.

At least for now.

She hesitated and he could practically hear her thinking it over and considering laying herself bare in this way. Gideon could have pointed out that they were already bared to each other, but this was different.

He stilled his hands, waiting for her answer.

"Don't stop." She covered the hand between her legs with one of her own, guiding him back to her clit and then lower, to push a finger inside her. Lucy moaned. "High-end dressing room. I've always wanted to have sex in a high-end dressing room—lingerie, maybe, if that's not super cliché." She tensed. "Crap. I'm doing it again. God, it's so hard to turn *off.*"

"I think we could make that happen." He kissed along her neck to growl in her ear. "I want to see you in green—that bright jewel tone."

She tilted her head forward, giving him better access. "I think we could make that happen." She echoed his words back to him.

"Charitable of you." He paused his stroking long enough to guide his cock into her. She clamped tight around him and he barely bit back a curse.

As many times as he'd slipped and imagined what it would be like to have Lucy in his bed, his fantasies hadn't come close to the bliss of reality. She was fucking perfection. Every move, every word, every gasp—Gideon stored them all away in his memory. He only had a limited time to accumulate enough to last him a lifetime.

A worry for another day.

Tonight he was inside Lucy.

Tomorrow could wait until tomorrow.

Gideon sat in Lucy's living room and ate reheated leftovers. She had a bright throw wrapped around her shoulders and her cat in her lap as she tried to arrange her food in an order that she could actually eat. He reached over and plucked the cat out of her lap.

Or he tried.

In reality, Garfunkel had no intention of going anywhere against his will. He let loose a yowl that raised the small hairs on the back of Gideon's neck. Before he could react, the cat hissed and swiped claws across his forearm. He cursed but managed not to chuck the horrid little beast. Instead he dropped the animal the short distance to the floor.

"Oh, my God!" Lucy shoved her food containers to the side and grabbed his wrist. "What were you thinking?"

He gritted his teeth as she dabbed at the blood welling in the scratches with a napkin. "I was thinking you'd have an easier time eating if he wasn't taking up so much space on your lap."

"You weren't wrong." She dabbed a little harder.

"But if you haven't noticed, Garfunkel is territorial. And he doesn't like men much."

"You think?" He took the napkin from her and pressed it hard against his arm. "It's fine. I should have known better." His lifestyle wasn't one that allowed for a pet, but if it had, Gideon would definitely be a dog person. Cats seemed to be little assholes as a general rule, and he had a feeling if he tried to adopt one, he'd pick the biggest asshole of them all through sheer karma.

Though Garfunkel has a solid running for that title.

"I'm really sorry."

"Lucy, it's fine." He grabbed his food and joined her on the couch. "How are you feeling?"

"Unwound." She leaned her head against the back of the couch and gave him a sleepy smile. "I'd forgotten how relaxing good sex could be."

Good doesn't begin to cover it.

He bit the comment back. It was sheer pride that made him want to say it and he didn't have a right. Not in the current situation. He was here for a specific purpose and he couldn't afford to forget that even for a moment. Lucy wasn't for him in any permanent way. This was a window into the world of what could have been in another life, if things had fallen out in a different sequence of events.

But they hadn't. So here he and Lucy were.

"What made you pick those particular men?"

It took him a few seconds too long to make the subject change with her. He didn't want to talk about other men while he still had the memory of her body against his and the smell of her on his skin. It felt wrong on a whole hell of a lot of different levels. An intrusion.

Except it wasn't.

Lucy had asked him for a specific set of things, and sex had been an afterthought. Just because it wasn't an afterthought for Gideon didn't mean he could snap at her for keeping her head in the game. So he did his best to do the same.

"They're all ambitious men who have reputations for being honest and are old enough that they're likely thinking about settling down with one person. I've personally placed both Mark and Liam in jobs, so I did all the research and then some. They have solid histories. Neither has any record of being a cheater or abusive in any way. They're good guys—as good as anyone is." And he'd checked. Even with only twenty-four hours at his disposal, he'd done extensive research and even gone so far as to call a few of their exes, though Gideon wasn't about to admit that to Lucy. None of the women had said anything to raise red flags.

She speared a green bean with her fork. "And Aaron?"

"He's the best of the best. I actually tried to poach him for a client last year and he wouldn't give me the time of day." When she raised her eyebrows, he shifted, something like embarrassment sifting through him. "There's more to it than that, of course.

He's got an excellent reputation, and Roman is actually friends with him."

"Your pitch is overwhelming." She laughed softly. "But then, this is what I asked for, isn't it?"

He didn't like seeing that look on her face, as if she was resigning herself to a life half lived. "Lucy, if you want to change directions on this thing, we can do that. Even if you go on dates with these guys, nothing is set in stone."

"I know you mean well, but I would very much appreciate it if you'd stop trying to talk me out of this."

He tried to rein in his temper, but he'd held himself too tightly under control the last two days. Too careful. It wasn't Gideon's natural default, and it had started to wear on him. He glared. "I'm not trying to talk you out of shit. I'm giving you options. You want this to have a chance in hell of working, you need to stop being so goddamn defensive. I'm helping you with this bat-shit-crazy plan, so I need you to throw me a bone once in a while."

She set down her fork. "I think you should leave."

Fuck. He started to apologize but stopped. Lucy might be fragile in some ways, but she wasn't broken. He had to remember that and stop treating her with kid gloves. And yet letting her make what might be the biggest mistake of her life because he felt guilty over her last relationship was a shitty thing to do.

He wasn't sure what his other options were, but he'd have to figure it out. Fast.

In the meantime he needed to get the hell out of there before he said something they'd both regret.

Gideon stood and buttoned the last few buttons on his shirt. "I'll email you the details tomorrow."

"Okay." She still wouldn't look at him.

He hesitated, but there was nothing left to say. Sex had changed things. Having concrete proof of how deep the connection ran between them was enough to set him back on his heels. She felt it, too. There was no way she didn't.

Now he just needed her to actually admit it.

CHAPTER SEVEN

"I'M SORRY—did you just say that you have a *date*?"

Lucy swirled her white wine, not looking at her little sister. "You don't have to sound so shocked by it." She hadn't wanted to confess her plan, but it twisted her up inside not to be able to talk about it with at least one person. Gideon hardly counted, especially since his reactions were hardly consistent with what she'd expected—and *her* reactions weren't cooperating, either.

"I *am* shocked. You've been all work, work, work. When did you have time to set up a date?" Becka leaned over and snagged a chip from the plate in the middle of the table. "That's not a dig, by the way. That's just facts. I'm on three freaking dating websites and *I* have trouble finding dates who aren't candidates for 'but he seemed so nice.'"

Lucy sighed. "They can't all be serial killers, Becka."

"It only takes one." Becka frowned. "Besides, we aren't talking about me. We're talking about you."

Now that push came to shove, she didn't know where to start. Or if she even should confess any

of it. In truth, if she hadn't had these drinks set up
with Becka already, she'd be at home, moping. It had
been two days since she'd seen Gideon and, aside
from a few emails confirming her first date, they
hadn't talked, either. She knew she'd been an ass, but
it wasn't like Gideon to avoid a conflict.

Not that there had to be a conflict. There didn't.
She just didn't want him to think that their having
sex meant he could push her into not going through
with her plan. She'd made the decision. He had to
respect that. If that meant he didn't want to continue
with their lessons… Well, that was something she'd
just have to deal with.

*Unless he doesn't want to continue for a differ-
ent reason…*

"You okay?"

She blinked and tried to focus on her sister's face.
Becka changed her hair color with the seasons and
today it was a bright blue that was the exact shade
of her eyes. Her lip piercing glinted in the light of
the little hipster bar where they always met up. She
had the cute-alternative look down to a science. *She*
never had problems with men, despite her lamenting
about dating.

Lucy tried to smile. "Just a crisis of faith. You
know, the usual."

"Don't do that. If you don't want to tell me, that's
cool, but don't pat me on the head. You don't have to
protect me anymore, Lucy. You know that, right?"

"It's not about protecting you." And it wasn't.
They'd had a fine upbringing. Decent—if distant—

parents. A solid middle-class lifestyle. Nothing traumatic happening to make waves in their lives.

But Becka was still her little sister. When they were growing up, Becka had been the shy one, the bookworm who was a little too odd to fit in with the rest of the kids in her grade. It led to bullying and, when their parents had failed to notice, Lucy had taken care of it.

She'd been taking care of her little sister ever since. Though these days, Becka fought her own battles.

But her sister had a point. Holding on to the turmoil inside her wasn't doing Lucy any favors. She'd talked about it to Gideon, but he wasn't exactly a neutral party. Neither was Becka, for that matter. "I just... I know it's been two years, but I still have Jeff's comments rattling around in my brain. It's pathetic and I should be over it by now, and I *am* over *him*. I don't know what's wrong with me."

"Nothing's wrong with you." Becka grabbed the wine bottle on the table and refilled her glass. "It's not like you had a monthlong relationship and turned around and let it mess you up for the rest of your life. You and Jeff were together for...what, like four years? You were going to marry him." She narrowed her blue eyes. "Though he better hope we never cross paths, because I'm going to kick his ass one of these days."

"Becka."

"Lucy." She mimicked her voice perfectly. "But that day is not today. Either way, I'd say you were having a normal reaction and that's that. Why's this coming up now? The whole matchmaking thing is kind of out there, but it's not like you're jumping into bed with these guys to give them a trial run." Becka grinned. "Though *there's* an idea."

She tried to imagine it—taking a single night with each of the guys on Gideon's list—and instantly rejected the idea. "No way." It felt wrong and she didn't want to spend too much time thinking about why. *I promised Gideon to be exclusive.* Sure, that was it. Definitely.

"Worth a shot." Becka ate a few more chips. "You'll be fine, Lucy. I promise. Dating is weird and it's hard to get to know people, but you have a matchmaker in your corner. It'll all work out."

She couldn't tell her sister that Gideon Novak was the so-called matchmaker in question. Becka had met him on several occasions and she'd lose her shit if she knew. Since they'd managed to get through this conversation without her thinking Lucy was out of her mind, she'd like to keep it that way. "I'm sure you're right."

"I am."

Lucy's phone rang and her heart leaped in her throat at the sight of Gideon's name on the screen. "Hello?"

"I'll meet you there ten minutes early, so be ready."

She blinked. "I'm sorry—what?"

"The date, Lucy. Please tell me you haven't forgotten about it."

She bristled at the irritation in his voice. "Of course I haven't forgotten. But I was not expecting you to be attending." She was nervous enough about going out with Mark Williams without having to do it under the watchful eye of Gideon. "That's unacceptable."

"My rules. Be there ten minutes early." He hung up.

Lucy set her phone carefully on the table and looked up to find her sister watching her. "What?"

"I know that move. The 'gently set your phone down so you don't chuck it across the room' one. Who pissed you off?"

"It's a long story and, unfortunately, I have to leave in order not to be late." *Not to be late to being early. I'm going to kill him.* She dug out her wallet and flagged down the waitress. "Same time next week?"

"Sure. You're the one with the crazy schedule." Becka finished her drink and set it on the table. She grinned. "And whoever that was that just called you, give 'em hell, sis."

"I plan on it." She set the appropriate amount of cash on the table under the ticket and rose. She accepted Gideon's direction in the bedroom because that was exactly what she'd asked for. She accepted his list of men for the same reason.

She refused to accept him taking control of every aspect of this matchmaking situation.

He vetted and picked the candidates, yes, but ultimately it was up to her and the individual men to see if it was something that could actually work. Gideon's role in this ended the second she and one of the men came to an agreement. She tried very hard not to focus on the way her stomach dropped at that thought.

It didn't matter.

What mattered was his trying to steamroll her on this. She had to have some freedom to figure out if she could stomach the thought of spending her life with the man across the table from her, and she couldn't do that with Gideon standing at her shoulder.

If he did, she couldn't shake the feeling that she'd compare every man to him and it would skew her perception.

Against Gideon Novak, who could compare?

Gideon checked his watch for the third time in as many minutes. Where the hell was she? He turned to look down the street again just as Lucy walked around the corner. She didn't seem particularly concerned to be running late—or happy to see him. He motioned to his watch. "We had an understanding."

"Wrong. You told me something. I disagreed." She crossed her arms over her chest, which drew his attention to her dress.

"What are you wearing?" It was a pale blue lacy thing that gave the illusion of showing more than it actually did. It clung to her body, the gaps in the lace showing a nude lining the exact same shade as her skin. At a glance, she might as well have been naked beneath it.

He loved it.

He fucking hated it.

"A dress." She touched it, a frown drawing a line between her brows. "Don't take that overprotective tone with me, Gideon. It's a good dress."

"It's inappropriate for a first date. He's going to sit

across that table and spend the whole time thinking about fucking you."

Lucy gave him a brilliant grin, her plum-colored lips mirroring the darkness of her hair, which she'd left in waves down around her shoulders. "Then it's doing its job. Now, if you'd please get out of my way, I can take it from here." She strode past him and through the door to the restaurant.

Jealousy flared, hot and poisonous, down the back of his throat. He didn't have a right to it any more now than he had before, but it was a thousand times more powerful now that they'd put sex on the table. Gideon followed her inside and hooked a hand around her elbow, towing her sideways into a small hallway that led to the coat check.

It was dimmer there than in the main entrance— more intimate. He pressed his hands to the wall on either side of her shoulders. "You make me fucking crazy."

"That makes two of us." She poked him in the chest. "You might be calling the shots in some things, but you have to give me enough space to breathe. The compressed timeline is already going to play havoc on my instincts—I don't need your constant presence doing the same."

He'd think about how his presence affected her later. Right now all he could focus on was the first part of the sentence. "If the timeline is too tight, then extend it. The only person who put this deadline in place was *you*."

"And it stands." She lifted her chin. "I'm already

late for this date. I don't want to have this conversation for the seventh time. Just give me some space to breathe."

He pushed off the wall even though it was the last thing he wanted to do. The truth was that he wanted Lucy, and it was fucking up his head space and messing with *his* instincts. He knew better than to push her, but he couldn't help doing it all the same. He wanted her and she wanted him—at least physically.

What if it could be more than just physical?

What if I actually played for keeps?

The thought stopped him in his tracks.

He watched Lucy greet the hostess and follow her deeper into the restaurant, but he couldn't move. This whole time, he had been letting Lucy take the wheel and guide things—at least to some extent. Gideon had handled her so goddamn carefully because he was well aware of the damage Jeff had caused her and he blamed himself, at least a little, because of it. That guilt was the same reason he hadn't pushed her to face the fact that there was more than just friendship between them.

But what if he did?

He couldn't hit this head-on—Lucy would tell him to get lost, and with good reason. She had her eye on the prize and she wouldn't be deterred by an outside force, even if it was Gideon.

If he could get her to change her mind, that would be a different story.

Gideon smiled.

Let her have her date with Mark. The guy was nice

enough, but Gideon fully intended to take her to bed until she was so wrapped up in him that she forgot Mark's fucking name.

A man looked up as Lucy approached the table the hostess had indicated. He was cute in a hipster sort of way, his close-cropped beard and glasses a combination that would have been strange five years before. Now it seemed like everyone had them. The only thing missing was suspenders or a bow tie. Instead, he wore a nice button-up shirt and a pair of slacks. When he rose to pull her chair out for her, she got an eyeful of his broad shoulders and clearly outlined muscles.

Too many muscles. Too much facial hair.

Oh, my God, stop. *What is wrong with me?*

He resumed his place and grinned at her, his teeth white and straight. "Lucy, I presume. Otherwise, this is about to get incredibly awkward."

That startled a laugh out of her. "Yes, I'm Lucy." She extended her hand. "That would make you Mark."

"The very one." He gave her a firm handshake, which she appreciated. Too many men—especially men who worked in corporate jobs—tended to give handshakes like they thought they'd break her. It drove her crazy.

Mark leaned back, his gaze roaming over her face.

Another mark in his favor—not ogling my chest. Lucy gave herself a shake. She had to stop overanalyzing every second of this date. Mark was most definitely not Gideon, and that didn't have to be a tally in the negative column.

It was just hard to focus when she could still smell Gideon's cologne from where he'd pressed her against the wall a few short minutes ago. It wasn't musky and strong like so many men she knew—it was light and clean and reminded her of... She couldn't place it.

Focus.

She gave a polite smile. "Thank you for agreeing to the date."

"When Gideon called me and explained the situation, I'll admit I didn't believe him." The corner of his mouth hitched up. "And then I asked him what was wrong with you."

She tensed and then admonished herself for doing so. He was joking. He didn't really think there was something wrong with her. "As you can see, I'm in possession of all my teeth."

"Not to mention beautiful and successful." Mark's easy smile made the words fact rather than a throwaway compliment. "I've heard of marriages of convenience, but I assumed they were the stuff of fiction. This whole situation is kind of strange."

"I can't argue that." She'd known it was a reach the second she'd called Gideon to put the plan into action. That didn't change the fact that she had no other option. "But I have to ask. If you think it's so strange, why are you here?"

He sighed. "I'm fucking up this small talk, aren't I? That was way too heavy to start in on."

"I don't mind. This isn't exactly the most conventional situation." She appreciated the frankness, even if there was something missing from this interaction that she couldn't quite put her finger on. Mark was attractive—there was no denying that—but... Lucy didn't know. It was off.

"In that case, I agreed to this because I've worked eighty-hour weeks for several years and that won't be stopping anytime soon. I don't know if you've been to a bar lately, but meeting people there is a joke. Everyone is on their phones or with their friends or not interested. Dating apps are even worse, in large part because women have so many nightmare encounters that they're edgy and distant. It makes it hard to really get to know a person when they're sure that you're going to turn on a dime and send a dick pic or freak out because they cancel the date." He shrugged. "It comes down to time. I don't have much of it to meet new people and jump through the hoops of first dates and second dates—and balancing the knife edge of showing that I'm interested without being too god-damn pushy." Mark sighed. "Sorry. It's a sore spot for me."

There was a story there—perhaps several.

The waitress appeared to take their order and then disappeared as quickly. Lucy leaned forward. "Tell me some of your dating stories."

He raised his eyebrows. "If there was a play-book for first dates, I'm one hundred percent sure it wouldn't include recalling dates with other women."

"This is hardly your textbook first date." She smiled. "My little sister runs the gauntlet of online dating, and some of her stories defy belief."

"I wish I could say she was making it all up." Mark

relaxed a little, just the slight loosening in his shoulders. She hadn't realized he was tense until it disappeared. He grinned. "If she's half as beautiful as you, she's seen more than her fair share of crazy on those sites."

"I'm sure she has." Lucy knew all too well that Becka had kept plenty of it back, sharing only the funny stories. That was what gave her away—there only seemed to be funny stories. Nothing dark, nothing worrisome. Nothing indicating she'd met anyone she had more than a passing interest for. "Tell me about them."

He hesitated, surveying her expression, but he must have seen only the interest she felt there because he chuckled. "I'd rather know more about you. Gideon said you're a lawyer."

"I'm a defense attorney." She had to wonder what else Gideon had told Mark and the other men he'd managed to get to agree to meet her. Lucy looked good on paper. She was confident in that, even if she wasn't in any other romantic aspect of her life.

But a lot of women looked good on paper and weren't going about marriage in such an odd way.

Mark leaned forward, expression attentive. "Do you like it? I've been fascinated with the court system since I was a kid. Too many *Law & Order* marathons, you know."

"It's not much like that in real life. There's a truly unglamorous amount of paperwork, and research can be tedious to the point where I've believed more than once that it might kill me." She forced herself to relax a little. "But actually being in court is exhilarating. It's like a game of chess but with higher stakes. I wouldn't trade it for the world."

Their food arrived and the conversation proceeded easily, her work moving into his work as cybersecurity expert, and then sharing a bit about their childhoods. Mark was as nice as he was handsome and Lucy waited through the entire meal for her heartbeat to pick up at the sight of his smile, or for her mind to leapfrog into what it would be like to get naked with him.

There was nothing but a vague pleasant feeling of spending her time in friendly conversation.

No sizzle whatsoever.

She'd asked for that, but she couldn't help comparing him to Gideon. They were different in so many ways. Mark was built lean like a blade—a very well-muscled blade—whereas Gideon looked like a Viking who had decided he'd bring his pillaging to the corporate world. His broad shoulders created a V that tapered down to a narrow waist and there was no way he'd be able to buy a suit off the rack with those powerful thighs.

Mark was attractive but missing a vital component she couldn't put her finger on. A sizzle. A flair. Something that screamed *life*.

I've been reading too many romance novels.

Or maybe she was trying to rationalize something that couldn't be rationalized. She didn't have a connection with Mark. That didn't mean there was something wrong with her—or with him. It just wasn't there.

Mark seemed to notice it, as well. He paid for their meal and sat back with a rueful smile. "This has been fun, but I won't be hearing from you for a second date, will I?"

She liked his frankness. She just wished she felt some kind of pull to the match.

Lucy pressed her lips together. "I can't say for certain."

"I get it." He stood and moved around the table to pull out her chair. "I'd love to get to know you better—as friends."

That was exactly it. She'd enjoyed the dinner. She wouldn't mind spending more time with him. She just couldn't imagine walking down the aisle to him, even in an arranged setting. "Thank you for a wonderful evening."

Mark pressed a quick kiss to her cheek. "You're something special, Lucy Baudin. I hope you get what you're looking for."

"You, too. She's out there. Don't give up yet."

He squeezed her hand. "Good night, Lucy."

She followed him to the door and allowed him to hail her a cab. It was only when she was on her way back to her apartment that she took out her phone and texted Gideon.

Heading home.

I'll be there in thirty.

Her stomach dipped pleasantly and she clenched her thighs together. There was no mistaking what would happen the second he walked through her door, and her skin heated just thinking about it.

She couldn't wait.

CHAPTER EIGHT

GIDEON STORMED THROUGH Lucy's door without knocking. He found her pacing nervously around her living room, practically wringing her hands, and stopped short. "What did he do?"

Her blue eyes went wide. "Excuse me?"

"Mark. Obviously he did something." He sliced his hand through the air to indicate her current state. "Tell me what it was and I'll take care of it." He'd thought Mark was a safe enough bet for the first date, but Gideon shouldn't have taken it for granted. If he'd stayed, he could've stepped in.

Lucy was still blinking at him. She burst out laughing. "Mark was a perfect gentleman."

"You don't have to smooth it over. It's my job to ensure you have solid dates, and if something went wrong, I need to know." He very pointedly ignored the fact that he almost hoped something had ruined the night. Mark was fucking perfect. If he wasn't essentially married to his job, he would have found a girl, gotten married and had a couple of kids by now.

She crossed to him and put a hand on his chest.

"Gideon, stop. Nothing happened. We had a nice conversation and decided to leave things at that."

Leave things at that.

Call him crazy, but he hadn't spent much time dwelling on what would transpire during—and after—the dates. Jealousy reared its ugly head and, even as he fought for control, his words got away from him. "Did he hold your hand?"

She blinked. "I don't know if I'd call it hand-holding—"

"Help you into your coat?" He took a step closer to her, crowding her and unable to stop. "Kiss you?" The thought of Mark in Gideon's current position, leaning down to take Lucy's mouth, made him crazy.

And, damn it, she saw it.

Lucy frowned. "What's wrong?"

"Nothing." *Fucking everything.* He kissed her to keep from saying anything else. Lucy responded instantly, her hands sliding up his chest to loop her arms around his neck, her body melting into his. Her instant yielding should have soothed him.

There were far too many "shoulds" when it came to Lucy Baudin.

He grabbed the hem of her dress and yanked it up as he tumbled her back onto the couch. Gideon had the presence of mind to catch himself so she didn't bear the full brunt of his weight. The break in their kiss gave him the chance to say, "You want this."

"That wasn't a question. But yes." She jerked his shirt out of his pants and went to work on the buttons. "I want to feel you."

He palmed her pussy. "Then feel me." He spread her and pushed a single finger into her. Lucy made one of those sexy fucking whimpers that he couldn't get enough of and yanked his shirt apart, sending the last few buttons flying.

She shoved the shirt down his shoulders. "I need you, Gideon."

He'd give every single dollar he owned to hear her say those words every single day of his life. It wasn't his destiny, but he sure as hell planned to coax her to say it as often as he could during their time together. "Tell me. Guide me."

"I, uh…" Her eyes shut for a split second as he circled her clit with his thumb. When she opened them again, there was new purpose there. "I want you in my mouth."

He froze. "Lucy—" *Fuck me, it's like she pulled a fantasy right out of my goddamn head.* He saw the exact moment her confidence wavered and bit back a curse. He was so determined to give her everything, he was missing signs.

Gideon shifted to sit next to her on the couch. He stopped her from going to the floor with a hand on her shoulder. "Open my pants."

She didn't hesitate. Lucy undid the front of his slacks and withdrew his cock. She stroked him once and then sucked him into her mouth. Gideon had expected some sort of cautious exploration, but she went after it like she was desperate for him.

As desperate for him as he was for her. He pulled her hair back so he could see his cock disappear be-

tween her deep purple lips. A sight he never thought
he'd stand witness to. She opened her eyes and pinned
him with a pleased look, and he couldn't stand it a
second longer. Keeping one hand holding her hair
back, Gideon pulled her dress higher, baring her ass
completely. He squeezed her ass and then ran his
hand down until he could push two fingers into her.

Her eyes went wide then slid shut and she sucked
him harder, faster.

"You like that? You like me playing with your
pretty pussy while you have my cock in your mouth."
It wasn't enough. He was so goddamn desperate for
her that feeling her come on his fingers wouldn't do
a thing to take the edge off. He kept thinking about
her wearing that peekaboo dress across the table from
Mark and laughing at that fucker's jokes, and inspir-
ing a lifetime of filthy fantasies. "Give me a taste."

He grabbed her around the hips and lifted her until
her knees rested on the back of the couch on either
side of his head. Gideon waited for her to start sucking his cock again before he ran his cheek up her thigh
to her pussy. "So beautiful." He licked her, teasing.

Or at least that was the plan.

She was so fucking drenched and tasted so fucking sweet, he lost his precarious hold on his control
and gripped her thighs where they met her hips, raising her to his mouth and spreading her wider in the
same move. She moaned around his cock and the
sound drove him wilder. He licked and sucked her
folds, growling against her hot skin. *I've got my face*

buried in her pussy. Me. *Not that asshole she went to dinner with.*

Lucy reached between his thighs and cupped his balls, slamming him back into the present. She twisted up off his cock enough to say, "You like this?"

"Hell, yes, I do. I like every single thing you do to me." His world narrowed down to the taste of her on his tongue and the feel of her mouth wrapped around him. Her whimpers and moans drove him on, leaching every bit of rational thought from Gideon's head. He needed her to orgasm.

Needed to claim her.

Lucy couldn't tell which way was up—and not just because Gideon had her in the most impossible and erotic position. She'd barely made it home before him and now he had her upside down on the couch with his face buried between her legs as she sucked his cock. She took him deeper. He made her so damn crazy.

For once, she wanted to return the favor.

She shifted her hold of his balls, squeezing lightly. He made a sound she felt all the way to the back of her throat. Nothing mattered but the next slide of his tongue over her clit and the way his fingers dug into her hips, effortlessly holding her in place.

Her orgasm rolled over her from one breath to the next, and she sucked him with unmatched desperation, needing Gideon with her every step of the way. She could *feel* him holding back, trying to outlast her just like he had every other time since they'd started.

If she didn't do something drastic right this second, he'd move them somewhere else and she wouldn't get a chance to finish him like this.

So she played dirty.

Lucy pressed two fingers to his perineum. She'd read in so many books that it was a hot spot for men as well as women, but she'd never had the courage to try.

Gideon's response made the risk worth it many times over.

His back arched and his balls drew up. He hissed out a breath that made her clit tingle. "Fuck. I can't hold out."

She sucked harder, not willing to lift her head to tell him to go for it. She wanted this. She *needed* this.

He hesitated but she circled her middle finger against him and that was all it took. Gideon cursed long and hard against her skin, his grip spasming as his hips bucked up to meet her mouth. She took him as deep as was comfortable and then took him deeper yet. He growled her name as he came. Lucy drank him down, sucking him until he shuddered and gently lowered her to the couch.

Only then did she raise her head.

The look on Gideon's face could only be described as shell-shocked. He opened his mouth, closed it and shook his head. "Come here." Without waiting for a response, he pulled her onto his lap and tucked her against him.

She settled her head onto his shoulder. "That was…"

"Yeah."

How to put it into words? She might not be the more experienced of the two of them, but she wasn't stupid. That hadn't been like the other times. There was no lesson here that Gideon wanted to teach her. He'd come through her door like a jealous boyfriend and then delivered one of the most devastating orgasms of her life and now he was holding her like he...cared.

Of course he cares. He wouldn't have agreed to this if he didn't.

Just because he considered her a friend didn't mean the lines had blurred for him.

She clung to the thought with a stubbornness born of desperation. Lucy had a plan and she knew better by now than to deviate from it. The last time she'd done that, she'd ended up with Jeff, and that entire experience had screwed her up, at least emotionally.

It would have screwed her up professionally, too, if she processed pain in any other way than powering through it out of spite.

Gideon stroked a hand down her back. "Did I hurt you?"

"What? No." She leaned back to look at him. Not as shell-shocked now and the thread of guilt in his dark eyes made her heart hurt.

That was the other reason she couldn't allow the lines between them to blur. Gideon might be someone she cared about, and he might make her body sing, but he would never forgive himself for his role in Jeff's shitty choices.

He'd never be able to look at her without seeing

his friend's ex-fiancée. The one *he'd* had to take aside to let know she was being cheated on—and everyone knew.

Gideon frowned. "Tell me what put that look on your face."

"It's nothing." The very *last* thing she wanted to do was to bring Jeff into the room with them. It was hard enough to banish the memory of him without inviting him in. She almost settled back against Gideon, but the moment had passed. Cuddling and soft words wasn't what this was.

Lucy climbed to her feet on shaking legs. "Give me a few minutes to change."

"Sure."

She retreated to her bedroom and threw on a pair of leggings and one of her knitted sweaters. It felt too comfortable, but as he'd been quick to point out before, this wasn't about seduction. If he wanted her to dress the part, he would request it so he could help her strike the right note. She closed her bedroom door behind her and made her way back into the main room. "I need to go shopping."

"This instant?"

"Don't be silly. Of course not." Her laugh felt forced, mostly because it was. Lucy pulled a newly purchased bottle of wine out of her cabinet and took out two glasses. "Wine?"

"Yeah."

She poured them, still not looking at him. "The date with Mark was nice enough, but I think it's best I meet the rest of your list. That said, I'd like to be as prepared as possible, and I think I mentioned before that I have nothing in the way of seduction clothing."

Gideon snorted. "*You* are seduction enough, Lucy."

He didn't get it. But then, she didn't expect him to. She turned and offered his glass then took a sip of her own. "This may sound strange, but I dress well."

"I noticed."

She ignored that. "Walking out to face a judge or jury—or both—is terrifying. It's exhilarating, too, but taking that first step is like jumping out of a plane and hoping you remembered your parachute. Or, more accurately maybe, it's like stepping onto the dueling grounds and hoping like hell you prepared your weapons and they won't malfunction. I know that sounds dramatic, but it's what it feels like for me. My clothing is both armor and weapons combined. It allows me to take that first step without fear crippling me. I'm going to need that in the bedroom, as well."

There. He might laugh in her face, but at least she was being honest.

Gideon didn't laugh. He studied her with those dark eyes, mulling over what she said and the implications behind it, no doubt. She'd revealed far more of herself in that little tidbit than she had in a long while. Becka knew, of course—she was the one Lucy always dragged along on her shopping trips—but everyone at the office assumed that Lucy was just extremely into fashion and expensive clothing.

Finally he took a drink of his wine. "Do you have free time next weekend?"

Next weekend? It was Thursday. "That's eight days from now."

"I'm more than capable of counting, Lucy." He set the glass down. "Tomorrow, you'll meet Aaron Livingston at the weekly event Roman puts together. I'll be out of town most of next week meeting with several potential fits for a client."

Disappointment soured her stomach but she did her best not to show it. Of course Gideon wasn't exclusively focused on her predicament. From what she remembered, he usually had multiple clients at any given time and there was no reason to expect to be the exception to the rule.

It also meant almost a full week that she wouldn't see him.

No lessons for seven days.

Stop it.

She managed a smile. "I'm free next weekend, aside from a lunch date with Becka."

"We'll go shopping afterward."

Which would give her a chance to imbibe enough alcohol to feel a little fearless at the thought of picking lingerie with Gideon. Lucy wasn't feeling anything resembling fearless at the moment. She swallowed hard. "Okay."

His gaze sharpened on her face. "Tomorrow, wear something appropriate."

Just like that, her nerves disappeared. She drew herself up straight. "Excuse me?"

"You know damn well that you were playing with fire with that dress tonight. I don't know how the fuck Mark kept his hands to himself, but it's a small miracle. No other man would."

Meaning *he* wouldn't, which he'd more than proved by walking through the door and ravishing her right there in her living room. *I did a bit of ravishing myself.*

That wasn't what they were discussing, though, and she didn't appreciate his attitude. The whole point of this was to market her—for lack of a better word— to these men, and he was acting like she'd been out of line. It wasn't a dress she would have worn for work, but it was a far cry from indecent. He was acting like she'd shown up in a minidress with all her goods on display. Lucy glared. "I'll wear whatever I please."

"Wrong. You'll wear something that doesn't project sex."

"You can't be serious." She threw up a hand. "I am more than capable of dressing myself. The lingerie excepting, I don't need or want your opinion."

Gideon set the wineglass down and advanced on her, a forbidding expression on his handsome face. A muscle in his jaw jumped and her stomach leaped in response. He stopped mere inches away. "You wear some shit like you wore tonight and you won't like the results."

She could barely catch her breath with him so close. "What are you going to do, Gideon? Put me over your knee? I don't think so."

"Put you over my knee." His hands came down on either side of her, bracketing her in. Still, he didn't touch her. "Yes, Lucy, that's exactly what I'll do. And after I've spanked your pert little ass red, I'll bend you over the nearest surface and fuck you, date with another man or no."

CHAPTER NINE

"YOU KEEP STARING at the door like that, you're going to start scaring guests away."

Gideon didn't look away from the door. He couldn't relax. Truth be told, he hadn't managed to relax since he'd walked out of Lucy's apartment last night, his words ringing in his ears. They hadn't talked today, other than his text with the address and time to be here and her reply that she would show up.

The question of *how* she would show up was driving him crazy.

He didn't know which outcome he wanted. It would be best if Lucy listened to him and dressed in something that was less of a goddamn tease.

But a part of him wanted her to challenge him—to push him to follow through on his threat. It crossed the line and he knew it, but he was past caring. If Lucy's date with Mark had made anything clear, it was that Gideon couldn't stand the thought of her with another man.

He'd stepped aside for Jeff.

He wasn't about to step aside now. Not again.

None of those other fuckers would care about her the way he would. Their chemistry about set the apartment on fire, and they had a history of genuine caring between them—all of which Lucy said she wanted with whatever husband she picked.

He was the right choice.

He just had to find a way to make Lucy see that.

"Shit," Roman muttered. He stepped to the side, blocking Gideon's view of the door. "Don't make a scene. I invited Aaron here in good faith and you look like you're about to rip someone's head off if they glance at you wrong."

"I'm not going to make a scene." As long as Lucy didn't test him.

He hoped like hell she *did* test him.

"The expression on your face is about to make a liar out of you." Roman slid his hands into his pockets, still looking on edge. "You've already crossed the line with Lucy, haven't you?"

He'd crossed so many lines, he'd lost count. But Roman wasn't bringing this up now just for shits and giggles. Gideon jerked his chin to the side. "Get out of the way."

"No. Scene."

Roman stepped out of the way and Gideon went still. Lucy made her way through the tables toward the VIP section, drawing stares in her wake. She had on a little black dress, but to call it that didn't do it justice. It was so short, it made her already long legs look even longer. It was also strapless, the heart-shaped bodice adding extra curves to her body. Her hair was down in a carefully messy wave that made him think of fucking, and her bloodred mouth only drove the image of hot sex home. She nodded at the guy manning the entrance to the VIP section and then strode straight to Gideon. Closer, he realized there were little beads sewn into the skirt of the dress, giving an extra shift of movement with each step.

Without looking away from Lucy, he handed Roman his beer. "We'll be right back."

Roman cursed. "Whatever you're going to say to her, make it quick. Aaron will be here in thirty."

Thirty minutes was more than enough time to thoroughly make his point. He stood and prowled the last few steps to her. "Follow me. Now."

She wet her lips, her eyes already a little hazy. "And if I don't want to?"

"You do." He turned and stalked back through the VIP section to the hallway that led to bathrooms and two rooms for meetings or private parties. One held a table and chairs and Gideon had used it on more than one occasion. The other had several couches for a more informal touch.

He chose the boardroom.

He opened the door and walked in, Lucy on his heels. She shut the door behind her and glared. "This is ridiculous."

"If you really thought that, you wouldn't be here right now." He grabbed her hips and pulled her against him. She instantly went soft, even as her blue eyes sparked. Gideon dipped his hands beneath her dress and froze. "What the fuck, Lucy?"

"Hmm?"

"You know exactly what I'm talking about." He pulled her dress up, though he didn't need the confirmation. "You come in here with that cock tease of a dress and you aren't wearing panties." Jealousy and desire twisted viciously through him. "Were you going to give Aaron a little show?"

"Oh, please. Give me a little credit." She lifted her chin. "I'm proving a point. You, Gideon Novak, don't get to make my decisions for me. I appreciate your help, but that's where it ends."

She didn't want him.

He was good enough to fuck but not good enough to listen to.

He kept a white-knuckled grip on his temper because having a knock-down, drag-out fight here and now wasn't an option for either of them. Not to mention the fact that he didn't have a *right* to be pissed. She'd laid out the terms that first day, and if he chose to ignore them, that was on him—not on Lucy.

It didn't make how shitty this situation was any easier to swallow.

Gideon stepped back. "The table. Bend over it."

Her eyebrows inched up. "You can't be serious."

"As a fucking heart attack. I told you what would happen if you showed up like that, and you were all too eager to pick up that gauntlet. Choices have consequences, Lucy. This is one of them."

She backed toward the table. One step. Two. "The consequences being that you'll spank my ass red and then fuck me right here."

She wants it.

It didn't soothe his temper. If anything, it ratcheted it up a notch. She might want *it* but she didn't want *him*. "The table."

Lucy turned and, prim as a princess, bent over the table. She seemed to consider and then lowered her chest farther until the top half of her body was flush against the polished wood. The position left her ass in the air and had her skirt riding up so he could *see* how turned on she was by this.

"Which part is getting you?" He stood between her and the door and pushed her dress the last few inches to bare her completely. "The spanking, the defiance, or the fact that we're in an unlocked room where anyone could walk in—including your fucking date?"

She tilted her ass up, just a little, an offer that made his mouth water. But it was her words that sealed her fate. "All of the above."

Fuck me.

He placed a steadying hand on the now-bare small of her back. "Brace yourself." Gideon wasn't into pain play, and he didn't think Lucy craved more than some rough-and-tumble shit, so he delivered a smack to her ass designed to sting without any lasting pain once they were through. Her gasp was almost a moan.

Gideon alternated smacks, giving each of her perfect fucking cheeks three. Enough to redden them as promised, but not more than that. He slipped a hand between her legs and groaned when he found her drenched. "You're going to fucking kill me."

He pulled out his wallet and retrieved the condom he'd stashed there this morning. The crinkle of the wrapper sounded unnatural in the silence of the room, but he could barely hear it over the roaring in his ears. He nudged her legs wider and notched his cock at her entrance. "Next time, obey."

"Not likely." She used her forearm to muffle a moan when he shoved all the way into her.

Damn him to hell, but he loved that she pushed back. She'd been so timid in some ways their first couple of times together, and this defiance was more like the Lucy he used to know. He gripped her hips and pulled almost all the way out before he slammed back into her again. It was good—so fucking good— but it didn't satisfy the feral edge of rage he'd been riding for damn near twenty-four hours.

Gideon pulled out of her and flipped her around. She barely caught herself on his shoulders when he hooked the back of her thighs and lifted her onto the edge of the table. *Better.* But not enough. He yanked down her dress, baring her breasts. "Fucking *hell*, Lucy." He spread her legs wide and shoved into her, his gaze glued to the way her small breasts bounced with each thrust.

It wasn't enough to erase the image of her wearing that dress while chatting up Aaron.

Don't have a right to be jealous.

Don't give a damn if I have a right or not.

"Touch yourself. I want to feel you coming around my cock." He maintained his hold on her hips as she reached between her thighs and stroked her clit. Every thrust ground him against her fingers, the sensation as unbearably erotic as the sight of her touching herself while he fucked her.

Her body tightened around him and she cried out as she came. Gideon tried to hold out, but there was no fighting against the intoxication that was Lucy. He came with a curse. His breath tore from his lungs and he had to keep a death grip on the table to keep from hitting his knees.

It had never been like this for him before. He'd cared about women—even loved them—but the insanity Lucy drew out of him without seeming to try all that hard blew his fucking mind.

He stared into her bright blue eyes and wondered how the hell he was supposed to go back out into that club and pretend like he hadn't just been inside her.

As soon as she had control of her legs again, Lucy climbed off the table and fixed her dress. She could feel Gideon watching her, but she ignored him and pulled a pair of panties she'd stashed earlier out of her purse. She slipped them on and double-checked to make sure she wasn't in danger of indecent exposure. She straightened and froze. "What?"

"You just pulled panties out of your purse."

Heat flared over her exposed skin, but she forced herself to meet his gaze. "Yes, I did."

He didn't move, but he seemed closer. "I don't know whether to be impressed or pissed the fuck off. You baited me on purpose."

"Yes, I did," she repeated. "I was also proving a point. I won't allow you to control every aspect of these dates, but this thing between us is separate from that. For the duration, I'm yours." The words felt funny, as if she was declaring more than she intended, but she couldn't take them back without sounding ridiculous and giving them more weight than they deserved. *It's the truth. We're exclusive.*

But only sexually. There wasn't—couldn't—be anything more between them. She had her plan and Gideon hadn't held down a relationship for longer than two weeks the entire six years she'd known him. Even if Lucy was willing to bend on this—and she couldn't afford to be—Gideon would lose interest right around the time she needed him the most.

There would be no change of plans. They might fit better sexually than she could have dreamed, but that didn't mean anything in the grand scheme of things. She'd let good chemistry sideline her before—or what she'd *thought* was good chemistry. She wouldn't do it again, even if this felt as different from that as night to day.

"Mine for the duration." It sounded funny coming from him, too. Or maybe those were the butterflies erupting in her stomach.

She couldn't manage a smile, so she nodded. "Now, can we please go out there and meet this guy? Not to mention I haven't seen Roman in years and you hustled me past him so fast, I didn't even get to say hello." As ridiculous as it was, the thing she'd ended up missing most about being with Jeff was his friends.

Gideon had disappeared the second she'd broken up with Jeff and the rest of that group hadn't put up more than a token effort to keep in touch. To be fair, she hadn't tried, either. It was hard to look them in the face and know that they'd all had at least some idea of Jeff's extracurricular activities well before she had.

It doesn't matter anymore. I won't let *it matter.*

She didn't wait for Gideon to answer before she marched to the door and back the way they'd come. There was no helping her flushed cheeks, but she'd purposefully styled her hair a little wild in the event that Gideon was good on his threats. She might not be willing to admit it aloud—to him—but she was so very glad he had. The first two times with him had been wonderful beyond measure, but last night and tonight felt like the *real* Gideon. The man beneath the carefully controlled exterior.

She wanted more.

In fact, the last thing she wanted to do was exactly what she was doing—walking back into the VIP section. Much more enjoyable to slip out the back door with Gideon and go to one of their apartments to relieve the tension that only continued to rise the longer they were sleeping together.

It wasn't an option.

She ignored the way Roman glanced over her shoulder to where Gideon had no doubt just stepped into the room, speculation in his hazel eyes. Lucy gave him a big smile. "Roman, how have you been?"

"Well. Really well." He took her hand and stepped a little too close to be comfortable, his handsome face severe. She tensed and his next words did nothing to dispel the feeling. He kept his tone barely above a whisper. "I'm so sorry. If I'd have known he was going to be here, I would have passed on the information."

It took her pleasure-drugged brain several seconds to catch up. He wasn't talking about Aaron.

He was talking about Jeff.

She turned horror-movie slow toward the sound of a painfully familiar laugh. Jeff sat next to a pretty redhead and the entirety of his attention appeared to be on her. Lucy hadn't seen him in nearly two years—not since she'd thrown every single item he'd owned out their second-story apartment window—and she hated that he looked good. There was no extra weight, no puffy face that would indicate alcoholism, no slovenly appearance.

In fact, Jeff looked better than ever.

Lucy, no doubt, looked like she'd just been up to illicit activities in the back room—because she had been.

She looked up at Roman and didn't know what she was supposed to say or do. Jeff hadn't seen her yet, but it was just a matter of time before he did. She wasn't ready. She'd fought long and hard to get past the damage he'd done to her, but occupying the same space as him was enough to bring the truth flashing in front of her eyes.

She was still making her choices because of Jeff.

A hand pressed against the small of her back and Gideon's crisp scent wrapped around her. He stepped into view, blocking Jeff from her sight—or her from

Jeff's. If Lucy felt off center, Gideon looked ready to shoot fire out of his eyes at Roman.

"Hey, man, like I just told Lucy—I didn't know he'd be here or I'd have let *you* know. He just showed up."

She pressed a hand to her chest. *I can't breathe.* An invisible band closed around her, tightening with each exhalation until black dots danced across her vision. Two years later and he still had so much power over her. She hated it. She hated *him*.

"Holy shit. Look what the cat dragged in." Jeff's voice came from directly behind Gideon.

Roman and Gideon looked at her, identical expressions on their faces. Asking how she wanted to handle this. If Lucy so much as blinked, she had a feeling Gideon would sweep her out of there without hesitation—and Roman would block Jeff from following if he tried.

But that was what she was so very tired of—letting Jeff's bullshit dictate how she handled any given situation.

Lucy lifted her chin, giving a slight nod. Gideon frowned, but he and Roman parted, taking up positions facing Jeff and only leaving a small sliver of a gap between them—standing sentry between her and her ex.

For all his pleased tone, Jeff's blue eyes were cold. The redhead on his arm didn't seem particularly happy, either, and Lucy spent a worthless few seconds wondering what he'd told her about this encounter. It didn't matter. *Jeff* didn't matter.

Or at least, he shouldn't.

She put all of her not inconsiderable willpower into appearing surprised. "Jeff. I had no idea you came here anymore."

"Not often." The look he shot the men in front of her was downright lethal.

Apparently his friendship with them hadn't lasted any longer than hers had. Lucy had known that about Gideon, but it comforted her to think of Jeff feeling just as abandoned as she had, even on that small scale.

He didn't jump in to say anything else, so she went with the first thing that popped into her mind. "You look well." *Meaningless chitchat.*

"I am well. Better than ever, really." His gaze jumped between her and Roman and Gideon. "You three look cozy." There was no mistaking the undertone of the statement. *Which one are you fucking?*

Looking too much into this. Get hold of yourself.

Gideon surprised her by taking a step back and pressing his hand to the small of her back. "We were just leaving."

At that, Jeff's mask slipped. His brows dropped, the first indication of what had always turned into a huge fight—one she had no chance of winning. Jeff seemed to take in her dress for the first time, his gaze leisurely raking over her body, pausing at her breasts and her bruised-feeling lips. "You and Gideon, huh? You took a pretty high-and-mighty stance with me when you broke off our engagement, and now you're fucking my best friend. Classy, Lucy, really classy."

No matter how much she told herself that his opinion didn't matter, it still felt like he'd sucker punched her. "It's not like that."

"It's exactly like that." Gideon spoke over her. He slipped his arm around her waist, pulling her against his side. "You fucked up and lost her. That's not on anyone but you, so don't start spouting that bullshit." He looked down at her, his expression hard. "You ready to go?"

"Please." She didn't want to stand there any longer than strictly necessary. The fact she hadn't sprinted for the exit was a win, as far as Lucy was concerned. Asking anything more of herself was out of the question.

Gideon nodded and glanced at Roman. "Next time."

"For sure."

He didn't give her a chance to say anything further before he steered them out of the VIP section and through to the front door. But what else was there to say? Anything she could come up with on that short walk sounded defensive, as if they'd done something wrong.

Well, I am sleeping with him.

But not dating him. Even if I was—it's been two years.

Two incredibly long and lonely years.

Lucy couldn't stop her shoulders from sagging the second they turned the corner away from the club. "That was terrible."

"I'm sorry, Lucy." His hand on her hip tensed, as if he wasn't sure whether he should pull her closer or release her. "I didn't know he'd show up. If I'd thought for a second it was a possibility, I wouldn't have taken you there."

"It's fine." It wasn't, but she should be stronger than this. Being brought to her knees emotionally just from running into her ex was inexcusably weak.

It wasn't even *Jeff* that was the problem. It was the fact that with one look, one carefully worded sentence, he could trigger every insecurity she fought so hard to banish. *He* wasn't the issue.

She was.

"It's not fine." Gideon stepped to the curb and flagged down a cab. "Your place or mine?"

If she let him, he'd talk through this with her. Gideon might be gloriously rough around the edges with a temper that would do a Viking proud, but he never failed to be careful around her.

Except when she pushed him hard enough that he forgot he was supposed to handle her with kid gloves.

There'd be no pushing him tonight. He'd pour her a glass of something alcoholic, sit her down and demand nothing but perfect honesty about how screwed up she was in her head. He'd pull out her issues and do his damnedest to fix them. Or, worse in some ways, he'd be wonderfully understanding and tell her it was okay.

She just...couldn't.

So incredibly weak.

Lucy didn't look at him as he pulled open the back door of the cab. "If it's all the same, I'd like to go home alone."

Gideon tensed and, out of the corner of her eye, she watched him fight an internal battle. Finally he shook his head. "If that's what you want."

It's not. "It is." Maybe if she got some distance, she could get her head on straight again. It was so hard to think with Gideon so close, his presence overwhelming her in every way. She couldn't handle it.

Lucy just needed time.

He stepped back, releasing her from her internal debate over whether she'd like him to force the issue or not. "Text me when you get back to your place."

"I will."

He waited until she slipped into the cab to say, "See you Saturday, Lucy."

CHAPTER TEN

GIDEON MADE IT until Wednesday. Three long-ass days in Seattle while he met with the first of the prospective fits he had for one of his clients. The guy was an advertising genius, though he was a little too free spirit for Gideon's straight-edged client. It might not be a deal-breaker, but it was something to take into account.

He shrugged out of his suit jacket and stared at his phone. Lucy hadn't called and she hadn't texted after the one letting him know that she was safely home. He had left New York with every intention of giving her the space she obviously wanted, but three days out of town had given him clarity.

She was running scared.

Seeing Jeff had screwed her up, and Gideon understood that. She hadn't wanted to further break herself open for *him*, and he respected that.

But she was closing him out.

He tossed his jacket on the bed and dialed her before he could think of all the reasons it was a bad idea. She hadn't brought him into this to work her shit out—she just wanted a husband and sex lessons. *Too damn bad. She signed up for* me—*and that's what she's going to get.*

"Lucy Baudin," she answered.

"Hey."

A long pause. "Hello, Gideon."

He hated the awkwardness seeping into this conversation before they'd exchanged half a dozen words. If he let it, it would become downright painful. Unacceptable. Gideon had never met a challenge he wasn't willing to go around, over or through, and a simple conversation wouldn't be the thing that stopped him in his tracks. "How's your week going?"

"Long, and it's only Wednesday. One of my clients is being difficult, and I'm having to work around her just to help her, which makes everything twice as challenging."

"You'll figure it out."

"I always do."

He dropped into the chair next to the desk. This wasn't working. Lucy held herself distant—polite—but there was none of the intimacy they'd started building. He hadn't even realized it was happening until that softness disappeared. *One way to put them back on solid ground.* "You home?"

"Yes. Hanging out with Garfunkel and wading through some old accounts for my current case—and drinking wine. This kind of investigating always requires wine."

"Naturally." He settled back into the chair and kicked off his shoes. "What are you wearing?"

Her surprised laugh was music to his ears. "Phone sex? Really, Gideon? Isn't that a bit juvenile?"

"We already had this discussion."

The amusement faded from her voice. "I suppose we did."

"On second thought, don't tell me what you're wearing. Show me. You by your computer?"

"Always."

"Give me two seconds." He grabbed his laptop and brought it online. A few button pushes later and he had a video call going through to Lucy.

She answered, looking unsure. "I guess I can hang up now."

"Yeah." He set down the phone and shifted to get comfortable. She looked good. She sat on her couch in the middle of several stacks of files, one housing her cat, and wore a fitted tank top and sleep shorts. Her shirt was thin enough that he could see the faintest outline of her nipples through the white fabric, and her sleep shorts gapped around her upper thighs in a way that made his mouth water. "Hey."

"Hey." She spoke just as softly. "Nice shirt."

"Thanks." He pulled his tie loose and tossed it onto the bed. "Have to look the part, though this guy isn't formal at all. He's a big fan of flannel, hair gel and skinny jeans."

She laughed softly. "Poor Gideon. You'd look downright fetching in flannel, but I like you without a beard. I'll hold out judgment on the skinny jeans, though they present some interesting possibilities."

His cock went rock-hard at the desire warming her

expression, but he kept his tone light. "I'll be sure to pick up something while I'm here."

"You don't have to."

"I know." But he wanted to show her that he valued her opinions. Gideon had never owned a piece of flannel clothing in his life, but if Lucy thought she'd like the look, he'd give it a shot. He noted the hesitance in her body language and refocused. "You always lounge in that sort of thing?" He waved to her clothing.

"This? Yes, I guess so." She shrugged. "It's comfortable."

"It's sexy as hell." He set his computer on the desk and leaned forward. "Let those thin little straps slide off your shoulders. I want to see you."

"Right now?" She looked around as if expecting him to jump out of a closet and tell her it was a joke. Lucy tucked a strand of her dark hair behind her ear. "I don't know if I'm ready for this."

She might very well not be, but if she didn't want to talk to him, then he'd keep them in the roles she'd set out for them. "Close your eyes." He waited for her to obey. "How do you feel when you take everything you think you *should* be feeling out of the equation?"

"Warm. Turned on." She hesitated. "A little intimidated. It's different when you're here with me, touching me. There's no room for being self-conscious."

"I've been thinking about you for five long-ass days and thinking about all the things I want to do to you when we're alone again."

"Things…" She licked her lips, one of her tells. Oh,

yeah, she liked this when she stopped remembering the reasons she shouldn't.

He kept going, pitching his voice low and intimate. "That lingerie shopping date we have? I've been thinking about sitting there and watching you come out of that room wearing one of those getups. Maybe you'll tease me, make me wait for it."

"Like this." She used a single finger to inch first one strap off her shoulder and then the other. The upper curve of her breasts caught the fitted fabric and he had to bite back a curse.

"Exactly like that. You know how bad I want it— want you—but I think you've got a little sadist in you because you like pushing my buttons. Making me crazy."

"I do." Her lips quirked up in a smile. "You're so controlled all the time. I like seeing what happens when the leash snaps."

He liked that she liked it. Gideon spent most of his days aware of how he presented himself and how everything from his tone to his appearance to his walk could be interpreted by clients and prospectives alike. He never let himself relax, because even in a social setting, there was no telling who was around.

There wasn't anyone around now—no one but him and Lucy.

"If I was there, I'd tug that top of yours a little lower. Yeah, like that." He watched, mouth dry, as she inched it down, stopping just below her nipples and then baring her breasts completely. "Exactly like that."

"This feels so dirty." She opened her eyes and pressed her lips together. "Would you...?"

"Tell me what you want and it's yours." He craved her words as much as he craved her touch. One was out of the question for the next few days—the other she gave him after the briefest hesitation.

"Unbutton your shirt." She leaned forward, the move making her breasts bounce a little. "I love your shoulders. Your suits have this way of masking how muscled they are, and seeing you shirtless makes me feel like it's my birthday."

He straightened so he could slip his shirt off and drop it on the floor. They stared at each other for a few seconds, Gideon drinking in the sight of her while she appeared to give him the same treatment. He spoke the second he saw doubt start creeping into her blue eyes. "Your breasts look like they ache. Palm them for me."

She instantly obeyed and then took it a step further and lightly pinched her nipples. This time he couldn't hold back his low curse. "Yeah, just like that."

"Are you...? Will you...?"

He instantly understood what she meant. "You want my cock?"

"Yes. Show me." She writhed a little, her hands moving with more purpose on her breasts.

He tilted his computer screen so the camera took in his lower half. He moved slowly, teasing her, and undid his slacks to withdraw his cock. He gave himself a long stroke and was rewarded with Lucy's moan. "You like that."

"I like that a lot."

"Take off your shorts. I want to see you stroking that pretty pussy until you come for me."

She barely hesitated this time before she released her breasts and lifted her hips to slide the shorts off.

He stroked himself again idly. "Spread your legs—yes, like that. Show me how you like it the same way you did that first time."

She slipped her hand between her thighs, parting her folds to draw a single finger over her clit. It was the single most devastating thing he'd ever seen.

Gideon watched avidly, taking in every detail and imprinting it into his memory. It was shitty not being able to be there and touch her, but it allowed him a perfect view and the distance to appreciate it in a new way.

Lucy was fucking magnificent.

After the first halting touches, she gave herself over to her pleasure—to both their pleasure—and stroked faster. Her head fell back against the couch and her body bowed as she pushed two fingers into her pussy. "I wish you were here."

"Saturday. I'll make it worth the wait."

"I don't know if anything is worth the wait." Her words were breathy and her breasts quivered with each exhalation. She managed to open her eyes. "I'm close, Gideon. Are you close?"

He'd been teetering on the edge the second she'd taken off her shorts, holding on through sheer force of will. "I'm close." He spoke through gritted teeth. Pressure built in his spine and his balls drew up, his cock swelling at the sight of her stroking herself to orgasm.

Lucy let her head hit the back of the couch again, but she kept her eyes open and on him as she fucked herself with her fingers. Her breath turned even choppier.

"Next time..." He had to stop and restart the sentence when she gasped. "Next time, you'll bring out that toy of yours. I want to see it sliding into you, vibrating and making you crazy."

"*You* make me crazy." Her back arched and every line of her body stood out as she came with his name on her lips.

Gideon couldn't hold on after that. He stroked faster, harder. She lifted her head in time to see him come in several spurts onto his stomach. He stared down at it marking his body and wondered when the hell his life had taken a hard right turn. A month ago he would have laughed someone out of the room for suggesting he'd be participating in a video call with mutual masturbation, let alone with Lucy Baudin.

And yet...here they were.

He reached down to grab his shirt and wipe himself off, and checked on her. Lucy had slid down to lie on the couch, and she watched him with a sleepy smile. "You've got that look on your face."

Her smile widened. "What look is that?"

"One that says you're thinking filthy thoughts." He liked that look. A lot.

She swept her hair off one shoulder and it pooled around her head on the cushion. "That's because I *am* thinking filthy thoughts." She bit her lip and then rushed on. "What time do you fly in Friday?"

"Our appointment is..." He stopped short. A slow tendril of pleasure that had nothing to do with sex rolled through him. "You want to see me Friday night."

"If that's okay. I know you'll be tired."

"It would take a whole hell of a lot more than a few hours' plane ride to make me too tired to see you. Though I don't fly in until after eleven."

She smiled. "I'll leave the key with the doorman."

Fuck yes. He damn well knew he was reading more into that choice than he should be, but it was hard not to. That simple sentence, more than anything else they'd done to this point, signaled her trust in him. "I'll stop by my place to drop my shit and then I'll be there."

"Perfect." She stretched. "Thank you for this, Gideon. All of it."

Strangely enough, he felt like *he* should be thanking *her.* He'd spent a long time just going through the motions and, for better or worse, Lucy had woken him up. He wanted to keep talking to her, but a quick glance at his phone showed that it was well past ten on the East Coast. "Don't let those files keep you up too late."

"I think I'm done for the night." She pulled on her shorts and resumed her comfortable-looking spot. "I had this really gorgeous guy call and talk me to orgasm just now, and I'm feeling all loose and relaxed, so I'm going to jump in the shower and head to bed to read for a bit. One of my favorite authors has a book out and I've been dying to start it."

I wish I was there. He didn't say it again. It was one thing to put those words out there when talking about sex—it was entirely another to do it now that the desire had cooled.

It was the truth, though.

He wanted to be there to pull her into a relaxing shower, to exchange small talk about nothing important while they got ready for bed, to settle in while she read her book and he finished answering the last few emails of the day. Gideon wanted it so bad, he could barely breathe past the need.

He couldn't say any of that now without scaring the shit out of Lucy.

But he managed a smile. "You'll have to tell me about it when I see you."

Lucy gave him a strange look. "You want to hear about my book?"

"Sure." If only because it was something she was interested in and obviously passionate about—and had been for as long as he'd known her, though she used to hide them under a pillow when he and Jeff would walk into the room. Jeff had always made snide comments that he covered up as joking, and Gideon should have paid more attention to Lucy's reaction to those comments. He'd known his friend was a jackass, but he hadn't realized the depth of the damage Jeff was dealing her.

"That's nice of you to say, but we really don't have to talk about my romance novel addiction."

Damn it, she was doing it again. He leaned forward until his face filled the video screen. "I wouldn't ask if I didn't want to know. Nothing but honesty between us, remember? It interests you, so I want to know more. It's as simple as that."

She opened her mouth, seemed to reconsider arguing with him and shut it. "That makes sense."

"Because it's the truth." He stomped down on his anger. Hard. It wasn't directed at Lucy, and it wasn't fair to take his fury at himself and Jeff out on *her*. Gideon kept his tone low and even. "Enjoy the rest of your night, Lucy."

"You, too." She looked away and then back at the camera. "If you change your mind about Friday, I'll understand."

God, she was fucking killing him. "I'll see you Friday night."

CHAPTER ELEVEN

LUCY HAD EVERY intention of staying awake to greet Gideon. If nothing else, she was sure nerves would keep her alert until he arrived. She hadn't counted on the long day.

It had started at 5:00 a.m. when she'd gotten a call from the office that there was a new client on retainer and that Lucy was needed at the woman's home immediately. Things had only gone downhill from there. The client—accused of money laundering—was as high maintenance as they came, so Lucy'd had her work cut out for her.

Throw in the partners dragging her into a boardroom for a progress report the second she'd set foot in the office, and she was exhausted. Her other clients couldn't be shoved to the back burner, no matter how important the new one was, so she'd worked late to ensure she was ready for court on Monday.

All of it had added up to an exhaustion she couldn't fight, no matter how entertaining the newest episode of her favorite medical drama. Her blinks became longer and longer, and the next thing she knew, she roused to the feeling of strong hands sliding up her thighs.

That alone should have scared the crap out of her, but Gideon's scent wrapped around her, setting her at ease even before she was fully awake. She blinked down at him as he hooked his arms beneath her and lifted her off the couch. "I can walk."

"Humor me." He strode down her hallway without turning on any lights and toed open the door to her bedroom. She hadn't bothered leaving lights on in her room and Lucy regretted that when Gideon set her on the bed and stripped in quick, efficient movements. She moved to do the same, but he beat her there, carefully pulling her oversize T-shirt off. Since Lucy had been expecting him, she hadn't worn anything else.

His quick intake of breath was a reward in and of itself. She ran her hand up his chest. "Hey."

"Hey." He guided her to lie on the bed, quickly put on a condom and covered her with his body. "You looked comfortable on the couch."

"I was." She wrapped her legs around his waist and arched up to kiss his throat. "This is better."

"Agreed." He laced his fingers through her hair and guided her mouth to his, kissing her lazily, as if he had no idea of the need already building in her core. Need that only Gideon seemed to be able to sate. He took his time reacquainting himself with her mouth before he moved to her neck and collarbone. "I was going to wake you up in a very specific way."

"Mmm." She reached between them to stroke him.

"This is better." She notched his cock at her entrance. "I need you."

He slid into her in a single move and kissed her again with them sealed as closely as two people could be. Pressure built between them, but his big body kept Lucy pinned in place so she couldn't do anything more than shake. Even that tiny movement ratcheted up her desire until she couldn't stop a whimper of need from escaping. "Gideon, stop teasing me."

"I know I'm not supposed to say it, but I missed the fuck out of you this week."

Her breath got tangled somewhere between her lungs and throat. The words she was supposed to say lingered on the wrong side of her lips. *That's not what we are.* It might be the correct thing to say, but it wasn't the *right* thing to say—or the truth. "I missed you, too."

He finally moved, rocking against her. It wasn't enough, but that made it all the hotter. She did her best to arch, fighting against the weight of his body and loving every second of it. "More."

"Demanding," he murmured against her lips. "I waited seven fucking days to be inside you again, and I'm going to take my time and enjoy it." He dragged his mouth down her throat, his whiskers rasping against her sensitized skin. "I like having you like this."

"Furious?"

He chuckled, the low sound vibrating through her. "Needy. Wanting. As close as you'll ever come to begging."

"Would begging make a difference?"

His lips brushed the shell of her ear. "No."

Lucy shivered, her breath releasing in a sob. It felt too good and she needed more. But he was right—she loved every second of this. Their bodies slicked with sweat as he kept up those slight rocking movements, every single one inching her closer to oblivion. His pelvis created delicious friction against her clit, and she found herself talking without having any intention of doing so. "That feels so good, Gideon. Don't stop. Never stop." She dug her fingers into his ass, loving the way he growled against her neck. "I love this."

"I know." He slipped one arm beneath the small of her back and the other up her spine to cup her head. She'd thought they were as close as two people could be. He proved her wrong. Lucy slid her feet down to hook around his calves, grinding against him. Gideon kissed her as if he couldn't help himself. His tongue stroked hers, plunging deep, the way she wanted him to elsewhere. Right when she caught his rhythm, he withdrew and then stroked deep again, starting the process over. It made her crazy—crazier.

He knew. He always seemed to know exactly how close to the edge she was.

Gideon began to move. His hips mirrored the movements his tongue had made, stroking deep and then withdrawing before slamming home again.

Lucy couldn't think, couldn't move, couldn't even breathe. Her entire existence boiled down to the places Gideon touched her and his cock between her thighs. Pressure wound tighter and tighter, turning her into a wild creature with no thought but her own pending orgasm.

It hit her like a freight train and she let loose a keening cry that didn't sound human to her ears. Lucy couldn't do more than cling to Gideon as his strokes became more and more ragged and rough until he orgasmed with a curse. He dropped slightly to the side of her, but shifted to pull her leg up and over his hip, keeping them close.

She tried to get her racing heart under control. "That was some wake-up."

"It's good to see you, Lucy." Such a polite thing to say considering their current position.

I think I prefer hearing that you missed me.

With the post-orgasm bliss numbing her common sense, she couldn't quite shut that thought down. She crossed the line they'd drawn in the sand. "Stay."

"What?"

She ran her hand up his arm. "Stay. It's almost morning and there's no point in you cabbing back to your place and turning around to do it again in a few hours. Just...stay here with me."

"You sure that's what you want?" There wasn't a single thing in his voice to indicate what *he* wanted.

"Yes. If you want to, of course." *Maybe I misheard him and I'm wrong about this entire situation.*

Gideon delivered a devastating kiss and climbed off the bed. "Give me a few."

"Sure." She waited for him to walk into her bathroom and shut the door before she relaxed and sighed, staring at the ceiling. *What am I doing?*

He was back before she could muster the energy to second-guess herself. Gideon pulled down the comforter and waited for her to climb beneath it before he followed suit. She tensed, waiting for the inevitable awkwardness, but he just slipped in behind her and guided her so he could spoon her. He kissed the back of her neck. "Sleep."

Lucy thought it impossible, but the heat of him and the feel of safety being tucked against his big body lulled her circling thoughts to a standstill. Between one breath and the next, she slipped into a deep sleep.

Gideon woke to the smell of bacon. For one disorientating moment he didn't know where he was, but then the events of the night came rushing back to him. Lucy. Her apartment. Sleeping here. He sat up and scrubbed a hand over his face. *I told her I missed her and then I stayed the night.* For all his intentions of respecting *her* intentions, Gideon was doing a piss-poor job of following through.

Worse, he'd been so focused on himself, he hadn't stopped to ask her how she was doing after seeing Jeff again—a week ago. *Fuck me.* He stopped in the bathroom to brush his teeth as best he could with a finger and pulled on his pants.

He found Lucy in the kitchen, opening a series of take-out containers. She looked fresh and happy, her hair back in a low-key ponytail, and wore black leggings and a blue sweater that matched her eyes. She smiled when she saw him. "Morning."

"Morning." He took in the spread. "What's all this?"

"I think we can both agree that cooking isn't one of my strengths, so I popped out and grabbed something edible." She grabbed two mugs from one of her cabinets. "Coffee, however, I am capable of throwing together."

"Survival skill."

"Exactly." She passed him a full cup and her expression turned serious. "Can we have today?"

Gideon took a careful drink of the scalding liquid and contemplated her. For all that she appeared relaxed on the surface, there was an underlying tension there. "And after today?"

"I figure we're due a conversation, but we have plans today and I don't want to ruin them by talking this to death. I'm happy and I want to hold on to that."

Meaning that this talk wouldn't make her feel happy—or him, for that matter. Gideon already knew what was coming. He'd muddied the waters by showing up last night, and taken it a step further by staying and holding her while they'd slept. They hadn't talked about lessons after that first time they'd had sex, which was supposed to be the whole purpose of this exercise. She'd also been on exactly one date.

He had to fix that.

He would rather chew off his own arm than set her up on any more dates, but that was what he'd given his word he'd do. Lucy trusted him and he couldn't betray that trust. *Not again.*

Gideon forced an easy smile onto his face. "Sure, we can have today." He didn't want to have that talk any more than she appeared to want it, so he wasn't going to worry about a few hours spent without over-thinking things. "I thought you had lunch with your sister?"

"She got called in to cover a class and had to cancel." Lucy gave him a small smile. "I know we had planned for this afternoon, but I'm free all day if you are."

"I'm free." Gideon had been looking forward to this date all damn week, so he hadn't put anything else on his schedule.

Because that was exactly what this was, even if Lucy didn't realize it. A date.

Maybe she does realize it and that's why she's asking to shelve the conversation we obviously need to have until tonight.

She gave him a sunny smile. "Good. In that case, eat up while I jump in the shower." She pushed the food toward him, grabbed her mug and strolled out of the kitchen.

He spent half a second considering following her and making the shower one to remember, but if Gideon read the signs correctly, Lucy needed time. It had been that way with them from the start of this—she'd take a step forward and need time to acclimate. He could respect that. He *would* respect that. If he pushed too hard, too fast, she'd bolt, and this time he'd never hear from her again. It wasn't a risk he was willing to take, especially now when it felt like they were close to something that could actually be real.

If she'd take that leap of faith with him.

He ate quickly and cleaned up the containers.

By that time, the shower had turned off, so Gideon grabbed the bag he'd brought in the night before and hauled it into her room.

Lucy glanced over from where she'd just walked through the bathroom door. She had a fluffy towel wrapped around her, and though it hid her curves, the exposed skin of her shoulders and calves had him craving the feel of her. She narrowed her eyes. "You didn't go home last night, did you?"

There was no use in denying it. "Nope." He'd wanted to see her—had *needed* to see her—and the extra forty minutes it would have taken were forty minutes too many. He nodded at the bathroom door. "Mind if I use your shower?"

"Of course not. Go for it."

He didn't need to be told twice. Gideon showered quickly, pausing long enough to wish he had time to shave, but he wasn't likely to see anyone he knew professionally today. He paused in front of his suitcase. Lucy had been wearing casual clothes earlier, and it might make her uncomfortable if he used his last suit. The other option wasn't as comfortable for *him*, but he'd make do.

He had promised her, after all.

When he walked out of the bathroom, she froze. "You…" She gave herself a shake. "Sorry, I don't think I've ever seen you rumpled-looking before— not even in college."

He glanced down at his designer jeans and the flannel shirt he'd thrown over a white T-shirt. "I'm not rumpled."

"You are most definitely rumpled." She moved closer, taking him in as a small smile pulled at the edges of her lips. "You look like you should be standing on a porch on some mountainside, a steaming cup of coffee in hand while you contemplate whatever it is that lumberjacks contemplate." She ran her hands up his chest and over his shoulders. "I like it."

"Rumpled suits me."

"You don't have to sound so cranky when you say it." She smoothed down his shirt, actually leaning forward a few inches before she seemed to remember herself and took several steps back. "I'm ready when you are."

She wore a different variation of what she'd had on earlier: dark leggings, a long black T-shirt and a slouchy knitted cardigan thing. Her pants were tucked into a sleek pair of knee-high boots. *Rumpled* was not a word he'd use to describe her, but with her hair falling in careless waves to her shoulders, she looked relaxed. Almost peaceful.

He liked it.

Gideon pulled on his shoes and then they headed down to the street. Lucy paused on the sidewalk. "It's such a nice day."

He could pick up a clue as obvious as that one. "We could walk. It's only a handful of blocks."

"Are you sure? We didn't really talk about what your other plans are for the day and—"

"There are no other plans." He cut in before she could talk herself out of the whole day. "I worked all week. I cleared today for you, Lucy."

"Oh. Well…oh." She managed to look everywhere but at him. "I'm sorry—is this weird? It didn't feel all that strange when I suggested it earlier, but I think common sense has taken hold."

"More like nerves." He pressed his hand to the small of her back. "Walk with me, Lucy. What's the harm that could come of it?"

CHAPTER TWELVE

WHAT'S THE HARM that could come of it?

Lucy forced herself to look at Gideon. His expression was as open as she'd ever seen it, inviting her to take this first step with him. First step into *what*, though? It had been an off-the-cuff thing to tell him that she wanted today, but through her shower and then his, the importance of that statement—this plan—had grown to epic proportions.

It felt like a date.

Except she wasn't supposed to be dating Gideon. She was supposed to be dating the men Gideon set her up with.

He didn't look particularly concerned that they had left the boundary of their agreed-upon relationship in the rearview. He offered his arm, the old-world gesture so very Gideon.

She slipped her hand onto his arm and fell into step with him as if it was the most natural thing in the world. Maybe it was. She didn't know anymore. These days, it felt like up was down and down was up, and Lucy was bouncing somewhere in the middle.

"How was your trip? Other than having to fend off a city full of free spirits." She injected false sympathy into her tone. "You poor thing."

Gideon shook his head. "You mock me while you were here, safe in New York. The people on that coast aren't anything like *our* people. They chat." He gave a mock shudder. "You wouldn't last two days."

"On the contrary, I'm not nearly as cranky and antisocial as you are. I'd be fine."

"There is that." He pulled her to a stop at the curb as cars whizzed past. "It was a productive trip. One of my prospective fits looks like she'll work out, and I managed to source a secondary backup in Portland. Those two cities are filled to the brim with tech geniuses, so if I can lure either woman over here, they'll have jobs waiting."

A barb of something like jealousy embedded itself in Lucy's throat. He'd spent a full week in endless meetings between Seattle and Portland, and a few of the people he'd met with had been women. It shouldn't matter. Lucy had no claim on Gideon. Not really. They might be exclusive for the time being, but there was a looming expiration date. He could have plans to hook up with one of those women—or both—and Lucy didn't have the right to be upset about it.

That didn't change the fact that her chest ached at the very thought.

"Maisey Graham has been married to her high school sweetheart since the month after graduation, and he owns his own business, so relocation isn't out of the question." Gideon spoke low enough that she had to lean in to hear his words, very carefully not looking at him. "Jericha Hurley will be eighteen in two months, though she's damn near a certified genius and she's got her pick of companies vying for her attention."

He knew.

The ache in her chest got worse. She managed to breathe past it—barely. "It's none of my business."

"Honesty, Lucy."

She didn't want to be honest. She wanted to shove her head in the sand. They crossed the road and kept going down the block. She tried to pinpoint exactly what the problem was. *Easy enough—I'm jealous of the thought of Gideon spending time with other women.* Not just spending time, though. Having long meetings, likely alone, on the other side of the country. "It's not that I think you'd do that after you told me we were exclusive."

"The fear is there all the same." He set his free hand over hers and squeezed. "That's not something you just get over."

Maybe she would have. If she'd put half the effort into dating that she'd put into her career, she'd have worked through what was apparently a hair trigger. *Or maybe it wouldn't have mattered.* There was no way to tell, and it was a moot point. "We have to fix this."

"What?"

"This is another issue. I can't very well marry someone if the thought of them being alone in a room with a woman is going to send me into a jealous spiral. They're all businessmen, and so that sort of thing will pop up. There's no avoiding it." She latched on to the idea, turning it over in her mind. "We can start at the lingerie shop."

Gideon pulled them out of the path of foot traffic and guided her to the brick wall of a nearby storefront. He let go and took her by the shoulders. "Lucy, stop."

"Don't take that tone with me. I'm not being crazy."

"Everything about this situation is crazy. No, don't get your back up. It is and you know it, and I'm here willingly, taking part in it." He looked like he wanted to shake some sense into her. "You're asking me to… What? Flirt with someone in front of you? More?"

More?

Her entire body clenched as if trying to reject the very idea of Gideon doing *more* with someone else. *I am out of control.* "If that's what it takes."

A muscle jumped in his jaw. "No."

"Excuse me?"

He shook his head. "Absolutely not. You pick one of these assholes and he flirts with another woman in front of you—or at all—and you get out, Lucy. You hear me? That is not normal, and no man who respects his partner would put them in that situation where they have to wonder if something more is going on. I would never so much as look at another woman if I was with you—in your presence or not."

"But—"

"But nothing. There are a lot of gray areas in relationships. This isn't one of them. Short of there being extenuating circumstances that are agreed upon by both parties, there is a clear line and no one should be crossing it."

She stared. This was supposed to be all in theory—a test run of sorts—but Gideon spoke like it was a personal attack on him. *Because it is.* She didn't know what to do, so she slipped her arms around his waist and pulled him in for a hug. "I'm sorry."

He cursed, but he wrapped his arms around her. "You have nothing to be sorry for."

"I'm blurring the lines." She wasn't even sure where the lines were at this point. Having sex was one thing, though they hadn't even done *that* right because she was too busy enjoying herself to pay attention to whatever he tried to teach her. On what was supposed to be her second date, she was more excited about pushing Gideon's buttons than she was about meeting her actual date.

And now she was getting jealous.

He pulled her tighter against him. "We'll talk about it tonight." He stepped back and reclaimed her hand. "Come on."

Lucy didn't know whether to look forward to the conversation or to dread it. When she'd initially brought it up, she'd deluded herself with the falsity that she had everything under control. Twenty minutes into this day and she'd proved herself wrong half a dozen times. Gideon was probably going to sit her down and explain how out of line she'd been lately.

Let it go. You can obsess about every word and touch and meaning once he's left tonight.

Strangely enough, that made her feel better. Or maybe it was his fingers laced through hers as they walked down the street. Two blocks later, he pulled her to a stop in front of a boutique lingerie shop. "Yes?"

She took in the window display, a perfect blend of tasteful and risqué. The mannequins reclined on a lounging sofa, both wearing jewel-toned bustiers, ruffled boy-short panties, with garters and thigh-highs. One had on a lace shrug that looked like something out of an old black-and-white movie. "Yes."

She couldn't wait to get into that dressing room with Gideon.

One minute Gideon was leading Lucy into the lingerie boutique, the next, a whirlwind of a saleswoman had stationed him in one of the private change areas and led Lucy away. He blinked at the opening leading into the rest of the store but didn't move from his assigned spot. *That was smoothly done.*

Content to leave Lucy at the mercy of the woman, he surveyed the changing area. It was a clever design, each of the three doorways leading to a small sitting area and an individual change room. The whole setup created the feeling of an intimate environment for shopping for the most intimate of clothing. He approved.

Gideon hadn't decided whether now was the time to play on Lucy's fantasy of change room sex. He'd intended it initially, but their conversation on the walk over had put things up in the air. He'd already pressed her hard just by staying last night. Her showing signs of jealousy was a sign that she felt more than just sexual attraction, but it obviously set her off balance and made her uncomfortable.

He sat back and scrubbed a hand over his face. The truth was, he didn't know how to play this. He'd made his career on being able to read people and find good fits, but he was fumbling around in the dark when it came to Lucy. He felt like he was back in high school, trying to express interest without hanging himself out to dry and becoming the laughingstock of the school.

Except the stakes were a whole hell of a lot higher now.

The saleswoman had hustled Lucy into the change room so fast, he hadn't seen more than a flash of bright colors attached to hangers before the door shut. The saleswoman—a little Goth woman who stood five feet tall, if that—emerged a few seconds later. She had purple streaks in her black hair and a lip ring. She winked at him and raised her voice. "You let me know if you need any different sizes or want to try something else. There's a button in there that will ding me, but otherwise, I'll leave you to it."

"Thank you." Lucy's voice was muffled.

The saleswoman stopped next to him. "Special lady you have there."

"Yes." She wasn't telling him anything he didn't know. She lingered for a second, something obviously on her mind, but he didn't have the patience to deal with it when he could hear the slide of cloth against skin in the dressing room. "Thank you."

"Let me know if you need anything. We have coffee and water." She waited half a beat and then was gone, striding out the door and into the main boutique.

Gideon drummed his fingers on his knee and waited.

Then waited some more.

Five minutes later his frayed patience gave out. He rose and stalked to the dressing room door. "Lucy."

"Yes?" She sounded small and unsure.

"Do you need assistance?"

"No."

He stared at the door, willing her to open it. She didn't. Gideon sighed. "Is there a problem?"

"No. Yes. I don't know. I just feel absolutely ridiculous."

He considered and discarded several responses to that. None of them was worth the breath it would take to give them voice. "Open the door."

"It's fine, Gideon. This was a silly idea. Just give me a minute to change back into my clothes and we can find something else to do today."

"Open the door," he repeated.

Her bare feet padded over the tiled floor and he held his breath as they approached the door. And then it was open and a vision from every one of his fantasies stood in front of him. Lucy wore nude-colored thigh-highs, held up by an emerald garter belt. Its decorative lace almost hid the fact that her panties barely hid anything at all. And the bustier was a work of art, offering her breasts with peekaboo lace that showcased her nipples apparently by accident.

The whole thing was a goddamn tease and he loved it. "You look ravishing."

She put her hands on her hips, at her sides, and then finally crossed them over her chest. "*Ravishing* is a strong word."

"It fits." He stepped into the dressing room and shut the door behind him, unable to take his eyes off her. "If you don't like it, *divine*, *exquisite* and *breathtaking* are also accurate."

Her eyebrows inched up. "Do you have a thesaurus tucked into your back pocket?"

"Don't need one." He stopped in front of her and uncrossed her arms so he could see her. As with all things Lucy, both she and the lingerie were even better up close. Gideon stroked his hands down her sides and ran his thumb over the garter belt. What he found had him going to his knees in front of her. "Your panties are on top."

"Well, yes." A blush spread over her pale cheeks and down her chest. "I'd already decided to buy it based on the color, so I wanted the full effect."

There was only one reason to wear panties over the garter belt; they could be removed while leaving the rest of the lingerie on.

Gideon hooked the side of the thong with his thumbs and looked up her body to her face. "Yes?"

"Yes." The word was barely more than a stirring of the air between them.

He slid her panties down her legs, taking his time. "I'm buying this for you. Don't argue. This isn't a disagreement that you'll win."

"This getup is incredibly expensive." As he crouched, she lifted first one foot and then the other so he could remove the thong completely.

"Worth every penny." The garter belt framed her pussy to perfection, an offering he couldn't have resisted if he'd tried—and Gideon wasn't interested in trying. He guided one of her legs over his shoulder, a position that left her completely at his mercy. "Just a taste."

CHAPTER THIRTEEN

AT THE FIRST stroke of Gideon's tongue, Lucy forgot all the reasons this was a questionable idea. She didn't care. The only thing that mattered was his tongue lazily circling her clit. As if he had all the time in the world and they weren't in a public place.

A public place where every moan and sound could be heard by someone on the other side of the dressing room door.

She shivered, heat cascading through her body at the thought of someone listening. Someone knowing what they were doing. Someone thinking Gideon was so turned on by the lingerie that he couldn't wait for the time it'd take them to get home.

He'd had to have her right then and there.

His dark gaze met hers as he licked her again. "What are you thinking?"

She was thinking she wanted more. To be dirty. To break the rules.

Lucy reached down and tugged on his shoulders. Without saying another word, Gideon rose and let her guide him to sit on the bench that ran along the wall in the changing room. He watched her through hooded eyes as she undid the front of his jeans and climbed onto his lap. After a quick detour to her purse for a condom, she rolled it onto his length. He opened his mouth but Lucy pressed a single finger to his lips.

His eyes flashed in understanding and his lazy grin made her pussy clench. Lucy guided him inside her and sealed them together. She leaned forward until her lips brushed his ear. "Someone could hear."

"Yes." The word was barely more than a whisper. He reached up and pulled her bustier down to bare her breasts. "Hope you locked the door. She knocks on it and it'll swing right open. Give the woman the sight of a lifetime."

Her nipples tightened at the image his low words painted. It didn't matter that she knew for a fact the door was locked. It *could* be unlocked. Lucy held on to Gideon's shoulders and started to move. Each time she lifted almost all the way off his cock, her breasts brushed against his mouth and he kissed first one and then the other.

Thrust. Kiss. Thrust.

"Look at how beautiful you are." He gripped her chin and turned her face to the full-length mirror.

What a picture they made. Him fully clothed except for his cock disappearing and reappearing between her legs. Her mostly naked and riding him, her pale skin flushed with desire. Lucy couldn't take her gaze away from where one of his big hands held her hip while the other maintained its grip on her chin, to the look on his face as he stared at her in the mirror. She licked her lips. "*We* are beautiful."

He guided her back to face him. "Fuck me. Come on my cock. But be quiet or Agnes will hear."

The words unleashed the orgasm that had been building from the moment he'd slipped off her panties. Lucy buried her face in his neck and tried to muffle her cry as she came. Gideon looped an arm around her waist and lifted her to reverse their positions, sitting her on the bench with him kneeling between her thighs, his cock still buried inside her.

He held her thighs wide and proceeded to fuck her. She had to cling to the edge of the bench to keep from smacking against the wall with the strength of his thrusts. Through it all, his dark eyes swallowed her up, so full of things she couldn't put a name to. An expression almost like pain flickered over his face as he came with a muffled curse, hips still thrusting as if he never wanted to stop.

Lucy slumped back onto the bench and blinked at the reflection of herself. Gideon crouched in front of her, his dark eyes wild. He started to reach for her and stopped. "Your place. Now."

"We could…" She trailed off. *My place.* Despite the outstanding and filthy sex, she wanted more. She wanted skin on skin and Gideon's taste in her mouth. She wanted it all.

She nodded. "My place." She lifted her shaking hands to finish undoing her bustier, but Gideon beat her there. He undid the tiny clasps carefully, the delicate lace looking strange against his massive hands.

He slid it off her arms and folded it neatly on the bench next to her before giving the garter belt and stockings the same treatment. The panties finished off the pile.

He ran his hands up her legs. Lucy held her breath and arched her back a little. His pupils dilated, which was a reward in and of itself, but Gideon stood. "Get dressed." Then he was gone, snatching the lingerie off the bench and striding out the door, careful to not let it open too much.

She stared after him for a long moment before she dredged up the ambition to move. It was just as well he'd shown a little restraint or she had a feeling they wouldn't have left this dressing room for several hours. She wasn't sure if she was disappointed that he'd walked out or excited for what was to come.

Excited. Definitely excited.

She dressed quickly and paused to check her appearance in the mirror. Flushed cheeks, slightly wild eyes, skin a little too glowy. It was a good look, but there was no mistaking that she and Gideon had been up to no good behind the closed door. It was becoming a habit of theirs, though Lucy couldn't say she was sad about it. She liked the thrill of knowing there were people within hearing distance.

She liked that she was experiencing it with Gideon even more.

Lucy stopped short.

There it was. The thing she'd been doing her best not to think too hard about since their first time—since *before* their first time, if she was being honest.

There'd always been an attraction simmering between her and Gideon, even when she'd been with Jeff. She'd gone out of her way to ensure she'd never given him any sign of it, because she'd been in a relationship.

Because she cared about Gideon as a friend, and if something had happened between them, she'd lose him.

There was no Jeff standing between them now, and her feelings for Gideon were significantly more complicated. There was lust, definitely. Her body craved his like she'd never craved anything—any-one—before.

But there were…feelings.

She gave herself a shake. It didn't matter if there were feelings or not. She'd set out the terms and Gideon had agreed to them. Changing the rules with-out notice meant she really *would* lose him and she hadn't come all this way to falter now. She'd missed him terribly these last couple of years, and the thought of going back to her life without him in it felt like she had a gaping hole in her chest.

Gideon wasn't the keeping kind. A lot had changed, but she couldn't afford to believe *that* had. He'd settle down someday, with the right woman, but he wasn't there yet. Even if he tried to give them a shot for her sake, it would self-destruct sooner rather than later.

No matter which way she looked at the situation, the end result was the same—if she changed the rules now, she would lose him. If she saw her original plan through to the end, she retained the chance to keep Gideon in her life.

Lucy would fight for that, even if it meant hurting herself to do so.

She took a deep breath and straightened her shoulders. *I can do this.* Lucy opened the change room door and marched out. Gideon stood by the entrance to the boutique and she headed his way, very carefully not looking for Agnes. They might be the only people in the shop, but they'd been in that room far too long to be doing anything but exactly what they'd been doing. *Focus, Lucy.* She licked her lips as she stopped next to Gideon. "My place?"

"I changed my mind."

She braced herself. "Oh?"

"That meal might have been sweet, but it won't sustain us for what I have in mind for later." He gave her a wolfish grin that had her warming even as she tried not to read into his words too much.

It won't sustain us.

He didn't mean anything by it—of that, Lucy was sure—but it served as yet another reminder that this was temporary and any effort to make it permanent would backfire spectacularly. She put on her best smile. "What's the plan, then?"

Gideon's grin dropped away and he studied her for a long moment, seeming to see through her façade. Finally he nodded, almost to himself. "Lunch. Then we'll head back to your place to finish what we started."

Not a brush-off, then, but a detour. She kept her shoulders from sagging through sheer stubbornness. "I could eat."

"Good." He touched the small of her back and ush-
ered her out of the building. He didn't say anything as
they walked down the street, and she was too twisted
up inside her own head to try for conversation. Nothing she said right now would change the truth, and
the weight of it threatened to send her scurrying back
to her place to barricade herself in with Garfunkel
and the work files she still had to find time for this
weekend.

Their destination was a little restaurant on the second floor of a converted apartment building. They'd
left most of the interior walls up and designed low
lighting so that even in the middle of the afternoon,
it gave the illusion of a night tucked away. The hostess led them to a room that might have been a closet
at one point, though it had two doorways now and
space for a little booth for two.

Gideon waited for her to slide in and then took the
spot next to her. The hostess left and Lucy became
aware of a low jazz song playing in the background.
She ran her finger over the rough tabletop. "I didn't
even know this place existed."

"It's new. A friend of mine bought the building a
couple years back and construction just wrapped up
a few months ago. The bottom floor is split into a
clothing boutique and shoe store, and the third floor
is privately owned."

She'd definitely come down here to check out the
shoe store in the future. She twisted to face him,
but he spoke before she could. "What happened back
there?"

"Excuse me?"

"You know exactly what I'm talking about. You were fine in the dressing room, and when you walked out, you'd put a wall up between us."

She desperately didn't want to talk about this, but his jaw was set in an all-too-familiar way. There would be no getting out of this conversation, short of crawling over the table and making a run for it. Since that was beneath Lucy's dignity—and she didn't know for certain that Gideon wouldn't just chase her down—she sighed. "We have clear boundaries."

"Mmm-hmm."

That response gave her no indication of what he thought of that, so she hedged. "Very clear boundaries."

Gideon drummed his fingers on the table. "Is the problem that you feel that I'm threatening the boundaries or that the boundaries themselves are the problem?"

Trust the man to just lay it out there with no qualms. She fought not to fidget. "I value our friendship. I know it may not seem like that after not speaking for two years, but I missed you terribly during that time and I feel like we're almost starting to reclaim that lost ground."

The guarded look on his face cleared. "You don't want to jeopardize our friendship."

"Exactly." She didn't mention the theoretical pending marriage or what their friendship might look like once she'd picked a man and followed through on that. The marriage might have sex included in the bargain, but it would still be a marriage without love. Having Gideon in her life, even on the outskirts, wasn't something she was willing to give up.

Not now that she'd just gotten him back.

The waiter brought their waters and took their drink orders. Once the man disappeared through the doorway, Gideon turned back to her. "That gap in communication was as much my fault as it was yours. I let guilt get the better of me and figured that you didn't want to see my face any more than you wanted to see Jeff's."

"You...weren't wrong—at least, not at first." She'd been so hurt and angry and embarrassed that she hadn't wanted to see *anyone* for months after she'd broken off her engagement. The only person who'd ignored that was Becka, and even she'd had to come to Lucy. If Gideon had tried during that time, she would have slammed the door in his face.

By the time she'd gathered the strength to get back out into the world again, it was to find that her former friends had moved on without her. It made sense, in a way. She'd lost most of her good friends when she and Jeff had started dating—a sign she should have paid more attention to. He hadn't missed a beat after their breakup, and most of their friends had been his first, so they'd moved along with him.

It was Gideon's steady presence that she'd missed the most, but she hadn't known how to reach out to him.

Or if she even should.

I'm here now. We *are here now.*

She held herself steady. "Regardless, I feel like I just found you again."

"And you don't want to lose that." He said it almost as if musing to himself. When she tensed, he leaned back and slung an arm over the back of the booth. "I don't want to lose it, either, Lucy. I missed you, too. I'm still missing you, if we're going to be perfectly honest."

Her jaw dropped. "What are you talking about? I'm right here."

"Yes, you are." He pulled her closer, tucking her against his body. "But we haven't stopped to have a real conversation since you sat me down in your office and told me you wanted me to help you find a husband."

Lucy opened her mouth to say he was wrong, but stopped and thought hard about it. Was he? "We've... talked." But not like they used to. There had been nights where Jeff had passed out, or was occupied playing whatever his video game of the week was, and she and Gideon had sat and just talked. Shared things about themselves, about their dreams. She'd always chalked it up to being good friends—family, even—but even if they'd restarted their acquaintance, they hadn't reestablished the intimacy they'd once had.

Sex, yes.

Intimacy, no.

She frowned. "I guess you're right. God, I'm sorry, Gideon. I've been treating you like a prize stud."

He chuckled. "I haven't exactly complained. But

I do miss us, Lucy. Whatever version of your future you're aiming for, make room for me."

That startled a laugh out of her. "You're just as confident now as you were back then."

"Two years can change a person, but it can't *change* a person."

That was what she was afraid of. Lucy had fought hard to shed the timid woman she'd become while dating Jeff. She'd even mostly succeeded, if one didn't look too closely at her lack of dating. But she couldn't shake the fear that, deep down, she was still that mouse of a person who'd let her boyfriend say such horrible things to her—worse, who'd believed him when he did.

"I should have known." He spoke softly in the tiny space between them. "I said it before and I'll say it again—I knew Jeff was an asshole, but I didn't know the extent of it. I would have stepped in."

Her heart surged even as she shook her head. "If anyone should have seen the signs and stepped in, it was me. I let myself get taken in by him, and I almost married him because I was too stubborn and too naive to see him for what he was. If we're going to lay blame, there's plenty to go around." She covered his hand with hers. "I don't want to talk about Jeff anymore. He's taken up enough of both of our lives, and I don't want to give him even another second."

"I won't argue that." Gideon nudged her closer yet, until she was almost sitting in his lap. "I have the prettiest woman in all NYC sitting with me in a dark restaurant. I can think of a thousand things I'd rather say and do than talk about a piece of shit that we share a mutual history with."

She laid her hand on his thigh, enjoying the way the muscle clenched beneath his jeans. "I can think of a few things to add to the list." They were alone in this mini room within the restaurant. They could do anything they wanted to beneath the table and no one would be the wiser. "Gideon..." She slid her hand higher.

"Yeah?"

"What have you been up to since I saw you last?"

He blinked down at her as if he couldn't reconcile her ever-sliding hand with her words. Finally he relaxed, muscle by individual muscle. "After you and..." He looked away and back. "Two years ago, I looked at my life and decided I was done dicking around. I went after the biggest accounts I could find and went head-to-head with companies that had reputations stretching back before we were born." He laughed. "I figured I had nothing to lose, so I might as well aim for the stars."

"You've made quite the name for yourself." Even if her company didn't make a habit of contracting headhunters to fill positions, Lucy would've had to be living under a rock not to hear news of Gideon. He'd beaten out several more well-known headhunters and developed an excellent reputation in the process. He always got his man—or woman, as it were.

God help the woman he finally sets his sights on. She won't stand a chance.

The thought was bittersweet in the extreme. Lucy

cared about him. She wanted him happy...but contemplating him with another woman made her want to throw things. *Stop that.*

He's yours for the duration.

That will have to be enough.

But what if it wasn't?

CHAPTER FOURTEEN

GIDEON INSISTED ON DESSERT, if only to keep things going for a little bit longer. Lucy must have felt the same way because she didn't hesitate before she picked a particularly delicious-sounding apple cobbler to his cheesecake. The waiter—who was getting a significant tip since he'd made himself scarce in between checking on them—took their order and hurried off. The restaurant had filled up, though the only evidence of it they had was a low murmur of conversation by people they couldn't see.

He curled a strand of Lucy's hair around his finger. "You said we needed to talk."

"Don't we?"

He'd always liked Lucy's directness. Even when she was highly uncomfortable with the subject— like sex—she still made an effort to cut through the bullshit and be as honest as possible. Now he almost wished that she was willing to let the slow slide of afternoon into evening go on without following through on her words this morning. Gideon should have known better. "Yeah, we do."

She met his gaze directly, never one to shy away from a potential confrontation. "Shall I go first or shall you?"

Though he was tempted to let her take the lead, that was the coward's way out. Gideon knew what he wanted and the only way to give him a snowball's chance in hell was to go for it without reservation. So he let go of her hair and sat back. "Pick me."

She blinked and then blinked again. "I'm sorry?"

"Screw the others guys and screw the list I put together. They won't make you happy like I can, and you know it. I know you as well as anyone, and we match up in the bedroom and out of it. Pick me." *I love you. I've always loved you.* He didn't say it. He'd already pressed his luck by putting his cards on the table. If he threw that at her, she'd be gone before he finished the sentence.

She leaned forward and then shook her head. "What are you saying?"

"You know what I'm saying. I want you. You want me. We fit, Lucy. You can't deny that it's true." He held himself still in an effort to keep from reaching for her. Crowding her now was a mistake and using sex to cloud her judgment was a dick move. Not one that he was above, but if he wanted a chance—a real chance—with her, he had to do this right.

As right as he could do it when they'd started this thing with her dating another guy and then restarted it by bargaining for sex lessons in addition to her attempting to marry another man.

When you put it like that...

Lucy put her hand to her mouth and dropped it as quickly. "I don't know what to say."

Hell, he really had overplayed it. He didn't retreat farther physically, though he wanted to. Instead, Gideon gave her an easy smile. "It's fine. We're fine."

"No, I don't think we are." She rubbed her hands over her face and looked at him, her blue eyes so bleak, it broke his fucking heart. "Gideon, even with all the crap in our history and the two-year separation, you're one of the closest friends I have. I *care* about you. I don't know what I'd do if I lost our friendship again and…" Her hands fluttered between them. "We have irreconcilable differences."

"What are you talking about?" He reined in his reaction until she could tell him exactly what the hell she meant by that. *I was never on that goddamn list.*

"When's the last time you dated someone for longer than a few weeks?"

He froze. "That's the measuring stick you're going to use against me? Fine, Lucy. I haven't dated anyone for longer than a few weeks. I've been focusing on my career, and before that, it was school." He shook his head, frustration reaching a boiling point. "It's pretty rich that you expect me to roll with your limited dating history, but mine is the reason you won't consider me."

"That's not what I meant." She tucked her hair behind her ear. "Okay, it's a little what I meant, but the core concept is still the same. What happens when I throw all my other options out the window and say yes to you? Are you planning on marrying me? Because that's still the endgame, and rather quickly. Even if you *are* willing to take that step, what happens in a few weeks, months, however long, when you get bored—or, heaven forbid, you meet someone who you might actually love?" Lucy slumped in the booth. "No, it's not worth the risk. You'd realize that if you took emotion out of your reaction."

That was the problem—Gideon couldn't take emotion out of the equation when it came to Lucy. He'd never been able to. "I wouldn't do that to you."

"Maybe not intentionally. But eventually you'd resent me for pushing you into this choice."

He took a calming breath and then another. "You're not giving me much credit here, Lucy." She thought she had it all figured out, and he couldn't say a damn thing to dissuade her because it'd just be used as evidence of either how unready he was for that kind of commitment, or how much she valued their friendship. *Struck down because she cares about me.*

That brought him up short.

He was being greedy, but hell. The thought of her with someone else when they *fit* drove Gideon out of his goddamn mind. He took her hand, noting the tension there. "You've given me the worst-case scenario, and I respect that. Let me paint you a different picture."

Lucy hesitated. "Okay."

"You pick me. We get married, figure out living arrangements. Nothing bad happens. In fact, our quality of life improves exponentially. We force ourselves to take a few breaks from work a year and travel a bit.

We start working through that list I know you've put together. We make our house a home. Fuck, maybe we have some kids, too. And every night, it's just us. You and me."

Her lips curved in a faint smile. "I like how you added in my sexual bucket list."

"It's important." He ran his thumb over her knuckles. Gideon wanted the life he'd just described. He wanted to be able to shoot Lucy a text and meet her after work for dinner and then walk home together and make love on every goddamn surface of the place they shared. He wanted the lazy Sunday mornings and the long weekends away. He wanted to be able to call her when he nailed an account or to get her calls when she was victorious in court.

He wanted it all.

Lucy pressed her lips together. "What if it blows apart in our face?"

"What if it doesn't?" He kept stroking her knuckles as she relaxed against him, bit by bit. "But let's talk this out your way. You pick someone else. We stop sleeping together, but that tension isn't going to disappear. Your new husband—" the term soured his stomach "—picks up on the tension and it makes him uncomfortable. Because it will, Lucy. Even if the guy is interested in marriage in name only, he'll have a problem with it."

"But—"

"Trust me. He will draw the line in the sand, and you'll have to choose which side of it you're going to be on." Gideon hated seeing the worry all over her face, but if they were being real, it had to be said. "You'll pick him. You'll have to."

The waiter walked in carrying their desserts. He set them on the table, took one look at Gideon's and Lucy's faces and stepped back. "Let me know if you need anything. Enjoy." He dashed out of the room.

"I don't… This is too much." She picked up a fork and poked at her apple cobbler. "You just dropped a serious information bomb on me and I don't even know how to wrap my head around it."

"Then don't."

She twisted to look at him. "What are you talking about?"

"I'm not saying you need to make the decision this second." He nudged his dessert away. "But you need to stop thinking that I'm not an option. I am. Fuck, I'm the best option."

"Arrogant to the very end."

"I'm sure of my worth. I'm even surer of how good we'd be. We've more than proved it over the last two weeks."

"One of which you weren't even on the same side of the country." But she relaxed against him and allowed him to tuck her head against his shoulder. "I'll think about it, Gideon. I don't… I don't know if I can promise more than that."

"Don't let fear win, Lucy. You've gone down that road before and you already know how it ends."

The walk back to Lucy's place happened in a blur. She couldn't get Gideon's words out of her head and his big presence at her side eclipsed all else. He made it sound so simple—the easiest thing in the world. *Pick me.*

It wasn't that easy.

The picture he painted was an attractive one. More than attractive. She craved that life, craved the connection already strung between her and Gideon. But Lucy had seen firsthand how bad things could get when she let someone close and they turned on her. Gideon would never cheat on her—of that, she was certain—but there were so many ways a person could hurt someone they cared about. Most of the time, it was even unintentional.

If she married some near stranger and they did something careless or cruel, she could respond without missing a beat. They weren't close enough to hurt her. Gideon, though? He could cut her to the bone.

Aren't you tired of living in fear?

The voice in her head sounded a whole lot like his. She nodded absently at the doorman and led the way into her building. Fear had controlled every choice she'd made since she'd found out Jeff had been sleeping around on her. Fear that she'd never get out had prompted her to end things in a rather remarkable fight. Fear of failure had thrust her into a career that she might love but which she'd chosen for its earning potential. Fear of being hurt again kept her from giving dating more than a token effort.

What if she just…jumped?

Lucy unlocked her door and turned to him. "Come in?"

"Sure."

His presence filled her apartment, giving it a life that it seemed to miss when it was just her and Garfunkel there. The feline in question meandered up as if he just happened to be in the room at the same time they were. She bent to pick him up and turned to face Gideon. "What if we do a trial run?"

"Trial run." Neither his tone nor his body language gave even the slightest indication of what was going on in that beautiful head of his.

"Yes, a trial run." She warmed to the idea as she spoke. "I have a few months before I'll be down to the wire on this marriage business. A week or two shouldn't make much difference."

His eyebrows rose. "What do you think you'll know in two weeks that you don't know now?"

He had a point, but she wasn't about to admit it. Making any kind of decision right that second felt like too much too soon. She'd know in a week or two. She'd be *sure*—or as sure as Lucy ever was these days about things outside of the office. "What do you say?"

"Yes." He carefully extracted Garfunkel from her arms and set the cat free. Then he set his hands on her hips and pulled her slowly toward him until they stood bare inches apart. "I say yes, Lucy. If you need two weeks to figure this out one way or another, that's what you'll have."

Her throat tightened. "You're too good to me."

"You've got that backward." He sifted his fingers through her hair, tilting her head back so she lifted her face to him. "I'm taking you to bed now."

She blinked at the change in subject. But was it really a change at all? Anything left to say would just be rehashing what they'd already gone over. Left to her own devices, she'd drive them both crazy with her doubts. Better to let their obvious physical connection take over and push her worries to the back seat than to sabotage things before they had a chance to get started.

Gideon didn't wait for a response before sweeping her into his arms and striding back to her room. He carefully kicked the door shut, his gaze on the floor. "Woke up this morning to the damn cat watching me."

"He does that." She dragged her fingers through his hair and kissed his neck. "In his defense, you look absolutely marvelous while you sleep."

"You watched me while I slept?" He set her on the bed and backed up enough to pull her boots off, quickly followed by her leggings. "That's very creepy of you."

"You're in my apartment—that means I'm not creepy." She pulled her shirt off and tossed it away. "If I was standing on the fire escape outside your window and doing it, *that* would be creepy."

"A fair point." He nudged her onto her back and stripped slowly.

Lucy propped herself on her elbows. "Have I mentioned lately how much I enjoy you in flannel?"

"It might have come up once or twice." He dropped the shirt onto the floor and started on his jeans. "Careful there, or you might look up one day and realize I've grown a beard and started wearing thick-rimmed black glasses."

She laughed. "You don't even need glasses."

"My point stands." He hooked the back of her thighs and slid her farther onto the bed. She expected him to follow her to the mattress, but Gideon stepped back. He pointed at her. "Don't move."

"Okay…" She froze when he went to her nightstand and unerringly opened the bottom drawer. When he straightened, he had her pink vibrator in his hand. She shivered. "Oh."

He examined it. "This isn't a design I'm familiar with."

"You—"

He chuckled. "Give me some credit. I can figure out how it works." He thumbed it on, his grin widening. "Brilliant." He joined her on the bed and took up a position next to her with his head propped on his hand. "Spread your legs."

"This feels…" When he didn't immediately jump in, she had to search for something to fill the space. "Naughty." It wasn't quite the right word, but it fit.

"More or less than bending over that table and offering your ass to me?"

Her entire body went hot at both the memory and his words. "I'm not sure. It's not the same thing." There was no one here except them. No one to potentially walk in or witness. It didn't make the encounter less hot, but it had a different flavor as a result.

Gideon traced her puckered nipples with his gaze.

"More or less than stroking yourself on a video chat with me?"

She gave a mock frown even as her breathing picked up. "You've made your point."

"Have I?" He ran his thumb over the circular silicone portion of the vibrator. "I still have a few points to make. Spread your legs wider."

She paused just long enough to have his brows slant down—the reaction she was aiming for—and then obeyed. The heat in his dark eyes was nothing compared to the inferno blasting into existence beneath her skin. *What if it was always like this?* He pressed the vibrator to her clit before the thought could take root. The silicone perfectly circled her clit, the vibrations drawing a moan from her lips. The fact that it was *Gideon* wielding it only made the entire situation that much hotter.

"How often do you use this on yourself?"

She arched half off the bed when he lifted it away. "Often. Don't tease me. I was so close."

He grinned wickedly. "I know."

"Gideon." She couldn't stand the teasing even as she loved it.

"Next time we go out—" he touched the vibrator to her clit long enough to have pleasure almost cresting and then took it away again "—wear what I bought you today under your dress. Halfway through dinner, I'm going to tell you to take off your panties and slip them into my pocket."

She couldn't catch her breath. "Tricky."

"I have a better idea." He set the toy aside and idly

stroked her with his fingers. "There's a blackout restaurant I've been interested in trying."

How he could talk so calmly when she was in
danger of going out of her skin was beyond her.
"Gideon—"

He shoved two fingers into her, drawing a cry
from her lips. "I'll spend the entire dinner fucking
you with my fingers right there at the table. You'll
have to be quiet or the other diners will hear you."
He stroked her and slid her wetness up to circle her
clit before pushing back into her again. "Though, if
they're too quiet, they'll be able to hear exactly what
I'm doing to you."

She reached for him, only to have him use his free
hand to press the vibrator into hers. "Show me."

It took three tries to get her shaking fingers to op-
erate it while he kept fucking her with his fingers the
same way he'd described. She could picture exactly
how it would feel to sit in perfect darkness, her dress
up around the tops of her thighs, Gideon's big hand
palming her pussy as he gave the waiter their order
with none the wiser. She froze. "Don't the waitstaff
have night-vision goggles?"

He guided her hand with the vibrator to her clit,
waiting until she'd placed it perfectly to respond.
"Yes. They'll be able to see every single thing I'm
doing to you."

Her orgasm exploded through her. Lucy's back
bowed and she fumbled the toy, but Gideon was there,
his fingers still inside her as he repositioned it and
sent another wave of pure bliss through her. "Oh, my

God." She thrashed, though she couldn't say if she was trying to get away from him or closer. "Oh, God. Gideon. Please. Stop. Don't stop."

A thunk sounded as the vibrator hit the floor and then his mouth was there, soothing her oversensitized clit in long strokes. She laced her fingers through his hair, riding his face. "What are you doing to me? I don't... I feel completely out of control."

He lifted his head just enough to say, "I have no control with you, either, Lucy. I feel like a fucking animal. I can't get enough of you."

"Then get up here." She tugged on his hair. "You want me? Then take me."

Gideon hadn't bothered with a plan when it came to seducing Lucy into seeing things his way. All his damn plans went right out the window the second their clothes came off. Now, looking up her body into those blue eyes demanding he take her, he wished for a plan. This whole day was special. The start of their trial run. But more than that, it was the first time they'd spent time together without someone else between them.

Just Gideon and Lucy.

He wanted her to know how important that was to him, how close to perfect today had been. How much he cared about her. How much he wanted her in every way, body and soul.

In the end, Gideon did the only thing he could do. He crawled up her body and kissed her. She met him eagerly, her body already shifting to accommodate his, her legs wrapping around his waist and her hands coasting down his back to dig her fingers into his ass. As if they'd done this a thousand times before and would do it another thousand times.

"Condom," he rasped.

"I'm clean." Her lips brushed his with every word. "And…well, I'm on birth control."

He went still. "What are you saying?" There was no room for misunderstanding—not here, not now.

Lucy kissed one side of his mouth and then the other. "If…"

"I'm clean. I haven't been with anyone since the last time I was tested." He hadn't done anything to disabuse her of the notion since it'd be wasted breath, but Gideon hadn't had much interest in sleeping around in the last couple of years. He hadn't been celibate, but the demon driving him had disappeared right around the time Lucy had vanished from his life.

"I don't want barriers between us. I want you—all of you."

He wanted that, too. So bad, he could fucking taste it. "You're sure."

She wedged her hand between them and stroked his cock once, twice, before guiding him to her entrance. "I'm sure."

He didn't ask again. Gideon kissed her as he slid into her, inch by inch. There were no words to express his feelings at her trust in him. From the very beginning, she'd trusted him, but this was something else entirely. He kissed her with everything he had, everything he couldn't say. And then he began to move.

She rose to meet each thrust, their bodies moving in a dance as old as time, neither of them willing to break the kiss. He laced his fingers through her hair to tip her face for a better angle. She raked her nails over his ass, urging him to move faster, harder.

It was like flipping a switch.

He froze for one eternal second. Lucy nipped his bottom lip. "Stop being so careful with me. I can take it."

He knew that. Of course he knew that. Gideon tightened his grip on her hair with one hand, tilting her head to the side so he had access to her neck. He dragged his mouth down the line and then bit her shoulder. "Teeth?"

"Yes." She let loose a shaky laugh. "Just don't mark up where anyone can see."

Which was as good as saying that she *did* want him to mark her somewhere.

Gideon rolled onto his back, taking her with him, and slammed her down onto his cock. "Fuck me." He sat up enough to palm her breasts as she did what he commanded. Gideon sucked her nipple hard, urged on by her fingers in his hair and her hips slamming down onto him again and again. He took as much of her breast into his mouth as he could and bit her. Lucy cried out, her pussy squeezing him as she came.

He wasn't through.

He flopped her onto her stomach and yanked her to the edge of the bed. Gideon guided his cock back into her, paused to kick her feet a little wider and press his hand to the small of her back, and then he started to move.

He fucked her. There was no other word for it. She wanted it hard, and her hands fisting her comforter and the cries slipping from her lips only drove him on. He became a wild thing, slamming into her over and over again, driven toward a release he couldn't have stopped if he'd tried.

It wasn't enough. He was so damn close, and it wasn't enough.

Gideon covered her with his body, reaching around to bracket her throat with one hand while he slipped the other between her thighs and pinched her clit. "You're mine, Lucy. *Mine.*" The move bent her backward and she twisted to give him her mouth.

"Yes, yes." She bucked against him, grinding herself against his hand. "Yours. Always. God, Gideon, don't stop."

"Never. I'll never fucking stop."

CHAPTER FIFTEEN

A LAZY SUNDAY morning was the only thing Gideon wanted, but he'd agreed to breakfast with Roman weeks ago. He left Lucy a note and brewed her a pot of coffee before heading out. An hour—two, tops—and he'd be back with her. Simple.

He still had to talk himself out of turning around seven different times during the cab ride—and again when he climbed out onto the sidewalk. The limited timeline Lucy gave him rattled around in his head, and he had the irrational fear that if he didn't spend every second with her that he could scrape out, it wouldn't be enough and she'd leave.

She's not leaving yet. I have time.

Not enough. Never enough.

Roman stood outside the little hole-in-the-wall place, staring at a pair of guys smoking just down the way. Gideon stopped next to him. "You quit."

"I know that. Doesn't mean I don't miss it some-times."

"Miss the ability to breathe a whole lot more when you end up with lung cancer."

Roman rolled his hazel eyes. "Yeah, got it. Thanks, Mom."

"How's your mother doing?"

"Same as always. *Just swimmingly, darling.*" He gave a spot-on impression of his mother's breathy, high voice. Roman opened the door. "She and my old man are on that goddamn yacht somewhere. The Caribbean this week—either Saint Lucia or Jamaica."

"Worse ways to spend your retirement." He followed his friend into the brightly lit restaurant. If one could call Frank's a restaurant. There were exactly two tables and three chairs, and in all Gideon's time of coming here, he'd never seen them empty. Most people took their food to go, which was what he and Roman did. They turned left without bothering to talk about it—it was always the direction they took when they managed to carve time out of their schedules for this sort of thing.

They both finished their breakfast sandwiches by the end of the first block. Roman barely waited for them to cross the street before he started in. "What are you doing with Lucy?"

"None of your damn business."

"No, it's not, but you know me well enough to know that I'm not going to leave it alone. Explain. Now."

Gideon stopped walking and turned to face his friend. He didn't like the set of Roman's jaw or the tight way he held himself. "Why are you pissed?"

"Everyone with eyes in their head has seen the way you've watched her since she came into our group.

You've had a thing for her for as long as we've known her."

He crossed his arms over his chest. "You have a point. Get to it."

"My point is that you agreed to find her a husband—that's it. A husband that is from the agreed-upon list that I helped you put together." When he didn't immediately jump in, Roman glared. "I may be pretty, but I'm not stupid. You dragged her into the back room at Vortex and you two had sex, which means you've crossed so many damn lines, you're too deep into it to realize exactly how much you're fucking up."

He wasn't fucking up. He might have changed the rules with her, but she was on the same page he was. *More or less.* It was the "less" that worried Gideon. Lucy had put it all out there yesterday—her fears about the future and what it might mean for them— and he'd essentially steamrolled her.

Admitting that to himself and admitting it to Roman were two very different things.

Roman, damn him, knew it. He shook his head. "She gave you an opening and you just went for it, didn't you? Didn't bother to stop and think about the damage you were dealing because you were too busy thinking with your cock."

Enough was enough. "I would never hurt Lucy."

"You're hurting her *right now*." Roman raked his hand through his hair. "We all stood by while that piece of shit ran around on her, and we have to live with that. There's no making it right—not really—

but she came to you for help, Gideon. You do anything else than give her exactly the help she wanted
and you're just as bad as he is."

No need to clarify the "he" Roman meant. Gideon
gave his head a sharp shake. "It's not the same."

"Isn't it? You and me—and even him, though I
hate to include Jeff in anything—are not good men.
We're just not. We never have been—you don't get
as far in the world as we've gotten without throwing people under the bus along the way. I've made
my peace with that, and I thought you had, too, but
you've always had a white knight complex when it
came to Lucy. *She* is good—as good as anyone is. She
deserves a hell of a lot better than she's gotten up to
this point, and that means we owe her."

"Fuck, will you listen to yourself?" Gideon knew
all that. How could he not, when he'd thought it himself over and over again for years? But hearing Roman
say it felt different. Real. As if Gideon really had
been deluding himself all this time by thinking things
could work out between him and Lucy. "She and I
just work."

Roman's eyes didn't hold a shred of sympathy. "For
how long? How long until she wakes up one morning
and realizes you pulled one over on her? She asked
you for help, and instead of doing what you promised, you used her needing you to leverage a place in
her life. That's shitty, Gideon. If our positions were
reversed, you'd tell me the same thing."

He started to react, but stopped short. If Roman
had come to him with news that Lucy had approached

him for help, and he'd ended up sleeping with her and sabotaging her matchmaking plans… "I would have punched you in those perfect teeth."

Roman rubbed his jaw. "You have a wicked right hook."

He didn't smile, though it couldn't be more obvious that his friend was trying to lighten the mood.

Gideon tossed his garbage into a trash can and stared at the street. "I didn't set out to do this." *I love her.* But what did his feelings matter when he hadn't taken hers into account? Lucy'd had years of playing second fiddle to some asshole—she didn't need Gideon coming in and starting a replay, regardless of his intentions. He'd never cheat on her, would do everything in his power to make her happy.

She didn't choose me.

That was what it came down to. If she'd given him any indication that she had started this process with some sort of feelings for him beyond friendship, he would have a right to ask for more. Yesterday she'd even gone so far as to try to explain that she didn't want to lose him as a friend, and he'd leveraged that fear into getting her to agree to give them a trial run.

His shoulders slumped. "Fuck me, you're right."

"I'm not saying it to be a dick." For once, Roman sounded downright apologetic. "You're my friend, and if she was any other woman, I'd say to hell with her plans—play dirty. But this isn't any other woman. This is Lucy we're talking about."

And, because it was Lucy, that changed everything. Gideon took out his phone and stared at it for a few moments. He knew what he had to do. The honorable thing—the thing he'd promised to do.

He had to set her up with another man.

Lucy woke up disorientated. The day before had been an emotional roller coaster, and she'd seriously looked forward to spending a lazy Sunday with Gideon, letting their time together ease her concerns over the whole thing.

Then she'd woken up alone.

She touched the side of the bed Gideon had slept on, but it was long since cold. Telling herself there was nothing to worry about, she went through her morning routine and then headed into the kitchen. A full pot of coffee sat waiting, along with a sticky note with a hastily written explanation. "Breakfast with Roman. Back soon." Lucy smiled a little and poured herself a cup of coffee. If he was occupied for a little bit, it wouldn't hurt to check her emails and make sure there was nothing requiring her immediate attention.

He still hadn't arrived by the time she was done with that, so she scrambled up a pair of eggs and went back to work on her files. Normally she had no problem losing herself in the facts she was compiling, but Lucy couldn't help keeping one eye on the clock as an hour stretched into two.

Did Gideon feel as strangely about what happened yesterday as she did?

Maybe he had regrets.

She wished he was there so his presence could keep her from second-guessing every single thing she'd said or done yesterday. Had she been too honest at dinner? He'd said he wanted honesty, but there was honesty and *honesty*. The sex had been even more outstanding than she'd come to expect, both the tender touches and murmured words and the rough and possessive...

"Stop it." She poured herself a third cup of coffee and headed for her living room. Obsessing over what Gideon did or did not regret would only drive her crazy. *Crazier.*

Work would steady her. Work *always* steadied her. It was her job that had gotten her through the worst times of her life, the ability to lose herself in the facts and how to use them to create the story she wanted the judge or jury to believe.

Except this time it didn't work.

Lucy kept glancing at her phone, waiting for a call or a text or, hell, a smoke signal. Something from Gideon. Something to prove that he didn't think this whole thing was a terrible mistake. Something to reassure *her* from deciding she needed to find a different way to accomplish her aims.

When her phone finally buzzed, she dropped the paper she'd been staring at for five minutes without reading and snatched it up. It was from Gideon, but only a few words.

The Blue Lagoon 7pm.

She hesitated, wondering if she'd missed something, and typed out a quick reply.

Dinner?

Yes. Wear something nice.

Lucy waited, but no information was forthcoming. She glanced at the clock. Two hours until he wanted her there. *Where has the day gone?* She could keep pretending to work, but the nerves bouncing in her stomach spoke of the futility of it. Something had changed with Gideon, and she wasn't sure it was a good sign.

Yesterday he'd been almost in her face with how much he wanted her—wanted *this*—and now he was playing least-in-sight. She'd thought Gideon was too direct a man to ever disappear on a woman, but she should have known better.

She'd watched him do it before, hadn't she?

She and Jeff even used to joke about the Gideon Special. He'd grow distant from whoever he was dating, showing up more and more at their place, and if the woman didn't allow him to fade gracefully away, he'd take her out for dinner and cut it off.

Kind of like the dinner he had planned with Lucy tonight.

She shot to her feet. "No. I'm being paranoid." Gideon wouldn't have said the things he'd said if he was planning on turning around and dumping her on her ass. He wouldn't have changed the perfectly good set of rules to push her to put her heart on the line.

Oh, my God. My heart is on the line.

She sat down heavily. She'd known she cared about

him, of course—hard to be friends and not care about someone—but her heart being in danger had nothing to do with friendship and everything to do with deeper feelings.

Real feelings.

The same kinds of feelings that made a person blind to another's faults and left them emotionally bloodied and bruised. She didn't want that. She'd actively worked to *avoid* that.

And yet here she was.

She got ready, mostly to escape the doubt plaguing her. It was fear talking—it had to be. Having a meltdown about their first speed bump during this trial dating thing they had going was just going to prove how unready to date or marry Lucy really was.

Obviously something had come up with Gideon that required his attention and prevented him from coming back to spend the day with her. Just as obviously, if it was important enough to need his presence then it would make his sending her a bunch of texts impossible. He'd arranged dinner tonight and paused in whatever he was doing long enough to let her know that they had plans, and *that* was a good sign.

She was overreacting.

Simple.

But she didn't feel any better two hours later when she stood in front of the Blue Lagoon, shivering in the cold beneath her thick coat. *This is fine. Everything is fine.* She walked inside and gave Gideon's name. The host smiled welcomingly and led her to a semi-private corner.

Lucy caught sight of a man sitting there already, but her steps stuttered when she realized he wasn't Gideon. *What the hell?* There was nothing to do but keep following the host. She started to reach for his arm to let him know that there had been some mistake, but as they came even with the table, she recognized the man. *Aaron Livingston.*

No. Oh, Gideon. Why?

She had to fight to keep her expression neutral as Aaron rose and smiled. "Lucy, it's been a while."

"I'm surprised you remember." She let him pull out her chair, her mind racing a million miles a minute. Gideon had set this up. It should have gone without saying, but she still couldn't wrap her mind around it. Twelve hours ago he'd told her that he wanted her to pick him—only him—and now he'd set her up with another man.

Aaron resumed his seat. "It's been a few years, but you're not a woman one forgets." He smiled charmingly, and though she could recognize why *BuzzFeed* had labeled him one of the hottest bachelors in NYC, his perfect features did nothing for her.

They also did nothing to explain why he was *here*.

You know why he's here, just like you know what it means.

If she was a better person, she'd sit and make small talk with Aaron and keep her eye on the prize—the whole reason she'd put this plan into motion in the first place. A husband.

But Lucy couldn't focus on anything beyond the fact that Gideon had set her up. She lasted a full thirty seconds before she pushed back her chair and rose. "I am so sorry, Aaron, but I've got to go."

"Go...?" Those keen dark eyes took her in. "You didn't realize you were meeting me, did you?"

"I'm really very sorry." She headed for the exit as quickly as she could without actually running. Lucy made it onto the street before she found her phone at the bottom of her purse. She dialed Gideon's number and listened to it ring and ring and ring before clicking over to voice mail. She hung up without leaving a message.

That was the moment she should have stopped. It was clear Gideon didn't want her, that he'd misled her horribly. She didn't give a flying fuck. He didn't get to put her in this position and then avoid dealing with the fallout.

She scrolled through her contacts to find Roman's number. It wasn't one she'd used more than once, and that was years ago when she'd planned Jeff's surprise birthday party. *I was such an idiot. Apparently, I am still* an idiot. She dialed, holding her breath as it rang. He'd probably changed his number by now—most people did at one time or another.

But she recognized the cultured, masculine voice that answered. "Lucy?"

She lifted her arm to hail a cab. "You're going to tell me where he is, Roman, and you're going to tell me right this instant."

CHAPTER SIXTEEN

THE SECOND GIDEON heard the buzzer being pressed repeatedly, he knew it was Lucy. He hadn't even tried to hide. He'd known what he was doing today and, as sick to his stomach as it made him, Roman was right—it was the right thing to do. Hurt her a little now and set her back on the path she'd carved out for herself.

Knowing that did nothing to prepare him for the fury on her face when he opened the door. "Lucy."

"No, you do not get to *Lucy* me as if nothing's changed." She pushed into the apartment and spun to face him. "What the hell was that tonight, Gideon?"

He kept his expression stoic, knowing it would make everything worse. "I'm just doing what you contracted me for."

She actually took a step back. "You've got to be kidding me. You're going to take that stance now? What happened to you wanting me to pick *you*?"

"I was wrong." It actually hurt to say the words aloud, and it hurt more to see the naked pain on her face. He forced himself to keep talking. *A little hurt now, rather than a big hurt later.* "This was fun, but you were right when you pointed out that I'm not the keeping kind." She'd survived her breakup with Jeff. She'd bounce back even faster from this mistake with him.

Because that was how she'd see it in a few weeks—a mistake, a bullet dodged.

"You're serious." Lucy shook her head. "What happened between leaving my bed and writing me a note and…" She trailed off. "What did Roman say to you?"

She always had been smart. He let nothing show on his face. "He didn't have to say anything. A little distance was all I needed to realize that we aren't suited."

"Aren't suited." She pressed a hand to her chest as if he'd reached out and hit her there. Gideon felt like he had. She finally took a deep breath and lifted her chin. "You're a coward, Gideon Novak."

He flinched. "What the hell are you talking about?"

"You. Are. A. Coward." He could actually see her putting the pieces of herself back into place, though her bottom lip quivered, just a little. "Last night was too good and, I'll be honest—it scared me, too. But the difference between you and me is that *I* fought that fear and focused on how good it could be." She raked him with her gaze. "I'm not fighting for this. I spent too long fighting to be with someone who didn't even try. I won't do that again, Gideon. This was barely a bump in the road and you've already jumped ship. Fine. So be it." Her lower lip quivered again, but she made an obvious effort to still it. "I chose you, and you didn't choose me."

It felt like she'd stabbed him and twisted the blade. "Lucy—"

"No. Your actions speak just as clearly as your words and I'm not stupid. I understand." She drew herself up. "Consider our contract terminated. Keep the fee for all I care, as long as I never see you again."

Gideon watched her walk out of his apartment—and out of his life. He shut the door softly behind her and walked to his kitchen and stared blankly out the window. *It's done.* Something that took so much effort to coax into being, decimated in the course of a single day.

He braced his hands on the edge of the counter, an anchor to keep from chasing her down and trying to explain. There was no explaining this in a way that accomplished the severing of their relationship and left her pissed off enough to leave him behind for good. As much as he'd hated hearing it, Roman was right. Gideon hadn't been thinking straight from the second Lucy contacted him. If he had been, he would have set her up with someone else for her matchmaking needs. He wasn't qualified for either of the things she needed from him, and he sure as fuck wasn't an unbiased party.

Letting his own selfish needs overshadow hers, and then convincing her to see things his way...

Yeah, there was no explaining that away. Cutting Lucy loose was the best thing he could have done for her.

He let his head drop between his shoulders. The best thing for Lucy, but he'd be riding this wave of pain for the foreseeable future. Getting out of town might help, but the memories of what they'd done here and elsewhere would still be waiting to ambush him when he returned.

No, better to stay and push through the worst of it.

A band around his chest formed, blisteringly hot and so tight he exhaled in a rush. He'd just ended things with Lucy.

Ended for good.

Gideon slumped against the counter. He'd known that woman for six damn years. Had been respectful of her relationship with Jeff and never said so much as a word out of line. Had backed the fuck off and left her alone after things had imploded so she wouldn't have to look at his face and see a constant reminder of the lies she'd fielded.

Through it all, a small part of him had been sure that it would work out. One way or another, he'd find a path to Lucy. That he'd win her if he was just patient enough.

He huffed out a pained laugh. He should have known better. He'd been so busy putting her on a pedestal, he hadn't stopped to ask what *she* wanted. Worse. He'd ignored what she'd wanted in favor of his own desires being met.

She hadn't picked him.

If he hadn't forced the issue, if he'd just stayed in the place she'd designated for him, he could have maintained their friendship. Would it be painful watching her marry another man? Fuck yes. It would have ripped his still-beating heart out of his chest to

smile and congratulate her on picking a man who'd
do as a husband.

But less painful than standing there, realizing he
was never going to see her again.

Lucy wandered the streets for hours. She'd intended
to go home, but the thought of four walls closing
her in was too much to bear. It wasn't any better on
the street—the city itself boxed her into place, preventing her from running until she couldn't breathe,
couldn't think, was too tired to process the level of
Gideon's betrayal.

He blamed himself for not telling her about Jeff's
cheating sooner. She knew that. She'd even used that
to ensure he wouldn't say no to helping her.

She'd also foolishly assumed that, when push came
to shove, he'd get over it.

Lucy looked up and breathed a sigh that wasn't
quite relief. She dug out her phone and called. Her
sister answered on the first ring. "What's up?"

"I don't suppose you're home?"

All joking disappeared from Becka's voice. "Yes.
What's wrong? What happened?"

Burning started in her throat, making it hard to
swallow. "Buzz me up?"

"Yeah, right away."

She hung up before her sister's concern had her
breaking down in the street. The walk up the rickety
stairs to the tiny apartment Becka insisted she loved
was a lesson in torture. As if her body knew she was

almost safe and had decided now was the perfect time to break down completely.

Becka opened the door as she lifted her hand to knock. Her sister wore a pair of brightly printed workout pants and a sports bra with more straps than was strictly necessary. Lucy stopped short. "You have class."

"I already got someone to cover for me, so don't even think of turning around." She stepped back. "Now, get in here and tell me everything while I make some tea I threw together this weekend."

That almost brought a smile to Lucy's face. "Is it better than the last batch?"

"The last batch was the exception to the rule, though thank you very much for reminding me of it." She made a face. "I couldn't get the taste of licorice out of my mouth for days, no matter how many times I brushed my teeth and drowned myself in mouthwash."

"Live and learn." Her voice caught, because living and learning was exactly what Lucy *hadn't* done. She'd been so sure she knew her path, and yet the first chance she had to take a detour that would ruin everything, she'd jumped in headfirst.

"Sit. Immediately." Becka took her coat and purse and tossed them onto the threadbare couch. Then she guided Lucy into a chair at the small dining room table and headed for the stove. The loft apartment meant Lucy only had to rotate a little to keep her sister in view.

Becka got hot water going in an ancient-looking

kettle and doled out loose leaf tea into two wire tea steepers. The few minutes it took to get the water boiling was enough to calm Lucy's racing thoughts a little. "I'm sorry to drop in like this."

"What are sisters for if not to be there when you need them?" Becka poured the hot water into two mugs and brought them to the table. "This is about Gideon."

She started to deny it, but what was the point? She'd locked down everything after the Jeff fiasco, and all it had done was completely isolate her from the world. Maybe talking through it with her sister was the right choice.

"I... He changed the rules on me. I had a fully fleshed-out plan, and every intention of following through on it, but I didn't anticipate *him*. Our connection. He showed every evidence of wanting more with me—we even talked about it and he said so in as many words—and then I wake up this morning to find him gone." She had to stop and focus on breathing for several moments. Even with the break, when she spoke again, her voice was strained. "I thought we were meeting tonight, but when I showed up to dinner, he'd set me up with another man."

Becka's blue eyes, so like Lucy's, went wide. "I think you're going to have to rewind to the part when you woke up alone. You had *sex* with Gideon?"

She'd left out that part of the plan, hadn't she? Lucy cleared her throat and stared at the ever-darkening water of her tea. "We've been sleeping together since the initial agreement. It started out as a way to get my confidence back sexually, but things…changed."

"They'll do that when sex is involved." She shot her sister a look, and Becka gave her wide eyes. "Not that I would know, of course. Your dear little sister is most definitely one hundred percent a virgin."

She snorted. "I'd believe that if I hadn't caught you and…what was his name?"

"Johnny Cash." Becka laughed. "Don't look at me like that. I know it wasn't his real name, but I was eighteen and he was hot." Her smile fell away. "So Gideon pulled a bait and switch on you? That's seriously shitty, Lucy. I never pegged him for the type to play games like that, but I've been wrong before."

"We Baudin women don't have the best of tastes in men."

"You can say that again."

She was tempted to let them skirt into safer territory, but the raw feeling inside her only got worse with each minute that passed.

Lucy pulled her mug closer. "I promised myself that I wouldn't fall in love again—that I wouldn't even put myself in the position to do so. Feelings and caring on that depth only cause pain. I didn't expect him. I couldn't fight against the connection or the way he made me feel." The burning in her throat got worse. "I thought we had a chance, Becka. A real chance. That maybe I didn't miss my chance at a happily-ever-after, and maybe it could be with Gideon."

"Oh, Lucy."

She laughed, the sound vaguely liquid with unshed tears. "That's very foolish, isn't it?"

"It's hopeful. There's nothing wrong with hope."

Except it was hope that had gotten her into this situation. It was because of hope that every beat of her heart felt as if someone were stabbing her. Hope had driven her to lay her heart bare for Gideon, and it'd gotten crushed in the process.

She took a drink, ignoring the way the hot water scalded her mouth. A small pain compared to her emotional wounds. "Screw hope. I want nothing to do with it anymore."

CHAPTER SEVENTEEN

GIDEON DIDN'T LOOK up as the door to his office slammed open. "Whatever it is, I don't want to hear about it." Keeping the damn door shut in the first place should have been enough to discourage anyone from coming in—anyone except Roman, that was.

But when he finally looked up, it wasn't Roman kicking the door shut behind him.

It was Becka Baudin.

He stared for a long moment and shook his head. "No. Whatever you have to say to me has already been said, so get out."

"It might have been said, but it wasn't said by me." She ignored his command and marched over to drop into the chair across the desk. She wore tennis shoes and neon-green workout shorts tiny enough to have him concerned about frostbite. When she shrugged out of her huge coat, she revealed a fitted tank top in an equally eye-searing pink. How it managed not to clash with her bright blue hair was beyond him.

"What the hell are you doing, walking around New York in *January* wearing that? You're going to freeze your ass off."

She blinked and then shook her head. "You have a lot of nerve. I could appreciate that if you weren't such an overbearing, selfish asshole." Becka jumped back to her feet. Gideon caught several of the men from the cubicles gravitating toward the windows of his office and stalked over to close the blinds.

"Put on some damn clothes."

She pointed at him. "Sit your ass down and listen to what I have to say, and then I'll leave and take my apparently inadequately clothed body with me." Becka pulled her ponytail tighter. "What the hell are you doing with my sister?"

"Nothing."

"No, shit." She looked like she wanted to throw something at him. "You know, Lucy doesn't get why you pulled that sneaky little trick with the date."

"I—"

"But *I* do." Becka paced from one side of his office to the other. "I might not have been around her and Jeff as much as you were, but I was around enough. I know you've been holding a flame for my big sister for years, and I know *you* were the one who broke the news to her about Jeff being a cheating bastard."

He started to cut in, but she spoke over him. Again. "That must have been a head trip for you, huh? Hard to break up their relationship, even if it was the right thing to do, because you were in love with your cheating best friend's girl. That muddies the waters."

"Actually—"

"I am not through." She glared, her blue eyes practically luminescent. "When I'm done talking, then you get to talk. Until then, sit down and shut up."

He didn't sit, but he did give her a short nod. Obviously she wasn't going to be deterred from whatever she was trying to accomplish. After what he'd done to Lucy, the least he could do was stand here and take a verbal lashing from her sister. "Fine."

"Good." She took another lap from one side of his office to the other. "So, you're carrying around a boatload of guilt, and playing the martyr and letting her try to move on with her life." She shot him a look. "Martyrs aren't sexy, by the way."

She sure as hell wasn't holding back. "Noted."

"So, as my sister is telling me the insane deal she put together with you, I can't help wondering what your motivation was. For screwing her, I get that—it was fulfilling a lifelong dream."

He couldn't let that stand. "No."

She stopped. "No? Which part? Screwing my sister being a lifelong dream or—"

"Stop saying that. Fuck, Becka. I didn't manipulate your sister into bed with me. *She* came to *me*."

She propped her hands on her hips. "Aha. It wasn't the sex, then. It's the guilt." She pursed her lips. "Guilt isn't any sexier than martyrdom."

"Why are you here, Becka?" He needed her to get to the point of this verbal thrashing so she'd leave. She wasn't saying anything Gideon hadn't already gone over more times than he could count. He'd replayed every step and second-guessed every action. It all added up to a mistake he couldn't take back.

He still wasn't sure if the mistake was agreeing to help Lucy—or leaving her.

"My point is that you love the shit out of my sister and have for years, but you decided to be the guilty martyr and make an executive decision about what she *should* have." She stared him down. "Tell me I'm wrong."

"She should—"

"Sweet baby Jesus." Becka rolled her eyes. "Here's a tip—take 'should' out of your vocabulary when you talk about my sister and her future. You might care about her, but ultimately, you don't get a vote. She's an adult. She can make her own choices. And she chose *you*, you asshat." She shook her head. "The question is whether *you* are willing to choose her instead of your idealized version of her." She snatched up her coat. "If I had a mic, I'd drop it, but you get the picture. Woman up or don't, but unless you have a good grovel prepared, I don't want to ever hear about you contacting my sister again." She strode out the door, leaving a trail of startled and appreciative gazes behind her.

Gideon dropped into the chair behind his desk and stared at his dark monitor. Becka hadn't said anything he didn't already know. And yet...

And yet.

He drummed his fingers on the desk. The last twenty-four hours since the fallout with Lucy had been the worst of his life. He hadn't slept. Food wasn't of interest. He hadn't even been able to work up the resolve to get good and drunk. Every time he turned around, he caught a trail of her summery scent, and the few times he'd been on the street, he'd looked for her distinctive stride even though he knew better.

He'd had his dream in the flesh—Lucy in his bed and in his life—and it'd been better than he could have imagined. He already knew she was driven and kind and had a sense of humor. He knew she loved Chinese takeout and discovering little hole-in-the-wall restaurants no one had ever heard of. He knew her parents were MIA, but she had a wonderful relationship with her sister.

He couldn't have anticipated the passion that flared between them. Hoped, yes, but even that hadn't encompassed reality. Lucy met him every step of the way, *challenged* him every step of the way. She brought fun into the bedroom even as she made him crazy in the best way possible.

And now he'd never touch her again. He'd never be able to show her a new place that he discovered. Never call just to chat with her because he was thinking of her. Never spend those fantasy lazy Sundays they kept talking about.

He'd done that.

There's no one to blame here but me. I had it all and I shit it away.

Even if he tried to make things right, Lucy would likely tell him to get lost. She *should* tell him...

He went still. *Fuck me, Becka is right.* He and Lucy had been doing just fine before he'd started obsessing over what *should* happen rather than what *was* happening.

He'd done this. He'd ruined it.

Gideon had known that, but the truth drove home hard enough to have him rubbing the back of his hand across his mouth. He felt like the biggest piece of shit in existence to have been so close to everything he'd ever dreamed of romantically and for *him* to have been the one that made it combust.

He drummed his fingers faster.

Could he fix this?

Should—

No. There was no more room for *should*. He was head over heels in love with Lucy. If she'd have him— if she'd forgive him once again—he'd do everything in his power to ensure that he never hurt her again. Not like this. Never like this.

He straightened. He'd fix it. Tonight.

Right now.

CHAPTER EIGHTEEN

LUCY CRASHED AND burned in court. There was no other way to describe it. She'd bungled the opening statement and then made an ass of herself getting into it with the prosecuting attorney until the judge called a recess until the following day. She strode out of the courtroom, her throat tight with shame and her skin hot. *I screwed up.*

No matter how frustrating or crazy her personal life got, she had always—*always*—found refuge in work. With her clients, the world made sense. It didn't matter what case they had leveled against them, she had a knack for finding the right facts to turn things in their favor. That click was her favorite thing in the world.

She'd lost it.

Two days since Gideon had unceremoniously dumped her, and she'd spent the entire time going through too many boxes of Kleenex and watching movie after movie while clutching Garfunkel. She hadn't touched her files. She hadn't checked her email. She hadn't done anything other than sit there and feel sorry for herself.

It didn't make *sense*. Work was her everything. Work was the reason she had contacted Gideon to begin with. Dropping the ball there was inexcusable.

Why? Why can't I focus?

She knew the answer. She didn't want to face it.

But Lucy couldn't keep on like this indefinitely. If she didn't recover tonight and fix the mess she'd made today, she could kiss her promotion goodbye and it would all be for nothing. Facing down the ugly truth required more courage than she thought she had.

She hit the street and turned a direction at random, needing the movement to untangle her thoughts. Three blocks later and she was no closer to unveiling the truth.

Coward. Just like you called him.

Damn it. Lucy stopped short. "I love him." The comment earned her a few looks from people walking around her, but she started moving again before anyone could get pissed about her being a human roadblock. *I love him.*

She'd loved Jeff, but it was...different. Even if they'd been planning their wedding when she'd found out that he'd cheated on her, her connection with Jeff had never come close to what she felt for Gideon. Her heartbreak at the time hadn't made her miss a step at work. If anything, without the stress of trying to juggle her emotions over Jeff's nasty comments, she'd been free to focus solely on what was most important—her job.

The only problem? Her job didn't hold up against what she felt for Gideon. Every time she tried to work, she caught herself wondering where he was or what he was doing—or who he might be with.

The last was her own personal demon. Lucy didn't think for a minute that Gideon had dropped her on her ass and gone off to hook up with someone else. No matter what he'd said about not being the keeping kind, it was his fear talking—not reality.

He cared about her. He wouldn't have taken the noble route if he hadn't. It was a stupid choice, to be sure, but she understood that he was trying to protect her. He just wasn't giving her the benefit of making her own choices.

That was the problem.

That was the thing she didn't know if she could get over.

Liar.

Gideon might have pulled the trigger on ending things, but only because he'd beaten Lucy to it. She hadn't fought for him—for them. He'd tried to do the noble thing and, instead of telling him where to stick his high-handed attitude, she'd just walked away. So much easier to retreat than to put herself on the line and be rejected by him.

Lucy wove through the crowd of people on the corner and stopped next to the building, staring at the stream of yellow taxicabs. She'd projected herself. She couldn't even blame her history on her reaction. What she felt for Gideon scared the hell out of her. She *knew* he cared about her—loved her, even. They hadn't shared so much for it to be anything less than love. He wouldn't have told her to pick him unless he was one hundred percent serious. That wasn't how Gideon operated. He didn't play games.

Honesty. He demanded perfect honesty—and he'd given it, as well. She mentally played back everything he'd said to her. Nowhere in there was him telling her that all he'd wanted was sex. No, he didn't think he was good enough for her, so he'd cut her loose. *High-handed, but so very Gideon.* He'd chosen *her* happiness over *his.*

She needed to put herself out there. To tell him that *he* was her happiness. Lucy had lived a decent life the last couple of years. She'd been perfectly content, but she'd also cut herself off from anyone that would make her feel deeply enough to hurt her. She'd barely tried to date and hadn't attempted to reach out to friends she'd lost touch with.

She'd been the coward.

That stopped now. If Gideon didn't want her— didn't love her—he could damn well tell her to her face. That was the only acceptable reason for him dumping her. Anything else they could work past as long as they were together. Lucy would make him see that. The man might make her fumble her words a bit, but she'd power through it to get the truth out.

Her phone vibrated and she almost ignored it, but the only way to make her Dumpster fire of a day in court worse was to ignore a call from her client or one of the partners. But when she dug it out of her purse, it was the last number she expected to see there. *Roman?*

Lucy frowned and answered. "Hello?"

"I owe you an apology."

She blinked. This situation kept getting weirder and weirder. Roman had never called her before, and she couldn't think of a single reason he'd have to call her now. Unless... Her heart lodged in her throat. "Is Gideon okay?"

"What?" His shock seemed genuine and then he laughed, breaking her tension. "Shit, I guess I owe you two apologies. Gideon is fine last I saw him, which was yesterday. I should have realized you'd think the worst."

Lucy let loose the breath she'd been holding. "Okay. Sorry. I just thought..."

"Logical. I should have considered it." He cleared his throat. "Look, I fucked up, Lucy. I never asked your forgiveness for not telling you about Jeff, and then I went and compounded the issue by letting my guilt prod me to give Gideon some truly shitty advice."

She'd known that something had happened while Gideon was with Roman to push him into action, but she didn't hold it against him. Any of it. "Gideon's strong-willed. He wouldn't have been pushed into doing something he wasn't already considering doing."

"Still."

She smiled at the stubbornness in that single word. It was no wonder the two men got along so well. They were cut from the same kind of cloth. "Consider yourself forgiven."

"I'd actually like to make it up to you. Before you

tell me it's not necessary, know that I realize it's not necessary and that's how good apologies work."

Amusement curled through her, though she wished he'd get to the point so she could hang up and call Gideon. "What did you have in mind?"

"What are you doing right now? A friend is doing a soft opening of his restaurant and I have a table reserved so we can talk."

"Right now?" She looked around. "I guess that works." Damn it, she wanted Gideon, but if she was going to get him to come around, it wouldn't hurt to have Roman on her side. Maybe she could use the lunch to mine for information. The thought buoyed her disappointment a bit. "Text me the address, please."

"Will do. I'll meet you there." He hung up before she could ask him any further questions.

Lucy frowned. *Strange.* Her phone pinged almost immediately and she frowned harder because she recognized the address. It overlooked Central Park, though it used to be owned by someone else. It must have cost a small fortune—or large one—to purchase. She set the information aside and stepped to the curb to flag down a cab.

The ride was blessedly short, all things considered. Lucy kept looking at her phone, but now that she was going to meet Roman, she didn't want to call Gideon until afterward. Just in case he wanted to talk immediately. Her stomach did a slow flip-flop. *Please be willing to meet with me.*

To her surprise, the restaurant was actually the

top floor of the building. After getting off the elevator, Lucy stood in the entranceway for a solid thirty
seconds, just taking in the opulence of the place.
It screamed wealth with its polished white-marble
floors and subtle gold accents. Nothing déclassé, but
there all the same.

A well-dressed man strode over, a practiced smile
on his handsome face. "You must be Lucy. This way,
please."

She followed, taking in empty table after empty
table. "I thought this was a soft opening?" Surely
there should be *some* people there. *Good Lord, did
Roman invite me here to shove me out a window?* She
pushed the thought away. Hysterical was what it was.

"It is." He chuckled. "Just a *very* soft opening."

That wasn't an answer at all, but she allowed him
to lead her into what appeared to be a greenhouse.
The air warmed enough that she unzipped her jacket.
Flowers of every color and shape lined the walls.
There were even trees in the corners, which made
her smile despite everything.

She was so busy looking at the foliage that she
didn't realize the man had left—or that she wasn't
alone—until she turned around and found Gideon
standing in the doorway. Lucy froze. "But—"

"I'm sorry for the cheap trick. I wasn't sure if you'd
agree to see me if I called." His dark eyes drank her
in and she actually felt his longing even across the
space between them.

Lucy shook her head. "Gideon, you have to *stop*.
If you want to see me, call me and say so yourself

instead of trying to manipulate things into a perfect setup." Now that she had him here, though, she was just glad she didn't have to have this conversation over the phone. She lifted her chin. "And if you love me, you stay. You don't choose the self-sacrificing route because you think you know what's best for me. You sit down and have a damn conversation where we talk it out."

His smile wasn't all that happy. "I fucked up."

"Yes, you did." She wasn't about to let him off easily, no matter how much she wanted to cross the distance between them and feel his strong arms wrap around her.

"I'm sorry. There's no good reason to explain why I freaked out, but guilt makes people do crazy things—like walk away from the woman they love because they think it's what's best for her."

"*I* decide what's best for me."

His dark eyes took on a tinge of sorrow. "I know. And we both know that I don't deserve to kiss the ground you walk on. Not because I love some idealized version of you, but because you're *you*. You're a good person, Lucy. The best kind of person. You are funny and kind and sexy as fuck, and I might not deserve you..." He took a step forward and then another. "No, I *know* I don't deserve you."

"Stop saying that," she whispered.

"Maybe we both fucked up. Fear makes for all kinds of mistakes, and what we have between us is wildfire." Gideon stopped in front of her and went down on one knee. "But, Lucy, I'd gladly spend the rest of my life burning for you." He withdrew a ring box from the inner pocket of his suit jacket. "I love you. I've loved you for six goddamn years, and I convinced myself that the right thing to do was to stand back and let you be with someone you deserved. I fought every single damn day not to pull some underhanded shit and steal you from that douche."

She reached out with shaking hands and touched the ring box. "Gideon—"

"I know you wanted a safe and pat marriage to some guy you don't give two fucks about. I can't offer you that, Lucy. But I can offer you a husband who will love you beyond all reason, even if he occasionally screws up. I can offer you a safe harbor, a full life and more sex than you know what to do with. I *am* offering you that."

She couldn't catch her breath. In all the scenarios she'd played out over the last few days, she'd never once imagined Gideon, down on one knee, offering her everything she'd spent two years being too terrified to admit she wanted. "Gideon."

"Yes?" He didn't look scared while he waited for her answer. He looked totally and completely at peace for the first time in as long as she could remember. As if he was exactly where he wanted to be—where he was meant to be.

Lucy stepped forward and tangled her fingers in his hair. "Steal me."

His dark eyes went wide. "That's a yes."

It wasn't a question but she answered anyway. "That's a hell yes."

He gave a whoop and shot to his feet, sweeping her off hers in the process. "I love the shit out of you, Lucy. I'll spend the rest of our life making up for six years of missed opportunity."

She kissed him with everything she had. "Maybe it was good that it took us six years to get here and more than a few missteps along the way. There's a right time and place. This is *our* time and *our* place." Lucy kissed him again. "I love you, Gideon. So, so much."

He stepped back enough to slip the ring out of the box and onto her finger. It was…perfect. The simple silver ban framed a princess-cut diamond that was big enough to have her shooting a look at him. "Wow."

"Funny, that's what I say every time I see you." He pulled her back into his arms. "Wow. This woman is mine. And I'm hers."

"Yes and yes and yes." She smiled up at him. "Always."

* * * * *

Wanting more?
Read on for a sneak peek of
Katee Robert's next Mills & Boon Dare,
MAKE ME CRAVE.

*Roman's story is far from over! He's got his eye on
an up-and-coming business, but when the owner
takes off on vacation, he follows her to paradise to
convince her to sell. The only problem? He doesn't
realize the gorgeous blonde he just met and the
stubborn business owner are one and the same...*

SHE MADE IT to the restaurant with minimum fuss and found it practically deserted. Allie paused in the doorway, wondering if she'd misunderstood the woman who'd checked them in. Maybe it was closed?

"Looks like it's just you and me."

She jumped and spun around. The man stood a respectable distance away, but his sheer size ate up the space and made her feel closed in. She froze. *I'd recognize those shoulders anywhere.* As if to confirm, his gaze slid over her body as if reminding himself of what she looked like with nothing but what she'd worn on the beach. She tried to swallow past her suddenly dry throat. "You."

"Me." He finally looked her in the face, and she rocked back on her heels. The man was Adonis. There was no other way to describe his blond perfection, from his hazel eyes to the square jaw to the cleft in his chin to the body that just wouldn't stop. He might be wearing a shirt now, but the button-down did nothing to hide his muscle definition.

He held out a wide hand with equally perfect square fingers. "Let me buy you a drink?"

"We're at an all-inclusive resort."

His lips twitched, hazel eyes twinkling. "Have a drink with me."

Oh, he was good. Charm practically colored the air between them, and she had the inexplicable impulse to close the distance and stroke a finger along his jawline. To flick that cleft chin with her tongue.

Allie gave herself a shake. "Since we're the only ones here, it'd be silly to sit apart."

The look he gave her said he saw right through the excuse, and why not when it was pathetically flimsy? The truth was that this man was a magnet and she suspected she'd be drawn to him even in a room full of people. He waved a hand at the empty place. "Lady's choice."

"How magnanimous of you."

"I try."

She laughed and headed for the table in the middle of the small patio. There were half a dozen tables, and she picked a spot that put her back to the building and presented the best view of the ocean through a carefully curated gap in the foliage.

He eyed the view and then the chair across from her, and then picked it up and set it diagonally to her, rather than directly across. "Nice view."

She turned to agree—and found him staring at *her*.

Allie wasn't falsely modest. Life was too short to play games with body shaming and pretending she didn't have access to a mirror. She was pretty—beautiful when she put some effort into it—but her body wasn't the type someone would expect a gym owner to have. Sure, she had muscle beneath her softness, and she could keep up with the best of them in her spin classes, but she'd loved food just as much as she loved to sweat, and her curves reflected that. Some guys had a problem with that, though she didn't keep them around as soon as comments about "Should you really be eating that?" started.

This guy looked at her like he wanted to put her on the table and feast on *her* for dinner.

The desire stoked the flame inside her that had kindled the second she saw him. She leaned forward, checking his left hand. No ring. No tan lines to indicate there ever was one, either. "What brings you to West Island?"

"It's paradise, isn't it? Who wouldn't want to come here to get away from it all?"

That wasn't quite an answer, but she got distracted with the intoxicating way his mouth moved when he spoke. *Get a hold of yourself, Allie. You're in danger of panting.* She took a quick drink of water that did nothing to quell the heat rising with each second she sat next to him.

Luckily, a waiter appeared to save her from saying something truly embarrassing. He outlined the menu for the night and took their drink orders, and disappeared as quickly as he'd come.

They were in the middle of one of the most beautiful places Allie had ever seen, and she couldn't manage to tear her gaze away from this stranger. She licked her lips, every muscle in her body tensing when he followed the movement. She opened her mouth, but he beat her there, taking her hand and running his thumb over her knuckles.

The touch was innocent enough, but she felt that light movement in places that were most definitely *not* innocent. She didn't have to look down to know her nipples now pressed against the thin fabric of her sundress.

His smile was slow and sinful and promised things she never would have had the gall to ask for. "This is going to sound unforgivably forward, but what do you say we get out of here and go back to my villa?"

It was crazy. More than crazy. She didn't even know his name, and she sure as hell didn't know anything more pertinent about him.

But there on the softly lit patio with the scent of tropical flowers and the soft shushing sound of the tide coming in, she didn't feel like Allie, gym owner and mother hen—the responsible one who could never afford to do anything crazy or make a misstep because too many lives depended on her.

Here, she was just Allie, a woman. A woman who desperately desired the man staring at her mouth as if doing everything in his power to keep from kissing her right then and there. She licked her lips again, secretly delighting in the way a muscle in his jaw jumped. "Yes."

"Yes?"

"Yes, let's get out of here."

LET'S TALK
Romance

For exclusive extracts, competitions
and special offers, find us online:

f facebook.com/millsandboon

⊙ @millsandboonuk

𝕏 @millsandboon

Or get in touch on 0844 844 1351*

For all the latest titles coming soon, visit
millsandboon.co.uk/nextmonth